HIS THRONE OF EMBERS

MOLTEN CROWN

BOOK TWO

RENEE APRIL

His Throne of Embers
(Molten Crown #2)

Edited by Lydia Fuller
Cover design by Dayna Watson

ISBN 978-0-6455708-5-4 (paperback)
ISBN 978-0-6455708-4-7 (hardcover)
ISBN 978-0-6455708-6-1 (digital online)

www.skynation.info

*For my audio drama actors, who brought the cast of Her Crown of
Fire to life with their incredible voices.*

The Tellamer Sea
The Kellatrae Ocean
The Lumic Sea
The Edipae Ocean
NORTHANDRELLIA
LOTHERIA
GOWAR
ABDOOR
STANTHOR
Norrimoor
Thurin
Numin
Riverdoor
Lotherian River
The Great Road
The Academy
Fairhaven
Castor

CHAPTER ONE

THE WATER SURGES around my waist, pulling and tugging at me. I press against it, my legs burning, breath rasping in my chest as I reach forward through the tumult.

Just a bit further!

Pain rages, dull and constant, but I file it to the back of my mind and lunge forward, catching the metal bar at the end of the little pool. The jets of water cease immediately, and I hang my head as my lungs heave.

"Well done, Rose!" Taylor, my physio, says proudly. She kneels down by the bar I'm hanging onto for dear life. "Now, you'd tell me if that was too tough for you, right? No pain in the leg?"

I open my mouth to respond, but my mother beats me to it. "It hurt her. And she's about to try to tell you it didn't."

I frown at her as Taylor turns back to me, a disappointed crease between her eyebrows. "I can't help you recover from this if you won't tell me when it's too much, Rose."

"It's taking too long," I manage between breaths. "I thought we'd be further along by now."

"It's been eight weeks," she corrects, offering a hand to help me out. "And you can't rush this kind of healing. We've talked about this."

I let her haul me from the pool, feeling ten times heavier than usual. Mum is there in an instant with a towel, but I take a moment to look at the offending leg that has landed me in very expensive hydrotherapy for two months. It's pale and soft from time in the warm water, but the calf muscle is gnarled with scar tissue and black threads. Taylor had queried if it was some kind of bruising when I'd first met her. I couldn't tell her it was the remnants of my own armour.

The clawed mace that had taken out a chunk of my dominant leg had very nearly killed me. I flex my fingers as the memories surge back like the water in the pool; Petre's lifeless body, the screaming man in my grasp, and flames...

Everything ablaze.

Though the scars on my forearms and face barely show under the fluorescent lights of the gym, the ones on my back show better. Mum always covers me up before the other trainers and members can get a look at them, but I remember Taylor's stuttered sentence when she helped me into the pool the first time. I feel the heat in my face grow as, even now, she avoids looking at me. I pull the towel tight around my shoulders and accept my mother's help towards the change rooms.

"You did really well today," Mum says as we pull into the driveway.

I say nothing, waiting for the follow up. It doesn't come, and as she switches off the ignition, she meets my look.

"What?"

"I'm waiting for the 'but'," I reply. "'You did well, but...'"

"No 'but'. I just thought you did very well for today's session."

"Oh." I take a moment and let that sink in. "Thanks."

"Do you need a hand getting out?"

I wriggle the toes of my right leg. The numbness has set in and I'm going to need to stretch to get any kind of movement out of the limb. "Yes, please."

Mum comes around the passenger side of the car with my cane and her work bag, and helps me out with one hand, offering the stick with the other. I take it like I would the hand of my oldest friend, the grip comfortable and worn. I lost my old one when Arno picked me up from the cobblestones of Fairhaven, broken and bleeding. Sometimes I remember it lying there as he carried me away and get inexplicably sad; the cane had been made for me by a man in Riverdoor, just after the death of my friend. I had lost my leg, and Petre, and received the cane in return. It felt wrong to abandon it to the fire of the village that I—

"Rose." Fingers snap under my nose. "You're doing it again."

I take a deep breath, returning to the present. "Sorry."

She plants her hand on my head for a second like she's going to say something, but then takes my gym bag along with hers and follows me up to the house, scaring a family of nesting birds from the eaves. I'm breathing heavily as I step over the threshold, but manage to kick my shoes off as Mum scuffs hers clean on the rug.

"Go sit down, I'll bring food," she promises, dumping both bags beside the shoe stand.

I watch her go for a second, then my gaze drifts up the stairs that may as well be Mt Everest in my hallway. Warm sunlight gleams from my open bedroom door at the top. I rest a hand on the bannister.

Then I curl my fingers and let my hand drop. It has been weeks since I've set foot in my own room. The smell of sawdust and wood glue stands testimony to Mum's efforts in between shifts as a travelling locum doctor to renovate the garage, so I have a bedroom on the ground floor. For now, I've turned the couch into a nest, complete with laptop and PlayStation. I hobble there now, falling gratefully into the worn cushions and picking up my laptop. I navigate to YouTube as I hear the microwave start up, then cast the videos to the big TV as Mum pokes her head in.

"Steak and mashed potatoes?"

"Yes, please. What do you want to watch?"

She looks aside, but then presses her lips together and smiles easily at me. "Anything but those miserable compilation videos."

I clench my jaw for a second, but manage to respond. "What about the dude making huts in the bush?"

"Oh yes, I like him."

I turn back to the TV and go to click on the thumbnail, but another catches my eye; an upload I've been waiting for. My stomach swoops as I'm faced with my own picture from the day I returned, bloody and hollow-eyed.

Top Five Mysterious Missing People Who Were Found reads the title.

I drum my nails on the laptop, then add to 'Watch Later'.

'Miserable compilations' indeed.

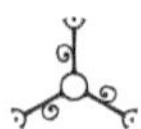

"I found another."

"Stop looking for them."

I pull apart the Crispy Burger bun and avoid Tyson's gaze. "I don't go looking for them. YouTube recommends them."

"Because you *went* looking for them."

A loud horn sounds in the distance, giving warning to the long train that curls around the corner and rattles along the tracks behind the chain link fence. We watch it from the warmth of Tyson's car, burger wrappings in our laps. I toy with my burger, knowing Tyson is eyeing it.

"How'd therapy go yesterday? Good swim?"

"It was good. She pushes me."

"Any progress on... on the... you know..."

I raise an eyebrow and look at him. "On the walking thing? No. I'm still Sticks McGee." I nudge my cane down the side of the passenger seat.

"I'm sorry."

I shrug, pulling the meat patty out of the bun. Tyson makes a pained noise. I wield the patty at him. "Calm down. Even this is a bit much for me."

"You still got the weird food thing?"

I nod and take a bite of the patty. Thanks to the magical blood in my veins, my body believes I should be existing off of unprocessed wholefoods. Which, in this day and age of adding sugar to literally *everything*, makes finding food I can eat quite difficult.

"Even the bun has sugar in it," I say through the meat. "The *bun*, Tyson."

He takes it from me. "That's what makes it so good."

Another train rattles past as we lapse into silence. One of the carriages lumbers past, covered in bright swirls of spray paint that just say 'Graffiti'.

"Well that's a bit meta," I say.

He exhale-laughs, and I know what's coming. I slide down into my seat and push my head into the headrest.

"You can't keep watching those videos about us, Rose."

"Why not?"

Tyson balls up the burger wrapper and ditches it into the bag. "Because it's not healthy. We've moved on. We're back. We need to live in *this* world now."

There's something in his voice, but I turn my head away, looking out the window at the stars. Different stars shone in Lotheria; somewhere back there I had a book with all the constellations.

"Take up a hobby. One that *isn't* physiotherapy. Go back to school, get a job... something, Rose. You can't keep living back there. I need you here, Rose. I—"

"The video today," I begin, "the newest one... it called us 'victims'. His theory is that we were victims of human trafficking and managed to escape."

Tyson leans into the driver's side door, as though to get a better look at me. I avoid his gaze.

"We were victims," he says.

"You might've been."

"Kaya forced you—"

"She didn't *force* me to collude with her. I was the one that went seeking her out, I was the one that let her into the town, I—"

His hand catches mine as my chest heaves.

"Stop," he says firmly. "It wasn't your fault what happened there. You need to let it go."

I press my lips together. "How can you say that? Don't you want to know if they're alright? Craige, Arno... Amisha?"

Laela.

Her name goes unspoken between us. The fate I left her to is too much for us to discuss in a dark car over burger wrappings. Tears burn in my eyes as I look away.

"I know you loved her—"

I shake my head fiercely. "I don't know what I felt for her. I don't think I'm capable of love." I turn back to him as a rebellious tear streaks down my cheek. "Would someone that loved her leave her there to the Halvers?"

His grip tightens on my hand. "It's *not* your fault."

"Yeah," I whisper. "It is."

CHAPTER TWO

THE STREETLIGHT FALLS DIRECTLY between the crack in the curtains. I don't turn my head, or roll over, or inch down the couch; instead, I let the light cross my eyes and keep me awake.

When I sleep, I dream. I remember.

Images sweep across my mind's eye, and suddenly I'm back in the town of Fairhaven. Tyson on the executioner's stand, the Halvers charging through the alleys and streets with weapons held aloft...

The darkness that had swept through my veins as fire replaced every rational thought.

The fire rages. With a screech of burnt timber, a support gives way and everyone stumbles towards the inferno. Cinders fly into the dark night as the riot rages behind me.

Another voice, familiar. "Have you got her? She needs to stop this fire."

When Arno nods, his hand shakes me somewhat. "She's deep, but I'll get her out. You get your boy."

I squeeze my eyes closed, feeling the itch of tiredness. Though I could hear everything being said that night, I could not respond. I was completely incapable. Forming words would've been as difficult as cutting stone with my bare hands.

The fire took even my words from me.

I raise my arm from the blankets and look at the runes I put there. The queensblood Kaya and I stole had burnt her, a woman physically unable to feel pain, to the point where she refused the power of a monarch. The woman had given up a crown because she could not stand the agony of accepting the magic that came with it.

I had carved into my own skin shortly after, with the threat of Laela's death over my head. Only the blade had caused me pain, to which I was no stranger... but the pale queensblood, trapped in an ice block for years, had fled to me like a stricken ship to harbour.

The runes were of my own design, from the language I'd been developing as part of my application to become a Rune Master of Lotheria. That dream had been pushed aside for the ambitions of others.

I let my arm fall back to the blanket. When had I last acted on my own accord? Even now, I go to physiotherapy at my mother's request. I see Tyson when he texts me.

I pick up my phone and scroll through his messages from the last few days.

> Hey, wanna grab burgers?

> How are you doing today?

> We all good?

> I just wanna make sure I haven't done anything wrong.

> Hey, how are you?

My thumb hovers over opening one, but the read receipt is a commitment I can't manage right now. Heat burns in my cheeks as I let the phone drop again. I should respond, let him know I'm okay. He hasn't texted for two days—the longest we've ever gone without speaking. Even being transported to another world couldn't break us apart.

But coming back seems to have done the trick.

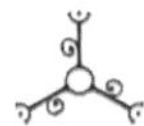

I close the door gently behind me, and limp down the driveway. The cool night air brushes my face, bringing the scent of damp soil, old exhaust, and the possibility of rain. I pause at the road, resting on my stick. The warmth from my blankets is fading behind me, like leaving a comforting hug.

I pick a direction, and start walking.

My midnight walks began three nights after I'd arrived, gasping, on the shores of the river. Tyson had reached desperately to me as though afraid I'd disappear under again—and this time, he would not be able to follow. I'd grabbed his hand, allowing him to tow me to shore, and had spent the last eight weeks regretting that simple action.

What had transpired in Lotheria since we left? It had at least been a relief to find out that time was linear in both worlds; only a year had passed since our disappearance. Surely, not much could've gone to hell in eight weeks.

I wait dutifully at a traffic light, though no cars cruise the road. Following the rules, even arbitrary ones, feels right and good at the moment.

We'd walked to the Narralong police station—well, Tyson had. Halfway there, he'd simply picked me up as I sagged by his side, my back bruised and blood on my lips. Later, doctors in green scrubs like my Mum's would tell me I had three broken ribs and severe bruising around my spinal cord. Somehow, I'd avoided extra damage to my legs.

Tyson told them we'd been in a car crash.

Huddled in blankets at the police station, our parents had been called. Tyson's had walked stiffly to him, barely sparing me a glance as I stared at the door and waited for Mum to enter. She'd swept through like a thundercloud, her expression unreadable.

"How are you feeling?" she'd asked, kneeling beside me.

"I'm okay."

She'd rested her hand on my knee and looked me in the eye, and that's when I saw it.

The guilt.

We were hauled to the hospital. Mum had stood in the room as they'd cut me from my Lotherian clothes, the rough trousers and shirt Laela and I had gathered together in the Halver camp. They were tossed unceremoniously aside and I was glad; I was able to dump them before the cops requested them for evidence.

A collective hush had fallen over the room as my scars and injuries were catalogued. I was wheeled into an X-ray room and made to stand on my shaking leg. The diagnosis didn't surprise me; I was just glad it wasn't worse.

"Scarring on the right palm," the doctor had noted. "Both inner forearms, three on the left cheek and..." She paused when she got to my back. "Several long healed lacerations on her back."

Several. The word stood out to me. I'd gone under the whip so many times the injuries were indistinguishable from each other.

The police took statements, added our injuries to their reports. Tyson came up with the story quickly, about us heading to the city on the bus, when some guys asked if he was interested in a job. They lured us both to a site where we were jumped by a bunch of dudes. His voice wobbled as he lied, and I'd filled in the gaps smoothly when he wavered, my eyes fixed on a distant spot in the room.

Finally, we were released. They gave me pain medication but I threw it out when I got home.

As I staggered up the stairs, in blinding pain and sensory overload, I'd passed Mum's room. There was a small box on her bed, and she stood over it, her knuckles pressed against her lips. She looked up, caught my gaze, and said the words I'd been turning over in my head ever since.

I'm so sorry, chickadee.

The pedestrian light blinks as I amble across the road. There is no traffic and no hurry, but I quicken my pace so the light doesn't stop before I reach the other side. Once there, I resume my leisurely pace as my leg throbs, howling at the midnight exercise. But I ignore it; the clacking of my cane is strangely comforting in the dead of night.

I head towards the town centre, the closed shops empty and hollow, washed in the stark orange light of the streetlights. I prefer night time to day now. There are fewer people, fewer questions... less noise. Part of me wonders if I became a nightowl during my strolls around Fairhaven, ending up at Laela's or Tyson's, my one little taste of freedom under the Headmaster's rule.

I think about the long flight of stairs up to my room, how much more comfortable I would be in my own bed if I just bit down on the pain; the climb pales in comparison to my walks around town, but I know which one I can live without. I would go crazy if I couldn't leave the house. It's a necessary sacrifice.

A shout catches my attention, and my steps halt immediately. It was a barked laugh from a group of guys, sitting outside the burger place, lounging on the low fence. I can see the light from their phones as they watch a video together, lit cigarettes between their fingers.

They're between me and the bridge, which is where I like to go.

I contemplate for a second, shrug to no one, and continue forward.

The tapping of my cane gets them first. A few curious faces look up toward me, and I nod.

"Evening."

"How's it going?"

"Not too bad," I reply, as is custom.

"Yeah righto."

"You're that chick from the news." Another pops forward, phone temporarily forgotten at his side. "That's wild."

I finally come to a stop. "Yeah, that's me. From the news."

"No shit," a few of them say.

"It's Rose, right? Rose Evermore?"

Bloody hell. Last time I saw this guy I'd shoved and yelled at him in front of his friends. Jacob stands from the fence, his hair still long and greasy. He flicks a cigarette to the ground.

"Shit, I *thought* it was you that disappeared, but people wouldn't shut up long enough to work it out."

"Yeah, it was me. Got grabbed from the city."

Jacob shakes his head. "That's cooked. They grabbed both you and Welles?"

"Yeah." The story had circulated and set up some kind of operation in the city. I felt kind of bad about the funds being poured into the search for imaginary kidnappers. "They were moving us from one place to the next when we, you know... got away."

Jacob takes a fresh pack of cigarettes from his back pocket, lighting one between cupped hands. He tilts his head. "And that's when you got..."

Even he's too polite to look directly at my leg. I remember Laela asking the exact same thing, and tighten my grip on the cane.

"Mhm." I tap it against my shoe. "Three broken ribs, and a chunk of my leg."

There are some 'oof's and sympathetic mutters.

Jacob moves over and pats the low log fence beside him. "Feel free to sit."

My leg does need a rest. I step forward, saying, "You're not gonna kidnap me, are you? Coz it kind of sucks."

They laugh. A few of the guys have gone back to watching loud videos on their phones. I sit beside Jacob as the smoke from his cigarette curls around both of us before being swept downwind.

"What've you been up to?" I ask, wanting to keep the conversation off myself.

He shrugs. "Not much. Odd job here and there, but you know how it is."

I smile weakly. "Sick of this shit hole town?"

"Yeah... sick of this shit hole town. Just waiting for an opportunity to get out."

I squint into the sudden breeze. "Well, I can't recommend the city."

He laughs, holding the cigarette between his teeth as he combs his long hair back with his fingers. "You smoke?"

"Nah. But thanks."

We sit together on the fence, watching the others. They joke around, punch each other in the shoulder, laugh at clips on their phones. It's normal. Weirdly comforting even.

"What was it like?" he asks suddenly, tapping ash to the bricks.

"What?"

"Being... gone."

I rest my chin on the handle of my cane. "It's real easy to forget this place exists."

"That's a relief."

I smile. "But I saw some shit too."

"Yeah... 'course you would've."

I shoot him a quizzical side look, but as far as I can tell, he's being sincere. Mum has tried to talk to me. Tried to get me into therapy. But somehow a midnight conversation with the local delinquent is the most comfortable I've felt in months.

Because he won't judge, I realise suddenly. *He's been to the bottom of the barrel and seen it and come back, too.*

"Some crazy stuff happened," I begin, and swallow hard. "Watched a friend die."

He shakes his head. "Shit, man. That kinda stuff can mess you up."

I clench my jaw. "I think it was my fault. He was trying to stop something bad from happening to me."

"Don't get stuck in your head about it."

"Trust me, it's real easy to. I shouldn't have needed protecting."

"What the hell were you meant to do? Look at ya." I glance up, and he nods towards me. "What are you, five foot two? How big was the other guy?"

I try to recall the northern commander. "Big. Over six foot? I dunno. He had a knife."

He had Petre's knife. He'd stabbed my friend with his own blade, like it was a point to be made.

Jacob pokes the cigarette at me, and the tip flares brighter in my presence. "Bad people do bad shit, alright? That's just how the world goes. Good people get caught up in it. Unless you started it, you were just there. You think your friend would regret getting involved?"

I couldn't imagine Petre, with his sense of noble duty, standing by and watching me get shanked. The vision would haunt him; much as it does me.

There's a lump in my throat, so I just make a non-committal noise and go quiet. He smokes in silence next to me for a few minutes.

"Sometimes, Evermore... people are just shit. Whenever you ask yourself why someone has done this, or someone has done that, it always comes back to—"

"People are just shit," I recite, and he nods.

"Exactly."

We're interrupted by his mate who wants to show us a video of a guy stacking it off a motorbike. The phrase 'full send' is thrown about with some admiration. After a while, they decide to head to the servo for snacks—an invite is even extended to me.

"Gonna head home and get some sleep," I tell them. "But thanks."

They pile into a beat up Commodore, Jacob last to get into the passenger side.

"See you 'round, Evermore."

And I begin to walk home, contemplating the weirdest conversation I've had in recent months, with my shoulders lighter than when I began.

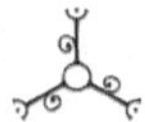

The cashier leans across the counter, her eyes on the sheet of paper I've given her. Her eyes flick to me.

"Would this be your first job?"

I fold my hands on my cane and nod.

She snaps her gum. "You finished school?"

"Uh..." Technically, no, I hadn't. *Got sucked into an alternate dimension*, I imagine saying. *The extra curricular activities were trying not to die, trying not to die, and, oh yeah... trying not to die.* "I'm in my final year."

She scans some lines of text, then pierces me with another gaze. "Looks like you've been in your 'final year' for a few years now."

I opt for a helpless smile. She drops my unimpressive resume on the counter. "Look, we've got some job openings coming up for school holidays. You need some basic maths and good customer service."

Ringing up tills, got it. I try to look excited and fail. Then I imagine telling Mum and Tyson that I have a job and let their genuine excitement leech through.

"One more thing." She chews her gum for a second. "This job has a lot of standing hours. Your shifts can be up to nine hours long."

"Uh huh."

I wait for her to look, and she does, using her head nod as a question. "You need the stick?"

My fingers tighten on the handle. "Yeah... I need the stick."

"Right..." She falls silent. An announcement comes on over the PA, cutting through the hits from the nineties which play constantly throughout the store. "These can be long hours," she says again.

I get the message. My stomach sinks, and I pick up my resume from the counter.

"Thanks for your time," I manage to say, and then limp from the store.

Outside, the brisk wind hits me. It's an iron-grey day, threatening rain—occasionally, the tired sunlight breaks through the cloud cover and ages the town a few decades. I sit heavily on the curb, ignoring the curious looks of shoppers.

I definitely prefer this place at night.

I look over my resume, the black text inked onto cheap paper. *Rose Evermore*, it says. *Eighteen years old.* Then it lists my address and my current year in school. Mum had wanted to add special interests, and I imagine what I could put.

Master of fire at seventeen summers. Potentially the youngest Rune Master to ever graduate the Academy. Next Queen of Lotheria.

I turn my wrist to look at the scars. Nah, that last one is a lie. It had been a stupid idea and one that marked me for life. Others my age would've gotten either an ill-advised tattoo, or—as is common in this town—engaged to their high school sweetheart.

They probably wouldn't have carved magical runes into their arms using the blood of a long-dead queen.

I half-wish I'd just gotten married.

I scrunch the resume into a ball and toss it into the nearest bin. It sails neatly through the air, landing directly in the one labelled 'Recycling'.

Can throw paper balls into bins despite the wind.

I stretch my legs out and rest my chin on my cane. *You can't keep living back there*, Tyson had said. But I don't want to live here either.

So where does that leave me?

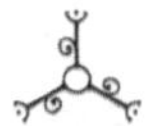

"Do you need anything from the shops?"

I shake my head, splashing hot foamy water over another glass. Mum bustles around, hastily writing a list and grabbing shopping bags. She pauses behind me, but I keep my eyes on the sink.

"Rose," she begins, and my movements still. "I think we should talk tonight."

I half-turn, keeping my hands in the water. "What about?"

Her lips part, but her eyes search mine as though looking for the words she's about to speak. "Just something that's probably long overdue."

It's too much to hope that she's going to address her apology and the mysterious shoebox. A telling off about my lethargic state is more likely. But, thinking back on everything she's done for me since I returned, I owe it to her.

I nod. "Okay. No TV tonight."

She nods, but her smile is thin and her eyes distant. I continue washing up as I hear keys jangle from her bag in the hallway, and the front door open and close. A few seconds later, her car pulls out of the driveway.

I scrub dried porridge from a bowl as though I can clean my mind along with it. Knowing we 'have to talk' always makes me anxious; I fear a similar situation is brewing with my now-absent friend. Eventually, I'll have to scrounge up the courage to get back in contact with him.

"Ugh." I let my hands splash into the sink, releasing the bowl to the bottom. It bounces gently as I dry my hands on a teatowel and reach into my back pocket.

> Hey, I'm sorry for the silence. Burgers tomorrow?

I click 'send' with a monumental amount of effort. But I'm not the only recently-returned teenager in my town; Tyson needs me as much as I need him.

I turn back to the sink but, before I can pick up the dishcloth, there's a knock at the door. A grin grows on my face, rusty and unusual, but my heart lifts with it.

Just like Tyson to not wait for any messages and just take action. I grab my cane and head to the front door.

"I just messaged you," I call as I reach for the handle. "You could've texted back."

I open the door, and the words die in my throat.

"Hello, Miss Evermore," Iain says.

CHAPTER THREE

I DRAW IN A DEEP BREATH, and then look up at him. I pinch myself hard on the arm.

"You're not dreaming," he says. He pushes past me, and I stumble out of the way.

There is a Headmaster in my house.

My grip tightens on my cane and I clench my jaw. "The last time I saw you, Headmaster, you were trying to execute my best friend."

He picks up a framed picture from the hall stand; a picture of me in pigtails and overalls, a young Tyson at my side. "You burnt my town down in return."

Heat grows in my chest. I readjust my grip on my cane. "And yet we're still not even."

He looks over his shoulder at me. "You haven't lost your attitude, Evermore."

Iain disappears into the house. I slam the front door and scramble after him, my steps uneven. In the living room, he pauses and looks around.

"Humble quarters," he remarks. "Are you comfortable in The Other, Rose?"

The question sets my teeth on edge. "The lack of murderous men and women *does* help me sleep at night."

Weirdly, he quirks a smile at that. He continues around the room, picking up objects at random. I remain in the doorway, my eyes never leaving his form, weighing up my options. In a hand to hand fight, he has me. The queenrunes on my forearms have been inactive since I left Lotheria two months ago.

And my fire...

I feel my left palm smoulder, and curl my fingers against it.

I can't use the fire again.

Not after Fairhaven.

"Iain," I say, and he pauses in flicking through a magazine. "What are you doing here?"

He closes the magazine and lets it fall onto the couch. "May we have some tea?"

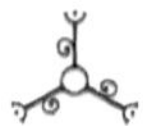

The Headmaster seats himself at the table as I dump boiling water into a mug for him. The seconds tick off loudly in the silence, the cat clock on the wall watching us both as its tail swings.

"I've never been to The Other," he remarks conversationally, as I slide the mug in front of him. He takes a sip and grimaces; I used the oldest teabag I could find in the back of the pantry and then dumped a ton of sugar in as well. "Won't you sit?"

"I prefer to stand, thanks." I hook my cane over the back of a chair and rest my hands on it. "How did you get here?"

Iain places the mug down. His neat dark hair is slightly askew, his maroon tunic damp. I frown; a sliver of white linen peaks from beneath his sleeve. A bandage?

"The river," he says. "Did you really think we kept the entire supply of queensblood in the vault?"

I don't respond, remembering the dark cavern filled with ice bricks—each held a sample of Academy student's blood and graded their magical abilities. The queensblood had been held separately.

"You destroyed the entire vault," he says, sipping the tea. "Did you mean to?"

The *caesis alledari*—the Sudafraen rune language—has a lot of uses for people and their blood. Destroying it had been a complete side effect of the magic I'd worked in the room, but not one I was upset about.

I press my lips together. "You shouldn't have had that blood."

"It is my school. They are my students." He drinks more tea, then pushes it away. "Is this really what counts as a beverage in your world?"

"What are you doing here, Iain?"

He steeples his fingers and leans back in his chair. He looks me over with an unreadable expression in his dark eyes. "I need you."

My lips part slightly. "What?"

"Lotheria is in turmoil. The Halvers were driven from the town, but they fled north. I'm sure you can imagine what they found up there."

The civil war had been in its infancy during my time at the Academy. Orthandrell, the people of the northernmost region of Lotheria, had been fighting for independence against a rising tide of apathy from their southern rulers. I'd killed several of their men in a border skirmish.

To have an army who couldn't feel pain, who fought to the death if commanded, with a woman at their helm who hated the Headmasters with every fibre of her being... the northerners would welcome them with open arms. The half-souls might even forget the northerners were the ones who actually killed their soulmates.

"I fail to see how that's my problem," I say, but my voice wobbles. There are people I still care about in that world, and Iain knows it.

"They no longer just want independence," he says. "They want revenge."

"Against you? I say go for it."

He taps a finger on the table. "Your attitude, whilst it may have been... amusing once, is not welcome in this scenario, Miss Evermore."

"You're in my house," I say. "Asking for my help. Which, I might add, I have no obligation to give."

He looks up at me, expressionless. "You burnt Fairhaven to the ground, Rose."

My stomach sinks. I fight to keep my face blank. "The Halvers attacked the town."

"With your information. With your support. Kaya Aule would never have been bold enough to try such a thing without an inside source. You are the reason the town lies in ashes."

My hand shakes, and I tighten my grip on the chair. "I didn't—"

He stands. "What you did or did not mean to do does not matter. Your actions, the consequences of your choices and decisions, has left Lotheria on the brink of ruin."

My lips part as I say, "I never meant for anyone to get hurt."

"And yet, they did."

I take a deep breath, steadying myself. "Why do you need my help?"

He lifts the mug, takes another long draught. "The powers you displayed during the battle. The fact that you escaped Lotheria through the river. The signs are clear, Miss Evermore. You are to be the next chosen queen of Lotheria."

Nerves thrill through me. "Even though you blooded and killed the last?" I fire back.

He blinks. "Yes. At the time, it was our chosen course of action to keep the peace."

I grind my teeth, but I have more pressing concerns on my

mind than the ongoing power struggles in the upper echelons of Lotherian society.

Iain thinks I am the next queen, chosen by the land itself. The runes I carved into my arms—which give me those powers—are hidden beneath my hoodie sleeves. It is a lie, one he has willingly bought and pursued.

"You think I'm supposed to rule?"

He hesitates a moment, and then nods slowly. "I think you are the next queen, though I cannot work out how the power was passed to a humanborn. More importantly..." He pauses for a second. "You seem to be the only person in both worlds who scares Kaya Aule and, by extension, the man she has allied herself with."

I let the words sink in. The last time I'd seen my co-conspirator, she was sprawled on the cobbles before me, broken, bleeding, and jeering. The sword in my hand had meant death for her. I was the one who'd beaten her with only one leg on the ground.

I clear my throat. "She's afraid of me?"

"We've sown rumours of you throughout the land. She thinks you're in Castor."

The capital city of Lotheria, three days south of the Academy and Fairhaven. A fortified city of a hundred thousand people, and the seat of power in the nation.

"I am not in Castor," I say unhelpfully.

"You will be," Iain replies.

He's so sure, so confident, that for a second I nearly believe him. But my hands are still soft from washing dishes in the sink, and Mum will return with groceries soon. Together we will make spaghetti bolognese and, instead of watching YouTube, we will have a mother/daughter talk. It is comfortable, simple, and easy.

But I don't want that. I don't deserve it.

"What do you need from me?" I ask, my voice raw.

"You will accompany me back to Lotheria, where you will be escorted to the palace in Castor. We will crown you as the new queen, the first *legitimate* one since Fleur. Your reign will unite the noble Lotherian houses slipping from our control. Under my tutelage, you will become a master of battle and strategy, just like the rulers of old."

"And I'll be your puppet," I say, my eyes on the cat clock.

His answer is unapologetic. "Yes."

My heart pounds as the front door opens and closes. I hear Mum scuff her feet.

"That is my mother," I tell him. "You are a teacher from the high school trying to convince me to come back. You will not say a word out of line."

Iain looks at me. "This is your chance at fixing what you left behind, Rose. Remember that."

I turn around as Mum struggles through the archway, carrying loaded bags.

"They'd run out of beef, so I got pork," she says, occupied. "I know it's not the same but—"

"Mum," I interrupt. "This is—"

She looks up, and drops the shopping bags. They tumble to the floor and spill their contents across the lino as my mother and Headmaster stare at each other across the room

And Iain says the single word which brings my world to a standstill.

"Lydia?"

CHAPTER FOUR

SHE DOESN'T RESPOND to the name, and at first I think he's gotten it wrong. Then she steps backward, away from me, away from Iain, her eyes wide with terror.

So much becomes clear in an instant; her understanding when I reappeared after a year away, why they couldn't find my name in the Academy records, why the queensblood burnt Kaya but not me.

It was my mother's blood.

Iain moves out the corner of my eye, and I grab my cane instinctively. I swing it at his head with both hands, but he catches it easily.

"You blooded my MOTHER?!"

His face is unreadable, his eyes on the woman behind me. I try to wrest my cane free of his grasp, rage boiling in my gut. Behind me, the stove bursts to life, four little fires burning steadily from the gas source. The runes on my arms seem to press deeper into my skin.

"Rose."

My mother's soft voice drifts across the kitchen. I stop struggling against Iain's hold and turn around as the stove burners die down again.

She stands, her hands clasped in front of her, eyes on me. For a moment, the instinct to turn to her is overwhelming.

My mother is the queen. The *true* queen of Lotheria. Her presence seems to fill the room as she holds up a hand.

"Iain, let go of my daughter."

To my surprise, my cane is returned. Iain steps back.

"I don't understand how this is possible," he mutters.

"And you won't," she replies. "Can you give us a minute? Rose, we need to have that talk."

The old shoebox sits on the kitchen table in front of me, innocent and crumpled from years of being hidden in her wardrobe.

"We didn't have YouTube in my day," she explains, and lifts the lid off the box.

Inside, yellowed newspaper clippings flutter at the disturbance. I slowly reach in and lift one.

MISSING WOMAN FOUND AFTER THREE YEARS

There is a picture of her. Younger, thinner, her eyes wide and gaunt. But it is definitely my mother.

I take a deep breath. "You were in Lotheria for three years."

She takes the article from me, staring at the tiny print. "Yes. I was about to graduate from the Academy."

I concentrate on breathing, my heart beating rapidly. "You knew about everything this whole time?"

She turns to me. "I tried to get you to tell me, when your magic first started manifesting. But I was scared, Rose. I was scared that if you knew what it was, you'd go. You'd seek it out."

"And then I did anyway," I say bitterly, leafing through the box. "But without knowing what waited for me on the other side."

She gently places the article back with the others. "Yes. I made a mistake. I should've told you."

"So you disappeared for three years, came back, and what— shacked up with a dude and had me?" I meet her hard gaze and hold my hands up. "I'm just trying to piece together the timeline."

She sits at the table, pushing away Iain's cold tea mug. "When they blooded me, they nearly killed me, Rose. They dumped my body in the river to send me back here, to get rid of any trace of me."

"But you survived."

"When they hauled me into that dungeon," she begins, her eyes distant. "They didn't know. No one knew at the time, except for me. I'd just returned from a trip north and hadn't made any announcement."

I sit opposite her, my leg numb from overuse.

She looks at me, eyes bright. "They drained me dry, of blood, of magic... of the will to live. I don't remember going into the river, or slipping below the surface. But there was a tiny little speck left... a star. It saved me." She clenches her jaw. "*You* saved me. My baby."

My lips part softly. "*I* got us home?"

She nods. "I think so. You were the only thing left untouched. I believe your magic sustained me and kept me alive until they found me on the riverbank."

I twist my hands together, bobbing my head. "Okay... okay, see, this is good. I'm learning I was a very accomplished foetus." The implications dawn on me. "So I was meant to be born in Lotheria? I was going to be a nativeborn mage?"

She pulls a wry smile. "The Greatcasts, our family line, are one of the great noble Houses. They rule Numin, near Riverdoor."

I'm not expecting it; the name hits me like a gut punch. "Riverdoor?"

"Yes. The Greatcasts are the biggest House in eastern Lotheria."

My vision clouds with memories of Riverdoor, how close to my ancestral home I'd been.

But another, more pressing issue suddenly surges to the forefront of my mind. "Is this why you never told me about my father?"

Her face is unreadable. "How could I tell you about him when he lived in a world you had no idea existed?"

"And now?"

Mum goes quiet, her eyes distant. "Rose..."

I grip her hands, bringing her back to me. "Tell me. You have no reason not to."

"Your father is... a complicated man. He's..." She falls silent for a moment, lost in memories. "He had his moments, good and bad. But I believe he's a good person."

I sit back slightly. "Not exactly the glowing report I was hoping for."

She looks up, her eyes searching mine. "You've never been in love, chickadee. People aren't always who you think they are. They're not simple, or easy. They can make you cry and feel on top of the world in the span of days. But when you love someone enough, you don't care."

I nod slowly, and heave a sigh. My mind is whirring, just like it did in my final days at the Academy. Iain's mere presence has necessitated a return to my old, paranoid way of thinking. "This is a lot to process."

She casts a look outside. "I know. And we don't have a lot of time to do it in. I don't know why Iain is here, but I can tell you this." She grips my hands and looks me in the eyes. "Do not trust him. No matter what he says, no matter what he does. Do you understand?"

I follow her gaze. Iain stands in the backyard, far out of

earshot, looking up at the sky as the afternoon begins to stretch thin.

"Completely." I turn away from the window.

My mother chews her lip, and her eyes go to the hallway. "And on that note... Rose, I have an idea."

CHAPTER FIVE

THE BACK DOOR screeches as the Headmaster lets himself in. "Am I allowed to return?"

"Do you want my honest answer?" I respond.

He approaches, eyes on my mother—Lydia. She stands behind my chair, her hand resting on my shoulder.

"What do you want with my daughter?" she asks.

"I need her to remedy a situation she created," he says. "As it appears Rose has followed in your footsteps in seeking dangerous alliances."

"You want her to return to Lotheria."

"That would be ideal."

Her voice is hard. "Hasn't she given enough to your world?"

Iain looks down at me. "On the contrary. I believe she took more than she gave."

"If we're measuring in lashes, sure," I retort, tugging my sleeves down reflexively. "Or did you forget about that?"

"We didn't authorise Hall's punishment of—"

"I'm not mad about the whipping, Iain. Of *all* the things we have between us, that is the last thing on the list."

He nods slowly.

Mum says, "She's not going back."

The Headmaster merely looks at me, and I answer, "Yes, I am."

"Rose—"

"He's right." I turn to look at her and she meets my gaze, questions burning in her eyes. I swallow. "I created the situation. I want a chance to fix it."

Because no one else has had the guts to look me in the eyes and tell me it was *my* fault. I've been met with soft, gentle rebukes, hand holding, carefully worded explanations of how I *had* to do this, and *had* to do that.

But for the first time since we washed up on that river bank, the gnawing guilt in my stomach is gone, and I know it's because I'm blatantly acknowledging the ugly truth of an inconvenient situation. I plant my cane on the floor and straighten my back.

"You aren't taking her anywhere."

Her voice rings out into the kitchen. I clench my jaw, but glance up at the Headmaster. He doesn't move, but his eyes darken.

"I implore you to examine what you think you can do to stop me, Miss Greatcast." His voice is low. "Your magical blood has run dry, and more than that, your daughter *wants* to accompany me."

"My blood ran dry because you bled it from me," she says. "Netalia tied me to the ice and emptied my veins as I pleaded with you, a man I considered a friend and a mentor. And now you're here to take my child away." Her voice breaks. "You are a monster, Iain."

"Yes," he says, "and one would do well not to cross monsters when armed only with words. Rose, come with me."

I let myself look at her, and my heart breaks as her eyes fill with tears. Mine do as well, but I walk, stiffly, from the kitchen—at the side of the man who nearly killed her.

"Rose."

Iain opens the front door for me, and I hesitate on the threshold. She's followed us into the hallway.

"Lotheria is the one place where I felt like I wasn't a mistake," I say, looking at the floor. "Where I felt like I could make a plan for the future... I was never meant for this world. And that's never been more clear to me than it is right now."

I step outside before she can answer, and the tears spill down my cheeks. But as we walk towards the river in the fading twilight, the pit in my stomach lightens with every step.

"That was dramatic," Iain advises as we climb down the riverbank.

I ignore him, carefully navigating the muddy slope. My shoes get stuck a few times, and I have to ease my foot free so I don't fall. When I reach the water, Iain holds his hand out, but I merely walk in beside him, splashing carelessly.

"Admirable," he comments. "But I need your blood."

I inhale, preparing for more pain only an instant before he grips my left hand and slices the back of it. Queensblood, white and shining, drips in shimmering flecks to the water.

It calms, stilling the strong current. An oval mirror forms between us, pushing the water outwards, sending tiny riplets against my knees.

Through the flickering white sparks searing the outside of it, I can just make out trees leaning over the water, and raindrops flicker across the surface though the skies of Narralong are clear.

It's raining in Lotheria.

I cast one more look back towards the road, where the sun has begun to set over the township. Iain surges towards me in the water.

"Your time here is done," he says. "It's time to return to what you wrought."

I am not done with Lotheria. Lotheria is not done with me.

Before Iain can lay another hand on me, I step forward into the portal.

CHAPTER SIX

For the third time, I am washed between worlds in a tumultuous current. I surface with a gasp, and strike out with my left arm and leg towards the bank. Speckles of rain hit me in the face as my feet hit the muddy bottom of the river.

"Miss Evermore!"

I look up, knee deep in the river. Eustace Greatree, first page of the Academy, is reaching towards me with a helpful expression on his face. I grip his hand, allowing him to guide me onto the shore. My leg, cold from the water, shakes rebelliously as I take a step onto land, and blankets are thrown around my shoulders.

"Headmaster Iain, we have your carriage waiting," Eustace calls. His hand presses flat against my back to guide me to the vehicle. Guards wait with tall halberds at their side, in full black plate armour. "We'll depart for the capital shortly."

"Castor?" I repeat with a broken voice, pausing with one foot in the enclosed carriage. "Not Fairhaven?"

I turn back as Iain pauses in accepting a blanket, his expression unreadable. "No... not Fairhaven. With the current threat from the Halvers and the... previous destruction, it is not currently habitable. As I previously stated, you will be residing in the capital."

The air leaves my lungs. More devastation sinks low in my belly. "The town is... gone?"

"Not gone," Iain corrects, approaching the carriage. "It still stands."

He doesn't elaborate. My chest rises and falls, and I tighten my grip on the carriage. "I want to see it."

"Miss Evermore—"

Unexpected heat sears through my blood, and I meet his gaze steadily. "Take me through Fairhaven."

Stillness descends on those gathered as Iain looks at me. No one moves for a moment.

"Very well. We will alter our route to go through the main township," he concedes. "But I warn you... what you will see is not pleasant."

The sudden strength fades, and I nod wearily. Relinquishing my grip on the doorway, I duck into the carriage, settling on the thick leather cushion inside. I flex my fingers in my lap and will my racing heart to slow.

At first, I think they're taking me through a burnt out forest. Blackened wood and charred remains lance skyward towards the iron-grey clouds as our carriages and mounted escorts pick through the cluttered streets. I watch the buildings and houses slide past the window, the curtain bunched in my fist. When we reach the main square, I utter a single word.

"Stop."

Iain knocks on the wall, and we slow to a halt. He makes no move to stand first, so I do, reaching the door as it is opened from the outside.

I jump awkwardly to the cobbles and move past Eustace. The platform where Iain had tried to reason with an angry mob, Tyson in his grasp hooded and bound like a felon, is a pile of lumber half-collapsed to the ground. The stone buildings fared slightly better, but some have fallen inwards, their thatched roofs long since incinerated, the mortar between bricks crumbling from the heat.

It is completely, utterly silent.

I move away from the group, a lump in my throat, and kneel to pick up some charcoal from the nearest building. It'd been a bakery; Petre and I had bought pies on the morning we visited the soulwitch. The non-magi who ran it had been pleasant and friendly, always smiling.

The counter is empty, burnt, and long since destroyed.

I crush the charcoal in my fist and let the fine black grit blow away. My eyes close as I recall Craige teaching Tyson the trick to distinguish between good charcoal and bad.

I wonder what he'd think of this.

Someone moves up behind me.

"It's all like this?" I ask.

"Yes," Iain replies. "We were unable to fight off the half-soul army *and* put out your fire. We chose the former."

Numbness settles heavily in my stomach. I stand, brushing my hand against my jeans, leaving a dark, sooty streak there. "Where did everyone go?"

"They left. Most fled to the capital as refugees. Others to outlying farm towns, or the surrounding forests to live off of the land. A few regiments of the guard have been assigned to capture the outlaws and bring them in."

I raise an eyebrow and duck my head. "Yeah, that sounds about right."

"What was that?"

"Nothing."

I swallow hard, stepping into the carriage and closing the door. Only when the Headmaster is out of sight do I rest my forehead against the curtained glass. The convoy lurches into motion, leaving the abandoned township behind in the fading dusk.

The next two days pass in relative silence. The greatroad twists and turns through the country, thick with forests and brush scrub. I'm reminded of our midnight ride north all those months ago, through trees that pressed close, and our ice-frosted gloves and scarves. We'd ridden to offer aid to a family the Headmasters refused to, blindly ignoring the threat in the north even after one of the biggest strongholds, Longrock, had fallen.

"Tell me of Riverdoor," I say around the campfire on our last night. Tomorrow, Iain has promised I will see the city walls. "Did the northerners press their attack?"

Iain hesitates for a moment. "Communication with Riverdoor has been scarce. The lord and lady no longer heed the call of the court, or their greater House."

My lips part in surprise, until I recall Hugh's fury at the Headmaster's indifference to his plea for help. My thoughts turn inwards as Iain continues.

"When we have crowned you, a messenger will ride with your summons. Either he or his wife will have to travel to answer in person, to confirm their intentions as a member of your court."

I clench my teeth, but nod. "I understand. I can do that."

"You *will* do that," Iain corrects. "It is in your best interests to unite your country as soon as possible."

"Is that your advice," I say. "Or your command?"

His eyes bore into me over the flames. "As the current ruler of Lotheria and your advisor, consider it both."

I lower my eyes to the campfire and reach out a hand to it. My sleeves are long and cover my scars, but I seek the warmth that has always comforted me. The queenrunes lie dormant as I cover my hands in flame.

"At least now we know why your fire whispering is so strong," Iain comments. "Your mother was queen, and so will you be."

Your fire affinity is stronger than most...

My mother had been a queen of Lotheria. My power had flowed from her. My heart sinks.

"And your rune work," he continues. "Fitting that you chose to major in it."

Curiosity shakes me from my reverie. "Why?"

Iain turns dark eyes towards me, the firelight reflecting within them. "I'm surprised your mother didn't tell you. Your master, Arno Veloquis, was her soulmate."

LYDIA

The young, dark-haired woman stood at her window, watching the sun begin to sink below the horizon. The man didn't knock at the door before entering, but she was turning towards him as he did.

"Wow, Lyd, look at you!" Arno was dressed in dark pants and a long coat with red trim. His golden hair was swept back and the short stubble on his chin framed a strong jaw; she knew for a fact it took him about an hour to get this 'uncaring' look perfect. "Where'd the dress come from?"

She grinned, and turned on the spot so it flared out in a narrow circle. "The Greatcasts sent it to me, with a lovely note."

"So they really like you, huh?" Arno picked up the note Lydia offered. He quickly skimmed it. "They want you to visit this summer."

She took the note back. "The Headmasters have agreed. They want me to meet my kin before—"

"Before they make the announcement." Arno closed the distance between them, and placed his hand on her shoulder. "How are you feeling?"

She shrugged him off. "I'm fine. Honestly, it won't change much."

Arno stared at her. "Lydia. It'll change everything."

She bit her lip and looked away. "Do I wish I could've just been a student? Yes. Do I wish I could've just studied Horticulture and travelled the world with you? Yes. But Lotheria, of all places, Arno, isn't fair. I'm grateful this is the hand fate has dealt me." Lydia stepped closer and straightened his collar. "It brought me here, to my soulmate. To you."

Arno grinned, and took her face in his hands to plant a rough kiss on her powdered forehead, then grimaced. "Why are you wearing so much of this?"

Lydia reddened and turned to the mirror in her vanity. "I'm not."

"You are! And you're wearing—" Arno nudged her feet. "Heels! You hate heels!"

"Jettais is bringing his brother."

"Oh ho ho ho," Arno declared, sitting heavily on her made bed and crossing one leg over the other. He gestured in the air like a fine lord making a proclamation. "The truth comes out! The sexy northerner has finally gotten Lydia Greatcast into heels... but will he get her into bed?"

She whirled in a flare of skirts, but he was ready and ducked the hand she swiped at him. Shimmering green mist curled from her palm as it passed. He yelped.

"Get your plant magic away from me! Last time you hit me with that, I sprouted roses in some very uncomfortable places."

Turning back to the mirror to continue fixing her makeup, Lydia smiled. "I know."

"But I'm serious, Lydia." Arno's tone darkened as he stood up again. "You're about to be crowned queen of Lotheria. You have to take that into account going forward."

She frowned at his reflection. "I know. Have I been behaving like I haven't?"

"Not yet," Arno admitted. "But I've seen you with crushes before. And Kynan—"

She faced him with a hard stare, her earlier humour nowhere to be seen. "Please don't say his name within these walls. It wouldn't surprise me if they have listening runes all around this place."

"They don't. I checked."

"And he's what, Arno? From the north?"

He held up his hands defensively. "There's a lot of bad shit happening up there at the moment. The Araspires have been saying a lot things—"

"They're *one* House."

He caught her hand. "They're *the* great noble House of the north, Lydia. And you know it."

Nerves fluttered in her chest. Suddenly, the evening seemed darker. She took a deep breath.

"Well, no matter what's happening in Orthandrell, we need to focus on what's happening here tonight." She faced him with a smile. "Your masterwork, Arno. What you've been working on for three years."

"*Almost* three years," he corrected. "But you're right. We should focus on what's important."

"You?"

"Me."

She grinned as he gathered up her things. But his words lingered, and her smile faded as they left the room.

CHAPTER SEVEN

THE STONE WALLS of Castor rise tall beyond the southern moors. The carriage comes to a halt, and I unlatch the door before we stop.

"Welcome home, Miss Evermore," Iain says, as though he personally constructed the city.

I limp away from the party—stiff after days in a carriage—and look over my new home. The greatroad continues down and across farmland, the fields bare but the soil rich and dark. Small houses cluster together in communities, their chimneys smoking with little figures working outside in the yards. A great gate made of black wood is crested by two tall watchtowers, their enormous blood-red flags unfurling in the breeze.

"Miss Evermore, will you ride beyond the gates with me?" Iain asks. His coat flaps in the wind as he holds a hand out. "Come, I will help you mount up."

I've ridden no other horse beside my own, Echo, during my time at the Academy. A great sorrow rings through me as I recall Iain's words—that the stables had been opened during the Halvers' attack, and all Academy horses had fled into the lowhills. I just hoped desperately that my beautiful horse had been taken in by a loving family somewhere far away from all of this.

The mare they bring me is sleek and white, intelligence gleaming in her dark eyes. I run my fingers down her nose, and finger comb the pale forelock between her alert ears; someone has brushed her mane and coat very recently.

She is a horse fit for a queen—the queen Iain believes me to be.

I take a deep breath, and hand my cane to the waiting guard. Iain cups my knee and hoists me into the saddle, my feet finding the stirrups easily. I twist to retrieve my cane from the guard, but he has vanished.

"My—"

"You will get it back when we reach the palace," Iain says. He rides up next to me on his own horse. "This is the first time you will be presented to your people, though they do not yet know your name. The rumours we seeded in the far north have not reached the southern city.

"This is your second chance to make a good first impression, Miss Evermore. Do not squander it."

He kicks his horse into a canter, and mine follows as though towed on a line. The dirt of the greatroad is churned beneath her hooves as the wind streams past my face. As I follow the man through the farmlands towards his city, I forget everything for a moment. The rhythm of hoofbeats, the rushing sound in my ears, drowns out everything but the ride.

I brace my right leg as much as I can, and stand in my stirrups, letting the motion of the horse roll freely beneath me. Her pace increases until we're flying along the road at a gallop. I sit back down and lean forward, the reins tight in my grasp as we pass Iain. A grin spreads across his face and, surprising myself, I return it as we pull ahead.

A few people appear along the sides of the road, drawn by the caravan we travelled with. I slow my horse to an easy canter as Iain catches up, my cheeks warm and chest heaving.

"You are a good rider," he comments as he draws even.

"I enjoy it," I respond, wary of the compliment. I rub my mount's neck. "She is a wonderful horse."

"Her name is Iotha," he tells me. "Named for the god of sea breezes in Sudafrae."

It is the first time he has mentioned his homeland to me. Kaya had told me he was originally from the land in the east, as was she, but to hear him speak it willingly—conversationally—is shockingly intimate. I look away, playing with Iotha's white mane instead.

"She deserves the name," I say.

"And of the position she holds in your stable," he continues. "Iotha is the Queen's Mare, a title held by only a single horse at one time. When you ride, or hunt, or travel, Iotha is the horse you will be seen astride. Her likeness will be depicted in the art of your great deeds alongside your own."

I let his words roll over me, my stomach churning, and then urge Iotha into a trot and ride ahead. It takes me a bit to get into the rhythm of riding at this pace again, and I bump along like a sack of potatoes until the gate looms over me.

It remains closed even as we get closer. I peer upwards to the stone watchtowers, taking in the wooden walkway that crosses the gate. I can see men moving between the gaps, though no one hollers down to question why a single rider waits below.

Not until Iain, and the rest of the caravan, arrives is the order shouted for them to be opened. Iotha shifts uneasily, tossing her head. I don't try to calm her, my eyes on the city beyond.

"Welcome to Castor," Iain says, and then adds, "The seat of your power and reign."

Houses and buildings cluster close to the walls, the wide street bustling with people carrying baskets or towing mules. The city peels downhill, thousands of thatched and tiled roofs slating the landscape in muted greys and yellows, separated only by thin cobbled roads or alleys, until it reaches the harbour below. The seabreeze sails over the districts, bringing a flurry of city smells to my nose. I squeeze my eyes shut and blink a few times.

"You are used to open fields and small towns," Iain says, beginning to ride forward. "The stench is worse by the walls."

My horse follows his lead, carrying me further into Castor. Here, the houses are ramshackle, almost shanty cabins, impermanent structures with thin smoke curling from the hides that serve as scant shelter from the weather.

"Who lives here?" I ask.

"Mostly villagers fleeing the rumour of war. Enough farms were burnt by the half-souls on their way out of Fairhaven that the very real fear of raiders encouraged them to pick up and seek safety. They cluster here by the walls as they attempt to make a living in the city."

I look over the few who stop to watch us go by. Their clothing is ragged and threadbare, the fires guttering in the wind and almost expiring against the damp wood they're trying to burn. I take a deep breath, closing my eyes and seeking the warmth that lingers in my blood. As we pass, each hearth and stove is strengthened, flickering bright and strong against the grey day, drying the wood it consumes. I can feel the heat from every fire as we journey through the districts.

The slender fingers of exhaustion begin to creep up as I ride through the city, but I tighten my grip on the reins and bear down on my fire magic. My vision blurs as I instead see the fires and hearths inside the cabins instead of the road. A ringing begins in my ears as something dampens under my nose, and suddenly Iain's fingers grip my arm.

"Warmer months lie around the corner," he says, and hands me a cloth. I press it under my nose to stem the flow of blood. "Their fires need only keep them for a few weeks more."

I take away the cloth and stare at the bright red blotch on it. Never before has my fire tired me so; in fact, using it has always been comforting... when I was in control. But I can feel a little chain of sparks behind me, and the magnitude of the magic I was trying to work suddenly catches up with me, and I sag in the saddle.

"Eyes up, Miss Evermore," Iain warns, and rides ahead. The click of horseshoes against cobbles wakes me slightly, and I refocus on my Headmaster.

A white stone bridge stretches tall over the sea inlet that nearly divides Castor in half. Ships sail far beneath it, and the wind nearly blinds us. I squint against it, my eyes drawn to the structure that crests a rock spire, looming over the city.

Tall towers pierce the low clouds, with blood red flags unfurling from their points. Guards patrol behind the crenellated walls, and it takes me a second to recognise the palace; for surely no other building would be allowed to loom from the highest point on the coast.

We wind up a twisting street towards the palace gate, joined by more guards. They escort the caravan past the few shops and houses who've managed to find a sturdy area to anchor their buildings, though the cliff falls away to the inlet below. Rainwater gushes from a gutter in the wall, cascading to jagged rocks. A sudden breeze sweeps spray towards us, and my horse tosses her head.

"I know," I mutter, leaning forward to rub her neck. "Me too."

As Iain welcomes the guards, my eyes are fastened to the gates. I get the feeling that once I venture beyond them, they'll close behind me for a very long time.

But I chose this. And it's with that certainty that I follow Iain into the palace courtyard with the others.

CHAPTER EIGHT

THINGS HAPPEN VERY QUICKLY once we're inside the gates. The rest of the caravan arrives, and we are directed towards the stable wing by a small army of manservants. Iotha crunches across the gravel as I look up at the large manse which will serve as my new home. The whole building has a presence that seems to lean down and examine me, an ancient aura that locks itself into the rock spire it's built upon —a promise that it will never be brought down by siege or fire.

As I wait for assistance to dismount, I look closer at the wall beside me. Against the rough rock, small vines twist and grow, digging into minute cracks and absorbing the rainwater that soaks the stone. I reach out a finger to stroke a deep red leaf, and it furls into itself at my touch.

"Sorry," I mutter to it, and turn my attention to the guard who waits for me to dismount.

Griffin offers my cane to me. I blink at him for a second.

"It usually works better if I'm on the ground first," I tell him.

He tucks my cane under his arm, and helps me dismount. "Oh, I remember. Good day, Miss Evermore."

"Good day," I respond, wobbling in place even with my cane

in hand. I try to flex my toes but they're slowly numbing and I'm not sure if I'm successful. "Are you stationed here now?"

"Believe it or not, this is where I've always been stationed. Though I did spend a lot of time in Fairhaven last year."

Of course. Griffin was a captain in the Governor's Black Guard. He oversaw the security of the city, in service to Governor Malico. Which meant being sent on errands, such as informing the next of kin in accordance with the old laws, or retrieving renegade students when they disappeared from the Academy in the middle of the night.

"Miss Evermore." Iain's voice cuts through my response to Griffin. "Come with me, please."

I give Griffin a wry look, and then limp over the gravel to Iain's side. He waits, eyes fixed on the captain behind me.

"I didn't realise you were friendly with Marks," Iain says as I amble closer.

"We bonded after he brought me back from Riverdoor," I respond. "We had a bit of time to talk on the road."

"He is non-magi."

I press my lips together for a second. "He is also a captain of the Black Guard."

Iain turns away. "Come, I will show you the palace. Also... your friends await."

The air leaves my lungs; I haven't seen my friends for months. Not since I said goodbye to them in their tent and promised to return. A mixture of excitement and dread fills me as I scramble up the stone stairs behind him, emerging into a vast, empty foyer. Inside, the air is heavy and stale, the rapid tap of my cane echoing off of the walls. Unlit golden sconces and long tapestries hang from the stone walls, and I shiver as the cold sinks deep into my clothing. The building is utterly still, until Iain's voice echoes around the room.

"Lotheria's rulers have always lived within these halls," he begins. "Be they queens, kings, or governors. Malico lorded here for seventeen years."

I follow him down the corridors of the empty, silent palace. "Where is he?"

Iain glances down at me, and I see something that gives me pause; unease behind his eyes. I'd caught him off guard.

"Malico's services were no longer required. He was only our placeholder in Castor until we found a worthy queen."

It's a vague answer, insultingly close to a lie. I let it go. "And what makes me a worthy queen, when my mother was not?"

The question bites sharper than intended, and I am surprised when Iain replies, "Because there is war now, and a queen is needed to rally support in her people."

Of course. Why give up absolute power in peacetime?

"You said my friends were waiting?" A small tendril of hope curls in my chest.

Iain nods. "After the attack, the education of our next genera-tion of mages was moved here, to the palace. They reside in the western wing and are barred from the main chambers of commerce and office."

He goes on ahead, but I take a moment to process this infor-mation. The corners of my mouth tug upwards as my heart races, and I hasten to follow the Headmaster.

I follow him into the heart of the building, deep within halls and countless rooms. The cold is fiercer here, and settles into my bones. I shiver, my breath misting in the air before me.

The throne room is long, with tall stone columns carved with scenes from history. They are faded and chipped in places. At the end is a dais, with one solitary throne. The ceiling arches high above, with an enormous glass window set into the stone, filtering muted daylight into the room. The second floor has a gallery to allow standing observers. I walk down the centre, towards the narrow throne.

"You will be crowned in this room," Iain says as I reach it.

"Your noble Houses will crowd the halls while the city cheers for their queen. The bells of the palace will ring victorious, and the northern spies will have something to take to their leader."

My earlier elation dies away in the face of cold logistics. "It's all for show," I say, my voice ringing against the walls for the first time. I sound small and weak against the majesty of the large room. "You'll use me for theatrics and posturing."

Iain steps up beside me, his eyes, too, fixed on the throne. "Not completely. When you have settled into your new role, I will educate you on what the half-souls and the northerners have done since your departure. Then, you will understand why we need you."

He rests a hand on my shoulder for a second, then removes it and turns away. His touch lingers even after he withdraws.

He climbs the steps to the dais but I remain on the floor. "You nearly killed my mother in pursuit of this power, only to bring me here nineteen years later to give it back. I don't trust you to have my best interests at heart, Iain, or the country's."

The Headmaster says nothing for a moment. I swallow hard, every sinew in my body tensed like a drawn bowstring as I wait for his response.

He reaches out and touches the throne lightly, then lets his hand fall.

"I did a terrible thing to Lydia Greatcast," he murmurs. "To a woman who considered me her friend and mentor. You must believe I never meant for it to go as far as it did."

I say nothing, but in my mind I see the town of Fairhaven burning, alight with my escaped fire. I don't lower my gaze as he turns towards me.

"This"—he taps the throne—"is a path to redemption, Rose."

He lowers his voice, and I strain my ears.

"For both of us."

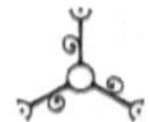

We leave the throne room together, lost in our own thoughts. A bell tolls outside, and I hear the chattering of voices. I perk up, going to a window.

"Your friends," Iain says behind me, and I spot the long, slate-grey cloaks of Lotherian students moving from one wing of the palace to another through the wide courtyard. They move in groups of two or three, but one trails behind.

Suddenly, something sings in my chest. The student pauses, looking in our direction as though he can see into the shadows.

My breath leaves my lungs.

Phoenix.

My soulmate.

The last time I'd seen him, he'd crossed blades with Iain on a burning platform in front of rioting villagers, setting Tyson free from unjust execution. The Headmaster in question steps up beside me.

"You allowed him to come back?" I ask, my voice small.

Iain says nothing for a long moment, his eyes on the courtyard. Then he says simply, "He bested me."

Phoenix remains in the square as the other students move on. I could emerge into the sunlight, allowing him to see me. But instead, I stand in the shadows, and eventually he turns and follows our classmates.

"You are ashamed," Iain comments in a low voice.

"Yes." I withdraw back to the corridor, and he follows. "Phoenix did what I couldn't. He saved Tyson without destroying an entire village."

"His decisions during the Battle of Fairhaven were surprising, for someone of his creed."

I'm pulled out of my thoughts by Iain's previous answer. "You let him come back to the south because he beat you in a swordfight?"

"Yes. When he asked to return, it felt fitting to honour his request, and it freed me of any obligation towards him."

I cast him a sideways look.

"Yes, Miss Evermore?"

"Nothing."

The excitement of seeing my friends has died down in the face of reconciling with the consequences of my actions. We walk together in silence for a few moments, until he breaks it.

"You have played Kingdoms, yes?"

I have, with Jettais and some other students. I tell him so.

"Good. Kingdoms is not just a time passer for academics; it is the game of rulers and kings, strategists, and leaders which ties into the very core of this land. Lotheria is not just rocks and forests... but you know this already." I nod, and he continues. "I myself hold the title of High Marshal amongst the ranked players, as has every queen that has passed through these halls. Their names precede them, their prowess in conflict at the helm of their memorial. I will be your tutor."

I frown. "I know how to play."

"For leisure and entertainment. I will teach you to *win*."

I hesitate, remembering the few games I played between classes; it was a fun pastime. I nod.

Iain leads me to a room on the first sub-level of the palace, carrying a torch. The heavy door is bolted shut, as though it protects a valuable treasure. The Headmaster produces a key and unlocks it, pushing the barred wooden door open and gesturing for me to go inside. I cast him a look, then tap past him, my cane echoing on the uneven flagstones.

The Kingdoms table takes up almost the entire room, a wide, roughly-shapen slab of oak with tiles carved upon it. I recognise the shape of Lotheria immediately, longer than it is wide, with the bays and harbours of the south biting deep into the landscape, the moors of Riverdoor and Numin flat and wide against the towering mountains of Orthandrell. It is ornately designed, my eye for rune craftmanship lingering on and appreciating the fine detail of every tile. I take a deep breath, reaching out a hand. I half expect Iain to stop me, and when my fingers meet the smooth grain of the table, I wait for the barked command to hold.

It doesn't come. I step closer as the Headmaster tends to the sconces around the room, sending golden firelight washing across the wooden landscape. He returns to my side as I continue my examination.

"This is the table upon which your predecessors learnt the art of war," Iain begins. "The games played here number in the thousands."

"It's stunning," I admit. "I only ever played on a fold-out board."

He nods sagely. "There are only two tables of this design in the world. Come, let me show you the tiles."

The walls are lined with cupboards and drawers. I move closer, noting the hundreds of thousands of miniature figurines, used to depict armies and soldiers for the game. They stand in various shapes and poses, with detailing in their paint hinting at their specialities and abilities. I reach up and lift down a small cavalry figurine, the horse in full motion with a flying mane. The rider lifts a lance upon the horses' back, in full helm and plate. There are many pieces I don't recognise, and I suddenly realise how little I actually know of the game.

Iain shows me the wide, flat drawers filled with interchange-able wooden tiles, some with different motifs painted on them.

"To display the change in season and weather," he explains, and a few tiles on the board move. I *do* know, from my games with Jett and the others, that this changes certain values of the terrain and will affect the pieces placed upon it, but I've always had to flip them manually. The table's enchantment is more complicated than I realised.

I drum my left fingers on my thigh, my eyes on the board. After a few moments, I realise Iain has fallen silent and is waiting for me to respond.

"Sorry, what?"

He surprises me by grinning. "I see the table has taken your attention, as it should. You were noting the landscape features when you first entered. Let us play a round."

My stomach swoops. "Now? We have the rest of our party waiting for us upstairs."

"They are preparing your rooms and settling the party. Besides, a Novice versus a Marshal? This will not take long."

That sounds suspiciously like humour, but I move around my end of the table anyway, to the tiny carved city of Castor, a perfect model of the city we just rode through. Guilt nips at me as I imagine people looking for us as we're sequestered away in the dungeons. I push the thought away and focus as Iain flips the token for who will move first.

He wins, gathering his armies as the table darkens for me, which is new. I will be unable to see where he places his figures until I march upon the location or successfully send spies amongst their ranks. I take a deep breath, and begin fortifying my city on my turn.

I've always favoured a defensive position in Kingdoms. I learnt early on that my classmates preferred to rush in and siege, with fire, glory, and chanting armies. I'd let them dash themselves upon the walls of my hold while I controlled the battlefield with archers and trebuchets, maintaining hidden supply lines so that my city continued on without disruption.

But I glance up as Iain focuses on his moves. He knows I've played before, and therefore probably knows my regular strategies. He will prepare siege weaponry with the intent of breaking my walls and resolve. Unless he knows I will think of this, and is preparing for me to sally out.

Kingdoms is a mind game above all else. I press my lips

together and gather large units of cavalry, sending them into the lowhills either side of the rich farmland that surrounds the walls of Castor; the same ones we stood upon to first gaze at the city. If Iain marches infantry and trebuchets to the front line, my riders will smash through it.

With my leftover resources, I muster as many archers as possible and line the walls with them. The sandtimer trickles down on the corner of the table. Neither of us speak. I solidify my supply lines, but know that if my cavalry is destroyed, I do not have the resources to retrain enough troops to defend the city.

Suddenly, the dark mist that hovers over the farmland tiles parts, revealing a large, varied army. Iain reaches forward, moving his siege weaponry as far as they can move on their turn, using the greatroad tiles to provide greater mobility.

He settles the pieces, and looks up at me. "We issue a challenge to the city walls. Your turn, Miss Evermore."

I take a deep breath, and reach for my cavalry units. Iain follows my movement, and I know the mist will reveal my figurines as it did for his. I keep my eyes on his, noting the complete lack of surprise as my horses ride forth. My heart sinks; he planned for this.

My cavalry dies upon the spears of his infantry that protected the trebuchets, buffed and strengthened by his chosen perks of longer, sharper weapons. I look closer at them on my turn, noting the small markings in the paint that signify the upgrades. Mentally filing them away, I surrender to the approaching siege and Iain nods to himself as we begin to pack up.

"You knew I knew your strategies," he begins as we clear the table.

"I thought you might."

"And you replanned appropriately."

"Not that it did me much good." The loss stings, though I expected no other outcome. I've always been a sore loser, and I struggle not to show it. Iain is a High Marshal. I am a Novice. The results speak for themselves.

I pause, a figure in my hand, as Iain approaches me with a book. "Every beginner should read this. I think you'll find it interesting."

I take it from him. It's *Critical Theory and Evaluation Tactics* by Olender Harvenspar.

"You showed initiative and critical thinking," Iain says, as I tuck it away. "This may work after all."

"Was that ever in doubt?" I ask, but he doesn't respond.

CHAPTER NINE

THE NEW MORNING, I am summoned to a room in the southern wing. I'm allowed to walk by myself, and I take my time answering Iain's call; I'll plead ignorance of the building's sprawling layout if he questions it.

The palace is located perfectly within the city, the crowning jewel. From its elevation, I can see every single district and bridge, the second, smaller rock spire near the sea, all the way down to the spits of land that jut out and form the natural harbours that give Castor its wealthy status as the capital. A ship is being towed into port from deeper waters, and I linger at the window to watch. My eyes flick to the flag, almost impossible to make out at this distance, but even from here, I recognise the flag of the Tsalski Empire—Amisha's home country. There are other flags beneath it; merchant symbols?

I tuck the information away and continue my search for the requested room.

The double doors are open, with a flurry of palace servants either guarding them or leaving them. They straighten to attention when I pass.

"Sorry I'm late," I say as I enter. Iain looks up from the large table and frowns at me. "The palace is way bigger than the Academy."

"And yet you found your way around, and out of that, quite easily," he counters. "Nonetheless, come inside so we can start."

The room is longer than it is wide, with tall windows looking out over the same harbour I'd been admiring. Two other men, dressed finely with neatly trimmed beards, are also in the room. I cast them a curious gaze as the double doors are locked firmly behind the last few servants.

"Lord Micah Chabin, Lord Harold Olinius, may I introduce you to Rose Greatcast?"

It's the name he addressed my mother with. I blink, unused to hearing the new combination. Both men bow sharply.

"So it's true then," Chabin says, coming out of the bow. He looks me up and down, but his eyes aren't unfriendly. "There were rumours, Iain."

"I intended there to be," the Headmaster says. "Why do you think I paraded her through the city?"

"Your Majesty," Lord Olinius says. He holds a hand out, and I take it; it's rougher than I expected from a nobleman. "I know that's not your title yet, but forgive me, it feels incorrect to address you without it."

It's a subtle stab at Chabin. I feel the corners of my mouth twitch.

"I'd prefer no title, if I can be honest with you both," I say, planting both hands on my cane. "Just 'Rose', will be fine while we're alone."

"A reluctant ruler?" Chabin questions. He rests a splayed hand on the table between us on stacks of carefully written parchment. "You don't want the crown?"

I consider my answer. "Not under these circumstances."

He nods. "I can understand that."

"Lord Chabin and Lord Olinius are the heads of two noble Houses here in the capital," Iain explains, looking between us all.

"I brought them here to discuss some issues the conflict in the north is causing us, and you are here to learn."

Before I can answer, the doors are opened again, and a familiar woman walks through them. Netalia removes her riding gloves as Iain makes his way towards her, and they embrace. My eyes follow her across the room, and the fire in my blood heats.

She'd tied my mother to the ice and bled her dry. That's what Mum had told Iain. I clench my jaw as she turns to me.

"Rose," she says simply. "I trust you're well."

She is dressed in riding gear, the close-fitting leathers providing a better look at her form than her blouses and skirts at the Academy ever did. She is well-built, lean with muscle on her arms. Her long white hair is tied into a long plait, her streak of black woven as the centre strand. A sword is buckled to her hip, a riding cape thrown over one shoulder to provide quick access to the blade should she need it.

Her dark eyes meet mine as I finish my assessment. The fire roars to be let out, but I incline my head to her.

"How are you, Netalia?" I ask, my voice steady.

"Tired," she replies. "The roads are not easy to travel."

"How is Mornington?" Iain asks. The two lords also turn their attention to the new arrival, and I take the moment to breathe deeply, calming myself.

Netalia sighs. "Burnt and salted."

My stomach falls; we passed through Mornington, stayed there for a night.

"The whole thing?" I ask.

Another town in ashes...

Netalia nods. "The harvests had just come in. The northerners apparently waited for it to be completed, and then swept in and raided the village."

Lord Chabin rubs his temples. "And it was a good crop too. They'd finally managed to get their fields producing well."

He turns towards the wall. I watch him, trying to gauge how bad the situation is.

"Salting the fields means it will be difficult, if not impossible, to get them to produce crops again," Olinius explains to me. "They've taken the last harvest for themselves and ensured we will struggle to get the same next year."

"Oh."

"My House provides advice and labour to the farmers of Mornington," Chabin says, turning back. "We'd worked those fields for a generation." He clenches his jaw and clears his throat.

I sweep my gaze back to Iain as he asks, "What are the villagers planning to do?"

"They rode with us to request housing in Castor," Netalia replies. "Under the old law of duress."

"The entire village?" I ask.

Netalia looks at me. "Yes. They are unable to eke out a living from the land anymore and wish to relocate."

I think of the shanty town within the city walls; they'll be living on top of each other.

"What do we do?" I ask.

"We let them in, of course," Olinius says. Iain glances at him. "We can't turn our own people away."

"No," Iain agrees. "But there are limits on what we can provide to them without taking from others."

I feel a headache begin to grow in my temples. I pull out a chair from the table and sit heavily, resting the cane beside me.

"To our other matter of business," Iain continues, and the others sit as well. "Riverdoor has not brought their goods south for the second month in a row."

"What goods?" I ask, and Iain reaches across the table with some papers. I take them from him, scanning. "Ore and stone?"

Olinius nods, leaning back. "We usually rely on their mines and quarries for the bulk of our building materials. We were already stretched thin after shipments from the northern mines stopped years ago, but the Lyons opened new ones with support from the Great-casts—your family, their lords. We could make up the shortage."

Iain had told me the Lyons had ceased all communication with the capital. Now, I understand that to mean trade as well. At the time, I hadn't understood how devastating that would be.

"My family runs the Blacksmiths Guild of the Southern Lotherian Region," Olinius explains. "We also own the forges and weaponsmiths in Castor. We are... very invested in the flow of raw materials to the capital."

"Rose," Iain says, and I look up at him over the notes I've been handed. "How would you suggest we make up the extra shipments we need?"

I blink at him. "What?"

The others sit in silence, their eyes on me. Nerves flutter in my stomach, and I swallow.

"Our main supply line used to come from the north," Iain explains. "The Araspire family ceased that line around eighteen years ago. Since then, the Lyons have taken up the mantle as our suppliers."

I nod, following so far.

"Now they have cut us off as well." Iain steeples his fingers. "What are your thoughts?"

Every single thought I've ever had clears my mind as expectant eyes turn to me. My mouth goes dry, and I buy some time laying the papers back down. I sit in silence for a few minutes, but when I look back up, I have nothing.

"I don't know," I say quietly.

Netalia tightens her lips, and looks back at the reports in front of her, but Iain holds my gaze. "In a game of Kingdoms, Rose. How would you address this issue?"

I picture the table in the dungeons below us, with its large tiles and set rules. The answer jumps to my lips. "I'd form a trade alliance."

Iain nods. "Good. With whom?"

I scan my memory. Amisha talked often about her homeland, and the ship in the harbour suddenly makes sense. "The Tsalski Empire. They have ore deposits on their larger islands."

Iain sits back and glances at Netalia, who is looking at me, not the information in front of her.

"Which is why," Olinius says, "two weeks ago, we established a trade agreement with the Empire. I believe their first shipment arrived this morning."

I place my shaking hands in my lap, and before I can stop myself I say, "My friend is Tsalskinese. She told me of an uncle who runs a forge in Kella Sur."

"Chances are I know him then," Olinius says, and smiles at me. Some of the nerves calm a little and I smile back at him.

But doubt gnaws at my stomach. Iain tossed me a question, and I fumbled it. I run my gaze over the papers strewn across the large table and see a multitude of tangled problems that lives depend on. I think of the villagers arriving in Castor this morning seeking shelter, and of the suffocating trade routes choked by conflict further north. How much did our shipment of ore from the Tsalski Empire cost? Surely it can't be cheap to send a heavy ship across the ocean.

I clench my jaw, simultaneously overwhelmed by the amount of information I have and the information I want. For the rest of the meeting, I listen closely as the lords discuss ongoing matters with the Headmasters, and accept the notes they hand me as though I understand them. I try to memorise each one, and am doing so when Iain taps me on the shoulder.

"We're going up for lunch now, Rose." He looks over the little stack of notes I've built in front of me. "I'll have copies of those made for you."

"Thank you," I murmur, and accept my cane from him. My leg is feeling good and rested, and I enjoy a few painfree steps as we all leave the room together.

"You did well with the trade question," he says.

I shake my head. "I don't think I did."

He pauses, letting the lords and Netalia go ahead. "You know, Rose, I did actually take my duties as Headmaster of the Academy quite seriously. I sat with the teachers and listened to their reports on their students."

I wait to see where he's going with this.

"The main feedback I got regarding you is that you're easily distracted, you daydream, and you find it hard to follow subjects you aren't interested it."

I wince; it sounds like all of my report cards ever. Good to know some things stay consistent across worlds.

"But," Iain continues, "when a subject *does* interest you, you are a quick learner and have a good sense of intuition. You only need to be shown pieces of the puzzle to put them together quickly."

I think of my time in Arno's office, writing runes and playing with designs for new ones.

"Running the country as its monarch won't be an easy task," Iain says, and we continue down the hallway after the others. "But I'll make sure you have all the information you could want on any subject regarding Lotheria's state of affairs. I can only hope you'll apply yourself as you did to Runes."

"I don't know yet," I reply honestly. "This isn't something I really thought would happen."

The Headmaster looks sidelong at me. "Either way, I'm pleased with how you conducted yourself within the meeting today. Lords Chabin and Olinius are the easiest ones to win over, mind you."

"How many others are there?"

"Leaders of the noble Houses? You've met two of nine. You will be introduced to five more later."

I nod, and follow him to the dining room.

That night, as the sun washes the western wall in tired light, I'm allowed to return to the expansive wing of the palace that has been set aside for my residence. The long room runs almost the length of the palace, separated into sections for sleeping and working. I bathe in the large marble bathroom, soaking in the hot water and sifting through the day's events in my mind. I stay there until the threads of armour in my right leg soften, and I pick at them absentmindedly. My thoughts begin to wander in a different direction.

Laela curls up beside me, her bare skin warm against mine. The furs around us hold the night chill at bay for now, but soon we will need to dress, lest we're caught with only a smile and my scars between us. Her fingers run up and down my ribs, raising goosebumps all over me. I squirm.

"Quit it."

She grins. "Are you ticklish?"

"Any person is ticklish when you poke them like that. Stop."

She does. I regret saying anything immediately. But then she sits up and lets the furs fall away from her torso, and regret is suddenly the last word in my vocabulary.

She looks me over, takes me in. Her fingers trace new patterns, down my ribs, to my protruding hipbones—she drums her fingers there as though in thought—but then continues down my right thigh to my knee. I take a breath as I feel her featherlight touch on my calf.

"Don't—" I begin, but she looks at me with steady brown eyes and I feel shame creep into my cheeks.

"You are beautiful, Rose. I thought that from the moment my father pulled you from that cursed river. Drowned and soggy, but you accepted mead from a stranger and reassured your friend." Her hand rests on my shin bone, her thumb lightly stroking the ruined muscle of my leg. "I watched you grow. Learn. How to sneak out of the Academy and bribe just the right people so no one ever knew. It's a gift, you know. To figure out who will and won't talk. You do it as naturally as breathing." She smiles slightly, caught in the memory. "You sought me out. At first I thought it was to find me." She lets her head roll back onto her shoulders, her dark brown hair curled and

messy from sex. She shoots me a look that would make armies fight for her praise; I will never in a million years master that look. "I don't think it was, at first."

I swallow. "That changed. I started coming to you."

"Only when you stopped being stubborn enough to realise you wanted to." Her hand moves to grip my calf, the warmth of her skin pressing against the gnarled remains on my once healthy leg. "When you came back with this... I worried I'd lost that part of you on the battlefield."

I don't look at her hand on my leg. I look at her face as she examines the old injury. Will she find it disgusting? The leg is not pretty to look at. It is ugly and ruined.

As though she can hear my thoughts, she relinquishes my leg and leans down over me. Her hair brushes my cheeks.

"You were beautiful then," she whispers, and drops a kiss onto my lips. "And you're beautiful now."

I close my eyes, and tears dampen my lashes.

Laela must hate me, if she's even alive. The little box I've knotted her into threatens to come undone, and I'm climbing from the bath before I can stop myself.

I cannot think about Laela. The guilt will drown me.

Instead, I dry myself off and limp to bed in silk pyjamas. The cavernous four poster envelopes me in finery, and I close my eyes, self-loathing sinking deep into my bones.

I did this. I caused all of this through anger and pain.

I pull my sleeve down and look at the rune scars again, but they are pale and inert against my skin. They've not flickered or whispered for months, as though Lotheria knows an imposter carries the blood of a queen.

I tip my head back on the pillowed headboard and know that I won't sleep, the deep ache in my leg throbbing from walking the halls of the palace. Spying the book on my nightstand, I reach over and pick it up, leafing through the first few pages.

One has been torn out, and my attention goes to it immediately, grateful for the distraction. It was neatly done, but the jagged edge along the spine remains. I light the lamp beside me, tilting the book to see if I can decipher the indent left long ago by the mark of a pen.

I trace the sunken letters, written in the clumsy hand of a child.

This Book Belongs To Iain Nevalas.

CHAPTER TEN

THE HERALDS' trumpets split the air and I wince from the noise, but keep my nose pressed to the window as Lillian—the same Lillian who once brought me breakfast at the Academy—clatters behind me. I can hear the booming announcement being read to the gathered crowd at the palace gate, but not the words being said.

"Do these windows really not open?" I ask, turning back.

Lillian is at my dressing table, her slender hands arranging small pots of paint and cream. I dread finding out the contents of each one. Her answer is curt. "No... ma'am."

I roll my eyes at her address, and tap my head softly on the glass.

I can hear activity around the palace again, which makes me want to disobey Iain's strict orders and go out to my friends. I've seen them walking across the yard between lessons, training in the evening; from this high up, it's near impossible to tell them apart.

Except for Phoenix. I can always sense him through our broken connection.

Because of course it's broken; I left Lotheria. Something ruptured like splintered bone the second my boots left the soil. In the daylight, I can see a thin thread of corded magic, spiralling through the obstacles between us; the frail wisp of the connection that could've been.

At night, I watch it glitter in the moonbeams. Sometimes, it twists and rolls, as though trying to repair itself.

The heralds were delayed by bad weather, and Iain was adamant that I would not spend time with my classmates until the announcement has been made. I'd spent the time wandering corridors, reading, and playing Kingdoms on a spare board, which lacks the soul of the one beneath the palace. The table fascinated me; I'd never seen such an intricate magic working. When my fingers rested against the wood, I could feel a tiny pulse throughout the grains, like a heartbeat.

My own thuds in my chest as I consider the upcoming announcement, and my eyes fall beyond the palace grounds, to the city and the walls. I count the days in my head since we crossed the gate, tapping my fingers against my thigh.

Just a few more.

"Ma'am."

I consider a fireball.

"You need to get ready."

She does my makeup, far too close to me for either of our comfort. I poke gingerly at a cheek and her eyes narrow in the mirror, as though contemplating the damage she could do with a single brush.

"Thanks," I say finally. "It looks good."

She holds out a dress. I resist the urge to let my chin rest on the dressing table in despair, and instead shrug out of my robe and let Lillian wrap me in the hefty gown of green silk. She fastens the laces at my back, pulling it tight.

Diamond earrings and a necklace—better suited to an older, more distinguished woman— are added to the ensemble, glittering at my ears and throat. I catch Lillian half-stutter something and the motion is so unusual, I let my hand fall from the gleaming jewels at my collarbone.

"What?" I ask.

There's a long leather case lying on the dresser. Lillian stands before it, her fingers on the latch. "Master Iain had one more instruction."

'Instruction'. Not 'request'.

I nudge her out of the way and she lets me, standing back. I open the case.

I take in the object inside and swallow the lump in my chest. Smoke curls up around my fists and only when Lillian takes another step back do I realise my palms are burning. I put it out, fighting the urge to rub soot-streaked palms across the dress.

"It's... a brace, my lady," Lillian says finally, as though I don't know. "For your leg."

"For my leg," I repeat softly.

"Yes."

"Why?" My tone is sharp. "Why do I need the brace instead of my cane, Lillian?

The maid hesitates. "Headmaster Iain said you did."

I turn and move slowly back to the window, my cane at my side, assisting me. After all this time, I'm so used to its grip in my hand that the idea of going without terrifies me. I swallow my fear. With Lillian's uneasiness, I won't show her this discomfort.

"Put it on," I say, and sit heavily in the chair before the dressing table.

It is metal and bolts, screws, and leather straps. She kneels on the floor before me and gently tucks my skirt over my knee. I feel like a princess at a shoe fitting. Instead, she lifts my wilted leg onto her lap.

The clanking of metal accompanies the tightening of the straps, and I think for a moment I'm going to pass out. Lillian rests my leg back on the floor as a sensation sweeps through my leg for the first time since the botched healing.

Pain.

I am used to numbness. I am used to muscle ache. But this is active, searing pain. I gasp, tears in my eyes, as needles of ice burn into my skin. Every touch of the metal is agony, gripping and pinching ruined flesh. My fists clench the chair beneath me. I didn't think the leg still had enough nerve endings for this dramatic of a response.

"Ma'am?" Lillian's voice sounds like she's in a fog, calling for me. I lift my eyes to hers. "Should I loosen it?"

"No," I gasp. "Wait."

I take deep breaths, willing it to disappear. I pound a fist against the table and swear in Tsalskinese, praising Amisha for teaching me the bad words first.

The bad words help a lot.

I imagine the smooth, round surface of a candle. Waiting for the touch of my knife. Waiting to be marked.

Everything stills.

I stand, leaving my cane against the dresser. My leg howls, sending a fresh wave of pain my way. But I tuck it away and bury it even as tears gather in the corners of my eyes.

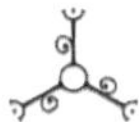

When the representatives of the noble Houses arrive, Lillian has dried most of the tears that had fallen, unbidden, as I staggered down the flights of stairs from my wing to this room. She'd carried two cloths; one for my eyes, the other for the rivulets of blood as bolts and metal threads had bitten into the soft, unyielding flesh of my leg.

I flex my hand on the arm of the throne. I have never missed the handle of my cane so much.

"Your Majesty." The man sinks low onto one knee, his wife flaring skirts in a practised curtsey. "Your return to Lotheria comes at the most opportune time."

There is movement from my right, as Iain hears the slight at the same time I do.

"Lord Fillegan," he says. "You have travelled far from your manse on the eastern wall. The crown appreciates your coming."

I set my jaw and do not speak. I had been beyond grateful to Iain when he instructed me to do just that. I could play a game of Kingdoms with relative success, but I could not dance the political dance of semantics and dialogue with these people yet.

"Let us be grateful you're the daughter of a great noble House and not a nothing mage from nowhere," Fillegan says. "Imagine the stir that would cause."

"Yes, imagine," I say, before Iain can intervene. "Luckily I'm just a humanborn who's spent a single year in this world."

They laugh politely, as though I've made a joke, but Fillegan leads his wife away shortly after. Iain sighs. "Why?"

The comment had jumped to my lips, aided by my shortened temper. "My leg hurts."

"The brace was a gift."

"For you or me?" I counter, and he frowns.

"It shouldn't hurt that much. The Carrier informed me you did not have much feeling in your leg."

"I don't, but what little there is screams for me to take this off."

Netalia shoots us both a furious look as the next nobles approach. I meet the ladies of Merrangold and speak with them under close supervision. The patriarch of House Temperhold is next, who gives me a rundown of his House's lineage and family tree. Iain finally manages to get a word in, and draws the lord away so the next can come up. I jump when Netalia leans close.

"He has a grandson your age. He's already put forth his name as a suitable kingsmatch."

I lean back. "A what?"

She just looks at me as I put the pieces together.

"I have to choose a king?"

"Of course you do. It's an opportunity for the noble Houses to tie their bloodlines to royalty and pledge their support." She stands, but glances down at me. "Think of it as one of your Kingdoms mechanics."

I try to let the thought roll through my head, but I just feel nauseous.

"Our last introduction of the day." Iain returns, having handed off Lord Temperhold to Lord and Lady Fillegan. "But I don't think he needs an introduction."

I follow his gesture to the figure standing at the bottom of the dais. Orin grins up at me.

My heart soars. I stand quickly, picking up my skirts, and running down the stairs. My leg screams but I ignore it, wrapping my arms around my old friend, who embraces me tightly.

He is so familiar, so comforting and real, that tears prick my eyes. Iain lets us have a moment, and then clears his throat. I relinquish my friend, stepping back as he bows neatly.

"Your Majesty," he begins, and I shake my head slightly, though I'm smiling. "I'm Lord Orin, representing House Thoreau. My mother and father hope you find me acceptable as their emissary."

"I do." I climb the stairs back to my throne to sit, and Orin follows me up onto the dais.

"House Thoreau sends their welcome to the new queen," he begins, hands clasped loosely before him. He's dressed like a nobleman, and it ages him a good few years. His red hair longer than when I last saw him, tied neatly at the nape of his neck. "Our tribute is currently being stored in the royal warehouses."

"The crown thanks you for your allegiance," I say, remembering the words Netalia taught me, but it's not what I want to say. I want to ask him if he's okay, what happened, how are the others, apologise for... well, everything. But Iain shifts at my side and I tuck the honesty beneath the pleasantries. "How does your family fare in the war?"

Orin's eyes flick to the Headmasters either side of me. "They are grateful for the upcoming military assistance the south has promised."

"And they will get it," Iain says smoothly, and I turn my head towards him. "In due time."

Orin inclines his head. "I will take my leave, ma'am, if you permit it."

"Of course."

I watch him head towards Lord Chabin and engage him in conversation.

"House Thoreau has also put his name forth."

The words ring hollow in the wake of our warm reunion, and for a second, I don't understand.

"His name—"

Netalia gives me a look.

"Oh."

"He would be a good match," she says conversationally, straightening to observe my friend on the floor below as he talks. "You two are friendly already and the Thoreau's allegiance to us has never waivered. It would be a good reward for them."

I look to Iain for rescue.

"Rose, don't mention the war," he says, and I sigh, knowing I'm getting a lecture instead. "We haven't officially declared it yet."

"But everyone here knows it's coming," I say, gesturing to the representatives chattering loudly.

"And they will be the ones to fund and fight it. But without proper legal proceedings, the casual mention of war will make them nervous. We need their agreement, and you assuming we have it already will be considered impolite."

I rub my forehead. "I'm not very good at this."

"It's alright," Iain says. "You don't have to be."

"I just have to be quiet."

"That's right."

I drum my fingers on the arm of my throne. I should feel

powerful and confident atop it, but I'm just a petulant piece on a Kingdoms board as far as Iain is concerned, a fact which annoys me more than it should.

When the doors are barred behind the nobles, I breathe a sigh of relief in the quiet. My mind is whirling with the information of the day, and I'm thinking longingly of the bath in my rooms above; perhaps the only thing that can provide any semblance of comfort for my aching leg.

Iain watches the guards leave, then steps up closer to me.

"Go upstairs. Have your maid remove the brace."

Netalia steps forward. "I commissioned it—"

"We need her able to sit through more than just a few hours," Iain shoots back. "Look at her."

The Headmistress looks down at me, and sighs. "I could fix you a tonic."

I frown, my forehead damp with sweat. "You're a carrier?"

"Absolutely not," she snorts. "I'm an alchemist."

"Huh." I never knew this, but surely they would've majored in their own subjects. I turn to Iain. "What about you?"

He lifts an eyebrow. "War magic."

"Of course," I retort. The words are quick, carried by impatience and pain. I unclench my fists. "Sorry."

"The offer stands," Netalia says, but I plant my hands on the arms of the throne and struggle to my feet.

"I'll survive," I say through gritted teeth. I can't imagine ever willingly drinking something she gave me.

Lillian is summoned from the shadows, and the Headmasters remain in the throne room as we leave, their heads together as they talk. My maid offers her arm, and I latch on.

I take a few cautious steps with her assistance, and then a few more as my stride adjusts to the new equipment. Belatha, the absent goddess above, seemingly takes pity on me and keeps me pain free and upright until we reach a darkened staircase.

Then, as though someone flicked a switch, my leg remembers

the intrusion and howls in agony. My knee buckles, sending me against the stone wall, and Lillian holds me up right. I silently beg her not to say a word, and she remains quiet.

In my rooms, she seats me at the dressing table. My chest rises and falls rapidly, processing the pain.

"I'll run the bath," she says, and moves swiftly to do so.

I wait until I hear the water running before pulling up the skirt of my dress. I barely pause to take in the ruined sight of the limb before my fingers are yanking and pulling at the buckles. The pain increases as I accidentally tighten the leather, squeezing more tears from my eyes as I gasp. Frustration surges and I rest my head in my hands. Carrier Bayde's words ring in my ears.

I cannot heal what no longer exists.

"My lady?"

I remove my hands from my eyes and look up. Lillian stands at the entrance to the bathroom, the door hidden in the gilded golden wallpaper. The sound of splashing echoes in the marble chamber within.

"Do you need me to attend you?"

I nod, and she approaches, undoing the buckles with difficulty; I'd tightened them too much. She dips a curtsey as I stand and grab my cane, my feet free of the delicate leather slippers she'd laced me into.

When the bathroom door closes behind me, I pull at the laces of my dress and step free of it. The long sleeves fall away, but a knot of scar tissue catches on a thread. I clench my teeth, forcing back the endless frustration and, as I step into the water, examine the inert scars on my arms.

I'd designed them myself—an alphabet I'd been developing in Arno's dungeon, to follow in the footsteps of my master himself. I knew he'd also written an alphabet, which he'd kept closely guarded, displaying little pieces of it at a time. The idea that little pictures could channel and change magic... it had filled me with the fire to learn. My first runework that day had cemented my love for the craft; setting a candle alight.

The rune for *burn* remains one of my favourites.

On my arms, there are eight runes in total, designed by my hand; borrowed from other alphabets and modified slightly, or of my own invention entirely. I'd been confident in theory, but as the days count on, I'm yet to see any display of power from them and my surety is waning.

Nerves bite in my stomach. How long will Iain, or any of the nobles I met today, believe me to be the next queen if I can't display any of the powers they think I have?

The door opens. "Is there anything else, my lady?"

I shake my head. "No, thank you, Lillian."

She disappears, leaving me alone in the cavernous bathroom. Beneath the water, my bruised leg is still tender to the touch. I blink tears from my eyes at not only the pain, but the sight of the limb. A year isn't long enough to grow used to it. I lean my head back against the edge of the bath and let tears flow down my cheeks.

"Rose."

I gasp, and surge upright. I search for where the voice echoed from, and freeze as a tall form unfolds in the corner of the room.

"Your maid is coming to ask if you're alright," Phoenix says. "Tell her you are, that you dropped something."

My breath is fire in my chest, but before I can respond, there is a light tapping at the door.

"Miss?"

I look to the door, and then back at my soulmate. He places a finger to his lips.

I press mine together. "I... I dropped something. I'm alright, Lillian, thank you."

We hear her footsteps fade away as she leaves.

"How did you get up here?" My cheeks turn red. "How long have you been there?"

"I looked away when you got in, and I can't see you below the water line."

"Thank you," I mutter, but honestly I'm mortified. I keep my leg covered; few people have seen it bare.

Phoenix approaches the bath and sits on the floor, facing slightly away from me to keep his gaze high on the wall.

"I knew it was you I kept seeing in the windows. When I heard the announcement, I thought they'd gotten it wrong though."

"So did I," I mutter, but the subtext of his comment still stings.

"Dena and Amisha want me to report back on how you are. And ask why you haven't come down to see us yet."

"Iain says I have to stay up here for now." I swirl my hands through the water. "But then I'll be allowed down, I think."

"Rose, what have they told you?"

I recount Iain's words in the Other. How Kaya Aule had gone north and found support with the Araspire family. How the Halvers and the northern army had made their way south, burning farms, towns, villages, despite their differences.

Phoenix takes a deep breath, his eyes moving from side to side as he processes the information I've given him. While he does, I look at him in earnest, drinking in the sight of him so close.

This man was intended to become my soulmate—the Lotherian way of binding mages together to enhance their magic. The power in our veins belonged together, until I'd severed it when I'd left. Regret rises in me, and I look away. An ally within the castle would be a boon, someone to confide in. To tell my secret to.

I want to anyway. Caution stays my tongue at the last moment. *I don't know if it worked.*

I rub my arm as he looks down at me. He goes to say something, but cuts himself off. I don't chase it; I'm remembering the last time I'd seen him, the square, the crack in the earth Arno had opened at our feet with a mere scratch in a stone. My heart aches for the man who'd been my master, my teacher...

"Rose?"

I shake my head back to the present. "Sorry."

He waves it away. "Don't be. I often live in my head too. I found it the one place where people don't talk so loudly to be heard."

I blink for a moment, and then a small smile grows on my face. "Was that a joke? Did you just make a joke?"

He lifts his shoulders, but the corner of his mouth twitches. I'm forced to concede that my once soulmate is an unreasonably attractive man, with broad shoulders and long dark hair he's pulled back into a tail. His strong jawline is covered in rough stubble, something that marked him as older than when I'd last seen him. He'd been fighting Iain on a burning platform.

"Tell me what happened after I left," I murmur.

"Rose—"

"I need to hear it."

He hesitates. "You know... of all the tales they use to warn Orthandrellian children of the perils of magic, the stories of half-souls frightened me the most—the broken body and spirit of the soldiers sent to claim our lands by the southern masters. In our bedtime stories and campfire tales, they are little more than crea-tures driven by a need to destroy." He pauses. "But I saw the truth that night in Fairhaven... that they are man and mind.

"I was armed. Many of the villagers were not. I saved those I could, but there were too many and I was the only one that seemed to be fighting for the common people." He turns his face from me. "There are not many Fairhaven refugees because... not much of Fairhaven survived, Rose."

I'd known this, but hearing it again digs deeper. I close my eyes and feel the loss.

"By chance I found a girl, in the middle of a burning building. She was digging through the coals with no regard for burns or pain. She fought and screamed when I pulled her away, and I nearly let go—but I recognised the house, Rose. It was the house we sheltered in after you'd been whipped." He glances at me, and then away. "I knew then who she was and the danger she was in. We ran to the lowhills with the villagers who remained. Some half-souls tried to pursue us, and I killed them."

Laela is alive. Tears of relief burn and hope surges in my chest. But his words are flat, as though he's speaking of the weather on a lazy afternoon. I recognise the look in his eye; it's the same way I deliver the story about Petre's death.

"There were others in the forest. Some who meant ill, and some who were displaced and confused. The trees weathered an odd visit for the next few days as we wandered, set up camp, and made alliances with those we thought we could trust. Then the Black Guard rode through and moved us on, taking some who resisted into royal custody."

I sit in the water and let this new information flow over me. "But you came back. You've returned to study."

He nods. "The guard made it clear I was going to be treated as a wayward northerner, who are now the enemy on sight. I decided I could make more change if I wasn't running for my life every day. I returned to the Academy and begged to be allowed to stay."

I can't picture it, but Iain had confirmed it as well.

"It's hard to imagine," I admit.

"I know. I suffered many sleepless nights. But sometimes we must humble ourselves and accept a loss in order to keep moving forward. Only when we give up entirely do we lose." He sighs. "That's what I keep telling myself, anyway."

I consider his words. I don't like losing under any circumstances—my most recent humiliation at the Kingdoms table comes to mind and sours my already fraying mood. But then I think of chestnut hair and bright eyes, and a new, real fear begins to creep into the pit of my stomach.

I force the words out. "And Laela?"

He lets the silence linger for a beat too long, and my heart pounds.

"She is safe. She is within the walls of Castor."

Relief washes over me as he explains how she'd trailed the caravan of students as it carried them to the capital, how he made sure she was safe and fed every night. At the gates, she'd merely stuck close to the carriages and been mistaken for a student.

And another knot in my chest undoes itself as I realise that, for a city on the edge of war, the gate security is very lax. It will be easy for someone to slip through.

"You did that for me?"

"At first. But as I got to know her, I came to understand why you are so drawn to her. She is a good person."

A smile tugs at my lips. Phoenix and I had rarely spoken in our first year, but I was already wishing I'd just gotten over my fears and connected with him.

"What?" he asks.

"I like the way you just... say things." I move my hand through the water again. "It's simple. I've needed simple over the last week."

"The transfer of power of the realm was never going to be simple, Rose," he remarks. "In fact, I'm surprised Iain and Netalia are announcing your legitimacy at all."

"So am I."

"It makes me nervous."

I look up at him. "Don't want to become a Halver yourself?"

"Not particularly. And you are also a good person."

I make a noise in my throat but don't pursue it. It's kind of him to say, but not necessarily grounded in fact, and I'd like to hang onto the sentiment before it's disproved.

I tell him about Iain coming to my world.

"How?" he queries. "How did they open the portal? I've always wondered."

"Queensblood," I say, and he frowns. I realise he doesn't know about the blood vault below the Academy. "Only a Lotherian queen can open the crossing between worlds, but they... they must've had some."

"Blood magic," he mutters darkly, and turns away. "I will keep my ears out and share the information with the others. Your friends are becoming powerful. And they are resourceful, and loyal to the idea of you."

Another reason Iain probably doesn't want me associating with them. "Thank you."

He stands up to leave. "Keep your head down and play by their rules, Rose. We'll find out what they're planning."

"Alright. Hey..." He pauses, and I take a moment to find the words. "I'm sorry we didn't bond last year. You would've been a good soulmate."

"Yes," he agrees softly. "But don't worry, Rose. I can still be a good friend."

CHAPTER ELEVEN

"THIS MOVE IS CALLED the 'Buckler's Row'." Iain pushes the small figurines into place. "Can you tell me why?"

I'm staring at the table, with its coloured discs and tiles and figures, but it's like the information has fallen out of my head. "No."

He heaves a sigh. His disappointment stings, but I shove it away under the layer of pain emanating from the leg brace. I grip the table, trying to cheat support from it.

"You are distracted today. What is on your mind?"

A whirlwind of thoughts blasts through my brain. It has been two days since Phoenix's visit and the announcement of my intended ascension. Plans for my coronation are well underway, as well as about a million dinners and noble introductions.

And above it all, Laela. I haven't been able to get her out of my mind.

"There's been a lot going on," I say finally.

Iain begins collecting up the figures. "That is true. The reception to your announcement has been..." He pauses, little soldiers in his hands. "Surprisingly enthusiastic."

I lift my eyebrows and take a breath. The gifts and courtiers and pledges of support are a little unnerving, especially as they all have an undercurrent of relief. I wonder if my Headmasters have picked up on it.

I watch Iain put a figurine down a little harder than is necessary, and note the crown on its wooden head.

I think they noticed.

"You and Netalia must be busier than ever," I begin. "Managing... everything."

Iain glances at me, and then away. He begins setting up the table for a campaign and nerves begin to flutter in my stomach.

"We are used to the volume of work from our tenure as Headmasters of the Academy. I assure you, it is nothing we can't handle."

I nod, and limp to my end of the table, which darkens. Silence falls in the long room as I begin establishing supply lines and economic structures to my tiny town, placing little buildings and farmland. The hexagonal wooden tiles flip themselves over, replacing their usual painted green terrain with tilled fields of rich brown. I smile slightly; the table never ceases to amaze me. An incredible feat of enchantment and—I suspect—runework, I've never seen anything as magically advanced in my entire time in Lotheria.

The game plays on, though my stomach begins to descend to my toes as my internal timer ticks on and I struggle to establish a military presence. By now, Iain and I have played enough that I know his methods—and sure enough, the blackened tiles surrounding my poor village lighten to reveal his small but effective army en route.

Hot fire rushes through my veins as they begin attacking my first building, and I push over my centre piece.

"I surrender," I snap, and shove away from the table. The brace bites into my leg, fuelling my frustration, and flames lick around my clenched fists.

"Not good enough, Evermore, I gave you plenty of time to

establish base defences. Doing so would have granted you the advance warning you needed to train troops to counter what—"

I wave him off, so incensed that I barely hear his frustrated sigh. He sweeps the table clear, wiping my village from the map as though to prove a point.

"You aren't improving."

"My leg hurts," I shoot back. "Why can't I have my cane?"

"The public look to you to lead. They cannot see you limping about with a stick in hand."

I yank up my skirt so he can see the bruised, dimpled flesh where the brace digs in. "And this is better? I want my cane."

"No."

"Iain—"

He meets my look. "Win the next skirmish, and you can have it back."

I stop, and make a disgusted noise in my throat.

"Fine. I'll win the next skirmish, and then you give me back my cane."

"For casual palace use only."

"For..." I take a deep breath through my nose. "And I want to see my friends."

"Soon. Just not now."

We play again. I drain my resources early, prioritising military and defence tactics over the wellbeing of my village. I have a wall and a small militia in place when my settlement tiles all begin to flip over, revealing red markings this time. The table clears and I see Iain's side, barely touched. He never even started building.

"Rebellion," he says, pointing to my now-reddened village. "You didn't heed their needs or concerns, and the people fought back."

I bite my tongue so hard it bleeds. I can feel my fire beating against my core, wanting to be released, but I hold it down, merely packing away my little buildings and letting the tiles return to neutral. To my relief, Iain begins unlocking the rows of cupboards so we can put away the figurines for the day. Together, we pack up our game, and I wait for him to release me.

Instead, he waits for me at the door. "We are going into the city."

It takes a second to sink in. I've been confined to the palace for nearly two weeks. Suddenly, the outside world seems very big and overwhelming.

"What for?" I question.

He holds the door for me and gestures for me to leave. "I want to take you somewhere."

He doesn't elaborate, and unease settles in my stomach. It clears somewhat in the fresh air outside, and I peer around the grounds as our horses are brought over. But there are no students outdoors, and disappointment slinks in instead.

Iain boosts me into the saddle, and I stroke the mare's pale mane as he mounts his own horse. Half a dozen Thornsguard—renamed by Netalia to follow traditional conventions of naming the guard after the noble House of the queen—follow us through the gardens, and I loathe to admit that it is more comfortable riding with the brace on my leg; without direct weight being placed on it, the contraption compresses the limb and makes it easier to hold myself upright.

The afternoon is crisp, clear, and bright as we begin the winding descent from the palace into the city proper. Gulls wheel about on the breeze above, and I can hear the clanging of ship bells from the docks. I shiver into the coat Iain insisted be brought down from my rooms.

"Where are we going?"

"The oldest place in Castor," he replies, riding alongside me. He is at complete ease in the saddle, one hand wound into the reins, the other by his side. "The city was built around it."

That tells me nothing, which means he wants the destination to have an impact. I want to ask more questions, but remain silent.

We ride across the bridge, heading towards the coast. I know there is a spire of rock on the headland; there is a lighthouse that beams a bright light across my windows every evening from it. The streets narrow and buildings lean in close; some of the Thornsguard ride ahead to clear the traffic. Curious faces peer up at us as we pass.

"Wave," Iain encourages, lifting his own hand. "Reward their interest in you."

I do so awkwardly, and the woman on the receiving end merely watches me ride past without a hint of recognition. My cheeks burn, and I drop my hand.

There's a chuckle from my side. "Don't laugh at me," I mumble at the Headmaster.

He rides closer, lifting my hand with his. "With confidence, Rose. You are to be queen. You wave like a stable girl."

I frown at him, letting him move my hand around. "I didn't realise that was a specific wave."

He relinquishes me. "Try again."

I shake my head and let my hand fall. "Seems more your thing."

We ride in silence for a bit, parting the foot traffic.

"You let your defeats and rejection weigh heavily on your shoulders," Iain comments. "They define how you think about yourself."

I say nothing.

"A defeat is temporary, Rose. It is a lesson."

"Maybe I'm tired of lessons," I shoot back, my temper rising. "You get annoyed as well."

"I don't fail often because I heeded the early lessons." He's insufferable. I roll my eyes. "I was much like you are right now. I felt every loss deeply and allowed it to set me back in terms of progress. It took over my thinking. It cannot take over yours."

"Why?"

He looks at me, his dark eyes unreadable. "Because I have a war for you to win."

I go to respond, but decide not to. I let his words roll over me and tuck them away for later consideration. Instead, I change the subject and try my earlier question again.

"Where are we going?"

"I want to see what you think of the Archives."

I've never heard of this place. "The what?"

"Knowledge is power in Lotheria," he says, somewhat smugly. "It is given only to those who can wield it."

"Mages?"

"Yes." He goes quiet for a moment. "And those who are willing to bleed for it."

The rock spire looms above the streets long before we reach it, and I realise we've ridden towards it like a beacon. I expect to see stairs carved into it and nearly break into a sweat, dreading the phantom climb Iain has surely prepared. Instead, a wide square opens in front of us, with people crossing it or visiting tall buildings either side. The sun has lapsed lower into the sky, and cold shadows stretch across the cobbles.

Sunken into the rock, a metal door waits.

There is no ornamentation, no gardens, no lights, or windows. Our horses are held by members of the Thornsguard as Iain helps me down, his hands wrapped tight around my waist. I stumble a little, numb in the leg from the ride, and peer up at the sheer rise of stone in front of me.

"The Archives," Iain says, and gestures towards the door.

It is the least welcoming place I've ever seen. Bizarrely, business carries on as normal behind us as Iain raps knuckles on the door.

It opens inwards, and he gestures for me to enter. A rough hewn stone passage leads into the spire, and the air is muffled and close as I walk awkwardly down its length. Iain follows, the door sealing us into the rock.

I take a breath, reaching for my fire. It curls sleepily in my veins, but the hot strength it lends—even temporarily—soothes me like a mother's hug. I need it, for, at the other end of the passage, a figure in a hooded cloak awaits us. It is dyed red in places, the rough fabric unhemmed and dragging along the floor. The person holds their arm out, indicating the larger chamber behind them.

I emerge into the room and try not to gape; they've mined into the middle of the spire. Ribs of stone arch high above us, and it's easy to imagine we stand in the belly of an ancient beast; I shiver in the gloom.

"She is here to see the book," I hear Iain say, and I turn.

"Book?" I query. "Singular? You said this was the Archives. I assumed it would be... I don't know, a huge library or something."

"It doesn't need to be," he says. "You'll see."

The hooded figure has waited for our conversation to conclude, and then leads us further in. A small pedestal of natural rock waits at the back of the chamber, with candles tucked into the recesses around it. They burst into flame as I approach, and the person who accompanies us pauses.

"Forgive her," Iain mutters. "She is young."

Was I supposed to stop them from burning? Uncertainty adds to the growing knot in my stomach.

But my desire to ask for clarification dies away at the sight of the book upon the pedestal. It is huge, taller than I am. The leatherbound cover seems stricken in places, as though the binding is too tight and pulls it taut. Within, the aged pages are compressed but shades of beige and brown edges are visible.

"Is this it?" I ask Iain, and he places a finger against his lips.

He steps up beside me, his voice low. "Show respect, Rose. This is the Lothericon. Some call it the War Book, or"—his eyes fall to it—"The Book of Blood. It is a place where knowledge is sequestered from the world, magic that should never have been discovered, inventions that are deemed to dangerous to exist. They are given to the Book, and forgotten. Few people are allowed to gaze upon the works inside, to judge the contents fit to return to everyday life."

It's his nerves that set mine on edge. I've never seen Iain properly unsettled before, but the Lothericon—the Book of Blood—has shaken him. I turn back to it, suddenly feeling like I shouldn't have taken my eyes off of it.

The cloaked figure steps forth, and demonstrates something with their hand out. I catch a glimpse of their bandaged arm before it's tucked back into the swathes of fabric they wear.

There is movement at my side; Iain has stepped between myself and the person.

"No," he says sternly. "She is not ready."

They lift their chin, though the drooping hood still covers their features. My breathing turns shallow as I wait for instruction.

"To gaze upon the Book," they say, and I cannot discern gender in their soft-spoken tone. "She must pay the price." Iain goes to say something, and they shake their head slightly. "You cannot."

He says nothing.

"Iain," I say. "It's okay. I'll pay it."

I have a few coins in the purse on my belt, but—as Iain nods and steps back—the person closes in and goes to pull back my sleeve.

I yank my arm away, suddenly very aware of the rune scars on my inner arms. They try again, more forceful this time.

Hide! I think desperately, and my pulse beats against my wrist.

They draw back my sleeve, and I barely catch a glimpse of pearl-white light as the rune scars, already thin and healed, sink deeper into my skin. I blink; I didn't even know they could do that.

"The price," they remind me gently.

I clench my teeth and nod, expecting a knife. But they walk me closer to the pedestal.

My hand is placed flat against the cover of the book and I wince, expecting it to be cold, sheltered here in the depths of stone.

But it is soft and warm to the touch. My eyes widen as the cover ripples.

Tendrils rise from the material, thin and blind, groping their way towards my splayed fingers. I try to jerk my hand away, but the attendant holds me in place with unexpected strength. I feel fire surge in my veins and the candles respond, flaring brighter, dripping wax down the walls.

"Rose," Iain says. "It's alright."

His voice, somehow, is comforting, and I stop fighting. The candles die down again. The tendrils find my hand and begin to creep across it, like the touch of an overly friendly stranger. They grow longer, seeking something, crawling across the back of my wrist, and tears spring into my eyes as I bear the feather-light touch. They reach my outer forearm, unblemished by scars, and pause as though considering.

Then they pierce my flesh and burrow down.

Pain screams along my arm, and I clench my jaw, refusing to utter a sound. White queensblood wells up around the tendrils and drips down my elbow to the floor, adding pale splotches to the red patina I now notice beneath my feet. Many have bled for the knowledge the Lothericon contains.

Many people have stood here and paid the price.

But even knowing that cannot stop the scream I muffle against my other sleeve as the flesh is peeled from my arm. Red lights dance in front of my eyes and the candles burn higher; I'm under threat and the fire in my body is responding.

Burn it, Rose, stop it from taking what's yours, how dare it touch you, how DARE—

A hand is placed between my shoulder blades, steadying me. I focus on that touch instead, as the tendrils finish clawing the flesh from my arm and roll it into a neat, slippery cylinder. Tears blur my vision as I look down at the white, bleeding mass it left behind; a rectangle, the size of a matchbox, has been torn from my arm. It roars with pain as the book withdraws.

The figure relinquishes me, and I wrench my hand from the cover as it withdraws with its prize. Another ripple spreads across the surface as my skin disappears into its depths, and I realise.

The pages, all different colours.

All different *skin tones*.

Iain removes his hand from my back. I put him out of my mind. Before me, the cover begins to lift, as though the book is stretching after a long slumber. It creaks like an old worn chair, until it rests, open, in front of me.

Iain steps up beside me, his eyes on my arm. "You may go," he says to the attendant.

To my surprise, they bow their head and step back.

"They are The Flayed," he explains to me, and I watch them shuffle across the cold chamber. "They have paid the price many times."

I can't imagine doing this more than once. "I have some things to say to you," I mutter to him, holding my bleeding arm.

"I have no doubt. I didn't realise they'd ask you to pay the price."

I snort. "Well, it's paid. What do we get?"

"I'm not sure. I brought you here to look upon the Book, to grow used to the idea that one day you will need to command it. I was not expecting The Flayed to be so demanding." He looks at the pages, creased and yellowed, and clears his throat. "Now that we're here, I need you to focus."

It's a tall order, with the screaming pain. I bite it back. "On?"

He hesitates, then looks at me out the corner of his eye. "Your master."

"Arno?" Shock temporarily blunts the pain. "Why?"

"He designed a rune alphabet. I need to see it."

I'm back in Arno's office, sketching runes in the candlelight. My pen is cautious and unsure, but his flies across the page. I remember the little shapes and the power they could wield.

"Can't you just ask him?"

Iain's face darkens. "Master Veloquis has made himself a difficult man to find, after submitting his work to the Book."

I turn back it, my thoughts whirling. My allegiance is to Arno, and if he gave his work to the Book of Blood, he could've been trying to hide it from Iain.

The blank page stretches before me.

"I don't know how it works," I say honestly.

"Think of Arno. Of your lessons with him, and anything he might've said to you."

Unbidden, the image of my master sitting behind his desk comes to mind. His long, unkept hair, the beard he never trimmed, the bright eyes that saw through me.

A small rune forms at the edge of the page, bleeding into existence. Iain grips my elbow tightly.

"Good, Rose."

I don't recognise the rune. I step closer to it, trying to read it. It glistens red on the page in the candlelight, wet and sickly.

Another forms next to it and professional curiosity takes over.

I shut my eyes, trying to remember Arno's voice, his body language, anything he ever said to me. It's likely Iain won't remember the runes anyway.

But when I look upon the page again, it is blank.

Disappointment rushes from my lungs, and I swallow hard. Iain relinquishes my arm.

"She is not worthy of the information she is trying to access," says the soft-spoken voice beside us.

Iain turns on the attendant. "She is to be queen."

They are unmoving. "The Book does not care. Titles and status are for the social world. Hard work and dedication are what add value to one's person here in the Archives."

Iain clenches his teeth. "We'll be back."

They incline their head. "As is your right of access as a citizen of Lotheria. The Book will be glad of your contribution to its pages. Good day."

My arm bleeds freely as we step out into the square. The heavy door closes behind us, and Iain sighs.

"Here," he says, handing me his handkerchief as our horses are brought over. "Clean yourself up."

I press it to my raw and bloody arm. The sensation of cloth against the wound turns my stomach.

"What did you want me to find?" Nerves suddenly spring to my stomach. "A rune alphabet?"

He mounts his horse, and I wait for the nearest Thornsguard to assist me. He waits until I'm atop Iotha beside him before answering.

"Yes. A Rune Master creating their own alphabet is not unusual. But the nature of your master's was; he claimed it could do things other magics could not, going so far as to carve some into the halls of the Academy itself. I have a mind to return there to study them." He glances at me in the evening light as I blanch at that information. Lanterns are beginning to be lit along the cobbled streets as the air grows cooler. "These designs could help us win the war, Rose, if wielded by a master of runes and tactics."

Cold realisation hits me as we begin to ride. "That's why you brought me back to Lotheria? You needed someone who could use runes?"

"The reasons for your return are much more varied than that, but yes. You are to be queen for the blood in your veins first and foremost. The country has chosen you."

I look away.

"Your knowledge of runes is advanced for someone your age with your education. The study of them has lapsed over the years, and now there are only two living Rune Masters in Lotheria. One, Arno Veloquis, has gone to ground."

I wait for him to continue, and when he doesn't, prompt, "And the other?"

He sighs, his shoulders dropping slightly. "The other has made it clear their cooperation with us will be... difficult."

"Difficult?" I repeat. "So much so that it was easier to shop in another world for a spare one?"

He meets me with a level gaze.

"Your master's master is one of the oldest living magic wielders. They do not brook my style of... governance."

A tiny hint of amusement lights in my chest, despite the pain.

"Can I meet them?"

"I pray you don't have to." He clenches his jaw. "Cursed be the day anyone is forced to meet Yoris Moon."

LYDIA

The hall was alive with music and laughter. Golden light glimmered from torches and magelight, cast high up into the vaulted ceiling, where glittering letters etched into the stone sparkled down onto the gathered guests like starlight.

"Arno, they're beautiful," Lydia breathed, her head tipped back to marvel at her soulmate's workmanship. "I can't believe you finished it."

"Believe it." Arno nabbed a glass of champagne from a passing page's tray. "Six months of my life, the biggest moment of my career and... you're ogling the northern boy."

Lydia jerked her gaze away from two men in the corner of the room. She'd gotten a glimpse of Jettais and his brother through the shining silks and suited pages and had temporarily lost the thread of conversation. "Sorry."

He nudged her. "Go talk to him."

Lydia turned and squared her shoulders. "No. It's your night and I'm here to support you, not flirt and giggle like an idiot. Now, where is the master?"

Arno grinned, then gestured with his chin. "Over there, talking to Iain."

Lydia matched the mischievous smile. "Oh, he'll like that."

The First Master of Runes had ridden from Castor two days previous, and had spent the time since going over Arno's application to the Runes Guild; the ceiling under which they currently stood. Scaffolding had been erected for the master to climb on, where the runes had been examined in minute detail through magnified glass of varying strengths.

Iain's gaze found the pair in the crowd and they knew they must relieve him. Looping her hand through Arno's offered arm, Lydia locked eyes with the Headmaster as they approached.

"Ten thousand hours of carving, gold leafing from the mines of Melacore shipped here over two oceans and applied with a dagger made from the tooth of an ulurair slain on the shores of Kella Sur." Arno cocked a grin at the Master and offered his free hand. "Arno Veloquis."

His hand was taken and shaken promptly by a smaller one, gnarled with age. Bright eyes glared over the rim of gleaming glasses. "And unfortunately, young one, you do not seem to have learnt a wit of grace while doing so."

The First Master stood at a solid five foot, making Lydia feel tall amongst the group. They kept their pale hair short and slicked back, their well-tailored clothes shimmering in the candlelight. Their glasses were often removed and polished on their waistcoat, before being returned to the straight, fine nose that now sniffed in Arno's direction.

"Runes are more than just elbow grease and blustering," they said. "Humility and patience must also factor in."

Arno frowned. "Did you not hear me say 'ten thousand hours'?"

"Yes, and I also heard the manner in which you spoke it." Their cane was tapped sharply on the stone floor. "Is this who you offer to me, Headmaster Iain? A boy with a chin sharper than his mind?"

Lydia hid her smirk in a long sleeve as the vein on Iain's forehead pulsed. "I apologise. Arno Veloquis, Lydia Greatcast, this is Master Yoris Moon. They were just telling me about your application, Veloquis."

Arno's arm tensed beneath her hand. "I'd be very honoured to hear what you have to say about my work, Master Yoris."

The master cocked their head at the student. "Ah, a little of the aforementioned grace. Good. Come with me."

They set off down the stairs and onto the main dancefloor. Couples scattered before the tapping cane, settling on the outskirts of the hall like disturbed butterflies. The band filtered to a stop at a look from Netalia, who watched with wine in hand alongside the governor of Castor.

"Talk me through your process," Yoris commanded, and Arno hesitated for a second as the eyes of the room fell to him instead.

Silence grew in the room, and Lydia's face grew warm. Taking a deep breath, she pressed her fingers into the crook of Arno's elbow, unseen by the room, and pinched him.

Arno took a sudden breath, his voice beginning to speak before his brain caught up with him. "I began with my own alphabet, Master Yoris. Developing a specialised language with a specific purpose in mind."

"Which was?"

Arno stood a little straighter. "To protect, to strengthen, and to repair. My runes seek out the smallest deficiency, the weakest element, the most minute damage in their design and reinforce it to be stronger than it ever could be originally. This hall, with hundreds of thousands of my runes, will never fall. Under siege, it will never break. Fire cannot scorch it, stone cannot break it." Arno's eyes took on a glint, and he turned slightly to address the room as well. "Time can merely dress its edges with character."

A murmur went through the crowd as Yoris' eyes widened behind their glasses. "No rune can interfere with the flow of time."

Arno turned back to the master. "Mine can. I can stop both physical and magical effects, having studied—"

A sharp rap of the cane on the stone floor halted his boasting. Only Lydia saw the slight shake of their head that accompanied it. Once again, she dug her fingers into Arno's arm, and he ceased speaking.

"Impressive," Yoris said loudly. "Your work is a fine art, young master Veloquis." They turned to the Headmasters and addressed Iain in particular. "I need a private place to continue the assessment with your student."

Netalia stepped forward in a swath of rosepink silks, but Iain held up a hand to halt her murmured offer. "My office is nearby. You will have complete privacy there."

Lydia remembered the place she'd been taken on her first day in Lotheria, before she was allowed to explore her new home. The fire in the hearth was long dead, cleaned out by dutiful pages, but Yoris approached the nearest brazier and scored a rune in the pitch with a long finger. The torch burst to life eagerly as though it had been burning for hours.

"Leave us, Iain," they said. "I will inform you how your student performs." As Iain left, the master's gaze fell to Lydia. "And you... you will not leave his side?"

She straightened. "No. I am his soulmate, the one who watched him work for—"

"I don't care, I don't care," Yoris interrupted, flapping a hand. "I, too, know the bond of soulmates, having one of my own, Miss Greatcast."

Lydia pressed her lips together and took a step back as the master turned to their student. "This halt in time you speak of... it is not wise to boast of such powers in hungry company."

Arno frowned, glancing towards Lydia. "Lyd would never—"

This time, he received a rap of the cane to his forehead. "Not your *soulmate*, dolt. The Headmasters. Iain, Netalia, and their grubby little friend and puppet, soon-to-be-governor Malico of Temperhold. Do you not see the greed with which they rule this school?" Yoris closed in and lowered their voice. Lydia strained to hear. "Soon, Fairhaven will not satiate their desire for power."

Both students were silent as Yoris continued. "The hungry are never satisfied. They will seek more and more until it consumes them. Runes with the ability to halt the effects of time, like yours, will be of great interest to them. It should be a priority of yours that they are *not*."

"My runes couldn't actually *stop* time," Arno protested. "They just stop…"

Yoris watched his face change, his brows crease slightly, and they nodded. "Yes. They stop the effects. Have you tried a rune on your person?"

Arno recoiled. "Though I may have studied them, my runes are not the *caesis alledari* of Sudafrae. They don't belong in flesh."

The master folded their hands on the grip of their cane. "Desperation makes people do things they would find abhorrent in kinder times."

Arno said nothing.

"I advise you to speak no more of the time element of your alphabet. Let the Headmasters believe you were speaking metaphorically in regards to the protection your runes can offer their halls." Yoris sighed, pushing their glasses up their nose, their eyes creasing as though in pain. "Though I must ask, *how* did you come to this discovery? Political implications aside, it is an incredible work of pure magic."

Arno clasped his palms together, as though to wipe sweat from them, but from the way his shoulders shifted, Lydia knew he was more comfortable discussing the mechanics of his language rather than the potential political fall out.

"The chamber below the Academy has interesting properties," Arno began. "After studying the apparent fluctuations in time, I was able to come up with a rune that protected the wearer against its influence."

"That chamber has remained nameless since I first came to the Academy as a wee student," Yoris said quietly. "Nameless and unused. I'm not sure there *should* be a use for such a place."

Lydia and Arno exchanged glances.

"The Headmasters want to explore its qualities," Lydia said. "As a place for testing the new students."

Yoris looked back at Arno. "Do you not see how their greed knows no bounds? To want to use such a place for a *test*? What do they hope to find?"

Arno raised his shoulders in a shrug, but Lydia again answered. "They want the new students, particularly the humanborn, to know the magic they wield. They hope that the chamber will reveal a glimpse of the future of that student, so that they might be able to guide them onto a path of greater destiny."

Now, the rune master's attention turned to Lydia. "The way you speak of them... you know much for a vine tangler."

Growth magic curled around her fingertips as she lifted her chin. "'Vine tanglers' can be more useful than you think, Master Moon."

A hand was lifted in parlance. "I meant no offence, Miss Greatcast. Tell me of your relationship to the Headmasters."

She looked to Arno, who simply looked back at her. She made a decision on the spot, and replied, "They are preparing me for the seat of power I must take."

The master said nothing, then brought their hand to their face to rest slender fingers on their jawline. "The next queen. Now, this is a surprise."

Lydia squared her shoulders. "I work closely with the Headmasters to ensure the transition of responsibility will go smoothly. I know how they think and what they want. I trust them."

"Oh, my dear." Yoris stepped forward, resting a hand on her shoulder. She felt their cool touch through the thin lace over her skin. "If either of you take one thing from this meeting, I warn you to holster that trust, and remember... Lotheria is not kind to its queens."

CHAPTER TWELVE

I'M deep in thought as we ride through the palace gardens. Our horses are led away as my cane is returned to me, and I expect the Headmaster to engage me in conversation. Instead, Iain speaks to one of the guards, and then begins to walk away. He doesn't look back.

I watch him go, then begin an uneasy journey across the gravel; the unstable surface is a nightmare to place my cane on securely. Two Thornsguard follow me inside.

"How do I get to the roof?" I ask them.

They exchange a glance beneath their golden helmets.

"We can show you the way, ma'am, but there are many stairs," one replies finally.

My leg twinges in anticipated pain, but I ignore it; I have both my cane and my brace. "Please, lead the way."

I follow them down the hallways, and one goes ahead of us up the narrow stairs while one trails behind me—I suspect to catch me if I suddenly topple backwards. Can't have the new queen murdered by gravity in her first week.

The climb is arduous. My heart thunders in my chest, roaring in my ears, as the brace digs almost to bone. I focus instead on the structure it grants, rather than the pain.

The Castor palace is taller than I realised. But when the door to the roof terrace is finally opened, I forget the strain instantly. A vista of ocean and city sweeps before us; I can walk the perimeter to examine the capital on all sides. The sun is setting behind the western wall, casting a breathtaking silhouette of the immense structure. I know the streets below me will already be enshrouded in cold shadow, but up here, the last rays of golden sunshine fall across us.

"Thank you," I tell the Thornsguard. "You can leave me up here. I just want some time to think."

They hesitate, and one says, "We'll wait inside, ma'am."

It's as good as I'm going to get. I nod slightly, and they disappear into the castle, closing the door.

I'm alone.

The strong wind buffets me, pushing me around. But I lean on the wall, folding my arms between the parapets, and let the cane rest beside me.

The Book of Blood found me decidedly unworthy. The queensblood refuses to answer my call.

Lotheria is rejecting me.

I pull my sleeves down and look at the runes I carved there; my left arm is half-covered by Iain's handkerchief, and the fresh wound seeps white blood through the cloth. I remember his gaze upon it, when I stood before the book; had he been remembering the last time he'd seen the queensblood? He'd drained it from my mother's veins and captured it in ice. Seeing it again had surely made him realise that I was, apparently, Lotheria's next intended queen.

The runes lie inert, merely scar tissue in the light of the setting sun. The earlier, ghostly flickers that rolled through my skin are now gone, perhaps still heeding my desperate *hide* command in the Archives.

I lift my gaze, catching sight of a flock of birds over the capital. They twist and twirl on the breeze, covering more distance in a few seconds than mere humans ever could. I think of the promise I made to myself, when I agreed to accompany Iain back to Lotheria.

I'd made promises before—to Tyson, to Laela, to Kaya. I'd made a point of keeping them where I could. But I'm quickly learning that promises are easy to make, and easier to break.

My eyes fall on the north gate. Promises had been made to me too.

Uncertainty drums anxious fingers in my chest as I look at the tiny figures in the city streets below. I take a deep breath; an ally against Iain and his plans would've been welcome.

In the courtyard, people are leaving the surrounding buildings. I recognise the walk of the Academy students, having made a habit of watching them in the evenings. I watch for my friends, but from this height, it is impossible.

"*They are loyal to the idea of you,*" Phoenix had said, and I file the information away.

Disappointment bites at the heels of that revelation as I reflect on my conversation with Iain; he'd needed a Rune Master, and both existing ones had refused to heed him. I'm here for the magic I'd studied and the blood in my veins. I'm a game piece on Iain's Kingdoms board.

I look at the capital laid out before me, smelling the smoke and salt of a healthy coastal city. In a few weeks, he'll place a crown on my head and rule with the closest semblance of legitimacy he legally can; we are no longer in Fairhaven, and the noble Houses here are harder to control than students and non-magi.

I'd promised, when I'd returned, that I would do better by my friends, my country, and myself; the Lothericon, the queensblood, and Iain, had tested me and found me wanting.

But I've been in this position before, and the men who'd passed judgement had burned with the trees in Deadman's Keep.

I remain on the terrace until the sun sinks below the horizon and the cool wind becomes cold. When I push the door to the stairs open, my cheeks are pink with the chill. Both Thornsguard stand quickly, and a pang of shame lights in me as I realise I'd kept them waiting out here.

"Sorry," I say, but they merely incline their heads.

"Headmistress Netalia would like you to find her when you are available," the nearest says to me.

I blink, hesitating before taking the first step down. "Why?"

"She didn't say. She wished to speak to you on the roof about an hour ago."

I hadn't been disturbed. "You didn't let her up?"

He meets my gaze. "You said you needed some time, ma'am."

I look closer at the pair; I'd wholly considered the Thornsguard at the behest of the Headmasters, but this is new.

"What's your name?" I ask the one who spoke.

"Ser Neal of House Undertoil."

"Thank you, Ser Neal." I begin my perilous journey down the stairs. "I've not heard of your House, I must admit."

"It is a minor one, Your Grace. Sworn to House Olinius here in the south."

Iain had explained there were nine major Houses throughout Lotheria—whose favour I would be courting for their support in the coming war. I'd met representatives of nearly all but two; House Araspire, who governed the north and had begun their insurrection almost nineteen years ago—the likelihood of them showing up at court was minimal—and my own house, House Greatcast. Likely, they didn't believe the missives from the capital, and I couldn't blame them.

It also strikes me that Ser Neal had called me 'Your Grace'; Iain had told me the staff of the palace were under strict instruction not to use the official titles until I'd been crowned.

"We must do our due diligence," he'd said, "and ensure the city will accept you."

We proceed down a few more stairs. I don't correct the knight's use of my title.

"Headmistress Netalia said she'd await you in the east-facing tearoom," he tells me when we reach the top floor. I'm desperately out of breath and red in the face, but I try not to show it. "Would you like to be escorted?"

I go to decline, but reconsider. "I'll find it much faster with your assistance, ser knights."

Ser Neal nods sharply, and leads me down another corridor. I can hear the chatter of palace staff around corners, echoing up from other floors. The place has seemed livelier since my announcement.

Netalia has chosen a long, expansive room which takes up much of the eastern wing. I shiver as I step inside, and the cold flagstones remind me of the Academy instantly. The Headmistress sits in an armchair beside an enormous window which overlooks the gardens. A chair sits opposite, a large, unlit hearth behind it. She looks up as we enter, but she does not stand.

"Rose. Thank you for coming to meet with me."

I nod at the Thornsguard, and they withdraw. "I'm sorry to keep you waiting, Headmistress."

She gestures towards the empty seat, and I reluctantly cane my way towards it.

"Don't be. The roof terrace is alluring for its temptation to stand and ponder. I've been up there many times since we left Fairhaven."

A serving girl enters, carrying a silver kettle in a heavy cloth, and pours the boiling water neatly into the floral teapot between us. Netalia ignores her, and lifts the teapot when she withdraws.

"Tea?"

I hesitate for a second, but it will be impolite to refuse. I want to know what she wants. "Please."

She pours the tea and hands it to me, watching closely as I lift it. The scalding liquid crests the lip of the cup.

I place it back down. "Bit hot," I say, with an apologetic smile.

"Let it cool," she says smoothly, and I cradle the cup as though I'm likely to take a drink at any moment.

"Ser Neal said you wanted to speak with me," I prompt.

She places her own teacup on the table between us, and lets her gaze drift across the window. She's chosen the darkest room in the palace, on the opposite side of the building to the sunset. The darkened gardens are vanishing into the gloom beneath us and, beyond the palace wall, there are few lights glowing in the districts below.

"I wanted, first and foremost, to offer my apologies." Her dark eyes flick to mine. "When Iain informed me who your mother was, I knew that would create ill will between us."

My grip tightens on the cup in my lap, and heat rises in my chest. An insult, a sharp retort, rises on my tongue, but I press it down. Instead, I make a non-committal sound in my throat, and also look to the gardens outside.

"Though it does explain how the blood passed to you," she continues. "From mother to daughter."

I smile tightly. "I thought the whole point of Lotherian queens was no hereditary title."

"And yet..." She lets the sentence trail off. "Though I've found over the years, the bond between mother and daughter is one of the strongest that can be forged, if fostered correctly."

I take a quick sip of the bitter tea. "Are you close with your mother?"

The corner of her mouth quirks, and she sips her tea. "That bond was not fostered correctly."

Despite everything, my curiosity piques. I've spent hours with Iain, playing Kingdoms, sitting in on meetings, being shown the castle. But Netalia has always been absent, from my schooling, to my arrival in Castor, and most of my introduction to the city. I know nearly nothing about the woman who has as much, if not more, say in my fate than her soulmate.

"Are all mages from major Houses?" I ask. "Are you?"

She looks at me. "A lot of mages come from the major Houses, yes. I believe due to mage marrying mage, their offspring carries their magical line. Hence our... discouragement of non-magi relationships."

I nearly roll my eyes, a rebuttal at my lips. But I need her to talk, not lecture. She continues.

"As for myself, I come from a small family near the eastern wall. A poor district." She gazes out the window again, and I follow her line of the sight. The city wall has disappeared into the night, lit only by the faint lanterns on the watchtowers. "All Lotherian children are tested for magic at four years old. The carrier who tested the children in my area was a drunken idiot." She lifts her eyebrows slightly, and sighs. "Unfortunately, drunken idiots are clumsy people. I'm told he fell down a flight of stairs, just days before I was supposed to leave for the Academy." Her eyes meet mine, and I go cold. "No carrier replaced him."

"Who tests for magic in that district now?" I ask, my voice low.

She smiles. "I do."

Our conversation lapses, and she pours another cup while I sit in silence. The room is growing cooler, and darker, as night settles over the capital.

"Humanborns have always fascinated me," she says suddenly. "Your bloodlines so strong they can be found even further from the slums—another world."

I feel like I'm being insulted, but I'm not quite sure how. I drink more of my tea, and stifle a cough as it catches in my throat.

"I'm just as shocked as you," I manage with watery eyes. "This is all so new to me. I still have a lot to learn."

"You do. Acknowledging that is a big step, especially for you."

"For me?"

"I read your reports, Rose. Admitting fault or ignorance is difficult for you."

Again, I fight down the kneejerk reaction to lash back at her. I get the peculiar feeling I'm being baited. Instead, I smile.

"I've learnt a lot in the last twelve months," I say. "I've had good teachers."

"A good teacher can make all the difference," she agrees. "Though some are worth heeding more than others."

"Oh?" I put my cup down. "Care to elaborate?"

"Not all teachers are born equal."

"You're right. Some are from the 'slums' on the eastern wall."

She goes quiet, and I wait to see what she does. Every fibre of my body has tensed in the silence.

"I'd advise you to heed those especially. An unorthodox education early in life can lead to interesting skills."

I wait in the silence, though my heart pounds at her words. Part of me wants to stand up and announce that I'm leaving.

Another part wants her to continue.

"It's getting a bit hard to see in here," she says suddenly, and goes to rise. "I'll fetch a maid to light the room."

I smile. "Don't get up."

The candles on various surfaces, the candelabra above us, and the hearth, have all been singing to me since I entered the room; waxed wicks desperate to burst into flame, the dried wood and kindling resting against the iron grate in the hearth. They all burst into flame now and golden light washes over the room, illuminating us both. The teacup, with its middling puddle of tea in its depths, was never too hot for me to drink. I just wanted to see what she'd do.

She settles back into her chair, her eyes on me. "Your control has improved. Elemental magic has always eluded me."

"It has its uses," I concede, and place the cup on the table.

"I always wished it would manifest. Your grandmother, or

great-grandmother, I suppose, has one most interesting to me. You will meet her soon, I hope."

The Greatcast family has not been present at court, nor have they responded to palace missives. She's managing to find a lot of sore spots to press. It stings, and I don't care for the conversation.

"Was there anything in particular you wished to discuss?" I ask instead.

She smiles in the warm firelight. "Not in particular, Rose. I just wished to reacquaint myself with you."

I clench my jaw for a brief second. "I hope the experience was satisfactory."

She stands, and I recognise my dismissal. Grateful for the opportunity to leave, I turn towards the door.

"I think we have a lot in common, Rose."

I pause. "Why do you think that?"

She doesn't answer immediately, and when I look, she's standing near the window, her eyes on the unyielding shadows.

"We've both been underestimated by people who meant us harm, but also those who are supposed to love us most. We'd both rather carve the path we think is right than tread the convenient one. And a shared surname does not guarantee us acceptance by those it should."

A chill goes up my spine. I'm running out of niceties.

"My mother loves me," I say, my voice low.

"And yet she let you leave, to face the crown, a war, alone." Netalia finally faces me, her hands clasped neatly before her. "Choose your allies carefully, Rose. Battle lines aren't only being drawn on the borders."

LYDIA

Lydia's breath felt like it was bound up in the wreath at her throat. Her eyes skated the horizon, searching the dimpled mountains for something her eyes could not see.

She'd never been this close to his homeland before.

The door opened behind her, making her jump. "The mistress will see you now."

She turned, one hand going to her throat. The prickly wreath of native flowers blended with the long silken gown of green, but she was having trouble keeping her thoughts and magic from the cut plants. She'd kept them alive as long as possible, but now their cries were going quiet, asking where the main stem was, the roots, why they couldn't see the sky anymore. She swallowed hard against the cacophony, and wondered again why the Greatcast Matriarch had seen fit to put a vine tangler in a posy of dying flowers.

She narrowed her eyes at the closing door, and grabbed the handle before it could settle into the arched doorway.

She was the next queen of Lotheria. She would not allow herself to be frightened of some old woman.

The long, narrow stairwell wrapped around the inside of her tower, the walk long and isolated. She had not been allowed to bring staff, which saved her from explaining that she didn't have any. Other students of noble birth took handmaids and manservants from applicants in Fairhaven, which provided comfortable employment and a steady pay purse each week for those selected. But Lydia, raised in a world very unlike this one, had grown up tying her own shoes and felt odd at the prospect of having someone do it for her, good intentions or not.

Now, part of her ached for someone on her side in this stone fortress.

The home of the Greatcast family, known as Thornsgrove in war time, was built on the banks of the river that divided River-door and Numin. The great manse rose tall from the riverbed, its walls made of greystone and pocked with age and lichen. She'd held her breath at the sight of it as they'd ridden over the low bridge, wondering what awaited her within its halls. The city had been charming enough, with red brick buildings and ivy growing over the foundations. It had been bright and clean, though the light hit the Greatcast castle in the evening and burnt the town with its reflection, the cold stone leeching away any hint of freedom.

The family had long been in attendance. Producing a steady line of mages, their pockets had been filled with gold and favours for as long as memory served. The Headmasters of the Academy had been more than pleased to reveal her true name on her first day in Lotheria, still damp from the river, shivering from head to toe in jeans and a t-shirt. The name 'Greatcast' had meant little to her.

Now, it meant everything.

Lydia took a deep breath, steadying herself outside the doors of the great lady's sitting room. A waiting manservant nodded slightly at her, and she gestured forth. The door was opened with the weight of a throne room door, and Lydia was bathed in the thick smell of lavender that gusted forth.

Her nose twitched. It was not true lavender, plucked from an unlucky bush in the limp gardens, but a scent brewed by an apothecary in the city. With enough time spent in the area, Lydia would be able to pinpoint which one.

"Lydia Greatcast, ma'am."

Lydia jumped at the manservant's voice, and met his eyes as he pulled the door closed behind her. She fought the urge to slip through the crack and run.

"My long lost granddaughter, is it?"

The voice cracked through the room, like an iceberg breaking against the shore. Lydia swallowed as her eyes adjusted to the bright light within, revealing a diminutive woman sitting in a wingback chair, a teacup and saucer within her grip. Her beady eyes ran up and down the length of her body.

Gennorin McKorthus Greatcast was immeasurably old, and had taken great lengths to keep it that way; even the Headmasters weren't exactly sure how Lydia was related to the woman. Her own haphazard guess put Gennorin at ninety or so years of age. Lydia mentally added another five years, as the woman set aside her teacup with trembling hands and lifted her arms.

"Approach me. Let me see what my blood in the Other realm has wrought this time."

Lydia swallowed, but kept her face blank. She dipped a neat curtsey as she approached, the flowers scratching at her throat.

Gennorin made a noise in her throat that Lydia had no idea how to interpret. "Sit down, girl. Have some tea."

Lydia sat, reaching for the tea service and pouring for her elderly relative first. Determination kept her hands steady even as her mind raced, but Netalia had trained her well, and not a drop was wasted.

"Dollop of honey," Gennorin instructed. "More than that, girl, do you think I lived to be this old on scarcities?"

"No, ma'am." Lydia chanced a look and caught a glitter in the old woman's eye. She tamped down the beginnings of a smile.

"You're taller than I expected. Prettier too."

Lydia offered her the full teacup. "Is that a good thing?"

Another grunt. Gennorin slurped the tea noisily. "Not always."

Lydia sipped her tea, having deliberately kept it bitter and sharp; she couldn't afford to relax around this woman. Her word of approval would mean everything in court. The nobility hadn't had a queen to accept for hundreds of years—and it would go a lot smoother if her Lotherian family accepted and spoke for her.

"A good thing you're of our stock, eh?"

Lydia looked up, noting Gennorin's eyes on her. "Sorry?"

"I can see you thinking it. Taking the throne, in front of a bunch of prissy nobles who haven't had to accept so much as a late dinner in their entire life. I bet our name being attached to yours will make that much easier to swallow."

"You speak as though I've not earned it." Lydia lowered her eyes to her tea and sipped.

"I'm speaking as though the convenience is too great to ignore."

Silence fell between them. Outside, the sun was setting, casting long rays of light against the tall glass windows.

"I was named a Greatcast on my first day in this world," Lydia began quietly. "The blood tests lined up true to that of my mage ancestors."

"Let 'em take your blood, did you?" Gennorin squinted. "Maybe you're not as sharp as they say." The old woman set her tea down. "Iain and Netalia have been in charge of that place since the old Headmaster died. They dissolved any laws that might unseat them, but they've become brazen with their rule. It is no longer a secret that they groom the council, and that young Temperhold student—"

"Malico?"

"—for a grab at power in Castor as well. And now you come along," the old woman grumbled. "Blood of the one family that could sway any naysayers, or flare them into rebellion. Not only do you take to your studies well, and grow a pretty frame and face, but you also carry the blood of the last queen, poised to become the next." Gennorin steepled her fingers and leant forward. "Tell me how you would view that."

Lydia considered. It was odd to hear such blatant, almost treasonous, comments against the Headmasters who were revered in Fairhaven.

But, as the view from her rooms reminded her, they weren't in the south.

"The land chooses the queen," she mused, thinking on the heavyset books she'd been given upon the discovery. "Maybe it shucks the Headmasters' rule?"

Gennorin's eyes bored into hers. "And what makes you think they'll give it over freely, girl?"

Lydia tried to swallow the heavy feeling in her throat, the dying flowers scratching at her throat. She raised a hand to them, feeding yet another tendril of power to the posy. They quietened, leaving her mind clear.

The words Gennorin spoke were worth considering. Since Arno's presentation to Master Yoris Moon, and the runes he'd displayed, the Headmasters had become cagey with their meetings, hiding behind closed doors, their voices muffled by Iain's clumsy muting runes. Not even her plant magic could relay to her the words they spoke.

"What other choice do they have?" Lydia said finally.

"Plenty. They could turn you into their puppet, they could kill you, they could take the blood that marks you as the landgifted queen." Gennorin shrugged. "Iain excels in strategy. He will become the first High Marshal since that poor mentor of his met his fate during the massacre. There are plenty of ways they can solve the problem of Lydia Greatcast."

She squinted, flexing gnarled fingers. "And on the topic of that name, we were discussing your legitimacy."

The room darkened in an instant. Lydia gasped, blinded, and fell back as a quick hand struck her across the face. She shook her head with ringing ears as the matriarch spoke in the eerie blackness.

"All Greatcast mages have strong magic. Let us see yours, Lydia."

A walking stick thumped the ground near her head. She went scrambling backwards on her hands and knees, her fingers still looped through the teacup handle. She stared into the darkness.

"Yours, mistress," Lydia called, "is night?"

This time, the stick caught her shoulder, and she whirled towards the blow, her arm smarting.

"They told me you were sharp, girl."

Lydia scrambled away, her ears wise to the sound of the crones' feet against the flagstones. She reached wide with her plant sense, the flowers at her throat curling upwards as they answered her call.

They were the only things that did.

The cane came down again, and she jumped away. No doubt Gennorin could see in the dark, and was having a right laugh at her frantic movements and wide eyes.

Lydia took a deep breath, closing them against the darkness.

The posy at her throat became her eyes, textured and coloured differently; the flowers did not see objects as she did, instead lending her whispers, hints of movement, and scents. Lydia touched the flowers, fingers questioning.

Two were common dalberries, found in most gardens in Lotheria. It sprung up everywhere and was favoured for its round white flowers. It was pretty, but useless.

The other two caught her interest. One, a blood poppy, reaped from the meadow she'd passed on her journey north. Her magic twined and twisted through its cells, gleaning hints of the power they could share.

But when she began to examine the fourth flower—a small, shy curlbright—Lydia realised.

She had a choice; she could play into the old woman's plan and end this farce, or she could use the blood poppy and display to her matriarch the kind of queen she could be.

Her fingers caressed the soft red petals of the poppy, her thumb brushing the short stem like a lover's cheek. Her instincts warred within her, even as she heard the woman's quick steps shuffling across the room to her.

Play the game, or end it.

Her fingers moved to the curlbright, a request in their grip. The flower responded, opening quickly with a bright flash of light like a snap of lightning.

Lydia had been prepared for it, and shielded herself. Gennorin stopped short, working gnarled fists into her burning eyes.

"An end to the battle it is." The darkness receded, the muted orange sunset replacing it carefully. Lydia stood, and delicately sat her teacup back down on the service, her chest rising and falling. "You did not use your queensgift."

"That wasn't what you were testing me for," Lydia replied evenly, sitting back down.

Gennorin gave a short bark of a laugh. "No, it wasn't. They told me my granddaughter was a vine tangler, and they were right. I apologise for ringing your neck in dying flowers, girl, but I had to give you something."

She rang a small bell, and the manservant re-entered, his face blank—though no doubt he'd heard the sounds of struggle within. In his hands he carried a small clay pot, filled to the brim with rich dark earth. Lydia gasped as the flowers at her throat strained towards it, like a thirsty horse to a river.

"That should keep them alive long enough for you to replant them somewhere of your choosing." Gennorin poured her a fresh cup of tea. "You can have any corner of the gardens you like. Take them all if you wish! Belatha knows we need a green thumb around here."

Lydia had seen the wilting gardens on her way in, and had already noted a dozen remedies that would assist the ailing plants. Her fingers itched for the soil and a trowel.

"What do you mean to do about your kingsmatch?"

Thoughts of the gardens fled her mind.

"Who?" Lydia asked unconvincingly.

Gennorin peered at her. "Your king, girl, the one who will reign next to you. Choose wisely, and from a good family. If you want my advice, pick a handsome one who will live to serve. You don't want him getting notions of power in his head." The walking stick was pointed at her. She recoiled instinctively. "Sit them on a throne, and you give them gravitas. A leadership they wouldn't have had before, in front of people who will idolise them. That choice will be the most important one you, or any queen after you, will make."

Lydia sat impassively, her face blank. But her hands tensed at the sharp words, and she busied herself transferring the dying flowers to the pot that would sustain them. She tended the curlbright first, the long ovular tendril tucking in on itself as though to sleep. The snap of intense bioluminescence had cost it dearly in energy. She stroked it tenderly.

"Think of him as one of your flowers," Gennorin said, but her tone was softer. "The curlbright is useful and serves at your command. The dalberries are pretty but harmless, a common sight that cheer all who lay eyes on it."

The matriarch paused to sip more tea, but Lydia's eyes fell to the remaining flower, knowing now the disturbing power hidden within the red petals.

And her thoughts turned to the one she would name king.

CHAPTER THIRTEEN

ON THE DAY I survive more than three rounds on the Kingdoms board, Iain allows me to see my friends.

We pack away the boxes, and the loss doesn't sting as much—instead, I am visualising his strategy, the thought process behind it, and how I will counter it next time. He catches my eye, and I know he's already inventing a new strat to throw me off balance.

I wonder if *Critical Theory*, the book he gave me, will have anything that might help me. I am itching to read when he breaks the silence.

"One of the gardens has been laid out for you," he begins, and any excitement I had begins to dry up at the idea of another meeting with a noble. "For you, the Thoreau boy, his soulmate, and the two humanborns. Also, against Netalia's advisement, the northerner."

Nerves spring into my stomach, and I just stare at him for a moment. "You included Phoenix?"

"The boy was to be your soulmate. It is a bond I do not take lightly, though yours may be broken. I am not a Carrier of the spirit to determine if it can be repaired, but I don't wish to stand in the way of it regardless." He meets my gaze. "We will need our queen at full strength."

I understand; a full strength that can only be achieved if the queen can bond with her soulmate. It was a nice six seconds to think Iain had some kind of goodness in him.

The garden they've set us up in is called the Dalberry Walk, and when I cross the little bridge into it, I'm taken aback by the sprigs of white berry-flowers that frame the neat lawn, a small pond skirting it. It's an unusually pretty place.

The clanking of armour announces the Thornsguard before they do it themselves. I turn to greet my friends, my heart in my throat—the last time I'd seen them had been in a camp of half-souls, on the eve of Fairhaven's destruction by my hand. Only Orin and Phoenix had spoken with me since.

Amisha meets my gaze evenly, and my heart sinks lower. Beside her, Dena and Theresa wear similar expressions. I gird myself against the conversation to come, trying to fend off the sudden sickness in my belly.

"Ma'am, Lady Amisha Ni Luh of the Tsalski Empire, Lord Orin of House Thoreau, Miss Dena Brungarra, Miss Theresa Goodman, and Ser Phoenix of House Araspire."

It takes a moment for his title to sink in. He watches me closely.

I manage to find my voice. "Thank you. You can leave us."

The Thornsguard nods, but to no one's surprise, does not leave me alone in the garden with a member of House Araspire. I now understand why, initially, Phoenix had to hide in my bathroom.

"Iain didn't tell you?" is his first query.

"He told me you begged forgiveness and pledged allegiance. You confirmed as much last time I saw you."

He nods, and leads the rest of the group to the table and chairs laid out for us, though my heart is slamming in my chest. I follow them, but don't sit. The others say nothing, their eyes flicking between us.

"Yes, and at the time I believed it. But now, with war closer than ever, it has become apparent to me that my pledge meant nothing, but my blood means everything." Phoenix turns and faces me. "I'm a ward of the Headmasters, Rose. Politely, I'm their honoured guest. Politically, I'm a hostage. I cannot leave, my correspondence is monitored, and if my family makes a move of aggression, I will be executed."

I grip the back of a chair. Iain had told me it was because Phoenix had bested him in a duel, that he felt honour-bound to grant his request. He'd lied as easily as he breathed, and I believed him. Bile rises in my throat. Orin, not Phoenix, is the one to reach for me.

"This is how war is done," he mutters softly.

"This is why the north haven't moved since I got here," I realise. "The Headmasters sent word to your family that they have you."

Iain's most recent words about keeping our soulmate bond alive ring in my ears. A blatant lie or a political manoeuvre Phoenix himself doesn't even know about?

"Sorry," I tell the others.

The women don't say anything. The anxiety deepens in my stomach.

"So, you actually actually met representatives of *eight* of the noble houses the other day," Phoenix says with forced lightness. "I didn't know how to tell you, Rose. For what it's worth, *this* Araspire sends his welcomes and regards."

"Thanks." I sit heavily. "How do you tie into all of this? What are your relations?"

He sits also, beside Dena. "My father, Aloysius Araspire, heads the family. I have three brothers, well... two, now. I left to join the Academy when I turned seventeen and it became apparent he would try to stop me, but my siblings remained. Unfortunately, there are plenty of so-called minor houses in the north who pledged to their lord instead of the usurpers, as they refer to the Headmasters."

A few maids cross the bridge carrying various beverages. We all sit in awkward silence as they leave pitchers and pots out. My stomach turns at the sight of the floral teapot.

"So you're the son of the instigator." He's given a name to the faceless enemy Kaya has forged an alliance with.

"It's a miracle they didn't kill him on sight," Theresa says, and Dena looks sharply at her. "There's been tension between the north and the south for longer than we've been at the Academy."

"But no one put it to the torch until Rose," Amisha adds, and it's odd to hear her usually warm voice so cold. Her analogy was not helpful. I take a deep breath, but meet her look.

"I need to apologise to you. To all of you." I stand so I can see them all again, despite my leg's waning patience. "I made mistakes which affected not just myself, but my loved ones and those around me. I can't promise that I'll ever be able to make it right. But I swear to you, I will try. It's the reason I came back."

Amisha looks away, her chest rising and falling sharply. I expect Theresa to lead the counter-argument. But Dena's voice catches me off-guard.

"You could've told us. You could've warned us about the Halvers, Rose." Another friend's comforting tone is lost to me as the edge in her voice roughens the words. "They came for the Academy as Fairhaven burnt, tried to break through the doors. If it hadn't been for the extra guards the Headmasters had put in place, they may have succeeded."

The subtext of gratitude towards Iain and Netalia sets my teeth on edge, despite my recent proximity and conversations with them. "They had Tyson on an executioner's platform," I remind them. I focus the words at Amisha, arguably his closest friend after myself. She clenches her jaw, looks me in the eye, but then drops the contact first. "They would've had his head if Phoenix hadn't intervened."

"And he intervened correctly," Dena finishes. "With words and a blade, not magic, Rose. Not *fire*."

I remember the darkness that had swept over me, accompanied by ember and wrath. "I know. I wish I'd done it differently. But I'm as new to magic as you or Theresa."

"We didn't burn a town," Theresa says pointedly.

I sit back down, gripping the table. White hot heat rises in my gullet.

They have no idea what it was like at the Keep, they sit there smugly and pass their judgement from the comfort of hindsight—

I steady myself and relinquish the table. Beneath my grasp, the pale wrought-iron has warped. Shame bites at me again.

I cannot keep losing control of the fire.

I sit in silence with them, their opinions, both spoken and unspoken, ringing loudly in my ears. My eyes burn with unshed tears of guilt, because I know they're right; we all make mistakes, but mine had killed people.

A girl, digging in the remains of her home...

There was only one conversation I feared more than this one.

"You are my friends, and I love you all. I would never presume your forgiveness and I accept whatever you decide."

Birds flit overhead, their calls distilling the tense afternoon. A cloudy sky boils with grey clouds promising rain, and a chilled gust blows our hair from our faces. Amisha glances at Orin, who frowns.

"I can't do anything about it."

She rubs her arms accusingly, as though a second-year weather mage can change an entire system. The soulmates hold each other's stern looks for a moment longer, and Orin cracks first. The tension around the table eases slightly as a reluctant smile grows on Amisha's face in return. She stifles it, and turns to me.

"Rose, it will take me a long time to understand how you did what you did. But I don't believe you capable of malicious acts with intent."

It's not quite forgiveness, but I grip it like a lifeline. I nod, accepting her statement, and then try not to look like I'm waiting for the rest to speak.

Phoenix pours himself a cup of tea, and offers the teapot around the table. "We've already spoken on the matter, Rose. I believe the nature of your magic is darker than you realise. We must work on that."

Theresa holds her cup out, and I watch the tea spill into it. Arno had held similar thoughts regarding my fire whispering.

"I've seen senior mages lose control of their affinities," Orin says next. "Sometimes I believe we don't control the power, but are merely conduits for it."

Before I can reply, Dena makes a sound in her throat.

"'It wasn't Rose who destroyed an entire town, it was her magic'. A nice way to avoid consequences," she says, and I try not to argue that I was about to counter his statement; hadn't I made it clear that I would take responsibility for Fairhaven? "Sorry, Rose, but it's going to take me a lot longer than these guys to get back to any semblance of normal with you. You ran off to Riverdoor with them and left Theresa and me behind, then you came back changed in a way we could never understand, and before we knew it, Fairhaven was a pile of ashes—*your* doing." Her gaze is severe. "I have no idea what you're capable of anymore."

She stands, and Theresa downs her tea before doing the same. They linger for a moment as Dena clenches and unclenches her fist.

"I thought I could get past this, but I just can't."

The knot in my chest tightens as they walk away, back over the bridge. The Thornsguard watch them go, and one peers over his shoulder at us. I pray to whichever god is listening that they're out of earshot.

"Rose—" Phoenix begins.

I hold up my hand. "Don't. I deserved that."

I sit in silence with my mage friends until the urge to cry the hurt out passes. My brain casts a wide net for a subject, any subject, that will get someone else talking.

One springs to mind. "The Thornsguard introduced you as 'ser'. Not even Griffin is 'ser', and he commands the city guards."

Phoenix nods. "My older brother knighted me against my wishes after... after a battle."

I frown at him, but a memory returns; when he'd won a sword from our training master. He'd wielded it with reluctant familiarity.

He glances at Orin. "I was on the opposite side of many conflicts with your family, and of the houses sworn to yours. You must know I never wanted any part of it."

Orin sets his jaw, but nods.

"How old were you?" Amisha asks.

"I was four when my father first took me into battle. He sat me in front of his saddle and made me watch the township burn. I know many mages must've died that night. Many of the half-souls who invaded Fairhaven may have been created during that fight." He swallows hard, sitting back in his chair. "Sometimes it feels like no matter how far I run, my past is right over my shoulder."

"What's he like?" I ask quietly. "Your father?"

Phoenix's gaze drifts to the ground. "He's the product of a generation of biases and scorn. He grew up being told by his father, and his grandfather, that it was on him to restore Orthandrell to glory in the absence of a queen and to stop pandering to southern lords and their taxes. When he became head of our family, it was he who stopped the trading of ore and minerals to the south. He told me it was unfair for the few to grow fat on the labour of many, and the resources of the land were gifted to us for *all* Lotherians to profit from, not merely the one who established the earliest claim."

"House Araspire and House Olinius had a deal," Orin says,

reaching for his teacup. "Your father acts as though he wasn't fairly compensated."

"In his eyes, he wasn't." Phoenix shrugged. "I grew up reading reports and newly drafted laws—I was the third son, set to become a steward of a minor house if I was lucky. My older brother, Aethon, is my father's heir, and my second-eldest brother will likely stay to support him in some way."

"You mentioned you have three brothers?" I prompt.

He hesitates, and Amisha sits forward, her hand out. "You don't have to explain in our presence."

"No, it's okay. I just haven't thought of him for a long time. Aris disappeared when I was ten. One evening I bid him good-night, and the next morning, he was gone. My father looked for him for a few weeks, but we never found anything." He's lost in thought for a second, his eyes distant. "I choose to believe he, like me, left on his own terms. I hope he's doing well."

"I'm sorry to ask." I reach forward to put my hand on his arm.

"My family is at war with all of us," he says, and shrugs. He doesn't remove my hand. "You have a right to know."

Orin nods solemnly, and Amisha rubs her temples. She's reaching for her cup as her soulmate collects the teapot she was clearly about to ask for.

A pang of loss hits me as I realise their bond has grown stronger in my absence. I look sidelong at Phoenix, wondering if he noticed too.

He clears his throat. "Rose, when is your coronation?"

"The seventh day of Candlemoon," I respond, and count the dates clumsily on my fingers against my leg; the calendar of Lotheria still doesn't come naturally to me. "Eight weeks."

"Have you chosen your crown?" Orin asks, setting the teapot down.

Iain had explained the crown tradition to me, how each queen designed her own. "I'm to visit the Olinius forge and choose the metals for its creation. I'm not sure what my options are yet."

Amisha looks at us curiously. "The Tideswept Crown of the Tsalski Empire passes from emperor to emperor. It is a symbol of royalty and governance. You design a new crown for each queen?"

"To set her reign apart from the previous one," Orin explains. "Besides, Fleur was buried with hers, and the people who know where her tomb is are long dead themselves, the information given to the Book of Blood."

Amisha is shaking her head. "Lotherian customs... I've been here nearly two years and I still don't understand them."

"And there is the matter of the kingsmatch," Phoenix mutters, lifting his cup, and I redden.

Orin, bless him, does as well. "Pressure from my family, Rose. I'm sorry."

"Don't apologise for wanting to marry me," I say, and it's such an odd sentence that the corner of my mouth tugs upwards. "That somewhat cheapens the offer."

He grins. "The offer is earnest. The Thoreaus would be thrilled to name the king consort amongst themselves."

I reach for a little cake, not because I want it, but to still my shaking hands. Marriage had barely been on my mind when I'd first tumbled into the river and crossed worlds; I'd been focused on graduating high school and the complications that came with it, such as finding a purpose in life beyond 'waking up to an alarm'.

Now, I was expected to marry soon, and well, for the stability of a realm I'd accidentally become the ruler of.

I bite into the cake. "Will I be told the other options for the kingsmatch?"

Orin shrugs. "Depends on the Headmasters."

"Do I have to choose from the set options?"

"They're not a menu," Orin says. "You will be queen, Rose. Your word will be law in the land. But you need to consider what law and precedent you're setting at every turn."

Silence lapses over the Dalberry Walk. Phoenix has withdrawn into himself, and Amisha's eyes are faraway as she watches the trees sway in the wind. The weight of my yet unforged crown sits heavily on my brow, and my arm itches fiercely; the toll of reading the Book of Blood is healing slowly and painfully.

"Have you heard from the Lyons?" Amisha queries gently, and I close my eyes for a moment.

"No." Other minor houses had sent representatives, to pledge allegiance and renew their oaths to my throne and their Houses. The Lyons had been conspicuously absent, but nor had they gone north.

"You'd do well to seek them out," Phoenix says. "Otherwise it appears lenient."

"I got their son killed," I say abruptly. "They deserve a bit of leniency."

"Maybe from Rose," he replies. "Not from their queen."

I clench my jaw. How I want to keep those identities separate. How I want to let Iain and Netalia rule in my stead, while I spend time writing runes, playing Kingdoms, exploring and travelling with my friends. But I'd made a vow on the rooftop terrace—that to fix my past mistakes and prove myself worthy to my friends, to the land, to the Book, I had to be better than the girl who burnt Fairhaven. I had to take responsibility, and I had to make sacrifices.

"I'll send for them," I say quietly.

Iain will be pleased at my willingness to wield power.

Lydia

The streets were warm with residual sunlight, even long after the ball of fire sank beneath the horizon. Lydia glanced at the woman beside her, still smarting from the verbal lashing Gennorin had given her when she'd dared offer assistance to cross the uneven cobbles. The Greatcast matriarch tapped along, her aged form hunched over her cane as the two ventured deeper into the city of Numin.

Even at twilight, the place was alive. Lydia had come to love it in her short stay with her family. They had visited restaurants, gardens, museums, and walked the streets almost every day. So when Gennorin had told her to dress well with sturdy footwear, she'd done so eagerly. Her sunset walks with her grandmother had become a favourite of hers, as had meeting various aunts and uncles who'd thought her lost to the Other. Gennorin had advised keeping her impending queenship quiet, and she had, merely enjoying time with her family.

The restaurant was a comfortable building of sturdy brick and panel. Vines climbed the walls, and Lydia reached out to it as she passed, receiving the plant's report of the happenings within. It was a very happy vine, with a larger footprint than she anticipated. For a second, she was overwhelmed with information and conversation from not only the restaurant, but the neighbouring buildings and the stables out back. She yanked her hand back from the vine, cutting off the flow of voices as her chest heaved. Gennorin, waiting at the door with a bewildered footman, quirked an eyebrow at her.

"What a lovely plant," Lydia said breathlessly, then hurried to catch up.

Inside, golden torch light washed the patrons in a soft glow. The clink of cutlery against plates, paired with soft conversation, immediately soothed Lydia, reminding her of the Academy dining room. Waiters circled around the tables, but their footman continued to lead them through the main floor and up a curling staircase. Above, a large balcony hosted an enormous round table laden with a lit candelabra and place settings for twelve. Lydia hesitated at the top of the stairs.

"You didn't say we'd be having company."

Gennorin, barely winded from the climb, tapped her cane

impatiently. "These are ten of the finest women in the region. They have come to meet with you."

"With... with me?"

The matriarch dismissed the listening footman with a wave. As he disappeared down the stairs, she continued, "Yes, you. Their future queen. You need to hear what they have to say."

Lydia, learning Gennorin's traits by now, saw determination in her great-grandmother's eyes and nodded, taking the seat indicated by her pointed cane. As Gennorin settled herself to her right, the wait staff appeared with jugs of wine. Lydia's eyes flicked to the high set windows as Numin's town clock counted eight on the night. She pressed her lips together, her thoughts set amongst her newly flourishing gardens on the Greatcast estate, then jumped as Gennorin set her wine glass down heavily.

"When they enter, do not stand. You outrank them despite your lack of crown. They will be looking for imperfection, weakness... do not let them see it. Use your vine tangler magic to listen to their words, not just what they're asking. Do you understand?"

"Yes, ma'am."

Gennorin leaned back, beady eyes looking her over. "Tonight, you are not a student of the Academy. You are Lydia of House Greatcast, Queen of Lotheria, Chosen by the Land. These women are here to evaluate you. And you, them."

A thousand questions burnt on her lips, but she merely nodded. Their dinner guests began arriving in packs of two or three, noblewomen dressed in rich velvet dresses and capes, which they handed off to the wait staff. Their eyes settled on Lydia as they took their places at the table, giving nothing away. To the waiters, it seemed a gathering of gossiping women. To Lydia, it seemed she'd been dropped in a pit of vipers.

The polite chatter continued until the women were left alone. As conversation from the restaurant downstairs filtered up, the heavy silence made them seem impossibly isolated.

Lydia gripped the table, filtering her magic through the wood-grain. Though few women leant on or touched the wood, she could sense their anticipation through their mere proximity. She took a deep breath.

Her wineglass had been filled, and she reached forward to take a long, languishing sip. Though her eyes were closed, she felt every woman's gaze land on her, and smiled inwardly.

"Thank you for attending dinner with me tonight," she began, replacing the wineglass. She took the time to settle into her chair. "My grandmother has spoken highly of all of you."

Gennorin had uttered not a word about the attendees, but one or two looked pleased. The others flicked their eyes to the matriarch, who sipped her own wine in response.

"And your grandmother has told us almost nothing of you," a woman responded. She was dressed in navy silk, the sigil of a table wrought in rich brown thread upon her breast, her hair coiled and pinned on top of her head. "Just that we must meet you as a matter of state importance."

"National," Gennorin corrected, her voice sharp. "Lydia, this is Merrin of House Nithewaite. She and her lord husband rule the castle of Spearhold near Thurin."

"Though our seat is not known as Spearhold currently." Her eyes were dark over the rim of her wineglass. "It's peacetime, Gennorin."

"Nithewaite?" Lydia said. "I know your daughter. I didn't know Alena was from Thurin."

Merrin smiled tightly. "She doesn't talk about her family often then, I gather."

"That's not what I—"

"The good lady has the ear of the council, girl," Gennorin cut in, her fingers pinching Lydia's leg under the table. "The War Council in Gowar."

Lydia took her cue. "Do you have many dealings with them?"

Merrin quirked a half-smile. "My son, Jacen, chairs the Council."

"And mine sits as his right hand," another woman replied.

A few more chimed in, and soon conversation flowed. Slowly, over the course of entrees, Lydia realised that these women were positioned powerfully throughout the country—and some had travelled the length of the continent to dine with her.

Nerves fluttered in her stomach.

Directly across from her, a woman lacking fifty years on the others sat quietly. Her gown was white, embellished with lily in hand-stitched gold thread—Lydia could feel the old fibres of flax twined amongst the patterns—and a braided leather belt. Her blonde hair was twisted into a bun. Her eyes settled on one conversation, then another. Lydia sent a wash of magic towards her, and the tablecloth creased as the ripple of power passed beneath it.

The woman's gaze flicked to her, and she took her resting arm from the table, moving her wineglass into the path instead. It bumped awkwardly as the magic settled beneath it, then faded. As the glass rested back on the table, Lydia cleared her throat, ending three different conversations.

"I do not know your name," she said pointedly.

Chatter ceased, as each woman turned to the one she'd addressed.

"Lydia Greatcast," Gennorin began. "This is Cryelle Montau. She is the great-granddaughter of Queen Fleur."

Lydia blinked, stunned for a moment, then remembered her manners. "My lady—"

Cryelle held up her hand. "I am no lady. No title carries through the line of Montau from my great-grandmother. Your Headmasters saw to that."

The room darkened slightly, muffling their voices. Merrin rested her hand against the table, as golden threads spread from her fingertips. Lydia braced, waiting for a magical working, but, when nothing happened immediately, relaxed.

Until she realised that all sound from downstairs had ceased.

"What did you do?" she asked, her voice harsh in the sudden silence.

"Tonight's wine was donated to the restaurant by the Nithewaite family," Merrin supplied, lifting her own glass. "A vintage from our cellars. It *may* have contained more than notes of oak and blackberry."

Lydia shoved herself back from the table and ran to the balcony. Below, the restaurant was held in a bizarre tableau, as patrons sat at their tables immobile. Some with forks halfway to their mouths, others mid laugh or sentence. Her skin went cold as she took in the magnitude of the magical working on unwilling non-magi.

She spun, her voice sharp. "Who are you?"

Cryelle looked to the other women, then stood when no one else did. "We're here for you, Lydia. To see you on the throne." She lifted her wineglass and sipped brazenly, her eyes cold.

Lydia took a long moment before returning to the table of women. Gennorin welcomed her back by thumping her stick impatiently.

"We could not risk being overheard," the matriarch said by way of explanation.

"So you drugged the non-magi?" Lydia balled her fists. "These people did nothing to you."

Merrin frowned. "They will be unharmed."

Lydia ignored Gennorin's narrowing eyes and focused at the Nithewaite woman. "You worked magic on unknowing persons. These people are not your playthings. Undo it!"

Looks were shared around the table. Lydia went back to the balustrade, gazing out over the frozen restaurant. A couple caught her eye; their hands entwined, leaning towards each other, the poisoned wineglasses almost empty. She clenched her jaw, and called the queensgift.

"They are *non-magi*," Merrin insisted from behind her.

Lydia's eyes were layered in silver threads, examining the magic coursing throughout the scene. "They are your countrymen."

She followed a taut line of enchantment, glittering silver in the candlelight, and moved her hand. The magic fell limp, dissolving before it hit the ground. The woman it had bound blinked, and Lydia hastened her movements, until the occupants of the restaurant returned to normal.

"That cost me months of preparation," Merrin complained.

Lydia seated herself next to her grandmother. "Then I'll be interested to see what your talents can do when used for an honourable purpose."

"Privacy was my only concern—"

"Then speak quietly."

Lydia met her eyes and didn't shift. As the silence stretched, Lydia broke contact first, lifting her water glass and setting her gaze on Cryelle.

"What did you need to say to me?"

Merrin glowered, but attention was already moving away from her. Heads turned towards Fleur's last descendant.

"My family was always welcomed in court," she began. "But after Fleur passed unexpectedly"—the women at the table shifted uncomfortably—"we were granted nobility and our children were stationed well in society. The following month, an election occurred. A man was chosen to rule, from a well-born family. As the dust of new government settled, my family began to split— some sent to far countries as diplomats, a few early illnesses taking the older members who remembered the queen personally. One by one, our stars winked out and my name became nothing but a paragraph in a history book."

Silence reigned around the table as Cryelle spoke. She sipped from her water glass.

"And when we lapsed into comfortable complacence, a bill was quietly passed amongst the government that gave the Headmasters of the Academy power against their students and the populace.

Power was granted over the Black Guard and the legions of reserves. Diplomatic immunity both on and off our soil. Overnight, the Headmasters become untouchable."

"Iain and Netalia have served the mage community faithfully nonetheless," Lydia said quietly.

Cryelle tapped her finger against her glass. "Yes, they have. Until recently. When did you arrive at the Academy, Miss Greatcast?"

"Three years ago," she replied.

Cryelle smiled tightly. "And a threat to their power appeared."

"They welcomed me with other students," Lydia protested. "I learnt alongside my classmates, studied my major, made friends... last year they pulled me into Netalia's office and told me I was to be the next queen. The signs were there, my magic was changing. They began to prepare me to take the throne."

The corner of Cryelle's mouth tucked inwards, and then the woman softened. "I truly hope that is what happens, Lydia. But these are the people who installed themselves as a shadow government before they were forty. They orchestrated the transfer of silent, irreversible power to themselves. People willing to do that aren't the type to bow and step aside when a challenger arises."

Lydia thought of Iain and Netalia, their closed door meetings, and her stomach dropped.

"So what do I do?"

The women looked between each other, though no one spoke. Gennorin finally cleared her throat.

"Play their game," Cryelle advised. "Stay in contact with your matriarch. She can put out a call to arms across the country."

"We are but a faction of representatives at your control," another lady supplied.

Merrin Nithewaite said nothing.

"The time of the Headmasters is over. You have our support, Lydia Greatcast," Cryelle said, but a few women shifted. "Please try to stay alive long enough to call on it."

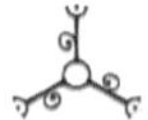

Lydia said nothing as she walked the lantern-lit streets with Gennorin. The old woman blocked out the light of the nearest, complaining it was too bright, that it affected her night sight. Without looking up from the cobbles, Lydia twitched her fingers and the glass cracked. The oil-fed flame guttered in the breeze and Gennorin fell silent, her night sight restored.

"They rattled you, girl."

"Yes."

"You shouldn't have antagonised Merrin. The House of Nithewaite is a powerful one, and they do not forget."

Lydia scowled. "She shouldn't have done that to the restaurant patrons."

"Pah! They would've been fine."

"That's not the point, Grandmother."

Gennorin waved her away, muttering under her breath. Lydia followed a few steps behind, feeling rotten.

"You have a choice to make."

"I do." Lydia lifted her gaze, seeing the shape of the land and buildings in front of her not through her eyes, but through her queensgift. She moved by feel rather than sight for the next few steps. "Do I betray the ones who have done nothing but support me and lift me up, on the say so of women who bewitched unknowing non-magi? Or do I take the risk that my closest advisors will slay me for the blood in my veins?"

"A difficult dilemma." Gennorin sighed. "But keep in mind I would not have had you meet with them if I didn't think their concerns were worth heeding."

"I know."

They paused on the stone bridge that arched above the river. Below, the water glistened in the lights of Numin, carrying river boats and ferries downstream, where they would eventually dock to trade in Riverdoor.

"I can shelter you no longer," Gennorin said. "The Headmasters have requested your presence back at the Academy."

Lydia swallowed, and turned from the river. Her night sight could not compare to her grandmother's, but the queensgift fed her the information singing on the winds—of ancient stone and prickling frost from the mountaintops.

Orthandrell is right there.

She closed her eyes, taking a deep breath, filling herself with the strength of Kynan's home.

"I could run away," she suggested half-heartedly, throwing a look to her grandmother.

Gennorin scowled. "They would hunt you anywhere you went. Across countries, across worlds. You are the biggest threat to their comfort and power. They will stop at nothing to snuff out your flame."

Lydia pushed off of the low stone wall and continued in the direction of the Greatcast manse. "And thus, I walk willingly into the lion's den."

Gennorin sighed quietly to herself. "Child, if I could stop it, I would."

Only a vine tangler could've scented the crushed grass and offended plants. Lydia's steps slowed as they entered the gardens, sending out a ripple of power through the greenery. Gennorin followed.

"What is it?"

Lydia went to respond, but a familiar scent swept past her on the breeze. She fought to keep the smile from her face, turning to her grandmother.

"I have sourmint that needs tending under the cover of night," she explained. "Go on inside, Grandmother. I will follow soon."

The matriarch grumbled a bit, but continued along the darkened path towards the main castle. Lydia waited for her to go, and then pushed into the garden, careful not to tread on any of her new seedlings she'd planted over the last week.

"Kynan," she whispered, and stifled a giggle as a strong arm swept from the brush and around her waist.

The tension of the evening melted from her bones as she kissed him, silence settling over their patch of the garden. He rested his forehead against hers.

"I didn't think I would see you before you left," he murmured. "I've been unable to get away from Norrimoor."

"I leave in the next day or two," Lydia replied, pulling him deeper into the garden. "How are things in the city?"

The northerner hesitated for a moment, and she took the opportunity to study him in the moonlight. He was older than his brother Jettais, with dark eyes and long hair that already showed a few pale strands at his temple. She ran her hand up his arm, revelling in the feel of his muscles and sensing them twitch under her touch; he was the strongest person she'd ever met, and the greatest swordsman she'd ever seen.

He caught her hand. "The city is restless, Lydia, the *state* is restless. Our calls for negotiation have gone unheeded."

Disappointment sank heavy into her stomach. "I urged them to respond, Kynan, I promise I did."

"I know." He kissed her fingers. "I don't doubt you. I doubt them. The entire region begins to."

She pulled him deeper into the gardens until they reached the manse wall, sitting on a low wooden bench.

Kynan brushed her hair back from her eyes. "What happened tonight?"

She explained about the restaurant, the women she'd met there. Caution screamed at her but she told him the names of the women, what they looked like, what they'd said. He watched her silently, letting her speak. Finally her words lapsed, and he pulled her against him, his fingers sliding beneath her collar to caress the soft silk.

"You have a choice to make."

"I do," she whispered, crushed against his chest. She closed her eyes, comforted by the rough fabric beneath her cheek, the smell of him, the sound of his heartbeat. "The Headmasters have been nothing but kind to me—"

"And of course, they would be. You can dismantle them, Lydia. They must keep you close."

"That still doesn't make it alright for me to betray them!" She pulled back and looked at him. "I sat at a table this evening with women who long for nothing more than to see them hang."

He stroked her cheek, his fingers gentle against her smooth skin. "My love, I am almost certain they did the same with their supporters." He encircled her in his arms. "War is coming, and we are drawing the battle lines. You have to decide which side you're on."

"Yours," she whispered, and kissed him softly. "I'm on yours, Kynan. I just don't know..."

"It's alright. Things can move slowly."

She rested back against him, but her heart refused to quieten.

"To openly oppose the Headmasters will be something I can never come back from. It will affect a lot of people."

"Yes."

She took a deep breath. "If I didn't... if I couldn't... would you still love me?"

His eyes were unreadable as he looked at her earnest face in the moonlight.

"Lydia Greatcast, no matter what happens in the coming months..." He kissed her gently. "I promise I will love you for evermore."

CHAPTER FOURTEEN

THE TALL, wide windows of the library overlook the palace grounds and wall. I watch a pair of uniformed guards walk between watchtowers, as a flock of blackbirds alights from the mismatched roofs of the city beyond. The sky is overcast today, shading Castor in pale browns and greys. A pot of tea rests on the sill beside me, its perfumed steam rising in spirals, and I lower my cup as I turn back to the board behind me.

Two manuals lie open next to my opposing camps on the Kingdoms gameboard. I run a finger down the page of one, then close it. Iain wants me to have memorised *Gilfrain's War Treatise* by the week's end, but truth be told, I've found myself already using his plays as countertactics to my own—and beating them. I'd finished every book he assigned me, and then sought more from the very library I stand in. The only one I keep returning to is *Critical Theory and Evaluation Tactics*, the book Iain gave me on my first day in Castor. I let my finger drift over the imprint of his name and count tiles with the other.

"Northern victory in four moves," I mutter to myself.

A few tiles give their warning tremble, and I pick up a figurine before it's knocked over. The tiles flip to the dark green of marshes, and I frown as a small cloud gathers above the board. I wave the condensation away, my hand dampening as I swipe the cloud from the air.

"Northern victory in six moves," I amend, arranging my armies to take advantage of the flooded swampland.

This board may not be as sophisticated as the one in Iain's dungeon, but it comes close. There are only two fully enchanted Kingdoms boards in the entire country, and the Headmaster has given me free reign of this one. I play against it almost every day, and it beats me less and less.

I give it a loving pat, and the board concedes. I gather the figures as the tiles flip to their neutral state, and begin to collect some of the padded boxes from below the table.

"Do you always play by yourself?"

I jerk upright and bash my head against the table. My first instinct is to swear but I bury it, my heart racing.

"Laela."

She wears the uniform of a palace maid, a black apron against black leggings and a white lace shirt. She's covered her rich, auburn hair with a black headcloth, pinned neatly at the nape of her neck, and looks every inch like she belongs in the palace halls.

Her eyes land on me. "Start talking."

The command is muffled by the rows of books behind her. I know the library is emptied and locked every time I choose to visit. Still, I cane towards her with the intention of pulling her deeper into the window nook, but as I draw closer to her, my steps slow.

"Laela..." Her name sticks in my throat. "I'm s—"

"Don't." She brushes past me. "Don't give me 'sorry' as your apology. 'Sorry' doesn't bring back the town you destroyed, 'sorry' doesn't unburn my village, my *home*, Rose. 'Sorry' is what you say when you're late for class, not to me. Not for what you did."

I take a deep breath as my heart races in my chest. My pulse thuds in my ears as I turn to face her.

"What else can I offer you?"

She folds her arms. "More than a two-syllable word. I want reasons."

I take a cautious step forward. "Would that help?"

"Neither of us know. But right now, as it stands, you left me at the half-soul camp while you and their leader snuck into the Academy on some magical mission I wasn't privy to. You promised to come back, Rose."

I swallow. "Technically, I did—"

"No, don't. Don't get smart with me, I know you. I know that this is hurting you, and it needs to." Her gaze bores into mine. "Did you even stop to think what would happen to me and Thompson if you didn't come back?"

"Of course I did!" I cane around the table towards her. "I left runes at the tent—"

"In the dirt. They lasted all of five minutes before the wind wiped them clean. I may not be a mage, Rose, but even I know that runes have to draw power from something." She shakes her head, turning from me. "Have you even asked for him?"

I'm silent for just a second too long, an unwilling question forming on my lips. She whirls back to face me.

"*Thompson.* The kid you used as a lookout, as a pack mule, as an informant for a *year*. He's nine years old, did you know that? Did you ever ask?"

My nerves are already frayed from the conversation with my friends in the garden. I bite back a sharp retort. "He wouldn't tell me even if I had."

"Because he wanted you to think he's older, so you'd ask him to do more." She presses her hands to the side of her head. "You never even asked after the kid you abandoned."

"Who am I supposed to ask?" I shoot back, my heart pounding. *Oh gods I should've made inquiries.* "You think I've got a messenger service in here? Dinner with my friends on the week nights? The Headmasters watch me day and night."

She rolls her eyes and fixes me with a hard stare even as I

disprove my own sentence in my head. "It must be very difficult living within a palace."

I close my eyes and concede. "I should've asked about Thompson. I don't know why I didn't."

"I do." Her eyes alight on the Kingdoms board between us. "Because you use people, Rose. To get what you want and need, like a door left open late at night, or a piece of information, or a letter delivered." She picks up a figure and looks at it. "We are pieces on a gameboard to you, and I was a fool to think I could be anything else."

I expect her to chuck the figurine—a tiny painted soldier with a spear—across the room, but she replaces it gently on the table and closes her eyes.

"That's not true," I tell her, my throat tight. "You're not just... things I use to get what I want."

She looks back at me. "That hasn't been my experience with you, Rose."

I lock eyes with her for a second, and then turn, shrugging the shoulder of my jacket down as I do. It's cold today, and the scars left by the lashes I'd taken for her stand out.

"I didn't have to take these," I remind her. I grip the cane tightly, my eyes on the roofs of my city. "I got between you and the whip. You said I'd bled for you."

Slight fingers replace my jacket and I jump—I hadn't heard her cross the room.

"Out of guilt," she says, and I turn back to face her. "You gave me the medicine that got me arrested."

Anger bites the words between my teeth. "Because your father—"

She slaps me. The crack of the hit echoes in the room before the pain registers, but I don't put a hand to my cheek. Heat begins to blaze in my stomach.

"We can stand here assigning blame to each other until your coronation, but don't you dare invoke my father's name in this," she whispers.

I take a breath, my cheek stinging. "He pulled us from the river. You said 'desperation does funny things to people'. I never asked for any of this."

"You never do. And yet... it keeps happening to you."

She steps away, taking familiar body heat and scents of jasmine with her. It'd been so comforting, so familiar even in a hostile situation, that a lump grows in my throat at its absence.

"Laela," I call, and she stops. "I will fix this."

She raises her hands and looks around. "How?"

"I'm going to be queen. I can change things now, with a crown on my head. I promise—"

She exhales, shaking her head. "Haven't you learnt your lesson about making promises in Lotheria yet, Rose? This world is anything but fair or just." Her voice echoes off the polished wooden floors, no longer absorbed by the gilded bookcases and leather tomes. "It's why in two months you'll receive a crown for your actions in Fairhaven and I"—her voice breaks—"I received the ashes of my entire family."

The floor falls away from underneath me, the fire in my belly going out. She's facing me with tears in her eyes, her hands clenched at her sides, waiting to see how I react.

I killed her family.

"No," I say, as though I can deflect the information, prove it to be untrue. "Laela, I'm..."

She straightens her spine and lets the words sit upon my shoulders, the knowledge that my greatest failure just worsened by a degree of millions. She wields her own magic, to hurt and harm, and watches me suffer.

"What are you going to do?" she asks, her voice low and dangerous.

I look up at her. "What?"

She takes a step closer. "How are you going to fix this, Rose? You said you were going to."

My lip trembles. "After the coronation, I don't know—"

"Then *know*. You can no longer live with one foot in this world and one foot in the other. It's time for you to grow up." Her voice heats. "How many times have you found yourself in a situation where someone else takes the blame—the hurt—for you? Stop playing the victim. Stop allowing yourself to be directed by the wants of others."

My eyes settle on the floor. I should stand up to her, defend myself, but she's right.

"You make so many promises, Rose Evermore," she says. "But they're worthless if you keep breaking them."

"I promised you a crown once." The words come from deep within me, remembering a happier memory. I see her recall the same one, and her eyes soften.

"Don't—"

"I promised to crown you in daisies and feed you sugared strawberries as my queen." I gesture out the window. "Look where we are, Laela. I can make that a reality."

She hesitates, and the slender victory that grants puts the fire at bay for a few moments. She hadn't expected the offers, hadn't thought I'd be able to hit back. But now I'm asking her to make a choice.

"You would name a non-magi as your kingsmatch," she murmurs.

I nod, though I can hear Iain's response without him even in the room. He will flay me bloody for this. A small smile quirks on the corner of my lips. "A crown of golden daisies and a seat beside me before the nine noble Houses."

Her eyes flick up, uncertainty swimming within them, and I trace her jaw, then curl my finger and draw her lips to mine. When I kiss her I remember all I've lost, and all I stand to gain.

But she pulls away. I let her.

"No."

I don't move. "Okay. I'm sorry."

Tears grow. "I *can't*, Rose. You lied to me. And that lie destroyed everything I'd known in my entire life." She hugs herself and tightens her lips. "I don't wish ill upon you. But I can never trust you, or love you, ever again."

Once, when I was little, I fell down the stairs. Mum told me later I'd somehow missed several steps at the top and then gone crashing down the rest. I'm falling now, that same swooping sensation deep in my stomach, untethering me from thoughts I'd had, dreams I'd dreamt, fantasies I'd constructed.

For a single, free moment, I soar.

But as Laela turns away to leave, I crash. I watch the woman I love walk from the room, leaving me with a gameboard and my books. I know I will never see her again.

Flames grow on my fingertips as she disappears. I don't stop her. The seconds that follow sear themselves into memory, and the fire grows.

I turn to the window, looking out over the city, thinking of the man who hauled me from the river and his wife who sheltered me after I took the lashes for her daughter. Both reduced to ash in the heat of my fire, my anger. I remember the comfortable void, the simple solution offered by the flames, and want to sink into it again.

But instead, I sweep the boxes off the Kingdoms table and scatter the contents to the floor, leaving them where they lay, and let my anger carry me from the room. Laela is nowhere to be seen, and I'm perversely grateful.

Belatha, the absent god, has seen fit to empty the halls on the way up to my rooms, and not even Lillian awaits me when I shove open the door.

I throw my cane aside. Yank up my pants leg, and grab the brace. Lillian has a way of putting it on so it doesn't hurt me anymore, but my hands don't know the same kindness and I relish in the pinch and bite of every buckle. It's tight—too tight—but when I stand I do it unassisted.

My eyes fall to the sword that has lain dormant in its sheath since it was gifted to me by House Olinius.

I draw it, and the steel gleams in the quiet room, reflecting my own pale, wide-eyed face back at me. I hold the sword level, looking at myself and hearing the excuses I'd served to Laela.

I lower the sword and squeeze my eyes shut, sending tears down my cheeks.

"I'm a liar." My whispered words grate against my ears and I make myself say it again. "I'm a liar and a coward and a thief."

The admission hangs in the air and dissipates, like the cloud above the Kingdoms board. I rest heavily on my right leg, absorbing the pain and embracing it. It is raw and honest and ugly.

I sheathe the sword and carry it with me from the room.

When Netalia showed me the training area in her tour of the palace, she did so with a large helping of irony. The first time I'd used a sword in battle had also assured it would be the last, but I'd stood and watched and allowed her to show me where the door was, how to unlock it, where training equipment could be found, and when the guards were likely not to be there.

As the clock strikes the afternoon hour, I know a fresh shift change has just occurred and they will be sweeping from the room to press out into the city. Just like I'd learnt the ins and outs of Fairhaven, so too was I studying the patterns of palace life.

That study pays off when I shove open the door to the training arena and find it empty. Straw covers the floor of the circular room, the earthy scent filling my nose as I crunch over it, moving towards the practice dummies.

I draw my sword and look at the figure in front of me; the rough outline of a human, a hessian sack stuffed with straw that pokes from the ends of its 'arms' and top of its head. There are a few dents in its sides from the blunt training swords offered to my guardsmen.

I flex my fingers on the hilt and lift the sword.

We are pieces on a gameboard to you.

I strike at the dummy's midsection.

I was a fool to think I could be anything more.

Out of guilt...

Steel sings through the air.

... the ashes of my entire family.

Again and again my blade cuts through the air and lances a piece of the training dummy off. When its limbs lie on the floor, bleeding straw from where I've struck it, I move onto the next one, Laela's words echoing in my ears.

You'll receive a crown...

My pulse thuds in my ears as my lungs burn for air. I know I'm pushing too hard, asking too much of my broken body but I don't *care*. For the first time in a year, there is a sword in my hands and I can swing it, so I do. I brace myself on my dead leg and let the mechanism there convince me my body is whole. Tomorrow, I will curse today's decisions, but right now, I am taking action and it feels good.

I move around the room, remembering my lessons, my training, the song of the sword in my hand that felt so right and natural until a split second mistake stole one of my few talents from me. Sweat gathers on my brow and runs down my neck, into the expensive clothes Netalia dresses me in, like the fancy little doll in a castle they always planned on having. Soon they will add a crown to my head and make me dance for the nobles, while they cement their chokehold on a country that begs in dark corners for freedom.

Tears join the sweat as I cleave the head from another figure. I raise the sword when I get to the next, but pause.

Someone has drawn a charcoal smile on this one.

Two dotted eyes stare at me as I hold my blade, chest heaving, sweat running. I lick my lips, indecision holding me in place.

I'd run a sword through the chest of a man who hadn't had time to look at me. I'd cut another down with borrowed war magic even as he'd raised his shield to defend himself. I'd burnt the rest of them alive.

The strawman smiles down at me as my lower lip trembles. All the borrowed strength rushes from my limbs, and the sword clatters to the floor. I drop to my knees beside it.

"Rose?"

Phoenix's usually soothing voice is hurried, and I hear the patter of heavy breathing behind his words. My once-soulmate carefully kneels next to me.

"What happened?"

I shake my head. If I open my mouth a whole lot of hard truths will come spilling out and I'll crack in the process.

"Laela came to see you."

I nod. My knees scream and I relent, sitting back and moving my legs in front of me. The brace clunks against the floor.

"She told me about her parents," I manage to say. "The ashes on her hands when you found her—"

"I would've told you before, but it wasn't for me to tell."

"I know." I wipe a tear from my cheek. "I had to find out this way. I had to face it, face her."

He sits beside me, glancing around. "What are you doing in here?"

I lift my gaze and finally look at him, then at the room around us. Scattered pieces of training dummies paint a clear path of destruction to our current seat, the sword beside me dusted with straw.

I heave a sigh. "I wanted to feel... something. I wanted to feel strong."

I press the heels of my palms into my eyes as though I can push the tears back in. Suddenly, there is soft pressure on my leg and I startle from Phoenix's touch.

"Let me see," is all he says, and I do.

He undoes my boot laces and sets it aside, then pushes my pants leg up to my knee. I know its bad—I can feel that it's bad—and I keep my eyes on his face. His expression is unreadable, but his lips tighten as the cooler air of the training room hits my bruised skin.

"This isn't strength, Rose."

My lower lip trembles again as the comment bites deep; another failure. I can't stop fresh tears from forming.

He begins to tug on a leather strap, pulling it back through the buckle. Blood rushes back to tortured flesh as the brace loosens, bringing searing, stinging pain. The tears flow silently as he removes the rest of the device, until it finally clatters to the floor.

For the first time, Phoenix looks at my damaged leg. He lifts it gently and probes the ruined calf muscle with his fingers, light glimmering around his fingertips. How could I forget? My soul-mate had minored in Healing alongside Dena. I expect the pain to wash away, for the bruising to fade and the cuts to stitch back together, but he lowers my leg to the ground.

"This is not strength," he repeats. "What did Laela Pike tell you?"

I'm not expecting to relive the conversation so soon, and I tell it haltingly. "She said I use people, like pieces on a gameboard. But I don't, Phoenix... I don't mean to."

He moves around to sit beside me again, leaving my leg painful and bloody. "So you believe you do."

I wipe my eyes on my sleeve and lean forward to roll my pants leg back down. "I don't know."

"You have the capacity for it. You read people well and you know what they want."

I sniff. "People keep getting hurt around me."

"Like you hurt Laela Pike."

"Yes." My throat is raw from crying and it hurts to say, but I push the word out. "Yes, like Laela. The one person I should never have been able to hurt."

"Why?"

I look up at him. He gazes at me steadily.

"Why what—"

"Why shouldn't you have been able to hurt Laela Pike?"

I clench my jaw. "You know why."

We sit quietly for a moment, then Phoenix nods. "You love her. It's why you interfered with her sentencing and took the lashes."

I say nothing.

"Rose, the Headmasters' Charter—"

"I'm fully aware of the bloody Charter!" I swallow hard and look away. "I don't... I don't love her, Phoenix. I don't think I love anyone anymore. I don't think I can."

A fear surfaces, sudden and brash. I hadn't tried to look for her, I hadn't asked after Thompson. Everything and everyone I'd tried to care about had become afterthoughts to me since I'd lain eyes on the throne I was promised.

Phoenix puts a hand on my arm, a soft, careful touch and, suddenly, my mind is filled with memories that aren't my own. It's almost a welcome relief.

Weak winter sunlight filters down from the overbearing peaks as the blood dries on my back. Fresh wounds crack apart, their healing interrupted, as the crowd gathers around me, waiting in hushed anticipation.

But he doesn't relent. The leather strap is lifted again.

I lift my hand from his as he jerks away. Phoenix doesn't look at me. I finally ask the question I should've from the first day we met.

"Why did you leave Orthandrell?"

His words are halting. "I told you. Freedom."

"From what?"

"Rose—"

"From whom?"

He turns on me. "From him. My father wanted a strong son who agreed with his statements of war. Who longed to wet his sword in battle. To follow in the footsteps of my brothers. And when I wasn't born with warcries in my ears and a blade in my hand, he decided to see if he could beat the bloodlust into me."

I lean back from the sudden heat emanating from him, but I've seen his scars. We carry the same marks on our backs.

He glances at me. "Rose, this would've been much easier if we'd bonded last year, rather than seeing it in fragments."

"Or you could just tell me." He shakes his head, and I continue. "Besides, if we had, you'd be a Halver right now."

"Better a split-soul than a half-soul," he mutters.

The term is unfamiliar. "What?"

"We lost each other before we bonded, and our magic was broken. We call them split-souls, though some refer to them as soulwitches."

The memory of a brazier in a wooden shed, surrounded by the frozen peasantry of Fairhaven, springs to mind. "We visited one, last year."

He blinks at me, then exhales. "Which is how you knew to avoid me. I always wondered."

"I wasn't avoiding you because... of anything you'd done," I say haltingly. "I wasn't ready to have someone that close to me. Living in my head."

"I understand. Now you know there are secrets I'm not ready to tell."

"And me." I take a deep breath. "So that's what the silver light I'm seeing is?"

He nods. "I believe it's the essence of our magic still trying to bond, or something else entirely."

We sit together on the floor of the training room, at an odd truce. I brush dried tears from my cheek and begin to massage my calf, avoiding the open wounds. Later, I'll clean myself up with salves and clumsy fingers that never learnt to heal, but Phoenix's hands replace mine.

"You're not alone anymore," he murmurs, and warm fire spreads across my skin.

The pain washes away, and I breathe an easy sigh. Bruises fade and the cuts close as his magic spreads across my leg, the headache in my temple beating a final tempo before vanishing.

"Thank you," I whisper, and he helps me to my feet. I go to continue speaking, but he clamps his hand over my mouth. A second later, voices echo from the hall outside. We freeze in the middle of the arena. If the guards were to enter and find him outside of classes, alone with the queen-to-be...

The voices fade, but my heart is thundering in my chest.

He quickly hands me back my boot. "I'll be close by if you need me."

"How will you know?

He quirks a grin at me. "I can tell when my friend is in trouble."

I swallow. Warmth spreads throughout my chest, filling the cold, hollow spot gouged out by Laela's words.

"Are you able to return to your rooms unassisted?" he asks.

"I'll manage. The first footman to see me without my cane will bring me one." I've now got an assortment of canes from around the castle, some of which I suspect are stolen from the older staff. "They seem to be under orders."

Phoenix suddenly steps close to me and pulls me into a hug. I'm surprised for all of a second before I wrap my arms around his torso and hug him back. He smells like woodsmoke and warmth. "Don't trust anyone, Rose."

"Wouldn't dream of it," I reply. "Now, go. Quick."

Pulling away, I give him a nod and turn to collect my sword. When I turn around, he's gone.

LYDIA

The horse sagged beneath her, breathing hard into the night. Lydia pulled her cloak tighter, burying her face in the fur lining. Kynan had warned her the north grew bitterly cold in the night—she'd thought she'd known what that meant.

Lantern light to her right indicated the greatroad heading towards Riverdoor. She stared wistfully to the small beacon in the foggy night, imagining riding instead for the large, established city with a number of inns. They'd have warm beds and full breakfasts, friendly smiles, and polite questions. She'd wake in the morning well rested and comfortable.

Muttering a prayer to Belatha, she knotted her fingers around the reins and urged the horse further north.

It had been days since she'd stolen the horse from the stables and galloped towards the fighting on the Orthandrell border. By now, the Headmasters would be searching for her, but they had no reason to suspect her destination. Not even she truly knew where she was headed; in her pocket, letters from Kynan were tied neatly into a bundle, their charcoal sketches her only clue as to his location.

For you, my heart, the sight that greets my eyes every sunset.

The roughly drawn mountain range, with its crags and peaks, had told her to head to the Shayde Mountains. After that, she would need to rely on hope and luck to find his camp.

She sipped from her waterskin, already feeling the slight touch of nausea that rolled in her belly. She smiled, resting a hand on her abdomen.

"Trust you to tell the time, little one," she murmured. This pregnancy had been like clockwork, with morning sickness waking her in the early hours of the morning. Her fingers curled as a smile shone on her face. Her eyes flicked to the darkened horizon and, with renewed vigour in their step, horse and rider continued into the night.

Despite her worries, she found their camp easily; they weren't trying to hide. Dozens of tents, their banners streaming from the peaks, stretched into the trees before her. Lydia swallowed sudden nerves.

They're growing bolder.

She lifted her gaze to the sky, where thousands of stars dusted across the cosmos. The moon was ringed in pale wisps, and long clouds sailed high above—she shivered as she wondered if it would snow. But her heart leapt into her throat as Kynan's familiar figure emerged from a nearby tent. He stopped short upon seeing her, and she dismounted with grace. She held the reins of her horse a moment longer than necessary, comforting the large animal as well as trying to soothe her own nerves.

"Lydia," Kynan said, and her heart soared at the sound of his voice. She turned to face him, heat rushing to her cheeks. "Come to my tent."

He held the canvas flap open for her, and she ducked inside, sighing gratefully in the warmer interior. A brazier held glowing coals, and she held her hands out eagerly to it.

"You're a hard man to get ahold of," she began, teasing in her tone.

He walked to the other side of the brazier, his arms folded. "Why are you here, Lydia?"

Her smile faded. "You weren't answering my letters. I came to see you."

His eyes were unreadable. "Why?"

"Because I love you and miss you." She set her jaw and lifted her chin. "Is that alright?"

Kynan sighed, tension fading from his frame. "Of course it is. Forgive me. The stress of war takes its toll."

He held out his arms, and she went to him. As she pressed her cheek against his chest, she could feel his heart thrumming as though he'd run a mile.

"You poor thing," she murmured. "When did you rest last?"

He pulled away. "Sleep is for men who don't command legions." He sat on a chair nearby, and gestured to the one beside it. "It's happening, Lydia. We are declaring our independence."

Nerves wriggled in her stomach. She rested a hand there, acknowledging the life within. Her eyes fell to the man she loved as she sat down, her fingers tapping an unsure tempo on her belly.

"We will keep casualties as low as possible, but this is the only way to get the attention of the southern leaders—"

"It's not," Lydia interrupted. "Kynan, Dawn Harbour approaches. The months of celebration and change—"

He snorted. "Festivals and revelry is your answer to war?"

She clenched her jaw. "No. My coronation will take place during Dawn Harbour."

Understanding lit his eyes as he leaned away, deep in thought. Something stung under her skin as his silence stretched on.

"With... with my coronation," she continued. "I can affect real change. I can choose—"

"Real change comes with complications," he cut in. "Compromise. We've had enough of that from the south, we're determined to—"

A flash of anger heated her stomach. "Kynan, would you shut up and listen to me?"

The brazier flared suddenly. Both of them stared at the coals until they died down again.

She grabbed his hand, drawing his attention back to her. "During my coronation, I choose my king. My *king*, Kynan. A choice that cannot be denied by any elected government. The old laws still reign above all else, even in the south. If I choose a king with witnesses present, the Headmasters cannot speak for or against him, no matter where he's from. They, and the people, would have to accept the appointment."

Kynan went silent, his hand limp in hers. She waited breathlessly as he stared at the floor of the tent, brow furrowed. Then, he withdrew from her grasp.

"They will not allow it," he said finally.

Her lips parted slightly. "They have to. The old laws—"

"They've dissolved older commandments and set precedence." He stood up and began to pace as she watched. "They'll interfere—"

"They *can't*, Kynan. They'd be ousted from power—"

"Then why haven't they been ousted?" he exploded, and she recoiled, eyes wide. "When they installed a shadow government, when they claimed established territory, Fairhaven, as their own jurisdiction, when they wrote the Charter of 917? Where was the outrage then, Lydia? Where do the people draw the line?" he finished, chest heaving. "There will *never* be a northman on the throne of Lotheria."

The words lingered as he turned his back. Lydia could feel her cheeks redden as tears burnt in her eyes. She stood slowly, her hand lingering on her stomach. Then, she let it fall.

"So you refuse the position of king?" she asked slowly, her words flat and monotonous.

He clenched his fist. "As if I could want a throne beholden to people who call me murderer in one breath, outsider with another. Such a throne could only burn me. Orthandrell is not part of Lotheria—it never has been. And we..." He took a breath. "We come from different worlds, Lydia. It's time we recognise that."

Her body went cold. A rush of breath escaped her lips before she managed to say, "Are we... are we done?"

Kynan stood looking into the brazier. Then he rested his hands upon it, and sighed into the coals. "Everything has moved more swiftly than I imagined. I thought things could be different, but..."

She heard his message with numb ears, but her back straightened. Netalia had been training her for the diplomacies that came with a crown. "I understand. But, Kynan, please know we could've done this differently. We could've negotiated, discussed terms, compromised—"

"We tried to—"

The dirt beneath his feet cracked. He stepped back warily, looking at her for the first time.

"You negotiated with the *Headmasters*, not with me. And I struggle to think how any common ground could've been reached if you spoke to them at all how you speak to me. For discussions to be had, Kynan, you must let the other side finish their sentences."

His face darkened, and he crossed the ground between them faster than she expected. She moved back, but his hand lashed out and gripped her chin forcefully. Despite the queensgift, despite her not-inconsiderable magic, Lydia felt like a doll in his grasp. Fear screamed through her as his fingers crushed her cheeks.

"You have chosen your side, then," he murmured. Once, his closeness was all she'd craved. Now, he was too close, too near. She fought to turn her head. "You've betrayed me, Lydia. I knew you would."

She struggled, trying to form a sentence, and he suddenly shoved her away from him. She fell heavily, her jaw aching, as he stood over her.

"Kynan, please—"

He rested his hand on the pommel of his sword and jerked his head to the front of the tent. "Get out."

Disbelief drove the air from her lungs as she looked out into the dark, frozen night.

"Kynan, it's the middle of the night, I have nowhere—"

His grip tightened on the sword. "Get. Out."

Hurt bit deep into her bones and she choked out a sob, climbing to her feet. The newest queen of Lotheria fled the tent and the man within it, as the first snowflakes began to drift earthwards.

CHAPTER FIFTEEN

A week after Laela's visit, I am collected early from my rooms for Iain's trip to Fairhaven. The footmen take my cane again as I ride through the city at the Headmaster's side, dread filling my stomach. Iain rides up beside me as my thoughts swirl into the mire.

"You did well in our games last night," he comments, and I latch onto the distraction.

"Thank you." His compliments are not as rare as they once were; our games of Kingdoms now stretch late into the night, as he teaches me every strategy and counterstrategy to offensive military tactics. So far, he has not been a fan of my main play, which includes building large walls and towers to shut my city off from the aggressive second player.

"You are not a turtle, nor will your impressive fortifications keep an enemy out indefinitely," he'd snapped during our last session. He'd actually approached my end of the table—a big violation of Kingdoms rules—to look at what I'd done.

The Headmaster had gone silent when he'd laid eyes on my harbour, the biggest I'd ever managed to build in a timed session, and the green trading tiles with other countries offboard. I would've had food, weapons, and materials for much longer than required to beat a less established enemy—just like the one he'd been playing.

That had been my first win, though he'd forbidden me to play the same strategy again. I cherished it either way.

"How is your reading progressing?" he asks, riding alongside Iotha and myself.

"I get a few chapters in here and there." It's a lie; I've become as obsessed with Kingdoms as I did with runes. My eyes burn with tiredness through the long sessions of court, state dinners, and parties thrown by the nobility. About the only time I actually pay attention is during the war meetings—and they've become more frequent as of late.

"And yet the library records indicate you're nearly halfway through the strategy catalogue," Iain queries, and my grip tightens on the reins. "Plus a few novels on historical battles that weren't on your reading list."

"I branched out. There's not a whole lot to do around here besides read and worry." I look ahead, to where our mounted guard leads us to the northern gate. "I mean, aside from now."

"The journey to Fairhaven has been scheduled since our return from the Archives," Iain replies. "I gave you ample time to prepare your mind."

As though a mind can be prepared like a potion or meal. In fact, having so much time to dwell on the trip had only granted me nightmares and restless sleep.

"Why are we going back to Fairhaven?" I ask, and I'm surprised at how steady my voice is.

"We are returning to examine Arno's runes. I need to understand them to unlock their power, and I'm hoping you can help me."

We pass through the city gates, and I lift a gloved hand to wave at those clustered nearby. I smile though I desperately do not want to, Netalia's recent lessons ringing in my ears.

"Why would I help you understand Arno's runes if he didn't

want you to?" I ask, sailing dangerously close to insubordination. "Arno was the one to show me kindness during my time at the Academy, not you."

"And I've apologised to you for that," he replies, as though our animosity can be swept under the rug with words alone. "But more importantly, we have a common goal, Rose. And that is to end the war before it destroys even more lives than it already has."

He urges his horse to the front of the column, our conversation apparently over. I watch him go, conflicted feelings surging within me. During our games, Iain is strict but informative, critical but constructive. A few times, late in the evenings during the sixth or seventh hour of our long campaigns, I mistake him for a friend. It is easy to forget the tyrant who dogged my steps during my year at the Academy.

I ride alone, thinking on our conversation, and as we pass an old wayhouse, I pull out a notebook full of Kingdoms rules and ideas. I turn to a new page, and begin to sketch deadening runes across the top of the paper.

It has been too long since I practised my craft.

When the trees clear, my horse stops without my command. The scent of old fire brushes past me and ashes drift around her hooves, as the rest of the caravan continues into the destroyed town.

The shattered structures, once buildings and businesses, thrust ruined black skeletons towards me accusingly. *There she is!* They seem to cry. *The one who brought us to the stones!*

The rear guard reaches me. My breath has dried up in my chest, and I blink little tears away as my heart pounds in my ears.

"Ma'am?"

I flinch at the sound, but cover it with a movement as though I'm turning to listen. I take a deep breath through my nose, and the smell of woodsmoke, perversely, comforts me. Fire has always been my strength. I linger in it for a moment.

I urge Iotha forwards without turning around.

When we reach Fairhaven, we ride through the burnt out ruins with little ceremony. The stable has been prepared for us by the remaining staff at the Academy. I dismount awkwardly, blinking away tears as my leg hits the ground, the resulting jolt referring up to my hip. Iotha, as the queen's mare, gets the largest stall. Fresh straw lines the walls, and I nearly trip over the glass bottle hidden amongst the hay. Freezing on the spot, I see a stableboy hurrying towards me to tend to my mare.

"Do me a favour and check Headmaster Iain's horse, will you?" I call, and he pauses. "The road was rough south of the town, and I thought I saw her limping."

He bows. "Yes, ma'am."

I flick him a coin and turn away before I see him catch it. Kneeling painfully in the stall, I retrieve the whiskey bottle from its hiding place.

A small scroll is tucked inside, slightly dampened with residual liquor. I pull the cork free, slightly amused that anything at all would be left, and fish around until I grip the parchment.

Your majesty,

If it behooves you, pleese meet us in the hortacultur students garden near the liberry at sundown.

Your loyal subjeks.

I crumple Maurice's note in my fist. A flash of fire illuminates my face, and I dust ashes to the ground as I stand, running a hand along Iotha's bridle.

"Leave the horse, Rose, the servants will see to her." I ignore Iain's command, combing her forelock with my fingers. A gift from the Headmasters she may be, but I adore her either way. "Come inside before it gets cold."

"It's *always* cold here," I argue, and immediately two manservants scurry from view—presumably to round up any and all cloaks in the vicinity. "Don't—"

"Let them go. Hurry up."

Iain sweeps his hand at me, and I follow, shuffling along on my braced leg. It can't look graceful, but the eyes of the staff are kept low and away from me. When we reach the first corridor, a number of coats are presented to me.

"May I also have my cane?" I ask before they all leave, and there is another flurry of activity and they all disappear.

Inside the antechamber, the air is cold and stale. My cane is delivered to me and I plant it carefully between the uneven flagstones as I follow Iain across the floor.

"We will eat first," he says. "And then we will meet with someone I think you'll find very interesting." I nod, but then he adds, "Unfortunately."

I have no appetite, my stomach heavy and leaden, and I can't fathom who he's referring to. The mystery nearly distracts me from the empty corridors, the dusty carpets, the utter silence that soaks into the bedrock of this once-bustling place. A sorrow lingers with me as I remember my classmates, the merchants and nobles, the ever-present foot traffic within the Academy.

It only worsens when Iain leads me to his old chambers. My eyes linger on the doorway where I'd once hovered at Petre's shoulder, as we levied them for assistance in retrieving the youngest Lyon son from the hands of a northern warband.

"I recall that moment as well," Iain says slowly, and my gaze is drawn across the grey room towards him. Despite it being noon, the sun is cloaked in clouds. The Academy is swathed in steely light that quickly fades to gloom in the corners, and my breath mists before me as I wait for him to continue. "The Lyon boy was one of many mistakes we've made."

I wait for him to continue, but his voice dies away in the stillness. "And the others?"

A knock on the doorframe makes us both turn. "Lunch, sir, ma'am."

Iain looks at me as the staff lay covered dishes on the table before us, and when he looks away, I know the moment has passed.

I don't press him for more information, but I let the words linger in my mind. *One of many mistakes...*

To my surprise, the food goes down easily—greasy chicken meat, seasoned heavily with salt, and limp vegetables, with a small fresh loaf of bread that we split between us. We eat in relatively comfortable silence, though I can feel him waiting for me to ask the questions, to persist in my questioning—he'd allowed a weakness, and he wants an opportunity to reinstate power, to repair the slip.

I don't ask my questions. I eat in silence.

I think he's almost relieved when another guard enters and bows sharply. "The Rune Master has arrived, sir."

I drop my fork and my breathing shallows.

"Rune Master?" I question loudly, and both men look in my direction. *Arno?* I try to make a joke of it. "You could've just asked me for anything runes related."

"You are not a Master, yet. Not of war, nor of runes." Iain stands, dropping the napkin on his empty plate. "Come on, Rose."

Did they capture Arno? Was he on the run? I struggle to remember if Iain had said anything about him previously.

If they hurt him...

My blood heats quickly.

I'll burn this place to the ground.

I follow the Headmaster to the antechamber. A lone figure stands in the centre of the room, and my terror fades to curiosity.

They, too, have a cane in hand.

"Master Yoris Moon," Iain says as we draw near. "This is Rose Evermore."

"The spitting image of her mother," the master says, their voice sharp. "How've you managed to hide that one, Iain?"

Iain clears his throat, discomfort rolling off him at the blunt question. "Rose has made contact with the Greatcast family, and they will be sending a representative to test her themselves shortly before Dawn Harbour."

Yoris sniffs. "Aye, and I'm sure they're itching to work with you again, after what you did to the last one. For her sake, I hope they send Gennorin."

"Who's Gennorin?" I ask, as a muscle twitches in Iain's cheek.

"'Who's Gennorin?'" Yoris repeats, and raps their cane on the ground. The guards and several footmen jump at the sound, and I file the movement away for later use. "Who's Gennorin? Gennorin McKorthus Greatcast is your great-grandmother, child. Matriarch of your family." Their eyes glint behind their glasses. "Great Lady of Numin and Riverdoor, though the Lyons no longer heed the call of their House."

"That's enough," Iain growls, sweeping a hand between the two of us. "I brought you here to talk runes, Master Moon, not needle at old wounds."

"You should know by now that I can't do one without the other, Iain." The Master fixes their glasses and ambles away to look at a nearby pillar.

I grin and follow the master eagerly, leaving Iain to speak with the other staff.

"You are too masterful at using that cane at such a young age," they comment as I draw closer.

I examine the grip of the cane in my hand; I've forgotten a time when I didn't use it, and a slow, forgotten ache for my full healthy body digs low into my stomach.

Yoris regards me for a second, then holds out their hand. "Evermore, was it?"

I take it. "Yes, though I suppose I should start using 'Greatcast' now."

Their grip is solid and dry. I can feel the wiry muscles of their hands through paper-thin skin. "Not until Gennorin has her eyes on you, young thing. I can't imagine what she'd do to an imposter."

I swallow hard, the scars on my forearms tingling. "Do I look like an imposter?"

Yoris eyes me. "You look like a prisoner."

I take back my hand and put it in my pocket, watching quietly as the Master goes about their work, tracing the lines of each rune closely. The entire ceiling is covered with them, and gold leafing has been pressed into the indentation of each mark in the stone. It glitters as though it is fresh. I read the alphabet like a text, the handwriting comfortable and familiar somehow.

At one point, the Master starts measuring the distance between the carved shapes—as though following directions on a map—and my gaze leaps ahead, following the logical progression of the design until I crane my head back to look at the smaller runes on the peak of the ceiling.

"I believe you studied under the tutelage of the artist of these designs," Yoris says.

My mouth goes dry. "Arno did this?" No wonder they seemed familiar.

"He did. It was his entry into the Guild, and earned him his master rank before he left the Academy. He came to work for me for a short time, but then your mother... disappeared, and he changed." Yoris looks at me closely. "Do you know what he did, Evermore?"

I swallow, thinking of the blood rune engraved behind my master's ear. "Is that why he went back to the Academy?"

The Runes' Master regards me for a moment, and opens their mouth to speak.

"My apologies," Iain says, approaching us. "Other business from the capital."

Yoris' eyes linger on me, then flick to the Headmaster. "You're a busy man, Iain. Time in the day must be limited for you."

Iain meets their gaze. "What have you found?"

"At least sixteen variants of the same shape so far," they reply, and I move closer to the conversation, lured by the opportunity to talk shop with a master. "It will take weeks of close study to even start cataloguing this alphabet, let alone finding the key rune."

"What's that?" I ask loudly.

Both of them look at me.

"Did Arno not teach you about key runes?" Yoris asks. "The single rune around which a design must be based?"

I shrug. "I only did one year of study. I was just starting Larussian nature classicals."

"Slow education," Yoris remarks, eyeing Iain. "No wonder I never received any applicants for the guild." Iain goes to respond, but Yoris cuts him off. "No matter. The key rune, girl, is vital to understanding the base of the alphabet. It links into every rune shape and must be the heart of the design or else the power cannot transfer. For a working of this size, the key rune would be incredibly intricate."

"And incredibly powerful," Iain finishes. "Rose, leave Master Moon to work. I have something to show you."

Key runes had been one of the first things Arno had taught me. They'd had to be for me to write with them at all. I remember the door to the blood vault beneath the Academy, a door shaped by rusted iron and a clumsy rune language; an impressive war mage Iain may be, but his runes have never impressed me. His key rune was what I'd plucked from the centre of the design, and the whole thing had crumbled into dust.

Feigned ignorance can be wielded as effectively as any weapon, was one of the first things I'd learnt from the book Iain gifted me. I was also fluent in Larussian nature classicals. The lie had come easily.

I bow my head and allow Iain to lead me away from the antechamber. We disappear into the depths of the Academy together, followed by two or three footmen, as my mind whirls through the new information I've been presented.

"What did you see?" Iain asks suddenly, and the sound of his voice in the quiet halls makes me jump.

"Huh?"

"In the rune design. I saw you looking, just as you once looked at the Kingdoms table. You see more than you admit, Evermore."

I press my lips together, though my heart beats a little faster. "I saw a bunch of runes. Arno never showed me those designs." I'm unable to keep the bitter tone from my voice. My master he may have been, but he kept that alphabet close, though I saw him work on it frequently. It had been one of the deciding factors for me in creating my own—though I'm slowly coming to the realisation that a Rune Master's alphabet is as personal as a family nickname.

"And what did you notice about it? The alphabet."

I limp at his side for a few steps, deep in thought. "It's insane," I say finally.

"Excuse me?"

"The design. It's crazy. Sixteen designs of a single rune? Countless rune shapes thereafter? The amount of power that ceiling must channel is just beyond me. What does it even do?"

Iain goes quiet, and for a second, I think he won't answer. Then we reach a familiar set of doors, and my stomach drops.

"Arno claims the runes can resist the pull and drag of time itself," Iain finally replies. "He studied the magical fluctuations required to harness that power in this very chamber itself."

A cold breeze sweeps up from the bowels of the staircase, and muttered voices brush past my ears. I take a deep breath, remembering the cavern. Inside had been pain, fire, and fear. I eye the stairs.

"You're asking a lot of questions about Arno," I remark. His name is heavy on my lips, but I begin the long walk down to the Chamber Beneath, leaning on the wall. "Why don't you just summon him and ask?"

"Your master has made himself unavailable to us, and his allegiances elsewhere, clear." My mouth goes dry at that, but before I can question him further, he continues, "To work with *his* master cost us more than we ever wanted to spend."

In pride or gold? I want to ask, but the descent is treacherous enough without an irritated Headmaster following me.

We reach the bottom of the stairs. I curl my hand into a fist, wet with grime and muck from the walls. Iain lifts a carved pendant from the hook and, with knowing eyes, I recognise Arno's alphabet.

"A temporary protection against the fluctuations inside. It doesn't last," he adds, his dark tone souring the note. "Just long enough to receive the lesson the Chamber wishes to teach."

I gesture. "So I don't get one of them?"

"Not this time. As his student, I want you to experience the Chamber as he did. Maybe something in your teaching will make his alphabet legible."

"And you'll be at my side?" I ask.

"Until the protection runs out, or the Chamber decides it does not want me there." I must look surprised at his candour, as he continues, "Do you think the old laws were written in ink by men of days past? Like the swell of the tides, or the phases of the moon, to defy the laws is to defy the very land itself."

His sentence ends too quickly, his voice echoing in the small room. I realise I'm waiting eagerly for him to keep speaking.

"Let us see what awaits you today."

He heaves on the door handles, and I can't help but wince at the cold blast of air that erupts. My hair is swept from my shoulders as I squint.

It's a cavern again.

I look to Iain, but he jerks his chin. I take a deep breath and step forward, my cane tapping at my side. The tone changes as we pass from carved flagstones to rough cave dirt, and I hear Iain follow me inside. Without warning, the door slams closed behind us.

Iain takes my arm, and together we shuffle to the side of the cavern. Fear has gripped me, and I can't help but search the darkness for the animals that attacked me last time.

"Wait," he says into my ear, barely louder than a breath.

My eyes adjust to the greylit gloom. At the mouth of the cavern, some distance away, a snowstorm is raging silently, but in here, we are completely sheltered.

Apparently someone else thinks the same thing—the hooded woman comes sweeping into the cave, her breathing ragged and loud. Snowflakes cling to her cloak, and she lowers her hood, wiping her eyes and sitting heavily on a rock.

It's my mother.

Younger and paler, but definitely my mother. I go to step forward as the cavern suddenly darkens, but Iain catches my shoulder and hauls me back. I nearly trip in the gloom, the noise echoing, but hold myself upright, spying another figure just in front of us.

I stop breathing.

It's *me*.

We watch young Rose, wide-eyed and motionless, atop her rock. I remember that damn perch. I'd been so afraid, so helpless. Barely able to conjure a spark on command.

I see the pack before young Rose or my mother does. The creatures had been resting in the depths of the cave during the storm, and now they rise at the intrusion, their skeletal bodies starved against the light.

I shove Iain aside, and begin to run. The cane in my hand falls away into dust as my injury fades and, for the first time in a year, I run with two strong legs beneath me. This is not borrowed strength from the fire, or biting punishment from a metal brace— this is skin and muscle and bone that was stolen from me by northmen.

Iain makes no sound as I run for the door. Because I know, any second now, that young Rose will do the same, and I must be the lesson waiting for her.

I turn as she falls from the rock, and the scene turns to glass. I press a hand against it, feeling nothing—it is as though the air turned solid between us.

Young Rose rushes at me, her eyes wide. I want to tell her it'll be alright, to reassure her, to take the pain that is coming for her.

But we all have our lessons to learn.

I lift my hand, calling the fire as easily as contracting a muscle. The flames dance over my skin, burning brightly in the dark cavern. She lifts hers in return.

I so desperately want to give her an encouraging nod, but I remain stoic. Her reflection. Her teacher.

My own.

Flames begin to gleam on her fingers. She turns towards a sound I do not hear, her fire nearly dying as she does. But then it returns in strength, and she drifts away from me, with growing confidence in her steps.

"Good luck," I murmur.

The scene darkens, and I stand in inky blackness alone.

"Iain?" I call, and the chamber swallows the syllables. A little of the fear young Rose had felt comes seeping back. "Iain?"

I understand it all at once. I have a lesson that I must learn, and the Chamber Beneath has decided he is not privy to its teachings. He hadn't stopped me running because he was no longer there.

The prospect is at once terrifying and comforting.

I'm in the grip of the old laws now, written by the land itself. The continent has veins of magic running through it, beholden to no one but the goddess that created it.

Magic I have stolen and cut into my arms.

My heart races, unsure in the face of this unknown entity. I fall to my knees, shaking my sleeves down. "If you want it back, you can have it!" I yell at the darkness.

Stillness is my response, and I expected nothing else. I remain kneeling, just in case deference is appreciated by ancient goddesses.

Light blooms around me, bright and magnificent. I shield my eyes, blinking away the spears of pain.

I'm ready for my lesson, I think, planting a hand to rise.

Soft carpet meets my touch. I look up and around at the inner hallways of the Academy, the stone ceiling arching far above my head. Taking a deep breath, I stand.

A gust of icy wind makes the gas lamps gutter in their housings. I shiver as it washes over me, turning back to the way I'd come, realising two things at once.

I'd turned on my bad leg, which is currently a normal leg, and the person who opened the door is the woman from the cave.

Due to the darkness of the cavern, I'd not gotten a good look at young Lydia, my mother. But here, as she nears the golden light, I see what Yoris mentioned. We have the same jawline, the same nose, even the same dusting of freckles. She pushes her long hair back, damp with snowflakes, and cups her hands to her mouth and nose. At first I think she's just warming herself until I see how she's shaking, the tears still glinting in the corners of her eyes.

I move forward automatically, my hand raised to comfort her, when she lifts her head and steps through me. Every cell in my body parts to make way for hers, and though she's moving swiftly, I feel every thread of her cloak and clothes scrape across my ribs and innards. I fall to my knees as she passes, pressing my hands to my torso, my chest—making sure everything is where it's supposed to be.

"That felt great," I call to the unseen entity that is the Chamber, or whatever controls it. I give a thumbs up to the ceiling. "Really awesome."

There is no answer. I scowl at nothing and get back to my feet, hurrying down the corridor where my younger mother is quickly vanishing into the dark. I stay on her heels, knowing now that she can't see, hear, or sense me.

The Academy looks the exact same as it did during my time of study. I'm still marvelling at the image of my mother walking through the same corridors I did after sneaking back in.

And the similarities don't stop there.

"Welcome back, Miss Greatcast," Iain says as we round a corner. I immediately stop, but his gaze passes over me. "Did you enjoy your trip north?"

"I did not," she responds sharply. "I tried to talk to him, but they're already on the war path. He threw me out into a storm, he..." Lydia clasps her hands to the sides of her head, bunching her hair and squeezing her eyes shut. "I sheltered in a cave until it was over and then came back... I don't know what to do now, Iain."

"I know. It's alright."

The Headmaster moves to embrace my mother. He holds her as she cries, patting her back. His eyes bore into mine, though he cannot possibly see me.

He closes them for a second, his hand lingering on the back of her head softly. She remains pressed into him, clinging to him for support as she weeps her heartbreak.

"I'm sorry, Lydia."

Then he looks up again, and nods towards me, as she gazes up at him. I'm confused until the guards move toward the pair.

"No!" I yell.

But the sound is swallowed by the nineteen years between us. I flail at the men who grab my mother, pulling her from the arms of her trusted mentor. She screams once, the sound echoing down the empty halls. Then a hand is slapped over her mouth as she struggles.

"Leave her alone!" I scream, my throat raw. Tears burn as anger heats in my chest. "Get off!"

My arms pass through the armoured men who begin to haul her along a familiar route. I feel leather and metal buckles claw across muscle and bone as I do, but I know where they're taking her and I know what's about to happen and I'd do anything to stop it.

"I don't want to see this!" I yell at the ceiling. "Make it stop! Please! I know the lesson I have to learn, just don't—"

But the ground is sliding beneath my feet and I'm forced to take a step. I follow, with widened eyes, as they drag my helpless mother into the dungeons where I once studied. I follow the route with knowing feet—but I'm unable to slow down or turn around.

We reach the blood vault, and Iain takes a moment before finding his own key rune, studying the design. The crueller side of me sneers at him for being unable to read his own alphabet when I found it immediately. But the petty emotion does nothing to slow the scene from advancing as the door disintegrates into rust flakes, and they carry her into the vault.

Netalia awaits inside, a shawl wrapped around her shoulders. Her breath mists before her as she ties her long hair back, more black than white at this time, and turns to a steel table set up beside a slab of rock.

At least, what I think is rock until a glass lantern is lit, the slim flame providing just enough light to make it glitter.

The iceblock I'd found my mother's blood in a year ago rests empty on the stone floor. The guards fight her onto it, and I'm proud of the struggle she puts up, kicking and biting. She thrashes, then goes still. I see threads of green work their way along her arms.

"No plants here, Lydia," Netalia says without looking at her, filling a syringe with a clear liquid. "We had them removed, roots and all."

She glares at Netalia, and my throat tightens as her familiar green eyes glint with silver, but the Headmistress merely lays two fingers on my mother's arm. I watch in spite of myself as dark fingers of magic spread like spilled ink beneath her skin, and my mother arches her back, a silent scream clawed from her throat. The blackened blood fades, and Netalia slides a needle into her neck.

The queensgift I've never been granted dies as the light goes out. I am introduced to a new reason to be wary of Netalia.

She's pulled tight against the ice. I swallow hard as I approach her head, watching her eyes begin to still. A tear rolls into her hair.

I reach out to brush it away, my finger passing through it. "I'm right here," I whisper. "It's okay."

At a motion from Iain, who stands in the corner with his hand to his chin, the guards leave. Netalia works quickly, inserting needles in the crook of my mother's elbows, and her wrists. She looks once to Iain.

"Do it," is all he says.

White, shining blood begins to fill the glass pipes attached to the needles. I watch the queensblood begin to seep into cracks in the ice. I kneel beside the block, watching it freeze in place. He approaches so quietly that I jump at his words.

"I'm sorry, Lydia," he says. "But the time of the queens is over."

I stand as her eyes roll towards him. Her lips part.

"Why?" she breathes.

Iain's gaze flicks to Netalia, who approaches to check the needle in her throat. The woman shrugs. "She's stronger than most. She'll fade soon."

"We taught you what happened after Fleur fell," he tells Lydia. "You remember?"

The barest hint of a nod.

"We cannot risk that happening again. Lotheria needs a stable government. One who can broker ongoing treaties and alliances with other countries."

He pauses for a second, not seeing the hatred in her eyes.

"'A queen passed must be returned to the bare earth with only the dirt and flowers as her coffin'," Iain continues, and I recognise the line from the book I stole last year. "I was there, the day they buried Fleur. It was the last real moment of Lotherian peace."

He's lost in thought, monologuing to a dying woman. Something in me can sense her life drifting away, down the glass tubes and into the ice beneath her. I want to shake him, scream at

Netalia—something. But I stay quiet, listening to Iain's rasping breaths.

"Do you know what happens when a predictable power vacuum occurs, Lydia?" He brushes a strand of her hair aside. "Chaos. Nobles with agendas and private armies, promises made over drinks in the nights of the months before. When Fleur began to sicken, alliances were drawn up in blood and ink at the mere rumour of her oncoming demise.

"The Dawn Harbour Massacre was only one night to most people, but it was the one night that changed everything for me. It *took* everything from me." He crouches next to the ice, Netalia watching as she cleans her knives and needles. "Peace during a single lifetime is not worth the price we pay between. We need everlasting rulership. Steady governance. Your time, the time of Lotherian queens, is over."

He goes quiet. Netalia waits, but her eyes linger on the stoic figure of her soulmate.

"Goodbye, Lydia Greatcast."

CHAPTER SIXTEEN

THIS TIME, when I land in the cave dirt, my leg aches fiercely just to prove I'm back in my own time. I remain where I am, breathing deeply. I can feel the weight of the building pressing down above.

And outside the doors behind me, Iain waits. I pull in a breath between dry lips. My hand curls in the dirt beneath me.

For a moment, I remain in that tableau. My leg goes dead, over exhausted from its tour of the past, and my body begins to shake with exertion.

I brush my lips with my hand, tasting salt; my mother's tears, and my own.

I turn and limp back to the doors, examining the area around me. It doesn't look so different from my first vision. It almost feels familiar now.

I press the doors outward, and Iain is waiting.

"Where did you go?" he asks bluntly.

His voice rolls up the staircase as I look at the base of them. It will take me hours to get up there alone.

"Rose."

I wave him away, angry and in pain. I cannot look at him without seeing the man who just bled my mother dry.

I pass him and he grips me by the arm. "What did you see?" he breathes.

For a moment, I feel my skin heat with coals. Iain doesn't flinch, though I know he feels it. I look into his eyes as they search mine for the experiences I had.

This man betrayed my mother and nearly killed her—indeed, until a few months ago, he thought he had. He held her and comforted her and then used her vulnerability to destroy her.

I should hate him. But his words from the past ring in my head, and the resounding mystery of them will keep me close to him for now.

"It doesn't feel right to speak of it," I say finally. "But it was informative."

At first I think he'll argue, but then he offers him arm. After a moment, I take it. I have to; there is no way I can ascend the stairs alone. Together, we climb the inverted tower, away from the Chamber Beneath and its mutterings. I remain arm in arm with the Headmaster when we reach the top of the stairs; without either my cane or my brace, I'm not going far without assistance.

"I have dinner with some of the leaders of the outer town-ships," he says, leading me down a hall. At first I think he's inviting me, until he continues, "So I'll have dinner sent up to your rooms."

I frown. "Shouldn't I be there? You'll be discussing the war, right?"

He hesitates, and I stumble forward. Footmen are already moving towards us, one with a cane in hand. "We are merely taking stock of inventories and storage. Just some light housekeeping."

"Can we play a match tonight?" I ask, accepting the cane. "There's a table in the library." I'd played on it in my first year.

"Of course. I'll see you then." He continues down the hall with the flock of staff bringing him notes, requests, muttered bits of conversation. I watch him go, then hurry to make my other meeting.

I wind through a labyrinth of halls to a small side door, avoiding the minimal staff patrolling the halls. Once upon a time, I'd watched from the library windows above as the Horticulture majors had used this door to visit their garden. Now, the door creaks open, heavy and unused, the courtyard beyond filled with neglected plants in their pots.

I push through the dry leaves and branches, to the centre of the courtyard. Once upon a time, this garden had been the pride of a class. Clay pots and earthen beds are overgrown with plants once carefully cultivated and looked after. Some are beginning to die. Some are entangled with each other as though in a lover's embrace, or battle. It's a lonely, forgotten place, and I hug myself as I wait.

"Evermore."

I look up. "Hello, Maurice."

The stable master folds his arms. "It's been a while."

"It has."

We look at each other for a moment, and I can *see* the unsaid words rolling off his taut arms and clenched jaw.

He grunts, then turns and begins to walk down the wide stairs that lead to the Academy grounds. I hurry to catch up.

"How's that leg of yours?"

It aches in the cold wind, from its journey to the Chamber. "No better than it was last time I saw you. Gives me a bit of grief every now and then."

He heaves a sigh. "Aye, I know that feeling," he says sagely. "The scars on my back warn me when rain is coming."

Maurice, too, had been whipped on the same day I'd taken Laela's punishment—for having a bottle of whiskey I'd given him. I wince at the memory.

"Maybe you're a weather mage, and you don't know it?"

"You reckon you're gonna hear me spoutin' about the clouds and the rain and the water catchments like your friend from Thoreau? Not bloody likely, girl."

The conversation falls silent, but he does turn to help me over the remains of the stone wall behind the Academy. We disappear across the training field, into the vanishing twilight, as the twisted trees of the lowhills beckon. My leg, having been battered against a stone stairwell and now drawn across the rough landscape, promises a world of hurt for me in the next few days.

A thin breeze threads through the trees and scrub, rustling leaves and bringing whispers to my ears. I pause, squinting through the undergrowth.

"Don't linger here, girl. The lowhills have been acting strange."

I notice now that Maurice is moving carefully through the forest, watching where he places his steps. "Strange how?"

He casts me a look. "Reckon all the land does is decide who gets a crown on their head?"

"Iain told me that some villagers sought refuge here," I say. "But they were chased out by the guard."

"That were an odd few days," he admits. "We lived amongst the trees for a short time, but the call of the land was strong, reverting us to hunters and gatherers. Not knowing friend from foe, the sight of a fire burning deep in the forest became a warning. Not of ravaging animals but of fellow man and their unknown intentions."

We continue through a small copse, the last of the daylight slowly seeping from the ground as a fog rises.

"In those days, I came to learn which is most dangerous, Evermore. And it's not the beast that charges at you with both eyes open... it's the man sitting across the fire from you, with naught but the clothes on his back and the regret in his belly." Maurice looks over his shoulder. "These trees saw a slaughter even before the guard rode through. It's no wonder they absorbed some of that bad energy."

If anyone else had told me the trees have a 'bad energy', I may have laughed. But standing amongst the forest—the runes in my arms tingling—I can almost hear the pounding hoofbeats, the screams of fleeing villagers. A thread of smoke reaches my nose and I turn, expecting to see the fire Maurice mentioned.

"Aye," he says gravely. "The forest remembers you."

That sends my blood cold. A new kind of fear seeps into my bones as we walk further in, and my arms begin to ache as exhaustion slowly takes hold of my entire body. When we reach the meeting place, a wide clearing with a small fire burning at the centre, my palm is bruised from gripping my cane so tightly, and my breathing is ragged.

"Sit," he instructs, and guides me to a rough stump. I do so heavily and lean forward, grasping my cane with both hands as I struggle to catch my breath. "You're out of shape, Evermore."

I try to think of a witty response, but pain makes me short-tempered and I've learnt better than to speak in anger.

"Remember," Maurice mutters suddenly. "He's had to remain hidden these past few months. The Headmasters would've wrung the blood from him if they found him."

"Who—"

But then I see who. Arno emerges from the trees, his beard longer, his eyes wary, and a surge of emotions fill my chest.

"You—"

My master shares a look with Maurice. "I knew she'd be mad."

"Don't do it around the fire," the farrier warns sharply, and I can sense the flames reaching out to me.

I take a deep breath, pushing them back. Arno had been the one to teach me to control my fire whispering, which makes it all the more annoying to rely on those lessons when he's the one I so desperately want to lash out at.

"Where have you been?" I ask angrily. "I've been back for a month, I didn't know if you were alive or dead—"

"I couldn't show my face around town without risking the Headmasters cutting it off," Arno interrupts brusquely. "I'm not sure if you know, Evermore, but they hate me right now."

Your master has made himself unavailable to us, and his allegiances elsewhere, clear.

"Didn't they always?" Jettais is next to enter the clearing, his beard rougher than I've ever seen it, coal-dark eyes flicking around as though doing a head count. "Keeping a Halver in their basement was sure to breed resentment, Veloquis."

"It wasn't my broken soul that pissed 'em off," Arno growls, but waves my teacher away. He approaches warily, like he would a wounded animal, and kneels in front of me. "I know you've been cooped up in that palace, Rose. I'm sorry we couldn't make contact sooner."

Pain and fear mixes in my belly, threatening to send my temper over the edge. I take a deep breath through my nose, my eyes flicking from one man to another, searching for something to centre my mind on.

Gather information. My critical theory book is very stern about operating without all available information.

"Who's 'we'?" I ask instead.

Arno and Jettais share a look.

"Not near the fire," Maurice warns again, poking it with a stick.

More figures emerge from the trees. Arno stands up and steps away, allowing me a close look at the newcomers.

Some I don't recognise. They're dressed in leather and furs, with crude weapons at their belts. They avoid looking directly at me, saving their attention for the man who follows them.

Craige, the Fairhaven blacksmith, is larger than I remember. His broad shoulders and looming presence seem to close half of the clearing in shadow, and his eyes rest on mine as though weighing the secrets I hold. I want to stand up, say hello to a familiar face, but any greeting dies on my tongue as the runes flare to life on my arms.

Silence, they caution.

Danger, they warn.

I say nothing as I look at the man I once considered a friend.

And that silence holds as my mother and Tyson follow him from the trees.

CHAPTER SEVENTEEN

"On that note, I have an idea."

"What?"

She'd gone to her medicine bag, digging through everything before I reached her.

"What are you looking for?"

"A syringe."

She'd produced one and swabbed the crook of my arm with rubbing alcohol, piercing my skin expertly as I watched the Headmaster in our backyard. Shining queensblood had filled the vessel, and my thoughts were dragged to that fateful night when Kaya and I had made our decision to irrevocably change the fate of our country.

I'd pulled my sleeve down and prayed the bleeding would stop before he noticed. "You're going to use this to cross the river."

"He'll take you to the palace." She'd hidden the syringe in the drawer where I'd found her lighter last year, though her smoking habit had slowed, if not ceased entirely. "I don't know what he has planned, Rose, but it won't be good. I thought he was my friend. He was nearly the end of me."

I nodded, and the backdoor screeched open.

It had worked. When we'd drawn my blood in the hallway of

our home, seconds before Iain returned to the kitchen, I had no idea of knowing if the queensblood would open the Lotherian portal.

There are no hugs. No happy reunions. They stand on the other side of the fire and watch me. I suddenly realise I haven't seen Tyson in months—his hair is shorter, and he wears the same leather armour as the others, a sword at his side. Something about that makes my heart sink, but I turn to my mother. Her face is older than I saw in the Chamber; the lines around her eyes are deeper. I look to her neck, wondering if Netalia's needles left any scars.

The words grind from me. "How long have you been in Lotheria?"

She presses her lips together. "Over a month."

It takes three days to travel from Fairhaven to Castor. My heart sinks further.

"Why didn't you come to the capital?

"We never would've made it to the palace," she says. "I considered coming south, but we decided to stay here, hidden and safe. We knew eventually Iain would bring you to Fairhaven."

I frown at that, running through some scenarios in my head. "That seems a big risk."

"One we were willing to take," Tyson says. His voice is deeper than I remember, and the look he's giving me is cold and calculating. "We couldn't get closer to the city. We had to wait for you to leave it."

"And if I never did?"

"It didn't come to that," Craige says, speaking for the first time. I shift my attention to him, noting how the strangers around the outskirts listen. "And we are here speaking with you now."

My stomach begins to thrum with nerves for some reason, and I fold my hands over the handle of my cane to still them.

You are always in control until you look like you aren't.

Remembering the textbook calms me slightly. These are my

friends, my family. I'd survived the conversation with Dena and Theresa—there are no new accusations that can be made.

"We knew Iain would bring you to Fairhaven," Craige continues. "Because Arno told us he'd want to examine the runes."

"In the antechamber? Your masterwork," I say to Arno, and he nods.

"My alphabet. Part of it, anyway... I've expanded on it since then, but I'll never outdo my greatest discovery." Firelight flickers over his face, and Mum moves closer to him, resting her hand on his arm. I watch the interaction silently. "Time runes, Rose. They defy the flow of time and halt the ageing process."

Expectant faces turn to me, and I fight the urge to shrug. I roll the information around in my mind. "Iain wants your time-defying runes?"

"One, in particular. The key rune can be annotated and changed, but will always perform its main task." Arno turns his head, folding his ear over. At this distance, it's hard to make out what I know is there—a rune for *halt*, designed specifically to stop his soul from decaying.

I put the pieces together. Sudafrae, Iain's homeland, is known for their blood alphabet—the *caesis alledari*. Runes carved into flesh; Arno and I have both practised the forbidden art. We both wear runes in our skin, powered by the magic in our veins. Iain, with the key rune for a time-defying language, could alter it, and apply it.

Peace during a single lifetime is not worth the price we pay between.

I stand up, moving away from them. The trees shift in a sudden breeze and the fire gutters.

"But you submitted your runes to the Archives," I say.

"Yes. The Lothericon wiped them from my mind. I cannot read or translate the ones I've already written."

"It should've removed them from the antechamber," Jettais says, and I turn to look at him. He shrugs. "When a work is accepted by the Book of Blood, it removes the magic and all traces of it from the world."

"Your alphabet defies it," I tell Arno. "Your runes defy the old laws."

What little colour was in his face drains from it. "I was just a stupid kid…"

"A brilliant kid," Mum corrects. "With incredible ideas."

"And not an ounce of sense in their application!" Arno shakes her off and walks away. I let him go, turning my gaze on the others.

"Why now?" I ask. "Iain has been in power with his soulmate for decades. The time runes have existed under his nose for those years."

Jettais folds his arms. "You destroyed their source of influence, Rose. I don't know what you were doing in that vault to begin with, but across the country, graduated mages changed their allegiances overnight. Even Governor Malico abandoned them, and hasn't been seen since."

The blood tags. The catalogued blood of every student to attend the Academy under the Headmaster's tutelage.

My face colours; when the queensblood, my mother's blood, had merged with mine, the resulting explosion had melted and tainted those samples. I can't even claim it as a victory because it was entirely by accident.

Not that anyone besides Kaya knows that.

"Iain is a rune mage—"

"A shit one," Arno puts in from the other side of the clearing.

"—but his blood runes kept the students in line and loyal. Unless, of course, their soulbond was broken. Or a stronger emotional tie presented itself, like a lover or a child." Jettais shrugs. "You freed a lot of people from bad dreams and unconscious impulses."

I open my mouth, but Craige steps forward. "We did not come all this way to discuss runes and maybes with you, Rose. Iain might want the time runes, he cannot get to them. He will ask you to interpret them, you cannot."

I bite down an argument. My own runes on my arms flicker into life again at his voice.

"What we want is change," he continues. "The country is at a breaking point. We have never had a better opportunity to implement that change."

His voice falls away, and I look at him closer. How the men around the camp respond to him, how Tyson turns to him, how my mother looks up at him. Firelight flickers deep in her eyes.

She moves towards him, her hand raised slightly, and I suddenly know why she remains by his side instead of mine.

The coals in the fire go white with heat and Maurice swears, stumbling away.

Craige meets my knowing gaze, and silence holds us both in its grip until he breaks it.

"You know who I am, then."

My mother looks from him to me, her lips slightly parted. I ignore her as the fire wraps around my core.

I've denied the magic for so long, fought its embrace every time, that it's with relief I fall into its depths. My blood turns to flames as warmth and numbness settle across my skin. My leg no longer aches.

"Tell me your name. Your real name," I say with a voice of ember and coal. "And why you've really come."

The other men look to him, but he doesn't break eye contact with me.

"My name is Kynan Alsain."

It means nothing, and everything, to me all at once.

My father steps closer to the roaring campfire. "And I'm here to take the throne."

CHAPTER EIGHTEEN

OTHER VOICES CLAMBER about the clearing, and it gives me the distraction I need to break free. The fire dies away, the taste of ash filling my mouth. The comforting warmth that filled my dead leg subsides, bringing back cold, aching pain. The campfire slumps, returning to its passive state, leaving us all in relative darkness, as I turn away from the sudden argument.

"We're not taking the bloody throne," Maurice is protesting.

"Kynan, that wasn't—

"—you're going to freak her out."

That was Tyson. I cling to his familiar voice and turn back. He's stepped closer to Craige—Kynan—but his eyes are on me.

"You're going to take my throne," I repeat, and it cuts through the arguments ringing the clearing. "Shall I consider myself a political hostage?"

Stillness settles over the meeting. I'd said it half as a joke, but seeing the look on some of the armed men's faces, I start to wish for my own blade.

I start to wish I'd brought Phoenix.

"You're not a hostage," Mum says finally.

Danger, the runes—my queensgift—warn again. My heart

thrums in my chest as I realise they're responding to me for the first time.

"An insurrection," Kynan clarifies. "A convincing of the people for a change in government."

Hands have drifted to weapons. I eye them off, then cane back to my stump and sit; my body feels hollow now, having held the fire within it. Every cell, every magical ounce of my blood, screams at me to be on my feet, alert, ready to run.

I cannot run. I cannot fight without hurting people I love.

But I can talk.

"And who shall be at the head of this... insurrection?" I ask.

Arno looks away and my mother thins her lips, looking to Kynan.

"We have someone in mind. Young, strong... and sympathetic to the people."

My heart slams in my chest as Tyson nods, looking at the ground. Kynan points to him. "The Headmasters were willing to execute him, and he stood his ground before them. The villagers of Fairhaven love him."

"His name was thrown around the campfires when we first retreated to the lowhills," Maurice says. "He became a martyr in their eyes."

And I am simply the one who burnt their village to the ground.

"You use Tyson to convince the people a rebellion is underway. You encourage them to rise up, you... arm them?" Both Kynan and Tyson nod, and I see the weapons at the belt of their followers anew. Rough, not made in a proper forge, yet sharp and deadly. "You storm the palace, and what happens to me?"

"You're kept safe," Mum says immediately. "You live a long and happy life with me."

"Reassuring," I tell her, and the hurt in her eyes pains me, but I ignore it. "And the Headmasters?"

A few chuckles do the rounds of the clearing, and it immediately sets my teeth on edge. It's a nasty sound. They've clearly discussed this so many times the outcome is clear to them.

"We do unto them as they would've him," Kynan says, planting a hand on Tyson's shoulder. I meet my friend's eyes and make him to look at me. "We remove the nobles, their Houses... by force, if we have to."

A few men add their voices in agreement. But after the war meetings, I know the military assets of each House located within Castor. I know the levies they can raise, the bannermen that will answer their calls. The Olinius forge has been working non-stop since our trade agreement with the steel merchants of the Tsalski Empire, producing good quality arms. Our soldiers will be better equipped, better trained than my father and his friends.

It will be a massacre.

I swallow my nerves, and turn to my friend. "You want them executed, Ty?"

"They would do the same to me," he replies, setting his jaw.

I let silence fall, my mind turning over the new information. I see Netalia looking out the darkened window at her old slums, the black magic she'd fed into my mother's veins. But Iain...

A hand is placed between my shoulder blades, steadying me.

"I did terrible things to Lydia Greatcast."

"The Lyon boy was one of many mistakes we've made."

My mouth is dry but I get the words out. The men have started talking amongst themselves, and my voice is drowned amongst theirs.

"No."

Mum hears it, and closes her eyes. When she turns away, I feel another part of myself crumble. I say it again, louder, resolve digging deep into my bones now.

"No."

The immediate silence indicates they all heard me. I stand up, holding onto my cane. I thump it firmly in the dirt, leaning heavily on it.

"Executing Iain and Netalia makes you as bad as them. You say you want a new era of peace, a new government, and yet you'd start in bloodshed, just like them."

"BECAUSE of them!" Kynan roars suddenly, and I step back, my calm facade faltering. His voice echoes around the clearing, those closest to him flinching away. My mother sets her eyes on him, but her expression is unreadable. "They drenched this land in blood, Rose. They ruled it with greed and corruption. They've dragged their governance on for too long, and now they are weak. Now we have a chance to change things. You stand between us and say 'no'?"

I lift my chin and look up at him, remembering the day he found me in the village. I'd never asked what he was doing so close to the Academy; a tradesman far from his corner of town. He'd healed my arm with a tonic, though I still wore the scars from my time in the Chamber Beneath. Craige—Kynan—had known much about my magic, more than a non-magi should. I'd queried it once; he'd dodged the question.

Compromise in the face of overwhelming odds. Survival today is a chance for triumph tomorrow.

I force a sigh, and hold a hand out. "Give me the opportunity to change things. A month, maybe two, is all I ask. A crown on my head, my words in their ears... we can do this another way."

"You have magic," Kynan mutters bitterly, and I'm surprised at the venom. Does he begrudge me, his own child, for carrying a gift he does not? "Use it."

"Iain has magic, too," I retort sharply. "I'd rather not get stabbed at a dinner function, or poisoned by his soulmate if I can avoid it."

Mum's expression darkens at my mention of Netalia, but she says nothing.

"Give me time," I say again. "Let me try."

I look at Arno. Of the people in this clearing, I'm starting to fear he knows me best. I've seen how my mother looks at my father, how my friend responds to his mentor. So I look to mine, in the hope that he understands the stakes of this conversation.

He's nodding. "She's right."

They round on him. "They don't deserve—"

"No, they don't... but the people do. The country does. Every time we hand over a crown, or lose one, there's blood." Arno clenches his jaw. "We've never had a peaceful transition of power, despite the stories that've been spun. But we've a chance for one now and I, for one, am not willing to sacrifice it for revenge."

Victory crests in my chest, but I don't show it. With my new ally, I turn back to the others. "Stay away from Castor. Don't do anything that would jeopardise my chance to talk them around."

He looks at me, eyes dark. I meet him equally, and wonder which parts of me are born from him. In his gaze, I see only bitter hatred; his mask as Craige the blacksmith has shattered entirely.

"I don't know you," he says finally. "Not really. You are the girl who burnt my village, who wields a power we can only dream of. And you ask to use *words* to fix a nation."

"I'm your daughter," I amend, and look at my mother. "I am parts of both of you. Your blood runs in my veins, and one of you raised me to know right from wrong. And it definitely wasn't you." Kynan narrows his eyes as my own bitterness leeches through my words now. "So I'll leave it to the one who did, to make the call. Mum... you know I can do this."

She hesitates, and it pierces me to the soul. Her eyes linger on mine and I let her see the earnestness, the desperation, the vulnerability I can hide from everyone but her.

My earliest memories are her, the good, the bad, and the uncomfortable. She was not always kind but she was always fair. I could reason with her as I grew older, barter for privileges and responsibilities. She always heard me out, with tired eyes and a cigarette between her fingers after a long shift.

It has always been just her and me. As I stand on the cusp of losing that, I feel another piece of myself go over the edge.

Kynan also looks down at her, his large figure looming over hers. She looks away.

"I'm sorry, Rose," Lydia says. "But it's the Headmasters... after what they did to me, it's a chance we can't take."

I thought I knew the depths of sorrow; Petre's death and Laela's final words had bruised and scarred me like a blade. But as my mother chooses my father, as she turns away from me and throws me to the wolves, I know I am losing something I will never gain back. I cannot even fathom the abyss I am falling into.

Tyson's eyes are on me, but I don't recognise him anymore. Kynan has him. Perhaps, thinking back on his apprenticeship, he always did.

Arno moves closer as the other men reach for their weapons. I see it happen as though through a lens of disbelief, as Jettais, my uncle, interposes himself between us, arms outstretched. But the men Kynan brought are eager for violence, and a taste of it is so close... I am only the young queen-to-be to them. I am not friend, student, or daughter.

I see it in their eyes. I saw it in the faces of the men I killed amongst similar trees.

This time, when the fire takes me, I do not show restraint. My fear feeds the flames and I walk forwards freely. I'm searching in the mire of shouting and movement for things I cannot see. They are not made of wicks and kindling, they are not waiting to burst into flames, but the cold, dull metal sings to a rune on my arms, and the queensgift graciously passes on the message.

Men howl as their buckles and straps begin to heat. Those who advanced quicker than the others fight to remove their armour as it begins to glow red, and the scent of scorched flesh is soon drowned by the ash and ember surrounding my form. I can feel my essence, what makes me *me*, beginning to spiral. In the face of what I've lost, I'm tempted to let go—to do what I do best.

To burn.

You make so many promises, Rose Evermore.

Her voice echoes in my ears. As my father raises a blade, my mother's scream in my ears, I come back to my own mind. The darkness inside beckons still, but I turn away from it.

I grip the blade as it comes down, the metal warping and twisting, though a line of pain sears across my palm—the one marked by Kaya's oath rune, when I'd sworn to protect the Halvers. Somewhere, she is laughing at me and my naivety.

I fling the melted blade aside and blaze inside an inferno. Kynan squints against the heat but stands defiant, and my anger rises.

Because of *him*, I've lost my mother again. Because of *him*, Tyson wears a stranger's face and speaks with a stranger's voice now.

I shove him in the chest, the strength granted to me by the fire enough to put him on the back foot. I grip him by the throat, by a roughly-made gorget, and watch as it begins to melt.

He cringes back from the sudden, searing heat; I see his skin begin to blister. And still, he does not fold.

"Kneel," I tell him in a voice of a thousand fires. The single word cracks and flares. "This is the magic you wanted me to use? The fire you wish to wield?"

He stumbles to a knee, but remains upright.

Hear him scream, the fire roars, and the gorget begins to glow. I curl my fingers beneath it and make him look at me.

"*This* is what fire does—it hurts, it burns, it destroys. You want me to use this on the Headmasters? Put Castor to the torch like I did Fairhaven? Is this what you want, *father*?"

A noise begins beneath the hissing and crackling of my fire. I hesitate, my fingers drawing away from his throat. The noise grows as I step back.

And my father laughs at me, his eyes bright. "That is *exactly* what I want, Rose."

CHAPTER NINETEEN

HIS LAUGHTER GROWS as I stare at him in horror. My fire flickers and dies, going out entirely, as I back away. His skin is scorched and reddened, but he does not appear to feel it, climbing to his feet as I stumble to my cane.

Arno gets in front of me, his arms wide. "Back off, Kynan. She's your *daughter*, for Belatha's sake."

My mother is crying, pulling at his arm, but he shakes her off roughly. He stabs a finger at me.

"One chance. You either put words in their heads, or blades in their hearts. And when you fail, when you fall, we will be there to put the city and its leaders to the torch, so that it shall rise anew." His eyes burn with darker fire than I could ever muster, and my heart stops in my chest. "Now run, little queen, with your soft words and your weak heart."

The clearing erupts in chaos. I finally reach my cane, then turn and flee. Their shouted arguments follow me into the boughs, but no one else does.

Darkness closes around me, and I hurry a few more steps, then sprawl over a large root. I lay in the dirt, tasting blood on my lip where I'd bitten it, and squeeze my eyes closed. Drawing my legs up to my chest, I take a few gasping breaths, shoving air back into my battered lungs, and the first sob is so ragged it's more a cough.

I cry into the night, pushing the heels of my palms against my eyes as though I can hold the tears in. My mother, my friend, and my mentor are not worthy of being cried over, and yet I do.

When I was younger, and somehow even more naive, I'd dreamt of coming home after school one day and finding my father in the living room. He was warm and comforting, everything a dad should be, and his absence was quickly forgiven by myself and my loving mother. He'd drive me to school and take me to sports, maybe run the barbeque at the events. He'd work somewhere well known, so when we passed it, I could point to the building and say, "My dad works there!"

He'd never had a face, this dream dad... I'd never known how to paint him.

But now I've seen his face and it was dressed with hate and scorn. I'd burned him in my anger and he'd laughed at my rage. He was a nightmare father, not my dream dad, and the little speck of hope I've carried in my chest for nineteen years is finally shattered and destroyed beyond repair.

I sit in the dirt, and contemplate vanishing into the trees. But a promise I made rings in my ears, a promise to myself, and I push to my feet.

I find the way back to the Academy and approach the dark castle. Guards ring the perimeter, and the relief that floods my system when I see them makes me feel so guilty I nearly start crying again. They move forward when they see me, halberds half-raised, but they pause at my voice.

"It's me." The tears are still in my words; I'd continued crying on my walk. "I went into the forest."

They lower their weapons as I limp towards them. One offers me his arm.

"You should be careful, ma'am," he says, and I recognise Neal of house Undertoil. "There are reports of dangerous people in the lowhills."

"Yes," I say, as he helps me inside. "I've heard that too."

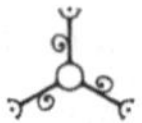

I should return to my rooms. I stand at my door on the ground floor, and contemplate the emptiness inside. I know I won't sleep; I will think and weep and greet the morning with heavy salted sorrow in my eyes.

I turn away, disappearing into the dark corridors. My footsteps, beleaguered and exhausted, know the way now. A crack of candlelight is visible beneath the door; Iain is still awake.

I raise my hand to knock, but then push the door open anyway. It swings wide, revealing my Headmaster at the table where we'd eaten, papers scattered across it, a tall candle half-melted and burning brightly. He glances up, and his quill pauses in its scratching.

"Rose," he says, and stands. I remain where I am, my stomach churning, as he rounds the table. His shadow blocks out the candlelight, and I feel him pick up my hand—the one with which I'd blocked my father's blade. Blood runs freely from a deep cut in my palm, marring the oath rune. His fingers tighten on mine. "Who did this to you?"

"People who were supposed to love me," I say, and I want to cry but it's all used up. I feel like a dry lakebed in the midst of summer; there's nothing left.

He tows me towards the table and sits me down, then goes to the door and speaks to a summoned footman. In a few minutes, a small tray of clean linen is placed next to me, a tiny cup of spirits beside it.

The blood is swept from my hand with the alcohol. The stinging jolts me into the present, and I'm almost grateful.

"An oath rune," he remarks, the design now clear. "I haven't seen one since I left home."

I look at it, and remember the night it was carved. My first experience with the *caesis alledari*... but not the last.

"Who is this one sworn to?" Iain asks.

"Kaya Aule."

"What did you promise?"

I lift my eyes to his. "That I'd do right by the half-souls. That I'd fight to better their circumstances and take care of them."

His expression deepens. We don't say anything for a few moments.

"You asked what my other mistakes were," he says softly. "The half-souls were one of them."

The cleaning continues. He begins to wrap my palm tightly, and the ugly wound starts to disappear from view.

"We sent them to fight for us, believing status symbols and jewellery were worth the lives it cost. But it wasn't about the Silver Wings, or the mirriam ore. It was about sending a message—that we owned Lotheria, all of it. And we would keep it, through blood and steel if we had to."

I say nothing. The freshly-cleaned wound stings.

"It was the wrong call. We were young, inexperienced, and eager to stake our claim. We ended up creating a lifetime of misery for students once in our care." He holds my hand in his for a moment, as though weighing it, then places it on the table beside us. "As I get older, Rose, as I feel my grip on power weakening... I wonder if all I'm leaving behind is a legacy of misery."

In the candlelight, his face is drawn. He has aged ten years since I stepped into the room.

"I want to make sure Lotheria prospers," he states simply. "Without the need for queens, chosen monarchs who sicken and die, leaving a country in chaos."

"Without me," I say.

He nods slightly. "Without your kind... yes. I wanted to use your name and your crown to unite the remaining noble Houses. To wipe out the unrest in the north, finally, and bring Lotheria together."

I take a deep breath, bundling this betrayal with the rest of the night's. I push the pain aside.

"I know." He looks up at me in shock. "I do actually read those books on strategy, you know."

After a moment, he exhales. "You are different to how I remember you."

I think of the scene in the forest tonight. My mother, my best friend, and their new allegiance to a man I don't know, and don't want to know.

"People change, Iain. Even if you don't think they can."

"I hope that's true. For my own sake."

I look at him curiously. "You want to change?"

"I want to do things differently. There has been so much hurt, so much loss, because of my actions."

I cast my thoughts to his soulmate. "Does Netalia share your sentiments?"

He meets my eyes with some of his old steel. "She does not. It has been a point of contention between us since you arrived."

I suddenly realise how little I've seen them together since coming back. Some of his earlier wording sticks in my mind.

"Do you think I'm going to get sick?" I ask. "You said that before. 'Monarchs who sicken and die'."

"You will die someday, Rose. Everyone does." Bitterness creeps back into his tone. "And when you do, it will happen all over again."

The words leap to my lips, the lesson from the Chamber now clear. "The Dawn Harbour Massacre."

He doesn't answer. The leaden silence of the empty building around us presses in, but for the first time tonight, I am calm. He will speak.

"I came over from my country as a boy," he begins. The candle gutters suddenly from an unseen gust. "I'd only ever known the outskirts of our capital, Ancana, and I was lucky enough that a visiting mage recognised the signs of magic in me. He arranged with my family to bring me to Lotheria so that I could be educated. I don't remember that family. I said goodbye to them in words and spirit when I boarded the ship.

"In Castor, the mage who had found me arranged for his House to take me in. Lotherian noble families often host wards, young foreign mages with no ties to this country. I lived with the House for my entire schooling, and when I think of my family, I think of them."

I know Amisha is a ward of House Thoreau, as Orin's soulmate. Iain's eyes grow distant, and I shiver slightly. The night chill is beginning to reach the innermost chambers of the Academy.

"I graduated. I moved to Castor, and lived with my family, as I was tutored in extra studies... in Kingdoms. I loved the city, I had my soulmate close by, and I loved what I did. I became the youngest Marshal in two decades, since my mentor had done it. He was the one who last held the rank of High Marshal."

Iain, at the onset of my teaching, had laid out the ranks of Kingdoms. I'd started as a Novice, working my way to Adjunct. In a few weeks, I will test to become a Sentinel, though it will require me to play against others for the first time. High Marshal is so far up the list I'd thought no one held it. The last rank beyond it, Warmaster, might as well be on the moon; no one had ever acquired the score to be awarded it.

But his mentor had achieved High Marshal. No wonder he was so good.

"When Queen Fleur started getting sick," he continues. "We were all called back to our hold. A manse in the south of Castor. When I arrived, Netalia in tow, we were greeted by armed men on our walls. The whole city was beginning to fear, Rose. You could sense it in the air, see the tension in the marketplace. More and more mercenaries arrived by ship every day, private armies bought and paid for by the noble Houses. The queen was about to die, you see... and power would be granted to those willing to bleed for it.

"Fleur didn't even have the courtesy to die during the day, or while I was home. Netalia had worried for her family, and we'd crossed the city to visit them. I remember the first fires, the sound of marching boots on cobbles, the screams of dying men. Her family's poverty saved us—the slums were overlooked by the nobles who battled for power.

"My House's allegiance had been with Olinius and Temperhold—a promise drawn up between the lords to secure positions and share favour. But men are hard to recognise at night, and friend spilled the blood of friend. In the course of a single night, negotiations of power were decided by the blade, and in the morning, the streets ran red with those who had lost, no matter the promises made in the light of day."

I'm held captive by his words, and when he stops speaking, the silence is too heavy.

"Your House?" I ask quietly.

He clenches his jaw. "When I returned, the manse was burning down to the foundation stones. They were the ones who lost. House Harvenspar ceased to exist that night."

I think of the book, tucked into my bags in my rooms.

Critical Theory and Evaluation Tactics by Olendar Harvenspar.

Iain's mentor... his family.

He clears his throat and looks away. "The Dawn Harbour Massacre... it was an ugly night, and the victors didn't see fit to release the true story of the queen's passing. She is remembered as an icon of peace, waging only one war during her lifetime... but few know another was waged because of her death.

"But I remembered, and Castor remembered... the non-magi were used as foot troops by Houses promising riches. They were sent against mages, armed mercenary corps... and they did not forget. When we took power, we sent for the men who had obscured the truth and altered it in their favour." He looks at me. "Netalia was always the one with the stomach for results measured in blood. They were old men by then, and they died easily, but she made it memorable. *Their* legacy is one of lies, and that version of events still lingers in corners of our country today."

His voice finally dies away. The candle has burnt low, but I steady it with a thought.

In a thousand years, I would never have expected Iain to be so candid with me, so honest. Caution screams at me against potential lies, but I'd heard the wounds in his voice, made fresh by recollection. I think, when I speak about the meeting in the woods, that my voice will sound similar.

He clears his throat, and moves away, not looking at me. "Now you know why I do what I do, Rose."

"It helps to know." The response is automatic. I'm running through everything in my head as quick as I can, but it's been a long day, and suddenly my body aches with tiredness.

Iain casts a glance at me. "So... Evermore. What do we do now?"

I flex my hand, acknowledging the pain the movement brings, and smile slightly. "Now we go back to Castor.

"And we try something new."

⁂

The next day, we leave Fairhaven. Despite everything, I slept well. My leg seethed with sharp aches and pains but, warmed beneath the blankets, it seemingly forgave me for the past twenty-four hours. A dull ache now resonates up my thigh, but it's become my new norm and I barely notice it as I mount up.

Across the yard, Iain avoids my eye. Honestly, I'm avoiding his too. Last night was too raw, too honest for the both of us, and I, for one, don't know how to navigate our new dynamic. So we both ignore each other, but as we prepare to leave the town, we end up shoulder to shoulder in silence.

A gust of wind stirs a flurry of ashes like blackened snow into the air. I can look at Fairhaven with new eyes now, though the regret still stings. Suddenly, I hope it never fades. I never want to forget what happens when I lose control.

I don't turn back to look at the remains as we leave. Beyond the ash and char lie the lowhills, and a loss I'm not yet ready to feel.

CHAPTER TWENTY

WE REACH Castor after three days on the road. The walls of the capital are barely visible through the fog that has rolled in from the sea. Fresh, ocean air sweeps towards us on the hills, riding the currents over the sprouting crops.

"Did you miss it?" Iain asks. "I do, every time."

I put my book away, squinting into the bright morning. "Why isn't the Academy established here?" We begin to ride down the hill, to the farmlands that surround the city. "Surely the capital makes more sense for the education of young mages."

"Fairhaven has always been the home of the Stanthor Academy. It was built before the town—Fairhaven grew around the Academy, to serve it. The castle was built by hundreds of non-magi, and the tradesmen who worked day after day built their homes around it. And," he continues reluctantly, "what better place to teach students of their burgeoning magic, where things might get out of hand."

I nod, my eyes downcast. The fire I'd begun in Fairhaven had only been put out after consuming the town. In Castor, it would've raged for days. And I am not the only mage wielding elemental magic.

Iain urges his horse into a gallop, and I follow with Iotha. Again, we race side by side to the city walls, and my heart lifts with the wind streaming through my hair. I recompose myself as we're let into the city, ahead of other merchants and refugees who queue along the sides of the road.

Castor is lively, the traffic flowing along the cobbled roads. From the gates—the highest point in the city besides the palace and the Archives spire—I can see the tiered houses and rooves all the way down to the harbour. There are ships anchored further out, their pennants flying high. I don't recognise the sigils from here, but I know why they're here; my coronation.

"Excellent." Iain points at one of the larger ships, sitting low in the water with a long, sharpened bowsprit. "That ship is from Syran."

"It's come from Gannameade?" I ask in wonder. The desert continent is far, far away from here. They must've travelled for weeks. "Why?"

But Iain says nothing. He rides ahead of the party, all the way to the palace, and the gates are open for us as we enter. I wriggle my toes in my boot, trying to get some blood flowing, and when I dismount, I have to hold onto my saddle for stability.

"Ma'am." One of the manservants offers my cane, and I take it gratefully.

The gravel of the large drive is awful to walk across with a cane, but I manage as the caravan mills about and begins to unpack. Inside, the palace has a charged air, and more staff than I've ever seen hurry about the halls, some stopping to bob a quick curtsy or bow in my general direction.

"How was Fairhaven, ma'am?"

Griffin appears at my side as I stand by a window, having taken shelter there to avoid the staff. He's in his dress uniform, not full plate this time. The stripes that mark him as captain stand out in gold on his shoulder.

"Dead," I say honestly, my eyes drifting over the busy halls.

"Quiet, and burnt. About the same, really. Why is the palace so busy?"

"The call for your coronation went out the moment you arrived in Castor. The first time," he clarifies. "The foreign dignitaries are staying within the palace. These are their servants."

My interest in foreign runes suddenly perks up. "Which countries?"

"A fair few, despite Lotheria's reputation."

I remember Amisha saying as much when I'd first arrived. I never thought I'd be on hand to see it.

"The Tsalski Empire arrived first, which makes sense. Shortest distance to travel and recent successful trade negotiations. Emperor Myrikan isn't in attendance, but his eldest daughter is. The princess has been here for three days. And Prince Fayyaad from Syran arrived this morning."

"Iain seemed particularly pleased about that," I comment. "Any idea why?"

"Oh, I know why. But I'll not risk the Headmaster's wrath to explain it."

I knock his boot with my cane. "Judge your allegiances better, Marks."

He turns serious. "I am, Evermore. The Headmasters are in power here. Not you, not the governor who ditched and ran a few months ago. Everyone knows it. Do you?"

I look closer at the captain. Griffin is in his mid-twenties, with early lines on his face and earnest eyes. Has he heard the tale of the peaceful death of the queen, or has he heard the truth?

Are the Headmasters saviours or usurpers to him?

Netalia approaches, parting footmen like the tides. I see her in a new light as she draws closer. Griffin inclines his head, and fades into the busy backdrop.

"Rose," Netalia says. "Welcome back."

"Thank you. How have things been here?"

"Busy." She looks around. "The season of Dawn Harbour begins soon, as do the festivities. We have much to celebrate."

"Do we?"

Her pale eyes are unreadable. "A new queen. New alliances. Rose, many foreign countries have sent envoys to treat with you."

We begin to walk, away from the bustling inner courtyard. "Is this unusual? The dignitaries, I mean."

She considers it. "I must confess I'm surprised at their... eagerness, given many outspoken opinions of our system of government."

"Both foreign and local."

She nods. "It's true. A number of minor houses have recanted their oaths to us in recent years, at the the time we need their support the most."

"You need a queen to sit the throne to win them back."

"His idea," Netalia says sharply. "He wanted to unite the Houses beneath a common banner, that of a queen, and of course, to have you read the runes. Which, I heard, you failed to do."

I shrug. "I was a first year runes' student. Besides, Yoris Moon can read them."

"Yoris Moon will read them in return for that which we're not willing to give." I look at her quizzically. "Our honest word, sworn in a blood oath, that we will not use them. Though they have enjoyed researching their student's masterwork without revealing the results to us."

"Are words the only tool you have to get information out of someone?" I'm dipping into cautious waters now, and the woman goes still. "I was led to believe you had other ways."

She smiles, and I realise too late I pushed a dangerous woman too far. My wrist burns with sudden pain and I drop my cane, a gasp in my throat. Black fingers spread within my veins, scouring and salting my blood as they reach higher. Agony nearly blinds me, and I fight the urge to double over. I can feel my skin beginning to peel back from the intrusion, and, for the first time, my fire does not obey my panic—it does not rise to defend me. For the first time since I landed on Lotherian soil, I am helpless.

The rot disappears as quickly as she summoned it. My chest heaves as I hold my wrist, still expecting to see my flesh blacken and open, festering in real time, from her touch. As my vision clears, my anger returns.

"If you ever do that again," I begin in a low voice, "I will burn you."

"You can try." Her fist opens and closes at her side. "Anyway, Yoris Moon is firmly entrenched in the noble community. They are related to House Fillegan and have used those connections to ensure their safety."

I shove the memory of pain to the back of my mind, thinking of the master, their cane in hand and their eyes glinting as they taunted Iain, and can't help my small smile.

Clever.

"And Arno—"

"Disappeared the second you did. It took us a while to realise, what with the town burnt to the ground, but when we went looking for him, he was gone. Neither reward nor threat could bring him to light." She heaves a sigh, as though this was some great quest she failed upon. "Runes is not a popular area of magic. Iain has a rudimentary knowledge, but when he tried to read the Book of Blood, it merely took his flesh in payment and remained blank. He cannot decipher those runes left in the Academy antechamber and thus, you were our remaining option. Your master called you a 'prodigy'."

The breath leaves my chest. Arno had been pushed to the back of my mind since the lowhills, but hearing his praise, even after the fact, brings tears to my eyes.

"Some prodigy," I hear myself say. "I'm not that good, I just read a lot."

She quirks a small smile. "Study is half the battle, Rose.

Learning the information before its application is a step not many move past."

I consider my next words carefully; my wrist still tingles with the aftermath of her foul magic. I tighten my grip on my cane.

"I wouldn't read the runes for you, Netalia, even if I could." Her smile dies away, and I look towards the city and sea, as though I'm not watching her every move out the corner of my eye. "Immortal rulers won't fix the problems in this country. Communication and good leaders will."

We stand, shoulder to shoulder, in silence.

"You are naive," she says simply, "as the young often are. I once longed to experience the innocence of youth again, but as I've grown older, I've seen people for who they truly are. I wouldn't trade that for the world, Rose. You have not yet seen the true face of those around you, those who smile and speak pleasantries but turn on you the moment it benefits them to do so."

I think again, unwillingly, of the lowhills. "I believe that most people, when given the chance, will do good," I say stubbornly, a small fire heating in my belly.

"Most people, when given the chance, will abandon you for the mere whispered promise of wealth and power."

Mum and Tyson, standing across the fire from me, slink into my head. Netalia is right, and that lesson in grief sinks deeper into my bones. I want to cry, to rage at how unfair it is—all I ever wanted was to be a good daughter, a good friend, but the moment someone stronger, more powerful and charismatic came along, they turned from me.

I clench my jaw, trying to work back the tears. "I want to believe and give the benefit of the doubt."

"Then I shall contact the mausoleum and tell them our next queen shall be along shortly."

I snort, suddenly reaching the limits of my willingness to put up with her, rot or no. "Why do you hate me, Netalia? What did I do?"

She glances sidelong at me. "You disrupted our hold on the Academy, burnt an entire town to the ground, then swanned across worlds to take the crown from our hands."

"You *brought*—"

"Iain brought you here, not me. He is your ally, not I." She faces me, her hands clasped in front of her, though her knuckles are white with restraint. "If I can give you any little piece of advice, Rose Evermore, any little scrap of information that will cling to that melon you call a head, it is this—get better at *lying*. And do it quickly. People who wish you harm are better at lying than you could ever hope to be."

I blink. "I hate lying."

"Why?" She raises an eyebrow. "Lying is a useful tool. Lying can be used to avoid conflict, disappointment, broken treaties. The sting of false words cannot compare with the wails of fresh widows. When you realise the peace and power that can be gained from the small twisting of reality, you will come to understand that I am right."

I say nothing.

"Read the runes, Rose. Carve them into our skin and give this country the immortal leaders it deserves—no more wars, no more power vacuums, no more fighting." She goes to leave, then pauses. "I know you think it is the wrong choice. But perhaps your first lie can be to yourself."

CHAPTER TWENTY-ONE

THAT NIGHT, there is a storm. I sit on my window ledge and watch the roiling skies dump curtains of rain onto the city. Netalia's words roll through my head as I twirl my cane across my lap, and the silence of my room wraps around me like a comfortable blanket.

Now, with some time between the meeting in the forest, I can begin to pick apart the threads that made up that hideous conversation. Mum had used the blood I'd drawn for her to cross the river. Somehow, for some reason, she'd brought Tyson with her; that part was unfathomable to me, but the answers aren't crucial enough for me to seek them. Instead, I think of the man I'd known as Craige.

Had I suspected him, during my year at the Academy? Had I known at all that one of the first people I met in Fairhaven was my long lost father?

I shake my head slightly, dismissing my own question. My bloodline had been far from my mind; I'd had enough practice at ignoring the absence of my father that it had become second nature as I'd grown older.

In the forest, he'd seemed larger than I recalled; he stood taller, he spoke louder, and he had a temper that I unfortunately recognised. When we'd met in Fairhaven, I had simply been a student, barely worthy of his noticing. But now, I was his daughter and the future queen—I was his ticket to power.

You shouldn't have let me walk out of that forest, I think.

He should've tried to convince me, win me over; clearly he had the skills to convince those around him of his ideals and plans. Mum and Tyson had stood shoulder to shoulder with him, against me. But he'd looked at me and seen an obstacle, a tool of the Headmasters.

I roll the cane back and forth, my eyes lowered to the glass in front of me.

Below, the inner courtyards of the palace are cloaked in darkness. Even the near-full moon cannot break through the thick clouds, and rain hammers to the ground. I think of all the serving men and women who opted to sleep in the stables, or on pallets in the hallways of the servants quarters. I can only hope they're dry and warm.

The foreign dignitaries had slowly started filling my schedule. I was surprised to find that I looked forward to spending time with them, to speaking with them. Deep beneath the waves of grief and disappointment, the harsh reality of learning what people are truly capable of, there is a small spark of new joy, one I'd only felt during my first few months at the Academy. An innocent curiosity, a childlike wonder of having a new world to learn remains, and I cling to it like a shipwrecked sailor.

I push my cane too far and it falls from my knees, landing with a soft *flump* onto the cushioned window seat. I leave it where it lies, instead letting my restless hands collect the next nearest thing to me.

It is the book Iain gave me, my first book on strategy and warcraft, written by his mentor. Holding it in my hands, feeling the smooth leather and stamped letters against my fingers, it seems heavier now, knowing the man who wrote it was murdered by his own countrymen. I open it and flick through a few pages, recognising some lines. Another small grief flickers through me as I realise I would've quite liked to meet Olendar Harvenspar, the man who travelled abroad and brought home a small, promising boy to teach him magic. Who gave him a home amongst his own children. Who was clever enough to rise to the rank of High Marshal, and write the book in my hands.

But Olendar Harvenspar reached too high, too far, and his family fell. Their House lies in ruin, and where ten noble families once made up the pillars of Lotherian society, now only nine remain.

I put the book aside and stare into the rain. A question that has been plaguing my mind for weeks is suddenly answered, a path laid before me as though someone spoke it into my ear.

Now, it's time to test how committed Iain is to this new idea, this way of doing things differently.

⁂

Two weeks later, they arrive at court. I'm having tea with the Tsalskinese princess, Layira, when a manservant brings me the news.

"Royal duties?" Layira asks. The princess is a delight, with laughing eyes and curious questions. Meeting with her has become the highlight of my week, and I was secretly thrilled when Lillian let slip that princess had also been cancelling other appointments to spend time with me. My maid had become quite chatty in the weeks since the Fairhaven trip—bizarrely, I think she missed me.

"Yes. I apologise for the short lunch," I tell the princess, looking for my cane. She laughs; we've been talking for hours, and the sun has crossed from one side of the garden to the other. She'd been telling me of the Tsalski Islands in such detail I could almost imagine I was there. "We'll reconvene soon."

"Only if you promise to take me into the city," she replies lightly. A servant hurries forward as she stands, a cloak in hand. Though the sun-warmed gardens were pleasant during the day, the shadow of the palace walls has reached long, cool fingers towards us, and even I shiver, though I'm used to the chill of Castor's evenings. "I want to eat as Lotherians do."

"Meat and cheese it is," I promise. "I hope you like mead."

"I like *our* version of mead," she says, and the conversation threatens to continue, so I quickly say my goodbyes with smiles and laughter before heading inside.

My heart is still light with Layira's presence when I cross the threshold of the palace. It takes a few murmuring wait staff, and the overall dour attitude in the hallways, before I recall who has arrived in the courtyard.

Dread begins to fill me, but I take a breath and try to disconnect myself from the feeling. I invited him here. I need to face the consequences wrought by the actions of the people I now represent.

Though a sour seed remains in my stomach at the thought of Iain and Netalia hiding on the upper floors and blaming a meeting with military officials for their absence at this meeting. I guess Iain isn't quite as ready to face his mistakes as he claims.

I'd requested to meet in the library, a wonderful room of intricately shaped shelves and aged tomes that *don't* try to peel my flesh from me when I open them. It also has the benefit of being completely and utterly silent, in spite of conversations being held in close proximity. I have my theories about that, but they'd fallen by the wayside in the face of the grimmer task I now turn to.

My cane thumps against the lacquered wooden floor as I make my way to the south corner of the library, away from my practice Kingdoms board. Just being in a familiar setting has calmed my nerves, but with each step, Rose's identity disappears into my queenly one. I've had to wear it more and more lately, like a suit of armour.

It troubles me when discussions go much more smoothly as a result; it lends credence to Netalia's words.

"Thank you for coming," I say to the figure, seated in the winged armchair facing away from me. They turn their head but don't stand, and my pride stings momentarily before their silhouette becomes recognisable.

"Your Majesty," Lady Matilda says in her low, melodic voice. Sudden nerves spring into my throat, though my gait continues forward uninterrupted. "You'll forgive me for not standing."

It's presumptuous, but I decide to give her the benefit of the doubt—Lady Matilda and I parted on amicable terms at least—and when I round the chair, I'm glad I did. A newborn infant is at her breast, swaddled comfortably and completely unaware of my presence. I smile and sit in the armchair opposite. Beside us, tall windows show us the tree canopies and southern walls, with open twilit sky soaring above them. Birds wheel in the thermals above the city and the flags uncurl lazily in the evening breeze. I take slight comfort in the picturesque scene before turning my full attention to the mother of my fallen friend.

"Rose," Lady Matilda says, by way of greeting, and I look about me for somewhere to set my cane aside.

"No titles then?" I query, tucking it between my armchair and the side table.

She lifts an eyebrow, adjusting her infant. "You didn't strike me as the type to care about them during your time in Riverdoor."

"That was before I had one."

"Ah." Matilda looks down at her feeding baby, though her fingers tighten slightly on the bundle. "Your missive makes a lot more sense now."

I let her words wash over me. "I was unaware that it was confusing. Every House, both noble and minor, have renewed their allegiance to the throne. The Lyons are pledged to my own House, Greatcast, and yet... you remained silent."

She nods, though her eyes are shadowed. "The Lyons were

pledged to House Greatcast, yes. Though I've heard Gennorin has not accepted you yet."

This is true. I shift. "She will."

Matilda meets my eyes, and my confidence falters. She has Petre's eyes, and for a moment I'm seeing the life slip from his again. I look away first, my heart thrumming in my chest.

"The crown has changed you."

The words are at my lips, Iain's voice in my ear. "For the better. I'm the leader this country needs, but first I need to make sure I have the support of those I can count on." I let my hand drift to the bell beside me, wondering if I should call for tea, but then I withdraw it. "We parted as friends, Matilda. You forgave me for Petre's death."

"For the death of my son, yes," she answers coolly. "Not for allying yourself with those who caused it."

"The men who killed your son are dead, by my hand."

"By your fire," she amends. "I saw what you did to Fairhaven on my travels here. I'm not so sure you're as discerning with your sense of justice as you think you are. Less so now, seeing the company you keep."

Her words burrow deep. I clench my jaw. "War threatens, Lady Lyon. From the north and closer than you know. Soon the Houses will resume their warnames, and the resources that accompany that declaration. Will the Lyon family pledge their banners to the Greatcasts if Thornsgrove must rise?"

"No," she answers, and places the infant to her shoulder, patting it gently. "Our men and our arms will remain where they are... at our manor, to protect what's left of my family."

I take a deep breath, and drum my fingers against the patterned arm of my chair. "Is it treason, or cowardice?"

Her hands do not still from their *pat pat pat* on the baby's back. "I beg your pardon?"

"I can't remember if refusing the call to banners is treason or cowardice. It's been a lot to learn in a very short amount of time." I reach for the stack of books at my left, placed there earlier by some of the library pages. Resting the top most tome on my lap, I thumb through it. "I did do some reading on Riverdoor. I wanted to get to know your land and people."

The baby burps, and the lady takes a moment to clean up the resulting mess. I watch the mother and child, trying to seem as though my stomach isn't threatening to do exactly the same thing.

"What do you plan to do, if not answer the bannercall?" I ask when she's done.

"It has been made clear to us in recent years, with recent events, that Riverdoor is expected to weather the storms alone," Matilda answers, as she settles the baby once again. "So that is what we intend to do. We will not spare men for a war that we did not ask for, when our similar requests went unheeded."

"I understand. Your family has been treated badly by the Head-masters. You should have had support when you asked for it."

"The Greatcasts did not help us either," she shoots at me. "Though we are their sworn men. They did not protect us."

"And I will speak on your behalf to my matriarch, when I meet with her." I lean forward. "I want to know your grievances, Matilda, all of them. So I can make sure you get the support you need in the event you need it."

She sighs. "It's too late for that, Rose. And you are not the one that needs to be promising support and apologies. But I daresay the mouths from which I need to hear it have found themselves... otherwise occupied."

I sit back in my chair. "I speak with their authority."

"Like I said"—she meets my eyes again—"your missive makes more sense now."

Time rests uneasily around us as a stale silence arises, neither of us willing to break it first. The baby fusses and whines, providing an excellent segue into conversation about the child's arrival, questions about travel—pleasantries. But I am learning more and more that politics and diplomacy are not pleasant.

I want Riverdoor back in the fold. I do not want Thornsgrove —the castle in which my magical family has resided for generations —to be fighting a two front war when the time comes. I need the east strong and united.

Matilda wants retribution, and thinks the only person capable of giving it to her has fled her very presence.

Which, I remind myself, *he has*.

"Harvestcall approaches," I say in idle conversation.

"Dawn Harbour is not yet done," she reminds me. "Or have you gotten so used to pretending there's a crown on your head you can no longer tell that there's not?"

The barb goes deep, but I let my gaze drift past her, into the shelves. The library is my domain; I haunt it like a restless ghost between meetings. It's become as comfortable to me as my own bedroom, and it is difficult for me to feel threatened here.

"My coronation approaches faster than anyone wants it, Matilda. But after the crowds disperse, and the ships leave, the call to arms will go out. Though in this case, the arms are pitchforks and sickles. Have you the workforce required for your fields?"

The baby burbles, but Matilda pays it no mind, meeting my eyes. She now knows what my next move is, like I can see Iain's on the Kingdoms board in the moment it becomes too late to counter it. And like my floundering troops and dwindling supplies, Matilda is destined to lose this argument.

To her credit, she continues. "Riverdoor doesn't have vast fields of emmer and grain, Rose."

I should be gracious in my victory, but heat rises in my gullet. "No? The seasons will soon be turning cold, though. Surely you've shored up your warehouses and stockyards?"

"Our orchards bore fruit and our livestock—"

I pick up another book and put it on the low table between us. Her eyes follow it as though it'll try to skin her if she doesn't watch it.

"It was only seven years ago that your stores ran dry for the first time," I say softly. "I know you were Lady of Riverdoor then. Petre would've been young, Samlin a mere thought in your future plans. How lucky you were to only have one child to feed."

Her anger grows swiftly. "How dare you—"

Mine flares as well. "How dare I? You start a fight you cannot win at the expense of the people who rely on you. You go to war on not one, but *three* fronts; Thornsgrove will not suffer a deserter on its doorstep and you know it." I take a breath; for a moment, I'd heard my father with each syllable. "I understand that you're hurting, I understand that you feel unheard, but personal squabbles *can not* stand in the way of providing for your people."

Like an anchor, she is drawn towards the book between us. *The Great Hunger*, it is called, and it was one of the more harrowing reads I'd found on the shelves. When the Lotherian River froze over—for the first time in recorded history—Riverdoor ran dry of stocked food and supplies. The city had nearly destroyed itself in desperation. Blood ran in the streets over the remaining loaves of bread, children were sent to the moors to hunt for beetles and mice, and any babies born during that dark winter season grew up on the thinnest of milk, if they weren't left in a quiet corner of the world for the elements to claim; one fewer mouth to feed was the only blessing the people of Riverdoor received from their absent goddess. When the snows had cleared, and the river thawed, the Greatcasts were able to send shipments of food and Carriers to the stricken city and end the famine.

Matilda looks away, her jaw clenched. I'd hoped not to use *The Great Hunger*, but maybe being reminded of her failures will prevent her repeating them; my fire lingers deep in my bones, but when I think of unleashing it, I see the town I burned and my laughing father. Matilda was Lady of Riverdoor and in charge of planning their winter stores. And here she is before me, half a year out from the same season, cutting off their trade routes and allies. Maybe she has done the smart thing, and negotiated for extra grain, rice, and salt. Maybe they brought in more livestock. Maybe they are prepared for what is to come.

Or maybe a mother received a summons and made a decision according to her grief.

When I watch her struggle for words, I know it's the latter, and I continue the negotiation.

"Pledge your allegiance to the throne, Matilda. Allow us to continue trading with you, to send you troops and provisions should the need arise." She says nothing, but looks at me, and I know she will accept. "And when you leave here, you will do so as the tenth noble House of Lotheria."

Her mouth goes slack, just a little. "Iain would never allow that."

"You said I speak with his authority."

"Yes, but..." She flounders, thrown off whatever track she thought I was going down. "There has not been a tenth House since Harvenspar. He would never allow them to be replaced—"

"And yet he did," I say gently. "Matilda, I am not a puppet atop a throne. I'm still the same person who followed Petre onto the moors, who killed men on your lands, who brought back your son from the ashes." My throat goes tight. "I hate that I could not bring both of them home. But I do have power now, and I won't allow my friend's family to cut themselves off from the world and place his remaining siblings in danger."

Crown or no, rank or none, I am flying *dangerously* close to being slapped. Her cheeks flush, from anger or grief, I cannot tell. But the babe in her arms keeps her grounded in her chair, and the moment passes. She lowers her head.

"Your Majesty," she murmurs, and I acknowledge the dismissal.

"Your minister is meeting with my clerks at the moment, waiting upon a runner with a message of your acquiescence. I will give it to him, and you will not suffer the coming months alone." I rise, collecting my cane, but turn back before leaving. "I need a warname for your House, Matilda."

She stands, the baby in her arms sleeping contently, a dribble of milk at the corner of her mouth. "Our manor does not have the fortifications required of a great House." She chews her lip. "I have a request. One that you may not be inclined to grant to us after our rebellion—"

"Matilda," I say, and dare to plant a hand on her arm. "You are my new House. I am to be your queen. What's a little request amongst friends?"

CHAPTER TWENTY-TWO

"Longrock," Iain intones, "fell long ago."

"Just over a year," I say, moving a few of my pieces around the board. I eye his arms as he does the same, but I cannot tell what he's doing. "They're not entrenched yet."

He sighs. "I gave you permission to raise the Lyons, Rose, not to begin the war early."

"Preliminary reports indicate that Longrock wasn't taken under order of House Araspire." I'd gone over them before accepting Matilda's request. "They claimed a rogue faction, not representing them, had acted outside of their wishes. They denounced them upon our inquiry."

Iain's eyes flick to mine, and he says nothing for a moment. I bask in the few seconds of silence, knowing he is pleased.

"And thus they cannot claim a move against the rogue faction as a move against them. You did well," he says. "I admit, having Longrock back under our control brings me comfort."

To his ego, not to his conscience. "Furymoor," I say.

"I'm sorry?"

"The Lyons chose their warname. 'Furymoor' is to be their castle."

He nods sagely, as though he was the one to spill blood on the moors. "What about their fighting forces?"

"I supplemented them." I move some cavalry up the board, and the hovering mist parts to reveal a small battalion of archers hiding in the surrounds of the tiny representation of Mornington. Iain draws a breath through his teeth as I ride them down, collecting his figures and placing them to the side. "You did this last time."

"The town provides resources and shelter," he argues, though he accepts the pieces I offer him. "Men need the promise of luxuries just as much as food and coin. How did you supplement the Riverdoor forces?"

"I promised reinforcements from Thornsgrove... from the Greatcasts." I look up. "Troops from the queen's own House seemed to be just as much a lure as... luxuries."

"A bold move. You don't have the support of House Greatcast."

"Yet," I amend, moving my cavalry onwards. I have a hunch, and it is proven correct when I find another two battalions of archers on their merry way to Mornington. They, too, are cleared from the map, and Iain goes still. I don't make eye contact as I remove those little pieces from the board as well.

His next words are heated with the loss of three archer battalions in the space of a short conversation. "You expect much from the House you just took a sworn banner from."

"Yes, I daresay they'll be quite angry with me." I move my forces up and continue reinforcing my position, knowing Iain likely does not have the ranged units to counter me. "They'll want to make their anger known. Probably through a petition in court."

I finish arranging my figures, and finally look up. Iain's gaze is not on his side, but on me.

"The Greatcasts refused to come to court to claim you," he says quietly, "so you made them angry enough to do so instead."

"All I need is an audience," I tell him, leaning forward on the table. "I just need to meet Gennorin, so she can see I'm Lydia's daughter, that I'm of her blood. She ignored my summons, but her pride cannot ignore this slight."

Silence falls over the room.

"I concede," Iain says finally, and for a moment, I think he means the conversation. But then he begins clearing the board.

There is the tiny sound of someone clearing their throat. We both look at the man in the corner, having completely forgotten he was there.

"The match goes to Her Majesty," Bernhard says, scribbling something in ink. "This grants enough points for her to test in the Sentinel range."

I can't help the grin that spreads across my face, nor the warmth across my chest. I'd been so concerned as to Iain's reception of my negotiations with Matilda, my attention had been drawn from the game. Now I realise that was probably a good thing.

The adjudicator gets both of our signatures, then begins to pack his things. At first I'd been nervous to have someone observing our sessions, but Bernhard has the particular talent of fading into the background—of not moving nor speaking throughout the duration of a game. It makes it easy to forget he is there.

I'd heard once that a pair of players actually had, and their resulting conversation of points forging and match throwing had been recorded by him as he sat in the corner, transcribing their plans to cheat and lie their way to the top rankings. Apparently the court case had merely been him reading that transcription aloud.

Sentinel. The slow warming of pride fills me, in a way I'd forgotten was possible. When did I last feel accomplishment for something I'd worked hard on? Seen the payoff of labour before my very eyes? I look at the copy of my test papers. Magic makes everything seem so easy sometimes; I would loathe to forget what true hard work feels like.

"Well done," Iain says, and though I listen for the bitter note in his vote, I cannot find it. "You did well to distract me with conversation."

"I think I distracted myself with conversation," I admit, and he laughs.

"Sometimes that does help. Come, Netalia has requested our presence for dinner."

As it seems too often these days, my good mood is pierced by the inevitable disappointment of reality. Netalia will not be pleased by my diplomacy; she will have thought of a hundred 'better' ways to have solved the problem, more than half, I assume, involving the Lord or Lady lying at the bottom of a set of stairs with a broken neck.

I flex my hand on my cane as we walk to her sitting rooms, wrapping my recent victory around myself like armour. Iain notices.

"You don't want to have dinner with Netalia."

"Not particularly. I've had enough disapproval from other people to last three lifetimes."

He sighs, resting a hand on my shoulder as we walk, but says nothing. For some reason, that makes it easier to bear than if he'd rolled out a speech of false praise and excuses for his soulmate's behaviour; the true nature of the situation had been acknowledged and sympathised with, and then we'd continued on.

Somehow the multitude of candles and a roaring fireplace still don't seem to be able to pierce the gloom of Netalia's sitting room. The table has been laid out for three, with Iain at its head. Netalia waits for us in an armchair near the fire, rising as we enter.

"Good evening," she greets, and I muster up a half-smile in the face of what promises to be an awkward affair.

We sit down, Netalia at his right and I at his left. A large sheaf of papers stand beside Netalia's cup, and I relax slightly; a dinner meeting. We're talking war and kingdom management. Much better than I thought.

"Wine, madam?"

Netalia indicates the server to pour and he does, moving around the table. I shake my head to him as Netalia straightens delicate spectacles on her nose.

"Rose, we need to discuss your kingsmatch."

I seize the server's arm. "On second thought, yes please."

Netalia watches the red liquid fall into my glass. "I know you've had several of your choices reveal themselves to you already, which is not how I'd prefer to go about things, but we need to discuss who you'll name at your coronation."

I take a sip of the wine, but it's sharp on my tongue and I grimace. "So that's how it works? I just name my poor husband to be in front of hundreds of people and he has to go along with it?"

"By placing his name in for consideration, he has already accepted." She looks at me severely. "They can withdraw at any time until the coronation. So far, none have."

I blink. Iain catches my eye, and the corner of his mouth twitches.

"As you know, your coronation will take place in the main hall. I will prepare a tonic for your leg the morning of; you will be on your feet for many hours." Netalia's eyes rest of the handle of my cane leaning against the table, and I make a promise to myself that no matter how many stairs I need to climb, no matter how many hours I need to stand, I'll never pour one of her poisons down my throat—I hadn't forgotten the rotting magic that had nearly claimed my arm. "Your crown still needs to be decided on."

"I will accompany you to the forges later this week," Iain puts in, and I nod. I've given the exact shape and make of my crown no thought after the Fairhaven trip.

"Once Iain places the crown on your head, you will name your husband to the waiting crowd, and he will accept."

She shuffles some papers, and I lift my wineglass again. Something isn't sitting right with me, like a pebble in my shoe, and her next few words roll off of me as I try to discern what it is.

"Orinius Thoreau," Netalia says, and I jump at my friend's name, though I knew he'd entered it. "He would be a good match. House Thoreau is the largest provider of grain in the country. We could do worse than to strengthen our ties with the breadbasket of Lotheria, especially at the onset of war."

She lays his sheet aside, and I note the distinct lack of Orin's picture on his... marriage resume.

We go through a few more—each noble House, and a few minor, has rustled up a son or a cousin to submit. I don't recognise any of the names, and their profiles cover only their family's accomplishments, not their own. By the time our main course is served, I'm much more interested in the roast pork they set before us.

"—a prince from Gannameade," Netalia is saying when I key back into the conversation she's having with the silence. "Fayyaad is the second son of the Hassar, a favourite with the local populace. An alliance with Gannameade would be extremely beneficial at this time." She looks over her glasses and slides the paper to me, the first time she's done so. I lay my knife and fork aside and pick up the prince.

Again, he has no picture. Twenty-one years old, served in the Gannameadan military—as is their custom for young adults coming of age—led a successful campaign against a bandit king in the Djhara desert... I realise I've stopped chewing as I continue reading about this prince.

"Next is—"

When she doesn't continue, I look up, but she is already holding the page to a candle. A small flame takes hold and begins to creep up towards the inked words.

But Netalia seems to constantly forget that the fire in the palace obeys me fully.

The page goes out, followed by the candle an instant later, the smoke curling around her hand. I reach out and pluck it from her grasp, and her expression darkens.

Ser Phoenix of House Araspire.

I frown, lifting the paper. "Phoenix put his name in?"

"As though we'd chose a nothing son from a rebelling House," Netalia snorts, lifting her wine glass. "Third, I believe he is."

I run my eyes over the page, nodding absently. "His older brother went missing though, so he's kind of second."

"Ran off, most likely. A wise choice," Netalia spits.

"He's knighted," I point out.

"By a traitor."

Battle experience, loyal to the south, friend of the queen...

I recognise the handwriting; he wrote this himself.

For the second time in hours, a warm feeling wraps around my heart.

"Even if he was first son of a noble House, the fact remains he was to be your soulmate before you... fled." My eyes flick to Netalia at that, but she holds my gaze steadily. "It would be unseemly for you to take him as your husband."

"Because soulmates aren't romantic, I get it." I put his paper down. "But we aren't. We never bonded, and our magic is fractured. We can never repair that connection."

Iain shifts uncomfortably. "House Araspire is in open rebellion against you, Rose. Taking their son as your husband implies you are attempting to placate them."

"Is that so bad? Have we ever tried diplomacy, or have we always reached for the sword first?" I'm using 'we' so Netalia doesn't derail the conversation about how I 'wasn't there' and it 'was a different time'. The fact remains that my former Headmasters used violence as a first resort. This war is merely the result of their egos having military capabilities.

"Araspire doesn't respect diplomacy or politics, and neither do their sworn houses. They will see the marriage as a declaration of your unwillingness to go to war," Iain says.

I snort. "A terrible thing, you're right. How dare I hold back against sending men and women to die for a bit of land."

Iain slams his hand against the table, and I jump as the cutlery rattles. "A bit of land, a castle, a town, a city... These lives are being affected already, Rose, whether you 'send' them or not. Do you truly believe Longrock was taken by a rogue faction, as they claim? They were pushing, searching for weaknesses, seeing how we'd respond. When they stole the Lyon boy from his bed, and you travelled north to burn the perpetrators, you won six months of peace in doing so."

Silence rushes in at the wake of his words. Any reminder of my actions at Deadman's Keep has the ability to shut me down, but not this time.

"They didn't continue their attacks because of me?"

"You responded to their claims with fire and steel," Netalia says. "And Riverdoor did not fall to the next 'illegitimate' raid as they tried to work out who you were and where you'd come from."

More words from the past sound in my ears. I look at Iain. "So when you said you regretted not helping Petre... it wasn't to get his brother back, it was because inaction made you look—"

"Weak. Yes." Iain spears a chunk of meat on his fork as though it is Lord Aloysius Araspire himself. "We miscalculated. It had only been a few years since our defeat at Thyssen."

A little more of the past unravels—Thyssen had been the mining town Kaya had been sent to win back; the single source of all mirriam ore in Lotheria. It was where she'd lost her eye and her soulmate, beginning her campaign against the Headmasters on the battlefield.

I rest my head in my hands.

Iain clears his throat. "Our mistakes of the past have informed the northern houses of our weaknesses and blindspots. Kaya Aule took her army to them, with a story about a girl who burnt a village. She has not been seen since." I look up at him, Phoenix's page lying beside me. "Every mistake we've made, Rose, has become an enemy faction bent on destroying us. We merely moved in to take power when it became clear no one else could be trusted with it."

"Which nobody asked you to do," I point out. "No one approved you, no one ordained you. You were never elected nor chosen, yet deemed yourself fit to rule, and you wonder why the Houses are rebelling?"

I feel both of their anger rise, and my fear of Netalia surfaces, but I lean into my own indignation. Gone is the easy banter between myself and Iain after a Kingdoms match. Now, the words that've been spoken to me in shadowed corners over the last two years rise to my own lips.

"'Chosen'," Netalia repeats, spitting the word. "It was the chosen rulers, the queens, of this country who drove it into the ground. When things got bad and corruption rose, the supposed leaders of Lotheria would sit and wait for their 'chosen'. The old laws created a people of apathy."

"The Dawn Harbour Massacre is only the most recent example of the dangers of the current system," Iain intones, and I know he's trying to placate us both. But I've got the bit between my teeth and Matilda's words in my ears.

"The power wasn't yours to take. It certainly wasn't yours to warp and change and mould an entire generation with!"

"And what would you be referring to with that?" Netalia asks, her eyes flashing dangerously.

I swallow my fear of her. "The Charter. The students under your command earning years on their ticket, to be paid back to you. You padded your coffers and made yourself comfortable, and wrapped yourselves in the reasonings of logic and righteousness. 'We *had* to take control, we *had* to do things differently...' Can't you see the damage that has been done since?" A thought bursts into my mind and I verbalise it before I stop to think. "You vilify Aloysius Araspire for daring to attempt the same things you did."

The silence that follows my outburst is deadly, but I can feel the runes on my arms singing. The queensblood roils in my veins, alive and active for the first time since the lowhills, and, bizarrely, I get the feeling it approves.

"Get out," Netalia says simply, and I hear the warning in her words. For a moment I imagine her trying it, the blackened blood spoiling in my skin, and the fire with which I would answer. She would be ashes in the carpet.

"Rose—" Iain begins, but I shove myself back from the table and stand abruptly, my heart slamming in my chest.

"You said you wanted change," I snap, and grab my cane. "I actually believed you were doing something different this time. But you still answer to *her*. She's sick and twisted and cruel, Iain. I had hope for you." I look at his soulmate, at her blank expression and dead eyes. "But never for her. She knows only how to use people."

"And you don't?" Netalia asks.

Once, that would've hurt, but now I laugh. "I'm an amateur compared to you, and grateful to be one. I've seen what will happen if I continue down this track."

Netalia, too, rises. "The accumulation of wealth and power?"

I snort, and gesture to the long, empty table. "Yeah, that you clearly share with all your friends."

"Rose," Iain says again, and I snatch Phoenix's page off the table, turning to face him.

"Don't." I point at him with my cane's handle. "I was actually starting to believe you gave a shit about me."

He doesn't say anything as I leave the room, my steps heavy and painful after a long game of Kingdoms only a few hours before. His silence is more telling than his words, and I hear the meaning between the unspoken lines.

Tears burn as I shoulder the door open, and neither of them try to stop me.

CHAPTER TWENTY-THREE

My father was right.

Put words in their heads or blades in their hearts.

The Headmasters will never change. This country, soaked in blood and learned in war, will never change. I was a fool to think I could herald it.

I tuck my feet in, the trickling stream dampening the soles of my boots. I can barely see the water in the moonlight, filtering through the canopy of trees overhead, but the dark is comforting in a way no one else has been lately.

I drum my fingers on my head, a thousand scenarios tumbling through it.

"Rough night?"

Something cuts through the gloom and I can't help but smile a little. "You put your name in for the marriage ballot."

Phoenix sits on the opposite side of the stream from me. "I did."

The gardens are always quiet at this time of night. We're sitting away from the manicured hedges and flower beds, in a rougher part that has been allowed to grow wild for some time. A small stream, designed to direct stormwater from the foundations of the palace, flows throughout it, ending in an artificial waterfall that spouts off the side of the spire the castle was built upon. It's as close to going for a walk in the wilderness as one can get in the middle of a capital city, and I love it.

"Why?" I ask him.

He shrugs. The moonlight is dim and I can't see him very well, but it somehow makes this conversation easier.

"Why not? We're good friends, Rose, and the conflict began with my House. Maybe we can end it with our marriage."

Warmth rushes to my cheeks at his words. But a colder part of me warns caution.

The legitimacy of the throne is one thing his family cannot seize through means of force. Marriage to you is the only way.

Internally, I scoff at the legitimacy of the throne—my rune scars tingle beneath my sleeves—but I know the part of me speaking; it is the harder, surer part of me born during sessions of Kingdoms. I push aside the first part, the giggling blushing nineteen year old, and look at my friend.

"We were once soulmates, Phoenix." Netalia's words ring in my ears. "It's not really done."

He shrugs again, barely visible. "A young woman from another world is to be queen of this one. This is not a time of tradition, Rose. It's a time of forging new paths... Look where following the old ones led. To a country divided, aimless, with the power hungry as our heads of state."

I clench my jaw and look away. He's right. Kynan was right. The Headmasters are the wrong leaders for Lotheria. "I'm not the queen this country needs."

He snorts. "Unfortunately for you, you're the only one we've got. The country and the gods chose you for a reason, Rose."

For the first time since carving the runes, I wish I *had* been the chosen queen—that surety, that hint of a reason, that whisper of faith required to select a woman and gift her the greatest power in the country, would've been a boon. Something to fall back on in my darkest moments of doubt.

But I pick at the scar tissue in my arms. I don't have that backing. I'm a lie, the false queen. My situation is no one's fault but my own.

I take a deep breath, closing my eyes. The wind picks up around us as leaves twirl from the trees.

"Rose..." The water splashes slightly as Phoenix steps over it. "What are you thinking?"

I say nothing, but I feel him sit beside me, his warmth pressing in at my side. Without opening my eyes, I pull down one of my sleeves.

He hesitates, then runs his fingers down my skin. I feel him trace the scars and my heart threatens to burst from my chest.

You are in control until you look like you aren't.

I will my racing heart to slow. He grips my forearm and turns it this way and that.

"What... are these?"

I pull my sleeve back down. "My rune alphabet. Designed to mimic all of the signs of a Lotherian queen."

He pulls back, sucking in a breath between his teeth. "*What?*"

I open my eyes and meet his. "I wasn't chosen, Phoenix. I designed and created this."

In all my time knowing him, I've never seen Phoenix rattled. I've seen him lonely, angry, lost... but never unsettled. And as he pulls away from me, I know I need to hold him to me now more than ever.

I seize his hand. "You said this wasn't the time of tradition. It's time for a new path. Walk beside me on it."

He looks at me in the dark, searching my face. I meet him evenly, a weight loosening from my shoulders as the lie I've carried all year is suddenly shared. A burden halved.

"You offered to marry me," I say. "You said you were my friend, and loyal to me. Or were they pretty words on paper to buy yourself more power?"

His hand tightens on mine, and his eyes darken. "I would never—"

"Then don't." I push my advantage, knowing he's off balance. "Support me, and denounce your family publicly. Pledge your sword to my throne, and House Araspire will have a new lord, recognised by the court and crown as legitimate."

He sucks a breath between his teeth, and goes quiet for a long time. Finally, he says, "You don't have the power to do that, Rose."

I smile in the dark. "Ask the tenth noble House of Lotheria that."

"There is no tenth noble House."

"Isn't there? I guess news travels slowly to the student quarters."

There is a beat of silence, then his hold on my hand softens. He leans away, studying me.

"I see it now."

I meet his gaze evenly. "What?"

"What Iain saw in you." His name is a bolt of ice to my chest. "Why he crossed worlds to retrieve you."

I don't ask what he sees. I don't want to know.

"I need an answer, Phoenix."

He smiles tightly. "I know your secret now. You won't let me leave without pledging to you."

I laugh. "What could I do to you? You're the greatest swordsman I've ever seen."

He doesn't return my brevity. "You've burnt men before, Rose."

My blood turns cold. "Never a friend."

Only a father.

He rises, and I do the same. We stand beside the stream for a few moments, looking at each other. The moment lingers for a second too long, and nerves begin to grow in my stomach.

Then, he sinks to one knee. "House Araspire is yours, Your Grace."

I smile, the tension melting away, and place a hand on his shoulder. I have another ally Iain and Netalia could never have expected. "I look forward to working together... Lord Araspire."

CHAPTER TWENTY-FOUR

HAMMERS RING out as another trickle of sweat traces a line down my spine. Journeymen and apprentices step out of our way as Lord Olinius leads Iain and myself across the forge floor.

"Apologies for the mess, Your Grace," he calls back to me. "But we've got few dozen orders due for delivery soon."

"It's alright," I tell him, stepping around a man carrying a batch of iron rods. I suspect the orders are mine, not that Netalia allows me to glimpse the paperwork she carries around like a weapon. "You have a lot of men."

"We put out the hiring word," he says as the three of us continue deeper. It's deafening in here, the sound of steel being beaten into swords and pikes reaching to the high ceiling. "As soon as we received our war funding."

I half-glance back over my shoulder at Iain. I know from my reading that the Houses usually receive their war funding at the same time—the declaration of war. This means the manse above us now wears its warname—The Forge. Olinius has always been the primary outfitter for arms and armour. I don't blame Iain for funding them first, but I do blame him for not telling me.

The Headmaster meets my gaze and does nothing.

We reach the back wall, where the lord keeps his desk. A leather apron hangs from a peg on the back wall, the large windows overlooking the rocky bay on the western shore. His desk has ink pots and paper atop it, but also long tongs and hammers. My fingers drift to the handle of one.

"That's—"

"A fuller, I know." I look up at Lord Olinius, Iain at my back. "You have the ingots?"

He inclines his head, sweeping his hand over another table along the wall. A small row of rectangular moulds rest there.

"I'll leave you to choose," Olinius says. "Just flag me down when you're ready to decide."

I nod, and he disappears into the chaos of the working forge. I step over to the table and begin to look them over. Iain follows me.

"Is your leg hurting today?"

I frown, not looking up. "My leg hurts every day."

He nods, going quiet. I know not to press; when he wants to talk, he'll ask about something else first to break the silence. I itch at my arm, and wait.

We've not been alone since the night I walked out of dinner. After Phoenix's pledge, I'd handed a footman a note for Netalia, telling her to make it so, and then locked myself into the library so she couldn't argue. There, I'd continued my mission of reading the entire catalogue and playing Kingdoms matches against the board until my fingers ached from moving small pieces.

I pick up a small bar of dull iron, turning it over.

"You were right," Iain says from behind me, and I stiffen. "We were never chosen."

I put the bar down and pick up another.

"We had no one to teach us, Rose. No way of learning wrong from right, how to treat with hostile parties, how to draw up laws. We did what we thought was needed at the time."

I turn to face him, a copper ingot in my hands. "Yet you seized power after the Dawn Harbour Massacre, knowing you had little experience in government. Why?"

He meets my eyes. "You will not want to hear it, but it is true. Someone needed to. The people were going to wait to be saved by the next queen, though she was likely a generation away." He lifts his chin. "I was the adopted son of a great House, and Netalia an educated mage with good connections. We were well suited to power."

We look at each other in broken silence as the rhythm of forging continues around us. I want to argue, but the same point of conflict serves no one. His time, and Netalia's time, as the shadow rulers of Lotheria, is over. He began this conversation for a reason though and, much like Phoenix, I see the opportunity, so I take it.

"I need you to promise me that you'll make changes, Iain. The Charter needs to go, yesterday."

He nods slowly. "That was wrong of us."

"You're learning."

He laughs unexpectedly, and I hate that my own tension melts away as he does. I hate that his approval holds such sway over my emotions.

"What else would you have us change?" he asks.

"Work with me. Rule alongside me, as my advisor. With all of us working together, we have a real chance of finishing this war before it begins. And"—my voice betrays me, catching in my throat—"don't pursue Arno's runes. Let them go."

The Headmaster looks at me. I can almost see the calculations in his head, much like when he stops to consider his next move on the board. I hold his gaze with mine; I've made my play.

"Rose... one day, we'll face the same problem. The death of a queen."

"Yes," I say. "But by my estimations, we have about sixty or so years before we have to worry about that. We've plenty of time, even without the runes."

He goes quiet, and I know the conversation is done. Iain will not give me a straight answer. I turn back to the ingots, to choose the one that will become my crown.

"Alright."

My fingers freeze on the next mould. I don't move, as though doing so will scare the word away.

Iain steps up beside me, and takes my hand from the metal bars. He doesn't bend the knee like Phoenix, but he lifts my hand in his. "I will cease searching for the key rune. You have my word." He hesitates, then adds, "My queen."

Victory soars in my chest. For a moment, my father's face flickers in my mind's eye, and I imagine shouting the words at him.

I won.

I swallow hard, trying to regain control. "Why, Iain? Why is this conversation all it took?"

"Because it wasn't just this conversation," he says. "You fought at Deadman's Keep and returned Samlin Lyon. You beat Kaya Aule, read the words of the Book of Blood—"

"Hardly any."

"More than most. You're the youngest ranked Sentinel since myself, you raised House Lyon, and recognised a new head of the Araspire family, which is causing the northern rebellion to lose any legitimacy it might've had with southern sympathisers." Iain releases my hand and turns the table before us. "All without a crown on your head."

I let his words wash over me, fighting the urge to denounce them.

"You were right at dinner the other night. We need a diplomat. Someone who fights with words and treaties rather than swords and armies."

"It might still come to that," I murmur, thinking of Kaya.

"And if it does, we'll be ready." Iain turns to gesture to the forge. "This is your power now, Rose. This and more."

Rows and rows of men work tirelessly, pouring liquid metal,

hammering lengths of iron, sharpening new swords and spear-heads. I think of all the little men on the Kingdoms board and their tiny weapons. Now, I will play the game with the real things, and the cost of losing is much higher.

Olinius strides towards us, ringing his hands on a rag. "Have we chosen?"

None of the metals are calling to me, having been a second thought for the entire time he'd been gone. I itch my arm again, and suddenly realise I've been scratching at a rune. One of them has activated.

"Not from here," I say, casting my gaze around the floor. "There's something else."

The rune tugs at me, pulling my skin much the way the Book of Blood did. I tuck the unerring sensation at the back of my mind and follow it back to Olinius' desk. There is no chair, but I pause on the spot where one would be, and tap the toe of my boot on the flagstone.

Olinius draws nearer, his brow knit in confusion. "There is a small lockbox under there, my lady, but how...?"

"What's in it?" I ask, and he kneels, pulling a key from his pocket.

The lockbox is indeed small, held easily in one of his hands when he draws it from the secret compartment. His rough fingers spin the dials on a delicate combination lock, and the lid comes away easily. He hands it to me wordlessly, and I look at the misshapen lump of ore inside.

"This one." I hold it out to Iain for inspection. "This one will be my crown."

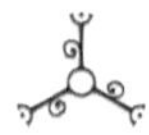

We ride together through the city, and I let Iotha have her head. She follows Iain's gelding through the winding streets of the city, their hooves ringing against the cobbles as the cityfolk part for us to pass.

Ahead, Iain beckons to me, and I ride to his side immediately, pleased to be summoned.

"You grow more and more comfortable in the saddle," he comments, and I reach forward to stroke the horses' neck.

"She's wonderful," I say earnestly. The mare never fails to brighten my day and greets me enthusiastically whenever I head to the stables. It's nice to be wanted by a creature with no other motive other than 'pats', 'carrots', and 'brushes'. "Thank you again."

Iain, too, reaches out and scratches at her mane. "You're more than welcome. As I said, a queen should have a mount worthy of the crown."

I grin. "Saying it like that makes it sound like she should be wearing one."

"Of course, that's what I meant," he responds, and I shove at him like I would Phoenix, but he just laughs and moves out of range.

I'm still smiling when I look forward again, and my arms go cold as all of the runes activate at once. A swathe of people are splitting for us to ride through, but Iotha, sensing my unease, dances to a halt. I soothe her out of habit, but my eyes are scanning.

"Rose?"

I ignore him. Our guards look to me, and then to the rooftops around us, beginning to encircle us.

Danger! the runes scream, but I don't need magic to warn me now. My own intuition is ringing like the palace bells.

Narrow buildings rise high around us, with clothing lines draped between each. Laundry hangs from them, blocking my view of the rooves, and I wait to see the latticed windows thrown open.

I suddenly feel very exposed atop my horse.

Something flashes out the corner of my eye, and I throw myself forward; the projectile whizzes past, landing with a solid *thunk* in the flank of Iain's horse. The gelding screams and rears, and Iain fights to hold his seat as men surge forward in the crowd.

Men with boiled leather armour and crude weapons.

Anger lights the fire in my belly, and I drop Iotha's reins to throw my arms wide. The dormant magic in my blood alights and I fight for control as it roars to the surface. Again, I seek out the buckles and blades of our attackers.

But the men do not flinch or wince, and I mentally scrabble to find something to bind my fire to. One of them closes in, and I see the knots of his armour, tightly lashed to his body. They're strongly padded underneath, enough to muffle any blow, bar perhaps a crossbow.

Their weapons are lacquered wooden spears, the tips sharpened to a point and fire-hardened; though I can warm the wood at its core, it will not burst into flame without my complete and utter focus. I grind my teeth at the obvious signs of my father's hand; he has rendered my fire whispering useless against his men. Instead, I draw the sword Olinius gifted me after our first meeting.

Around me, the cityfolk are screaming and attempting to flee. One of my guards pushes a woman out of the way, but the move throws him off balance, and a spearpoint finds the gap in his plates. He cries out as the assailant twists the weapon, using it to leverage him to the ground. I wrap my hand in Iotha's reins but she is already turning on the aggressor and, like Iain, I fight to keep my seat as the mare rears and lashes out with her hooves. I feel them connect and the man goes down, and I turn my horse to face the rest of the attackers, standing over the injured guard; my leg will render me useless if I dismount, and I have not an ounce of healing magic in me.

It's as though the streets are boiling—they've chosen their time to attack well, in the late afternoon when people are returning from outside the walls and heading to the taverns. I glimpse movement from the corner of my eye and throw myself back as a spear-point jabs where I'd been, but before the man can react, I grab the spear shaft and yank him forwards, meeting him with my new sword. The point enters his throat and bursts from the other side in a spray of red.

Then it's over, and I watch him slide from the blade, the spear limp in my grip. I snarl and cast it aside, my stomach heaving.

I've killed before, not just with fire—but with steel.

Iotha screams as a man grabs her bridle, pulling her snapping teeth from the second man who approaches from the other side. He's too close for me to bring my sword about but I clench my fist and lash out with the pommel. He dodges it, his hands grabbing my leg and pulling me from the saddle.

There is nothing to soften the blow, and I hit the cobblestones hard, feeling their rough edges break my skin. The air shoots from my lungs and I wheeze, struggling to rise. Before I can, my head is jerked back by rough fingers woven amongst my pinned hair. Suddenly, all I can see is the steel-grey sky and lines of drying clothes.

Thunder rolls through the clouds above.

Then, I am released. I fall forwards, the weight at my back suddenly removed as a sword flashes over me. Iain roars as he takes the man's head clean from his shoulders, then looks about for his next foe, standing over me. Maroon light flickers down the length of his blade, and the metal hisses as though it is being warmed.

War magic.

I haven't seen it since Petre granted the same boon to my weapon, though his cracked like ice. I know from experience the strength it grants; the man Iain just killed could not have wished for a cleaner execution.

The Thornsguard are beginning to push back the attackers, moving in a close-knit formation that lends itself to the configuration of the street. More crossbow bolts whiz past our heads and *thunk* into the surrounding buildings as the men realise they won't get close enough to stab me personally, but my fire flares again and the bolts that near me simply burst into flame and lose their momentum, the metal heads clattering to the street.

"Are you alright?" Iain is asking, holding out his free hand. I grab it and take a deep breath, knowing pain is coming. My leg screams as I stand on it unaided, and I make a mental note to always wear my brace while riding.

"Yeah," I say. "Just bruised and angry."

He pulls me behind him and meets the man who'd gotten through the Thornsguard with his sword. Wooden spear against war-magicked steel does not go well for him, and soon another body is flung to the cobbles. I try not to stare at his face, fearing I'll recognise him from the meeting in the lowhills if I do.

A distant sound meets my ear, distorted, but I turn towards it. Another attacker rushes us from the side, having hidden in the building until now, but his element of surprise is ruined by whatever noise he'd made. I step offline and cut him down, my blade slicing cleanly through meat and bone as Iain's magic flares.

"How did you know he was there?" Iain asks, and I frown at him.

"He made a hell of a noise coming out. You didn't hear it?"

Before he can answer, another group of men surges from an alley. Fatigue draws at my arms, unused to swinging a sword in recent memory, but the magic dancing on the metal lends its strength to me as well, and Iain and I fight together in unison. Our time at the Kingdoms table has taught us to read each other's intentions as though we shout them, and again and again, we act in tandem, an unstoppable force sharing one mind.

Then it is done, and I drop Olinius' beautiful, bloodstained sword to the cobbles, my fingers limp. The war magic fades from my body and my leg no longer howls, for it is numb. I stagger, unbalanced, but arms collect me before I can collapse entirely.

"You didn't wear your brace," Iain says, carrying me as though I weigh nothing.

"I never do," I gasp. "I'm starting to see its value now though."

A horse is brought to us, and I look about for Iotha, my heart in my throat, but the mare is gone. My eyes begin to burn.

"I'll send men to look for her," Iain promises, setting me on the ground and then boosting me into the saddle. "But you need to return to the palace, now."

I gather up the reins in one hand and look down at him. Neither of us need to speak the words that dance unspoken in the air.

They were here to kill us.

"What about you?" I ask, and my voice wobbles slightly; the battle-shock is wearing off, and soon my hands will shake, I'll likely vomit, and tears will be non-stop for the next few days.

"Once I've given orders to the men, I'll be right behind you. I promise."

I hesitate a moment longer, but Iain is stepping back into the swollen mass of soldiers, cityfolk, and corpses. Without his hand to steady me, I waver in the saddle. Soon, I'll fall.

I lean forward and my horse springs into action, the crowd parting for us to gallop along the street, away from the blood-soaked cobbles and the men that lie upon them.

CHAPTER TWENTY-FIVE

For the next few days, I am kept under constant supervision—for the first time, I do not feel like it's because of anything I've done.

Lillian seems to take the attack personally, keeping me wrapped in blankets and plied with tea. At first I'm surprised at her level of care, until I overhear her talking with another maid about how she's unlikely to find another station at this level. Strangely, it makes her ministrations easier to bear.

A personal guard is assigned to me, and I'm pleasantly surprised to find that it's Neal of house Undertoil. Our first meeting, outlining his duties and going over my schedule, ends in the two of us chatting amiably, until he clears his throat and apologises for his candour.

A report is drawn up, with Iain and I giving our statements in the same room. Netalia purses her lips as I describe the attackers.

"You speak as if you know these men," she says, and I hesitate.

"I've fought northmen before. I know their arms and armour."

She raises an eyebrow, while Iain, beside me, says nothing. He knows of the meeting in the lowhills, has likely come to the same conclusion I did—that this attack was led by them and the meeting was the cause. But he has not questioned me or pried for answers.

"Do you believe they were sent by House Araspire, or Kaya Aule?" Netalia presses.

"Why does it matter?" I ask irritably.

She closes her book with a snap despite the wet ink on the pages, and the gathered nobles jump. "I need to know which group of our enemies is advancing in their aggression."

The eyes of the room fall on me, and my nerves begin to hum. I fight the moment a little longer, then hear my own voice as though I'm not saying the words.

"The men were sent by my father, Kynan Alsain."

There is a beat of silence. Netalia's eyes widen, and she flicks a hand outwards as the other men in the room begin to whisper.

"This is now a private meeting," she says imperiously, her gaze on me. It takes a little while to clear the room, though finally the last leaves and the door is closed behind them. I can hear them muttering in the hallway, and know I've made a mistake.

Netalia breathes out sharply. "That would have been better off as a lie."

I grind my teeth. "You asked."

"Not expecting you to be stupid enough to admit who your father is, or that he's trying to kill you." She ticks off my actions on her fingers, and I wince, knowing she's right. "Kynan Alsain is a dissident these men know well. His outspoken support of House Araspire is common knowledge amongst the nobility.

"And now their queen is his daughter," she continues, pacing, "even if he hadn't attacked the pair of you, that knowledge would have been enough to seed turmoil throughout the capital." She turns in the centre of the room, facing us with her hands on her hips. "We need to crown you and announce your marriage. *Now*. Before this information has time to spread."

I think of the sheaf of husband profiles, and pale. "I haven't chosen—"

Another flick of her hand. "Then choose. And be quick about it."

"Enough." Iain rises, his form silhouetted against the tall windows. My rising panic calms as he looks over his soulmate. "Rose is in no condition to be making large decisions right now. The attack was sudden and brutal. She was forced to kill."

"She's killed before," Netalia replies dismissively.

"I don't enjoy it," I shoot back, unable to bite the words down. She meets my gaze evenly.

"Lotheria is an unkind world, Rose. The harsh reality of our lives demands harsh action be taken when necessary."

Her cold stare chills me to the bone, and I fumble for an answer. Before I can find it, she stabs a finger at me, and I recoil instinctively.

"I told you to get better at lying. Start practising while I clean up your mess."

She sweeps from the room, winning the argument by default. I swallow my anger and cross my arms, holding what little dignity I have left in my chest to stop the fresh tears.

"Should I not have told the truth?" I ask Iain.

He sighs, his shoulders slumping. "I do wish you'd told me first."

I huddle deeper into myself. "You never asked."

"I waited for you to tell me."

It stings. The truth of his statement brands me with a shame I'm tired of feeling, and I press the heels of my hands into my eyes as they burn.

When Petre was killed, it took the wall in my mind weeks to crack. This time, it only takes days.

The toll of killing, the knowledge that my father was behind an attack seemingly designed to end me, Iain's fresh disappointment, all weigh my shoulders down and, bizarrely, I think of my bedroom in the other world. I'd not spent a night there in years, the ability to climb the stairs leading to it taken from me by men like my father.

Loss grips me anew and the memory disintegrates. For so long, when I'd thought of 'home', I thought of the house that my mother and I shared for our entire lives. But now, I cannot fathom returning to that familiar street, the familiar door. Instead, I see my mother standing across a fire from me, beside a man I don't recognise, his words coming from her mouth, and I realise my house was never my home; my mother was.

He has taken everything from me, and more.

I clench my jaw but tears spill down my cheeks. An aching hollow opens in my chest so wide and deep I fear it'll never close.

A gentle hand draws me to my feet, and my cane falls aside. Strong arms enclose me fully, and I press my face into Iain's velvet jacket, wrapping my arms around him in return. The Headmaster holds me as the first sob escapes my lips, much like I'd once seen him hold my mother before betraying her, but even that image does not drive me to leave the comforting embrace.

"This world is harsh and hard, Rose. It demands more than what its people can give, and the life they are allowed to eke out is small and sparse in reward. I tried to change it. I got closer than most people, but I changed it only for those who would help me, support me, benefit me... and I know now that was wrong. You've shown me that was wrong." He sighs. "You are strong and loving in equal measure. You don't require proof of devotion or someone's mettle before fighting for them, shielding them. You are the change I tried to be. And if your father doesn't see that, it is his failing, not yours."

His words are gentle and kind, but a black monster rears its head inside me, and I pull away, choking on my words. "I cannot accept that, Iain. Don't say those things."

"They are true, Rose."

"No they aren't!" I stagger back a few steps, my leg aching as it hits the ground. "They can't be true, because if they were my father should love me! He should want me, no matter what!"

"The people in this world who truly care for you, will," Iain counters. "Rose, family is not bound by blood, it is the people you choose. They are the man or woman who stand above you in the rain so you do not get wet. They are the person who gives you the larger meal without a word because they know you are hungrier. *Family* is not born, it is forged. It is chosen."

His words stem the flow of despair in my chest, and I hold onto that kernel of peace for a second.

"I suffered many trials, living amongst the Harvenspars while not being one of them. But slowly I came to realise that a name, a claim, means nothing without love to bear it."

I have no words to answer his. My lips are unable to move, and so I merely look at the ground. I've never had anyone speak so openly about love and family. I don't know the proper responses. I think of the Greatcasts, and how important their name is to my rule. But I don't know them, and I don't love them. They are not my family—they are my potential allies.

Iain clears his throat, brushing a hand unconsciously over his now-spotted jacket. For some reason, the corner of my mouth twitches.

"It'll take me forever to clean this, you know?" he says, gesturing at the tear stains, and the tension melts from my body.

"I'm sorry," I tell him, and then I meet his eyes and our small mirth expires. "... I'm sorry."

He inclines his head. "I know. So am I."

In the wake of the attack, I begin seeking little moments to break away from my guard. When Neal is summoned to give a report on my movements, I hide in an alcove until his replacement assumes I'm in the library and strides down the hallway.

I breathe a sigh of relief, beginning in the opposite direction.

"My lady," someone says, and I look up to see a young man leaning against the top of the stairs. I do not recognise him, and the fire in my veins heats quickly. He begins to walk towards me. "I was hoping to catch a moment with you."

I take a step back as he draws near, and he bows deeply. "Prince Fayyaad, second prince of Gannameade."

I relax for a second, then tighten back up like a wound spring. A marriage prospect.

I'd have preferred an assassin.

Suddenly, I flush pink. The prince has never seen me up close before, certainly never with my cane, and I am struggling to climb the stairs.

"Rose Evermore," I reply in a small voice, and allow him to take my hand. His is not soft and warm; rough callouses shape a strong grip, and the surprise must show on my face.

"My mother is always trying to get me to use ointments and silk gloves," he says. "She dismays everytime I pick up a sword."

I'm smiling in spite of myself. "And yet we must."

"A queen who fights," he remarks. "Though that is unsurprising, given what I've heard."

We begin to walk. "What have you heard, Prince Fayyaad?"

"For starters, the reason for your cane." He gestures towards it, and my smile dies away, but he continues. "I heard that it was a wound received in battle, protecting the heir of a sworn lord."

"I guess that's true."

"The marks on your face were received in the same fight."

The man I'd burned alive had clawed desperate fingernails at my face. I haven't thought about them in a long time. I clear my throat.

"There is something admirable about a queen willing to sacrifice so much so young for her people." Fayyaad holds open a door for me, and bright sunshine spills through. I cross into a clear day, the first in weeks. "Though you should never have been asked to do so."

"No one did," I say, as he follows me onto the terrace. "I volunteered to help a friend."

The prince looks at me for a moment as fresh sea air gusts around us, laced with salt from the inlet. When Fayyaad doesn't answer, I walk to the wall and look out over Castor. The inner docks are busy today, with several long, shallow boats collecting their haul and preparing to row out to sea where their larger counterparts await. I know that they will be laden with grain and salt, our merchants taking advantage of the calm seas of Dawn Harbour to export the majority of their goods.

"What about you?" I ask. "Any scars with stories to tell?"

"A few." He rolls up the sleeve of his shirt and shows me a collection of scars that wind around his forearm. "Patrolling near the Kythas mountains, on the trail of some bandits that were giving the locals a hard time. Nasty *quazibs* that targeted the villages while the harvest was being brought in. We found their camp, and my men set about killing or capturing the murdering bastards."

I'd read about his battle with the bandit king. "You said 'your men'… so where were you?"

He grins. "Ah… I was hoping you wouldn't pick up on that." He holds out his arm again. "I was tangled in a fence one field over, being cut free from the wire by a farmwife. My horse saw a snake and bolted. Mine were the fiercest scars won that day."

I take his arm in my hands, examining the old injuries. "I bet that fence didn't know what hit it."

He chuckles. "It was hit by a panicked gelding and a prince who desperately did not want to end up the same."

That gets a laugh out of me. After a few moments, I realise I'm still holding his arm, but he doesn't pull away. I run my finger over one particularly deep wound, knitted together with softer scar tissue.

Fayyaad takes my hand, and turns it over. The oath rune stands out more than the ones I cut myself; Kaya did not have my skill with a knife. It is marred now, by the mark left from my father's blade. The prince runs his thumb over it. Goosebumps erupt on my skin.

"Bit chilly up here," I say, by way of an explanation he didn't ask for.

"What is it?" he asks of the scar.

I look at it, remembering a night time conversation in a tent. "A promise to someone I thought was a friend."

"Are they no longer?"

"I don't know," I tell him. "Last time I saw her, I don't think so."

He sighs, and gently releases my hand. "People are fickle creatures. Not every word they speak is directly how they feel. Actions over time are what prove a person's nature, not words spoken in anger or despair. If the friend returns to your side time after time, that should speak louder than anything shouted during an argument."

I watch birds circle the lower city. The sun is beginning to sink closer to the horizon, and when it disappears, I know they will light the great beacon in the lighthouse at the furthest point in the bay. It is one of my favourite times of day, and suddenly, I want to show it to the prince.

"You might be surprised to know that is not the first time I've heard those words of late."

He sits between the crenellations, my heart nearly stopping as I consider the drop at his back. "Power is a test for those who wield it. Not just for the individual, but those around them. When one gains power they often lose those closest to them, for its presence forces them to reveal their true nature, and few people are kind to the core."

The pool of self-pity is tempting to wallow in, but I spy a familiar look in his eye—as though he's seeing things far away.

"Who was it for you?" I ask quietly.

He doesn't answer for a long moment, tapping his fingers against the stone. "My best friend. She decided my person and friendship was less valuable than the path to power I now wielded, and decided to walk it, though it meant the end of us."

"I'm sorry," I say quietly. "I think I am experiencing similar."

He sighs. "Then you have my deepest sympathies."

We meet each other's gaze and smile tightly, then I look back to the city.

"If I can be forward, Your Highness," I begin, "why are you in Lotheria? It is a long way from Gannameade."

To my surprise, he doesn't hesitate. "My father, the Hassar, wants a treaty with your country. He has ordered me to lay the groundwork for the diplomats."

"Is that what we're doing up here? Preparing the way for our ambassadors by having an amicable conversation?"

"When I stepped off of that ship"—he points to the harbour, to a long ship with a sharp bowsprit—"I intended to try. I expected a soft woman from nobility and the right blood to rule this country with your strange rules around succession."

I want to respond, but say nothing. The prince sighs.

"In truth, it felt good to finally have a directive. 'Go here, woo her' might not seem like the noblest of quests, but it was something."

"Consider me wooed," I say before I can stop myself, and he laughs. "But I know what you mean. Sometimes I feel like a tool for the will of others. A figurehead, a piece on a gameboard. People meet me, but only see the others standing beside me."

"We live similar lives it seems. For that, you have my deepest apologies, as well as sympathies."

I say nothing for a moment, wondering what he'll say next.

The setting sun sets his dark skin to glowing, and his hair is untied, brushing against his collarbone in the seabreeze.

"You know, I've dealt with Lotherian nobles before," he says. "Bloodlines older than most cities, and an attitude to match."

I think of the Greatcasts, the matriarch I'm yet to meet. "They tell me my family is old blood," I say, joining him at the wall. I lean my cane against the stone, ignoring my aching leg; the sensation is too familiar these days.

"Of course," he says as though remembering. "You're from... The Other? Is that what you call it?"

I nod. "The Lotherian River is a portal to it. You don't have one in Gannameade?"

"No. Magic is very rare in any country outside of Lotheria. Most mages discovered off the shores of this continent are shipped to it for schooling."

Amisha had said the same, and Iain's story is a testament to its truth.

"My lady, if I may be so bold—"

"Rose, please."

"Rose. How can you rule a country you don't know?"

I look at him. It's a fair question, and one I don't have an immediate answer for. Instead, I turn my gaze to the lighthouse as the shadow from the palace reaches the far side of the inlet. Fayyaad follows my line of sight, just as flames bloom bright in the upper dome. Mirrors reflect the magical fire out over the water, casting a beam of light into the rapidly darkening ocean. All the ships in the harbour clang their deckbells in appreciation, and the sound carries to us on the breeze. A smile grows on my face.

"I'm learning," I say, as we watch the first sweep of the beacon over the harbour. "I have a good teacher."

"You and the Headmaster Iain are very close," he agrees. "I've seen you walking at his side. If I can be truthful, I waited until I saw you without him to make my introduction."

I look at him curiously. Iain has handled all of my noble meetings. "Why?"

Fayyaad turns to me. "Because I wanted to speak to *you*, not your advisor. You are the one I've been instructed to marry, not him."

The mention of marriage lances to my stomach, but I don't let it show on my face. "Are you sure? Iain takes a little while to warm up to, but he can play a mean game of Kingdoms and hold a conversation at dinner."

He laughs easily. "Iain is not the one set to receive a crown. You are."

"Ah." I look out over Castor. The sun is setting rapidly and more lamplight is being lit below, causing the streets to glow softly. Near the wall, I can see the fires of the refugees. "Is this another case of being pursued for the power I wield?"

"Of course it is." His frank answer catches me off guard and he stands, taking my hands in his. "Rose, I am the second son to a great nation, one which itself wields immense power. We have resources to share with you, soldiers and engineers, raw materials, and knowledge of warfare. We have long sought a tie to the greatest magical country on this planet, and now we have the ability to negotiate one.

"Yes, this is a case of power being traded for power, Rose. But the difference between whatever you've experienced, and this potential alliance, is that you walk into the agreement knowing it for what it is, with no falsities."

He's right; he is the better, more sensible choice for me to make. I look up into his eyes, and gently tug my hands free.

"You've given me much to think on, Your Highness," I say, and he bows, recognising his dismissal.

"Would you like me to escort you back inside?"

It's the perfect response, from a perfect choice. "Thank you, but no. I'd like to remain up here."

He takes a moment, then dips another bow and walks towards

the door as I turn back to the city. The great lighthouse beacon sweeps across the bay and I wish I, too, could have such simple guidance.

Turn your ship away, lest you smash upon the rocks.

Fayyaad's words echo in my mind, Phoenix's pledge right behind them. I squeeze my eyes close and wish I could look into their hearts, their souls, to find the words written upon them.

Phoenix potentially wanted me for the legitimacy only a crown could grant. Fayyaad had made no secret of that quest, though had promised benefits in return that would help us in the coming war.

Fayyaad is the reasonable choice. An alliance with Gannameade would be *beyond* valuable to us.

I sigh, sitting on the crenellations where the prince had, pulling my cane into my lap. The drop yawns on my left, but I feel steady and stable, tucked between ancient stone—though falling off the top of the palace would certainly earn me a place in the history books, perhaps for the wrong reasons.

Or maybe I could survive the fall—I'd done it before.

"They called me gods-touched, all last year," I say to the star-speckled heavens. "You dropped me on my face in the middle of the stable yard and I walked away from it. Then, you do nothing with me?" I dredge up her name from the depths of my memory. "Belatha. You had plans for me, I think. Surely it couldn't have been this."

There is no answer from beyond the wisps of cloud. I roll my cane between my palms, wondering how long I should wait for a response. But the god does not reply, and I shrug, turning my gaze back to the city and, by extension, the winding road up to the palace.

Suddenly, I sit up, the cane clattering to the rooftop. A caravan approaches the main gate, and I can see a flurry of activity as the guards on duty notice as well. I stand, leaning against the stone to try and see which banner they're flying.

My mouth goes dry as I recognise the sigil; my own, a golden rose on a maroon field.

The Greatcasts have arrived.

CHAPTER TWENTY-SIX

THE DOOR to the rooftop opens as I reach it, and Ser Neal bursts out, his chest heaving with exertion beneath his breastplate.

"My lady... ma'am." He inclines his head for split second. "The Greatcasts have just entered the grounds."

"I saw," I reply, caning towards him as fast as I can. My free hand goes to my hair—nothing a good brush can't handle. "Fetch Lillian. Send for Iain."

"I have," he replies, and a knot of anxiety unravels in my stomach. Inwardly, I thank the absent goddess for Ser Neal, wondering if she'll respond to gratitude above insolence. But neither gets a response immediately, and I follow the knight awkwardly down the winding staircase. "How did you know where to find me?"

"I checked the library first," he calls over his shoulder. "And the gaming room in the dungeons. The roof was third on my list."

A small smile grows on my face; not even Iain would have had such a list—he would've had me summoned to him instead, letting palace servants search the building from top to bottom.

"Have they asked for me?"

"Not yet. But they will, despite the hour." His voice is uncharacteristically sour, and I raise an eyebrow as we trek down the wide carpeted hallway of the upper floor. "To wake the queen and castle at this time..."

"It's only an hour after sunset," I point out.

"And the court is well closed and petitioners sent home," he shoots back, and my other eyebrow lifts. I'm quite liking this side of my bodyguard. "Yet the nobility arrives without notice, rousing every manservant and maid from their rest to tend to them."

He halts suddenly, and I waver, trying not to bump into him. "My lady—"

"I need to hear these things, Ser Neal."

"Of course."

But he falls silent as we enter my rooms, and Lillian hurries to set me at my dressing table. The soft candlelight allows us both to hide the weariness from our faces, and she quickly brushes the windswept tangles from my hair, pinning it at the base of my neck. My cheeks are ruddy from the seabreeze and she merely pinches them a bit before sweeping a brush over my lips.

"Scent?" she asks, her hand hovering over an array of delicate crystal bottles.

"Um, lilacs? Lilies? What do I normally wear?"

"Vanilla and bluebell," Neal answers from the door.

Lillian pauses, as do I, and then I nod. "Vanilla and bluebell, please, Lillian."

She dabs the crystal against my neck and wrists. The familiar scent rises to my nose. I look at Ser Neal out the corner of my eye, but he's studying the roof.

Lillian sends my guard out, and then helps me from my jacket, blouse, and breeches that I prefer for casual wear. She pulls a green silk gown from the press as I lace myself into a shift.

"What about the brace?" she asks, and my fingers halt on the lacings.

I eye my cane and the metal leg brace, resting next to each other at the end of my bed. The brace will allow me to appear more regal... normal. But it is a lie; I cannot walk unaided for long.

The cane is comfortable, easy, though if I allow myself to look at it too long, I find myself despising it and all it represents—all that I've lost. I don't wish to set myself up for loss tonight.

"The brace, Lillian, please."

She nods, and finishes helping me into my dress. As she fetches low boots, I begin to buckle my leg into the leather straps and metal rods of the brace. When I stand, I waver for a moment, and she holds her arms out to steady me.

"It's been a while since I've used it," I tell her, and she nods again.

"Take your time, my lady."

She helps me around the room, and the same warm flush of gratitude I'd felt for Ser Neal returns as she hovers around me.

"Thank you," I say, and she nods quickly and goes to move away, but I take her hand. "Thank you, Lillian."

She hesitates, looking at her hand in mine, then drops a low curtsy. "Your Majesty."

I smile tightly, and allow her to draw from my grip. I smooth the front of my gown, feeling the delicate golden embroidery against my fingertips. They shake, and I let out a nervous breath as the door opens.

"My lady, they've asked for you," Neal says.

I lift an eyebrow at him. "At this hour?" I ask in spite of myself, and he grins.

The warmth of his and Lillian's presence keeps me company as we walk to the throne room. I could've met the representative in a sitting room, one of my offices... anywhere with a lounge and a table for the tea service. But Netalia had cautioned against it.

"You must give yourself every advantage in convincing them of your heritage and bloodline," she'd instructed me a few days past. "The throne room carries more majesty than you can ever hope. Seating yourself upon the throne, without a crown on your head, suggests you've reached the forgone conclusion of their support."

Now, as Neal and I climb the wide stone staircase and two

manservants open the door to the hall, I grudgingly admit she was right, though my innards twist at the idea of her knowing that.

Torches are being lit along the walls, though the servants lighting them glance at us as we enter and hastily finish their work. I ignore them, gathering my skirts in one hand so I can stride along the length of the chamber towards the dais at the end. A chair is placed beside my throne so that I might easily speak to the person in it. The glass ceiling above allows the slender moonlight to wash everything beyond the pool of torchlight in pale grey, and I shiver.

"Shall I fetch a fur?"

"No, but thank you, Ser Neal."

I reach the throne and turn, allowing my skirts to fall before I sit. I smooth them out as the staff disappear through side doors, and the hall that had been bustling with activity suddenly falls silent, as though the room itself waits for our guests.

We needn't have rushed. The main doors do not open in the next minute, or the ten that follow. I rub my hands together, trying to work some warmth back into them, and hold up a single finger when Neal opens his mouth to offer the fur again. Slowly, impatience grows in my belly alongside the nerves. I drag up every memory of a lesson Netalia ever gave me, pinching my leg to fend off the heaviness of sleep.

The rattle of the door gives me a second's warning, jolting me into the present. A footman enters.

"Her Ladyship Gennorin McKorthus Greatcast of Numin, head of House Greatcast and Lady of Thornsgrove."

His voice echoes down the stone, followed by the sound of tapping. I place my hands on the arms of my throne and lean forward, straining to see in the gloom. Slowly, a hunched figure ascends into sight, struggling up the grand staircase, and I press my lips together. Until I got used to it, I struggled with that staircase too.

She emerges, one gnarled hand clutching a worn cane, the other gathering a fur about her shoulders. Her hair is the colour of steel, pulled to the nape of her neck, and for an old woman who has surely been travelling all day, she is surprisingly alert; her eyes bore into mine as though searching for a secret.

I clear my throat and straighten.

She doesn't pause, climbing the dais and drawing closer. As she sits in her chair, Neal steps forth.

"Her Majesty, Rose Lucinda G—"

"Say 'Greatcast', boy, and I'll put your knee out," the old woman snaps, pointing the tip of her cane at him.

I clench my jaw, but force myself to remain plain-faced. "Thank you for coming."

"You hardly left me a choice, did you?" Gennorin looks about. "No tea service? Biscuits?"

"I'm afraid they're still coming. We had to call the servants back from their quarters."

"Phagh." She stops looking, fixing on me instead. "Title a house out from under me, the least you can offer me is tea and biscuits in return, girl."

The Thornsguard in the room, Neal included, stiffen at that. I feel the barb bring sudden anger to the surface, but I don't react to it. I examine it like a new Kingdoms figure, wondering why this insolence wrought such a reaction—I've never cared for my title, or the reverence that comes with it... until now, apparently.

"You are referring to the Lyons," I say instead.

"Of course I am! Their family has been sworn to mine for generations, tithe and tax. My lands profited from theirs, their people from our protection."

"Protection?" I can't stop the word bursting forth, some of my annoyance burning within it. "The heir—"

"Was fine. Being schooled at the Academy until you dragged him north on a noble crusade." She turns her lined face to me finally, her eyes locked on mine. "The boy they took was a second son, and you traded the heir's life for his. No protection was given because none was required."

Silence falls in the throne room, her cruel words echoing. I feel my skin grow hot and know my chest is flushed, and dangerous words cluster on my tongue, aching to be said or shouted.

But then her silence and her gaze lingers a moment too long, and I recognise the game being played.

I sit back in my throne, the tension leaving my body. "My apologies, Grandmother. But I believed the Lyons require their own tax and tithe to fight the coming war, along with the ability to form and call their own bannermen."

She sniffs. "You did, did you? Under whose authority?"

I smile. "Mine."

"You do not have any authority," she counters. "You are a girl on strings, dancing like a marionette for your masters. Where are Iain and Netalia? Lurking in the halls to listen?"

"In their rooms, I expect. I did not see the need to summon them."

"No, you're right. Why do we need their voice when you speak with it anyway?"

A side door opens, and a footman enters carrying a tray of biscuits and tea. The sight of it turns my stomach, but Gennorin hooks her cane over the arm of her chair and serves herself, adding most of the honey to a single cup. She slurps noisily as I wait.

"Dismiss your men," she says, setting the teacup down on the tray.

My mask slips. "What?"

She flicks a hand. "Your men. The Thornsguard, as you've so ridiculously named them despite bearing none of my countenance. I will not speak freely with them present."

This wasn't *speaking freely?*

I hesitate, then look to Neal and nod slightly. He catches my eye for a moment, questioning the order, but I give him no other.

"Withdraw," he orders, and the other Thornsguard filter from the room. I keep my eyes on Gennorin as I hear his echoing footsteps leave the dais.

My grandmother grins. "You seem frightened of me, girl."

"You are the matriarch of a family I've never met and yet belong to, the ease of my reign entirely dependent on the support you may or may not give. Of course I am frightened of you, Grandmother, for loyal family seems few and far between these days."

Her smile fades. "You speak of your mother... of Lydia."

I pick at my nails, looking down at them instead. "Yes."

"Is she well?"

The note of concern in her voice makes me look up. "Last I saw, as well as one can physically be."

"And mentally?"

I take a breath, looking beyond her for a moment. "I did not bring you here to speak of my mother."

"You did not bring us at all, I might remind you. I came to seek recompense for our lost banners and lands."

"Yes, you did refuse my summons." I tap two fingers on the arm of my throne. "You housed one queen, why ignore the second?"

"Because I do not believe you to be she," Gennorin says, lifting her tea. "The line of the molten crown does not pass between blood, girl, but the worthy. Neither story nor rumour inclines me to grant you the latter. You are a child from the Other, barely a year into her schooling, who burnt a town to the ground and got her friend killed. You then fled the repercussions only to return a short while later claiming a crown on your head." She lifts a wrinkled finger and points at me. "I believe you to be naught but a liar, who tricked those around her into thinking she was the next gods-gifted queen merely because her mother was."

She's dangerously close to the truth. I reflexively turn my forearms as I lean forward, so the rune scars are pressed downwards.

"You know nothing of which you speak," I say quietly, hearing Netalia's words in mine and hating it.

"I know you brokered an alliance with a half-soul. I know you led them into Fairhaven with flame and fury, and the town lays in ashes because of it. I know what happened at Deadman's Keep and the magic you host in your veins." She clenches her jaw, staring into my eyes. "The north have stories of fire whispers who allow themselves to be controlled by their element. Fire burns, Rose, it consumes, and I believe it has hollowed you to ash and shame."

My heart pounds in my chest as my mind replays the columns of fire that swept over Fairhaven. I simmer as I take in the grand lady before me, dressed in her silks and fine furs, and my temper breaks slightly. "What would you know of shame?"

She barks a laugh. "I am the head of one of the great families of Lotheria. Our magical prowess is renowned and sought across the world, as is our friendship. We have negotiated marriages and treaties to strengthen our line since the beginning of this nation, and produced some of the most powerful mages in history. I have seen leaders rise and fall, and thought I could fathom the depths of their disgrace, but I did not know true shame until the girl who burnt Fairhaven claimed our name from under us."

My aforementioned fire flares, and I cannot hold it back. "You forget yourself."

"And you never knew yourself," she snaps. The edges of my vision darken as she raises a withered hand. "I wield the power of night, Rose. You of fire. Shall we test them against each other?"

Darkness blankets around us, but my hand shoots out and grabs hers. I can *feel* the magic she's working, and suddenly my vision is overlaid with strands of silver, highlighting the edges of every object before me. I can see Gennorin Greatcast as though a monochrome painting is brought to life.

"I did not bring you here to play games, Grandmother," I hiss, and the darkness fades. I blink, dispelling the white light from my eyes. "I brought you here to negotiate your support."

A slow smile grows on her face. "You may have gifts I have not yet seen, girl, but words are not one of them."

I release her, sitting back. She is right.

"Do you play Kingdoms, Grandmother?"

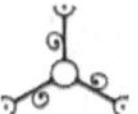

A small board is brought to us. We don't speak as it's set up, the footman hastily placing it on its own table. Boxes of pieces are brought to us; it won't be a full game, requiring the large table in the dungeons, but instead a death match played on a tiny Lotheria no bigger than a shoebox. Extra lanterns are brought over and set around us in a semicircle, so that we might be able to see the miniatures. At least, I will; Gennorin's eyes glitter with unusual magic, dark wisps playing at their corners. Her night magic allows her to see in the dark, but I am blind without the golden light of the lamps.

"You are ranked as Sentinel, I heard. Low or middle?"

"High," I respond, and catch a grunt of approval from my matriarch. "And yourself?"

"I never bothered with all that formal garbage. I play against others, and I beat them." She looks up at me. "You were hoping to form your strategy against my rank."

"Of course." I set up my end of the board smoothly. This smaller version does not have any of the magical elements of its larger counterpart. Instead, players must not 'see' the other's pieces, and randomly drawn cards dictate the changing weather conditions and diplomatic situations that may befall an army or settlement. Iain had drummed into me the importance of not looking at another player's pieces, a courtesy every good Kingdoms player must master. I could no sooner look at Gennorin's end of the board than I could willingly bite off my own finger. "Information is power in a game of Kingdoms."

"As it is in life," she intones, and sits back. "You may begin."

I'm not naive enough to believe it is because of my rank, on the board or off of it. We both know why this game is taking place; I know where she has built her settlement. Any other time, I would second guess my surety—but this is a battle for Numin, for Thornsgrove, and she wants to see how it would play out.

I use my first turn to assemble a swift cavalry, capable of riding the length of the continent and arriving battle-ready. I also send some foreign requests, usually answered by the table, but this time I draw cards, flipping over the worn wood to read the words inked on the back.

"In dim light, you look like her," Gennorin muses, and I place my card facedown.

"My mother?"

"Yes."

I nod, indicating her turn. I examine my own buildings as her hands busy. "Did you spend much time with her?"

"One visit, in the autumn of her final year. She came to Numin and I tested her."

"Like you're testing me."

"No, girl. I tested her as queen."

"Am I not to be afforded the same?"

The old woman looks up at me across the board, her beady eyes cloaked in shadow. "No."

I gnaw the side of my cheek, my leg beginning to ache beneath the brace. I bounce it lightly to work the blood back into it.

"Your mother was the first queen since Fleur. She was beautiful, kind, compassionate—her ties to our House, despite coming from the Other, were undeniable by all who met her. She was also smart as a whip. I suspect she got that from me."

She flicks her hand, and I take that as my cue. My little cavalry army, buffed by certain agreements, is ready to leave the city. I take an extra movement to add some more perks, opening the boxes the particular miniatures are housed in. I remove them from moulded velvet, placing them on the board.

"Lydia was beauty, grace, and empathy. She busied herself in the gardens as a vine tangler, and allied herself with the matriarchs of the other great families in a single dinner. She was the perfect queen Lotheria had been waiting for." Gennorin leans forward as I put down my last figurine. "She was everything you do not seem to be."

The little soldier falls over. I pick it up with shaking fingers. "You do not know me."

"You are the Headmasters' creature. For a long time I suspected they killed your mother upon her return. I never found out if that were true."

Her following silence indicates she'd like an explanation. I do not offer one.

If Gennorin Greatcast finds out they blooded my mother, she has the pieces to finalise her suspicion of how the crown passed to me. She will figure out I took the queensblood.

She will also never forgive my working with the Headmasters. She does not believe me capable of shame, let alone the willingness to fix it.

My leg bounces faster.

I draw a few more cards, read the words upon them, and place them down. "Your turn, Grandmother."

She busies herself. I look at the closed doors at the end of the throne room, wondering who stands outside of them. *Where is Neal? Has he dismissed the staff?*

I doubt it. Until this negotiation is concluded, no one in the palace will sleep.

Her turn passes in silence, and I offer up prayer of gratitude. Nerves thrum throughout my chest; this match of Kingdoms is the only chance I have to show Gennorin I can lead, that I can be the queen Lotheria needs.

She cannot leave without naming me 'Greatcast'.

My cavalry begins to traverse the greatroad, and my entire turn is spent travelling, with the exception of a few more cards drawn. The conflict between our armies is mere minutes away, and I fight to keep my expression plain.

"Your mother was courting a man during her time at Numin," Gennorin says, and my eyes flick to her. "She thought I didn't know."

My leg stills at the mention of my father. His name has only just been released to the nobility of Castor. Did it reach her ears so soon?

"He was from Orthandrell—not even a mage, my sources tell me. A non-magi dwelling in the shadow of the Araspires, believing their lies and sucking up their vitriol like marrow from a bone." She clasps her hands together, leaning back. "I had him investigated extensively, once Lydia left the castle. My spies brought back paintings of his likeness."

"Let me guess," I say, moving my horses up the board. *Nearly there...* "I look like him."

"No, you do not, and be thankful. He had a dreadfully dour countenance. But my spies are great artists—they capture more than appearances." She moves her pieces into view, and I sit back; pikemen, holding long spears in formations designed to stop cavalry. "They are experts in capturing the spirit of a person. The determination. The cruelty. The vindictiveness... these are the traits I believe you share with him."

"You looked at my pieces." Anger heats my chest.

She shrugs. "It was available information, girl. A good queen would've used it."

"It's against the rules!"

Gennorin retrieves her cane and stamps it on the ground. "Do you believe war is fought with rules? I should call you 'naive' if it didn't have such gentle connotations awarded it. You are a fool, girl, believing the world to behave as it has been commanded to in your presence, bowing to a crown you do not wear and never shall, if I have anything to say about it. You were given information, and you ignored it in the spirit of 'rules'. I did not, and I have won."

Her voice echoes down the hall. I flex my hands, curling them into fists, and then rest them on the arms of my throne.

"It is my turn, Grandmother."

"Oh, yes." She sits back in her chair, reaching for her tea. "A good queen would see her men die in her name, for her committed stupidity."

I reach forward, but my hand does not reach the small wooden horses of my cavalry. Instead, I pick up a box and open it, revealing intricate miniature ships resting in their velvet. Gennorin says nothing as I place them at the bay east of Numin, where the Lotherian River empties into the sea.

I lay a single card in the middle of the board, beside our pieces poised to fight a bloody battle.

Alliance accepted.

"You never learned all this 'formal garbage', including not to look at another player's pieces, so I will layout the rest of my strategy." I draw a finger from my ships to the city of Numin. "While my cavalry travelled, I spent the rest of my turns brokering a military alliance with Surac in the east. My ships, carrying Suracen troops from their capital of Zhul, will land in the undefended bay and march on the city within a turn. You did not build defences and sent your army down the greatroad to meet mine. Short of your citymen being rather good with rocks and arrows, Numin will be mine before your pikemen, wounded and tired after battle with my cavalry, are able to return. I'm offering you the chance to concede, Lady Greatcast."

Her eyes dart over the board, and I wait to see if she has anything up her sleeve. I have another wave of ships incoming, with siege mechanics and equipment onboard, but I calculated she would only think me simple enough to prepare a counterattack for the obvious cavalry charge. Still, nerves cause my fingers to tap restlessly against my throne.

"You conducted your alliance negotiations through the cards," she murmurs. "The only way I could not see it."

"Yes."

"Hmph." She sits back, working her jaw. Defeat stings—I've

felt it before—and everyone reacts differently to it. It took many losses to Iain before I stopped feeling the urge to blast the board into ashes at the appearance of his much larger army.

"As I suspected," she begins, sweeping a hand over the board, taking in our army placements. "Deception. Deceit. The two tools you deferred to immediately."

My mouth falls open. "I *won*, Grandmother, using the mechanics—"

Gennorin stands, pointing her cane at me. "You are *his* whelp, through and through. I will not suffer to see you sit on a throne with a crown granted by my good word, much less with my name attached to yours. My magic might be night but yours is darkness— and you will consume this land with your corruption and desperation to prove to yourself that you are not the girl who burnt a town, who colluded with the enemy and brought them to the doorsteps of your friends and family, and who actively betrays the memory of her mother by befriending the people who have ruined this country."

I stand as well, my fists clenched. "I beat you at a game, Gennorin. You lost within five turns. How well do you think you will fare on the real battlefield?"

"Oho! Threats and blustering—the Headmasters have taught you well. That is their first response as well." She gathers her fur around her, shaking her head. "I came here to lay eyes upon the girl who claims to be Lydia's daughter, who stole my sworn lords from under me, and who promises war with the north in coming years." She looks me up and down. "And when I return home, Thorns- grove shall take up its war mantle and my remaining bannermen will be called. When your armies march north, we shall see who claims the lands they burn."

I say nothing as she turns and steps off of the dais. Fury battles in my chest as the tapping of her cane narrates my defeat, as the matriarch of my family, one of the ten noble Houses, leaves the throne room promising retribution. I close my eyes and let the breath leave my lungs, tears stinging the corners of my eyes as the doors slam closed behind her.

I am so lost in my own despair I nearly miss the clatter of wood on stone, followed by a resounding *thud*.

I stare at the closed throne room door for a long moment. Then I gather my skirts and run, ignoring the brace cutting deep into my leg, the rods and bolts holding me upright taking their price in blood. I reach the doors and pull one open.

"Grandmother?"

Silence echoes in my ears. The staircase before me sweeps to the lower level to the wide foyer.

A cane lies halfway down.

My mouth goes dry. I approach it warily, my footsteps heavy. I pick up the cane, and finally look beyond it.

She must have hit the ground with tremendous force. Her limbs lie sprawled, one leg twisted and obviously broken. As the drumming of boots on flagstones reach my ears, I reach her body and kneel beside it, resting a hand on her cheek.

"Your Majesty!" Neal reaches us first. "Is that—what happened?"

"She... fell," I say quietly. "She must've tripped down the staircase."

My guard stammers for a few seconds. "Are you sure?"

I nod. "I heard it as she left."

I draw my fingers over her eyelids, closing the wide, staring eyes. I've gone numb.

We were just playing Kingdoms together.

Neal is saying something as other staff and guards gather around us. Their cries of disbelief are muted in my ears.

"What?"

"Sorry, my lady. It's not my place."

"It's fine, Neal."

"I just..." He pauses. "I only asked, 'what did she say?'"

I think to our game, our sparring of words, and the look in her shadowed eyes as she'd lost.

You are his *whelp*.

And then, another, hated voice whispers in my ear. And I realise I have a solution to my greatest problem.

"She..." I clear my throat and take a breath. The gathered crowd goes silent, the maids and footmen and guards waiting for me to speak. I look at Neal.

"She named me Greatcast, and heir of Thornsgrove."

CHAPTER TWENTY-SEVEN

I MISS my grandmother's funeral.

The brace was never designed for running; when I ran the length of the throne room, fear had fed the adrenaline in my veins and drowned out the screaming of my nerves. When Neal finally picked me up off of the floor, from beside Gennorin's body, my leg buckled and collapsed completely.

I hear the mourning trumpets from my bedroom, as I stare at the canopy of my bed and my leg is prodded, twisted, and pressed.

"Anything?" Carrier Bayde prompts, and I shake my head. He purses his lips and removes his spectacles. "You've done a marvellous job on it, Your Majesty."

"She wasn't thinking," Netalia says smoothly, standing from my dressing table where she's watched the carrier go about his work. "She was full of concern for her grandmother."

"And rightly so, apparently." The carrier looks to the sky outside, the steel-grey clouds threatening rain. "What a terrible thing to happen."

"Yes, it is." Netalia folds her hands before her. "How is her leg?"

Bayde sighs. "She's damaged it further," he says, and my

stomach turns. I swallow hard. "The bolts from the brace cut off her circulation further."

Silence falls across my bedchamber.

"Can I walk?" I ask finally, propped against my pillows.

He meets my eyes. "It's still too early to tell—"

My heart sinks. "Tell me."

Bayde rests a hand on my leg. I can't feel it. "The injury was severe to begin with, the repair work of very low quality. The trauma to your leg required a senior carrier, and there were none on hand in Riverdoor. Rokun, the Lyon's carrier, did his best at a moment's notice, but his best is my mediocre. Your insistence to walk, run, climb stairs... these have further damaged the limb, Rose. This is very serious."

I let out a shaky breath, blinking away tears. Netalia stands like a pillar of marble at the corner of my bed.

"Where's Iain?" I ask her quietly.

"Attending the funeral," she replies. "We decided one of us should in your stead."

"And you drew the short straw?"

She pauses for a moment. "He has been the one most often seen at your side. We assumed that, with your inability to attend, he was the closest to a representative you currently have."

I nod, turning my attention back to Bayde. My hands begin to tremble, so I grip the covers. "Will I lose it?"

The carrier hesitates, then shakes his head. "If it is treated properly over the next few days, then no. But I cannot promise that with any degree of surety."

I nod, blinking tears onto my cheeks as I stutter a breath of relief. "Okay."

He leaves a hand on my leg for a second longer and, as Netalia turns away, he mouths 'alright?' at me. I nod and manage a shaky smile, and he stands. "I'll write up your treatment plan. It will be intensive."

"She has maids," Netalia says, drawn away in her thoughts, her hand on her chin. My eyes go to her, and a dark anger simmers.

The carrier who tested the children in my area was a drunken idiot.

I'm told he fell down a flight of stairs.

Caution had warned me not to say anything as she'd spoken the words in her tearoom, but my suspicion had grown to certainty.

Netalia had killed my grandmother the same way she killed her district carrier.

It would have been an easy thing for her to listen to our conversation, to be a witness to my latest failure. I had been instructed to placate Gennorin Greatcast and win her support for the throne, but instead I had incited her to near open rebellion. The Headmistress would've done what was necessary to continue on their current path.

My hand curls into a fist atop my blankets, a welcome reprieve from the worrying numbness of my right leg. For a moment, I imagine calling the fire and unleashing it upon the woman who dogs my nightmares with her poison, her words, and her lies. But then the door opens as Bayde straightens from his writing, a sheaf of papers in one hand, and the moment passes.

Iain enters, resplendent in black velvet. His hair is windswept yet tidy, his beard combed, and he removes a heavy cloak to hand to the footmen who admitted him. The salted white hair at his temples grant him the look of seasoned wisdom, and for a moment, I could believe him to be king.

His eyes fall on me and, for a second, I loathe my relief at seeing him. Then tears flood my eyes, and he strides to my bedside, going to one knee.

"Sorry," I whisper, wiping at my cheeks.

He grips my hand and squeezes it, turning to Bayde. "Your prognosis?"

The carrier repeats what he'd told Netalia and I. Steeled to hear the words, they don't seem as bad a second time, but Iain's hand tightens on mine.

"What can we do to improve her chances?" he asks, and Netalia turns to her soulmate.

"She won't lose the leg. She'll be fine."

Iain ignores her. "Will she be in pain?"

Bayde's eyes flick to me. "She's always in pain. It is likely she will continue to be, in some capacity."

Iain turns to me, the question in his eyes. I shrug. "I tell you. It's not my fault if you don't listen."

He's silent for a long moment, and I brace for an argument. "I'm sorry. I didn't realise," he says simply, and I relax.

Netalia's eyes linger on us, heavy like a physical weight, and I lift mine to the carrier, inviting him to continue.

"There is an ointment I can make up," he says. "I'll apply some before I leave, then will send more up tonight. It needs to be applied every four hours, even during the night. It's harsh stuff... you'll need to wear gloves."

I'm nodding, but Iain cuts me off. "Of course. What else?"

"Regular massage will help. Stimulation of the remaining nerves and returning blood flow to the site is crucial for the next forty-eight hours."

I've gotten pretty good at massaging my leg. "Sounds like sleep is optional for the next few days."

"You must rest," Iain says. "I will tend you."

The room goes utterly quiet.

"She has maids—" Netalia says again, but Iain raises a hand.

"Is there anything more, Carrier?"

Bayde looks between them, but apparently decides to defer to Iain. "I have a student who will be able to work magic into the leg. It is delicate work, but I trust her. She is training to become my apprentice."

"Why not you?" Iain asks pointedly.

Bayde inclines his head. "I have the clinic to oversee."

Iain's face darkens, but I put my hand on his arm. "It's fine. Dena can tend me."

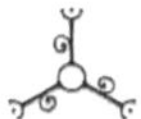

My former friend arrives at my chambers as the day turns to evening. She enters, her hair tied back, her Academy uniform replaced by white cloth breeches and a loose blouse. She sets her books and boxes on my dressing table, then turns to me.

"Hello," I say quietly.

She dips a quick curtsey. "Your Majesty."

I lean back against my headboard and take a deep breath. She begins to roll up her sleeves and draws nearer.

"Dena." She sits in the chair placed beside my bed. "I've earned your ire, I know it. I deserve it, and you've spoken as such. I know you won't forgive me—"

"Then why do you ask?" She reaches for my leg, but her hands are gentle as she works my bruised skin.

"Because I miss you. I miss all of you."

"Funny," she remarks. "As you've not sent for us once."

I consider that for a moment. "Would you have come?"

She pauses, light glimmering around her fingers. "Probably not, no."

I don't respond, letting her work in silence. Her lips thin further as she examines my leg, and I realise she's never been this close to the injury. I can feel the magic she's working into it warming me slightly, and if I were more relaxed, I'd be drifting to sleep. But I'm watching her face as she catalogues the extent of the damage.

"What was it?" she asks quietly.

"A mace." I look at the withered remains of my calf. "I believe he aimed for my head, but I moved forward at the last moment and he adjusted."

Dena's hands still, and I can feel her gaze on me.

"I waited to die. In the mud, far from home and everyone I loved." I look up and catch her eyes. "But I returned, thanks to him."

"Petre," she murmurs, and I nod. She turns from me, continuing her work. "You loved him."

It's half a question. I think on it.

"In a way. He was a good friend. I fancied him." It seems like decades ago through the fog of grief. "Maybe if he'd lived, I could've grown to love him properly. I certainly wanted to try."

Magic sinks beneath my skin, easing the ache that refers up my body and into my skull. She sits back as the light plays over us both.

"I'm sorry," she says finally.

Old tears threaten, so I just nod in acceptance.

"It's no excuse for what I did," I begin. "I know—"

"Sometimes excuses are just that," she says. "And sometimes they are important context." She begins her ministrations again. "I do not forgive you, Rose. You burnt a town to the ground and killed people. You brought ruin to our doorstep and uprooted us from the home we'd just grown to love. But your grief lends a certain allowance of grace to your actions."

"You sound very different to the Dena I used to know," I say quietly. "From the Dena I met in the gardens only a few months ago."

"You have your darkness," she replies, her hands working. "And I have mine."

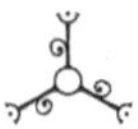

When she leaves, we do not part as friends; she curtsies goodbye and waits for dismissal, and I know that while the fracture may be understood, it is not—and likely never will be—healed. It twists a knife I thought I'd removed deeper into my heart, further marking me as another version of myself from the one who'd arrived at the Academy.

"Your thoughts are absent tonight," Iain says, moving his pieces down the board.

My eyes flick to him. It's nearly midnight, and we're waiting for the ointment to take effect. Bayde had cautioned supervision while his medicine worked. My leg is warming as though I'm holding it over a fire—though that sensation is getting harder and harder to recall. I shift uncomfortably.

"I was thinking about Gennorin," I say.

Iain hesitates as he draws a card. "Ah."

"I've been close to death before. I've been the cause of it. But..." My sentence trails off. Iain finishes his turn and looks at me, the candlelight throwing his eyes into shadow. "Violent death in the streets or on the battlefield is one thing, seeing someone you're related to thrown to the bottom of the stairs is another."

"I know it must have been shocking to see," he says quietly. "But, Rose, she was an obstacle."

"That doesn't mean she had to be killed."

Iain picks up a miniature, a little queen with a crown on her head. He hands it to me. "Rarely does a crown rest on a head without blood being spilled in its name."

I pause, the figure in my hand. "That's very pretty. Did you think of that yourself?"

"Gennorin's death bothers you."

I eye him. "Of course it does."

"Do you see why it had to happen?"

I shift, trying to stretch my leg. "She wasn't going to back our claim. She was going to oppose any moving of troops near her lands."

"And in doing so, send hundreds of men to their death." Iain looks at me. "Her own prevented that."

Just a small twisting of reality, Netalia had said.

"For peace and power," I mutter.

"And now you are the Lady Greatcast. You hold the lands that would've been turned into a bloodbath to assure a spited old woman she still had a part to play in Lotherian politics." He returns to the board. "For the price of one lie, Rose, you bought the lives and safety of every family in Numin."

"Yes," I say. "Just in time to toss them in the *right* war, right?"

He sighs. "You are insolent this evening."

"No." I move my miniature army up the greatroad. "I'm correct."

He says nothing. As his turn begins, I massage my leg with both hands. Five days of intense treatment, and the numbing ache subsides slightly from the strongest painkillers Iain and Netalia will allow.

Calloused hands, gloved in cotton, replace mine, and Iain nudges me out of the way. "This is why I'm here."

I don't say anything, but let him press and squeeze my leg. It looks tiny in his huge hands, but I can feel the bound up knots and tension begin to move around. It's not instant relief, but I know from experience that it'll feel a lot better in the morning.

"Is that good now?" he asks, and I nod.

"Thanks."

He rubs the back of his hand against his eyes, and the clock strikes one. I realise he'll have to be up in a few hours, covering my duties so I can sleep as much as possible. Still, I feel there is more to say and, selfishly, I want to keep him here.

"Netalia pushed her."

Heavy silence falls over the room. Iain removes his gloves, buying himself time. I wait, my heart thrumming in my chest, sensing a fight and building myself up.

"Contrary to your belief that we are attached at the hip, I cannot say, one way or another, if she did."

I snort. "That's diplomatic."

"It's the truth." Iain sits on the chair beside my bed, ignoring our Kingdoms game, and leans forward. "Rose, I was not there when your grandmother fell down the stairs. That's all I can promise you."

I eye him. "But Netalia was."

"Not to my knowledge. She told me she was going to walk in the gardens. I was meeting with Lord Olinius about your crown."

I chew on that information for a moment, but Iain isn't done.

"Besides... as we just spoke about, your grandmother's death bought the lives of thousands. Soldiers, yes, but families on the moors, in the hamlets and villages who would've been in the way of any marching men. This *needed* to happen."

I meet his eyes. "Gennorin Greatcast was never going to leave Castor alive."

He sits back. "We needed her cooperation."

"Or her death."

The sick thing is, I can see his point. It rails against every fibre of my being, churning every moral I thought I had into uncertain muck.

"Rose... I would hope that by now you trust me, in a sense," he says quietly. "Once I may have declared her death earned, necessary... but now, I only feel the loss prescribed by oncoming war. The decisions I made long ago, the actions I took, are coming full circle. And it is not fair that you are caught up in the web—but by some set of circumstances, you decided to become queen. The current diplomatic landscape, no matter who designed it, is now your inheritance."

I look at him. He meets my gaze steadily, but without expectation. He will let me tell him if I want, and if I don't, he will go on allowing me to believe he doesn't know. But I am tired of living lies—they make me feel like I belong to Netalia.

"How long?" I whisper.

"It took me longer than I'm proud of," he says, and I can't help my small smile, but it trembles as I wait for his reaction. "But your mother being Lydia Greatcast, your prowess in runes... I'll believe in a lucky coincidence if it serves me, but at some point, it pays to be suspicious of good fortune."

We look at each other a moment longer, then I break eye contact and begin to pull back one of my sleeves. In the candlelight, the scars are near impossible to see, but for once, he is looking for them, and for once, I am showing them. His hand cups my elbow as he examines the runes.

"How did you know which ones to choose?"

"I found a book," I say in a small voice, "in Arno's office. He never burnt them, as you commanded."

He seemingly pays my words no mind, turning my arm this way and that. I watch his face closely, my heart slamming in my chest. *This* is the moment I've been dreading for nearly a year— Iain Nevalas, Headmaster of the Academy and shadow ruler of Lotheria for over a decade, discovering my greatest secret.

That I falsified the power of Lotheria's great queens and stole the blood he'd once taken from my own mother. I have no right to the crown he's about to seat on my head, the crown that we've already killed for.

The crown that belongs to the mother I brought here, only for her to turn on me when she did.

"Are you mad?" I ask, and hate how pitiful it sounds.

He places my arm back on top of the covers. "Rose... I told you why Netalia and I took control of the Lotherian government after the Dawn Harbour Massacre."

"Because someone needed to."

"Yes." He looks at me, the lines on his face thrown into deep relief by the candle. "Lotherians wait, Rose... it's all they've ever done. They wait for a queen to come and save them, whenever the stars align and the tides allow and an absent goddess bestows great power on a single woman on the continent. They roll the dice with leadership and doing so resulted in a system that thrived on instability, that favoured the already wealthy, and granted more influence to those who already had it. I played my role in that. It's true that it went to my head, and I acted poorly—"

"Poorly?" I interrupt. "Iain, you were prepared to behead my best friend for existing."

He doesn't rise to my heated tone. "I know. I, and Netalia, had become addicted to ruling, and he threatened that rule. I was wrong. I hope one day I get to tell him that."

"He may not forgive you."

"As is his right." He leans forward. "Rose, when I realised what you'd likely done, I was angry with you. I felt cheated, spited... I felt as though you'd returned out of selfishness, to grab at the throne and deceive the people of Lotheria."

I swallow. "But you're not angry now."

One corner of his mouth twitches. "How could I be, when you've done exactly what I did in my youth? You didn't wait, Rose. You seized the opportunity to grant yourself a better position."

I hadn't though. I consider telling him I originally wanted to crown Kaya, to shake up the ruling nobility and force them to confront their mistreatment of the Halvers. But my oath rune remains benign on my right palm, and I stay silent.

"I'm not angry," he says, and I take a deep breath. He collects my hand and squeezes it. "I'm not angry, Rose. You have the makings of one of the greatest practitioner of runes in our time, you channelled your grief into change—though, not in the healthiest manner," he amends, and I can't help a little smile through growing tears. "You are so young to go through what you did."

"I burned a village," I whisper.

"I brought a country to the brink of war," he replies. "We have no business being at the top, Rose, yet we are. I've given up on trying to rule forever, for you, because I believe we can make good change together. I still want to try that, if you do."

I blink, and the tears streak down my cheeks. He wipes one away with his thumb, and pulls me against him. I lean into him, tiredness suddenly sapping my strength.

The lie is out. I no longer have to fight the daily fear that he'll somehow discover my secret. It had taken more from me than I'd realised, because at some point during all of this, I have come to care what Iain thinks about me.

I pull away, wiping my eyes. "I'm a bit tired. I might try and sleep, if that's okay."

He nods, looking away. "Yes, I should leave you to rest. I'll be on the cot."

"Okay."

Iain stands, collecting the medical paraphernalia around my bed. "Wake me if you need me, Rose. I'll be right here."

"Thank you."

I wait for him to settle on the cot, then snuff the candle out beside me with a thought. And as I lay in the darkness, I bask in the warmth of having someone nearby who cares for me with no secrets between us.

CHAPTER TWENTY-EIGHT

A week later, one particular morning dawns with a flurry of activity. Women swarm the room, Lillian and Netalia at their helm and, though I spent the previous two days tremulously wobbling on a tailor's stool, wrapped in measuring tape and stuck with pins, there is concern as they recheck me.

Lillian had fastened me into the brace before anyone else arrived, and already I can feel it numbing, the cold steel biting into my freshly-healed skin. Old pain has already begun to sprawl from it, and my eyes fall on the cane leaning against my dressing table. Today, I will have both; it is the only way I can walk.

"Rose." Netalia appears in front of me, her hands clasped. She is a moment of stillness in a room of activity, a liferaft in a raging ocean of silk, lace, and perfume. But I recall my grandmother's sprawled body across the flagstones, and meet her eyes blankly. "Do you remember what we went over?"

My mouth is dry, but I nod. "Yes."

She pierces me with that hawkish gaze. "Are you alright?"

"Do you care?" I ask her frankly.

Netalia blinks. "You are to be our queen. Of course I care about your wellbeing."

"Of course. How could I have ever doubted?"

My eyes remain on the woman as she leans to speak to Lillian, on the hands that likely pushed Gennorin Greatcast to her death. I curl my fingers into a fist, and the candles in their holders rise a little higher.

Despite her link to Iain, I cannot forgive her. Bitter rage fills my stomach as she stands at the door and meets my eyes easily. I look away, and the candle flames die down. I have not forgotten her deadly touch, the poison she can wield.

Lillian laces me into a dress; a long, dark blue gown with layers upon layers of sheer fabric. A tight belt pulls it in at my waist, the neckline plunging deep. My arms are left entirely bare, which makes me nervous until they approach with the cape made of the same blue material, with well-tooled leather pauldrons sitting tight on my shoulders. Somehow, Netalia has fashioned a dress that covers all the scars, bar the ones on my face.

"They should see these," she'd said, her fingers against my cheek. My skin had crawled at her touch. "Gifted to you by the northerners you killed. It will set the example of the queen we intend you to be."

And the scars on my back, the ones she and Iain had gifted me a lifetime ago, are conveniently hidden.

I step down from the footstool, grateful for the sturdy blue boots I wear; a chunky metal leg brace is not conducive to tiny, delicate footwear. I keep my balance as I'm guided towards a chair.

They brush and tug and pull at my hair, binding it tightly in a bun at the back of my head. Makeup comes next, though true to Netalia's words, they leave the scars bare. I suffer every touch of an unfamiliar woman, my eyes on the rain-soaked city outside the window. I tap my fingers against my thigh under the cover of my cape, counting to myself.

There is a knock at the door, and the entire room stills.

Netalia glances at me, then sweeps across the carpet and opens it. A footman waits on the other side, nearly bowed beneath the amount of flowers he carries.

"For Her Majesty," I hear him wheeze.

Two maids rush to Netalia's side and relieve the footman of the bouquet. They're carried to my desk and, even from here, their heady scent washes over me.

"Who are they from?" I ask, and Netalia approaches.

"There's no card. But an arrangement of this size could only be the prince."

A few of the maids give a little giggle, and I look between them, trying to spot the joke.

"Why would Fayyaad send me flowers on the morning of the coronation?" I ask, sitting still as Lillian continues her work.

"He tries to convince you. From what I understand, he made a strong argument for his candidacy as your kingsmatch."

"He did," I admit. "Prince Fayyaad is the sensible choice of my suitors."

Lillian diligently paints on, and the maids busy themselves tidying up, but I can feel the eyes and ears on us.

"He is," Netalia agrees. "A second prince is still powerful, and ties to Gannameade would do you credit."

Lillian moves away, and I pick up a paint pot to fiddle with. "I agree."

Netalia meets my eyes in the mirror. "Have you chosen?"

I hesitate, then twist in my seat so I can look at her. "I won't be naming my king today, Netalia."

For the second time in as many minutes, the room stills. Netalia's clasped hands fall apart.

"What?"

I turn back to the mirror, but Lillian doesn't approach, standing frozen with her brush. "I will not name my king during the ceremony."

"You *must* choose a king—"

"And I will. But not today." My eyes flick to hers in the mirror.

"Besides, all of my suitors, and my subjects, are to be at the feast after the coronation. I will get to spend more time with them, see how they engage in social settings, and how they treat my advisors and friends."

She straightens. "Iain and I are to be there as well."

"I said 'advisors'."

A slight victory thrills through me as she purses her lips, and her eyes dart around at the listening maids. She will not challenge me—not here, not this close to the ceremony, though part of me desperately wishes she would.

I chose my moment well, and I thank the mysterious flower giver for the opportunity.

"Very well," she concedes finally. "Are you ready, Rose?"

The room stills, and my momentary bravado leaves me. I want to shake my head and open my latest book—*Harriot's Tome of Treaties*—and curl up in my window seat for the next eight hours.

But they're waiting for my answer and there's only one I can give.

"I am."

The stairs down are an ordeal. Pain shoots up my leg with every torturous step, referring into my hip. I have a death grip on my cane, and lean heavily on Ser Neal who has come to escort us.

I can hear the rumble of voices as we reach the bottom of the staircase that leads into the main hall. I stand where my grandmother died, and my hands shake as I nod dismissal to Ser Neal and Netalia. They climb the stairs before me, and disappear into small hallways either side of the grand set of double doors, where a pair of footmen wait for me to approach.

The stairs yawn above me, and I may as well be facing a climb to the summit.

I start slowly, letting my stronger left leg lead. I place the cane and lean on it heavily as I draw my limp right leg after it. My shoe taps the stair before I place it, and I know I'm dragging it up.

My cheeks burn as tears grow in my eyes. I've had over a year to come to terms with my disability, but frustration grows quickly and often. I still remember the joy of running, of sword fighting, of riding with two strong legs beneath me; the Chamber Beneath had gifted me those sensations briefly, now lost to me forever. I think of the cavern below the Academy, the runes carved into the stone that Iain had coveted so dearly until I convinced him to believe in me instead, and I climb another stair.

My brow grows damp and my right palm aches, the hard scar tissue beginning to bruise against the handle of my cane. Kaya's oath rune has not pained me since she cut it into my skin and I begin to wonder if she was merely as bad at runes as Iain is. Hers had worked—she'd shown me the weeping wound at the height of her betrayal. She had not kept her oath; the taste of revenge had been too sweet for her to ignore. I, and the people of Fairhaven, had paid the price of her pettiness.

That anger succeeds in driving me up another stair.

My former friend had fled north, to Phoenix's father, and found common cause in the restless people of Orthandrell. Two disgruntled factions had formed a friendship against the leadership in the south, and now I was to be seated at its head. I'd seen the maps denoting the small skirmishes for pockets of land and—thanks to my habit of devouring every book on a topic once I've discovered it—I knew exactly what those lost parcels of land would cost us in terms of harvest, coin, and men.

My fingers twitch, as though I'm reaching for a figurine on a Kingdoms board, as I consider the strategies in my head. I can see the coming war laid out before me like a fresh set game.

And though I hate to admit it, I'm eager to play.

My appetite for battle had not been ignited by the skirmish on the streets. On the night Iain had cared for me, laid at the foot of my bed, and stood up for me to his soulmate, I had come to realise what exactly I had lost by having the extreme misfortune of Kynan Alsain being my father. *Family is not born*, Iain had said, but I remember the determination on the assassin's faces; they had been there for Iain, and they had been there for me. My father was the puppet of a man I'd never met, acting against the daughter he'd never claimed. And yet some small, sickly thread, something broken in my mind, clung stubbornly to the idea that he might change. That he might come to want me. If I could best him in battle, maybe I could prove to him that I am worthy of being his.

My head, I'm coming to suspect, is more broken than my leg.

I breathe deeply, then climb the next few stairs quickly. At the top, I sag for a moment, and the footmen start forward hesitantly. I hold up my hand to still them; bless them for wanting to help, but Netalia didn't grant the leave to, and I'm worried they'll be punished. The relief on their faces as they hold their stations confirms that suspicion, and I let the warmth of being right speed my recovery.

I wait until my chest stills and my heart slows, and then I nod.

The glass ceiling of the throne room lends muted daylight to the cavernous room below, and I'm taken aback for a moment at the sight of hundreds of people crammed into a room I've mostly seen empty. Nobles in colourful silks, feathered hats, and polished leather wait either side of a slim aisle, and a few incline their heads as I meet their eyes.

I recognise none of them; Iain told me that the great Houses would be at the front, but every minor house has sent a representative to ensure they are seen at the coronation of Lotheria's newest queen. This is the first time many of them have laid eyes on me, and I turn slightly pinker as I see a few curious gazes land on my cane.

At the end of the aisle, atop the dais next to my throne, Iain waits in black velvet. His hands rest on the pommel of his sword, and for a moment, I seriously consider seceding the position to him; I cannot look the part of queen as much as he looks like a king in front of the people.

But then he takes a small step back, and his hand lifts slightly, indicating the throne.

The tap of my cane echoes throughout the hall as I begin to walk. Murmurs follow in my wake, and I pretend not to hear them. Familiar faces, and then friendly ones, begin to appear in the crowd. My friends, dressed like the nobility they are, wait near the front with the other students. Amisha smiles at me, but her eyes glisten with tears. Orin looks similarly nervous, and I give him what I hope is an encouraging smile. His name is in the marriage ballot, and this could very well be his coronation too.

Phoenix, as the representative of House Araspire, a newly minted Lord, waits at the front with Houses Nithewaite, Chabin, Fillegan, Merrangold, Lyon, and Temperhold. I recognise Lord Olinius as well, and my smile to him is genuine. He returns it, and I remember the crown he has forged for me. It is here somewhere, and the bite of nerves return.

With myself as the representative of Greatcast, and Orin for Thoreau, when I ascend the dais, I do so in front of all ten noble Houses, for the first time since the Dawn Harbour Massacre. My eyes flick to Iain but his face is smooth, though I know he will have observed the same fact.

Iain begins the long intonation of my swearing in. The words blur and hum through the thumping of my heart in my ears, as hundreds of pairs of eyes examine my every movement, my every reaction. I imagine myself seated at a Kingdoms board with an eagle-eyed player, and my features smooth with the ease of hours of practice.

Iain's words do not still. There is no mechanic for me to refuse the crown. Once called, Lotherian queens can only serve.

The rune scars tingle as Lord Olinius approaches with a velvet box. Inside, seated safely, is my crown—the one I had designed, the one I intended to ignite a war of passion with.

Iain opens the box and lifts a circlet of broken, beaten silver. The odd faces are jagged and sharp, mirror bright in places but pewter dust in others. The last of our stored mirriam ore, Iain places a fortune on my head as whispers break in the crowd.

Soon, those whispers will reach Kaya, and the knowledge that I wear upon my head the metal her soulmate died for will send her into a predictable frenzy of hate and anger. She will be easy to outmanoeuvre—she is reckless when her blood is up.

The crown is heavier than I expected, and it digs into my skull. I resist the urge to adjust it as the hall surges to its feet, voices eager in supplication to the first crowned Queen since Fleur.

CHAPTER TWENTY-NINE

MORE WINE SPLASHES into the gold-rimmed glass in front of me. I lift it as the server turns away, managing a sip before another noble approaches our table.

To my left, Iain stands and bows deeply. "Prince Fayyaad, welcome."

He smiles. "Thank you. My father sends his regards and regrets that he cannot be here himself."

"Of course."

I stand and take Fayyaad's offered hand. "Your Highness. Thank you for coming to the ceremony."

The prince's eyes linger on me as though searching my words for hidden meaning. "I wouldn't miss it," he says. "The first Lotherian queen in a generation. Your country rejoices."

"Not all of it," I remind him.

"Every queen has her dissidents," he says. "No true monarchy is entirely at peace."

There is a strange splinter of comfort in his words. The weight of the mirriam crown is bruising my scalp already, and though the political play is worth it, my head is paying the price. Soon there won't be an inch of my body that isn't scarred or bruised in an attempt to pledge my allegiance to someone or something.

"Thank you for the flowers," I continue, and Iain glances at me curiously.

So, too, does the prince. "I, ah... I did not send any flowers, Your Majesty."

Awkward silence falls across us, and I clear my throat. "My apologies, Fayyaad. A large bouquet was delivered while I readied and I thought—"

"If I had not thought it too presumptuous, I would've," he says, and smiles. "But I thought we made the terms of a potential marriage clear."

Relief swims through me. *He hadn't sent them.*

My eyes alight on Phoenix, standing with my friends near the wall.

"We did. I apologise, the day has somewhat gotten away from me." I tear my gaze from my former soulmate, in time to grant Fayyaad the hand he requests. His lips barely touch my knuckles before he nods to Iain, and melts back into the crowd of my nobility.

"That was embarrassing," I mutter, sitting back down. "Why did I say anything?"

"It was a safe assumption," he says. "No other than a prince would be bold enough to send flowers to a queen on her coronation. Have you eaten?"

I shake my head and he summons a footman. The other guests have dined and drunk from our cellars for the last few hours, but every time I've lifted a bite to my lips, my stomach has curled in on itself. I'm terrified of being sick; the crown is heavy and the laces of my dress are tight. There is no way the act could be done neatly.

Iain doesn't say anything for the next few minutes, and I'm allowed to rest my voice. I focus on the golden plate in front of me, which has been swept away after every course by a footman, but it swims in my vision. My hand automatically reaches for my wine glass, but something stills it. I rest it back in my lap as Iain's summoned footman brings another platter.

"Try to eat some of this," Iain says, serving me himself. Rich, creamy potatoes are piled neatly on my plate. "I'm surprised you recognised Fayyaad."

"I haven't drunk that much," I protest, my vision sharpening as though indignant at the accusation itself. I eat a forkful of potato out of reflex and feel something settle as my stomach has something other than fermented grapes in it for the first time since the morning. I pick at a few more mouthfuls, eating between conversations with my new lords and ladies as they approach.

The Greatcast party, who came to Castor with my grandmother, attended the coronation. Now, they—a party of one of my cousins, three of Gennorin's ladies-in-waiting, and the seneschal of Thornsgrove—wait in the wings of the hall like consequences wrought human. They do not believe Gennorin made me heir; I can feel their disbelief weighing on me from their stares and close-knit murmuring. I allow them to watch me speak to my nobles. There will be a play to be made in the coming weeks, and I must prepare for it. The image and idea they have of me must be of a competent queen, called to duty, and not the girl that Gennorin rightly saw me as.

Black doubt lances through my stomach again as my dead grandmother's words echo in my ears.

A warm hand grips my left one, and Iain squeezes tightly. "It's nearly over."

I laugh, some bitterness making the sound ugly. "Are you sure? We've supplied the palace's finest wine to those very good at drinking it. Can you not feel their relief?" Iain's gaze follows mine across the crowd as my tone cools, my tongue loosened by drink. "They finally have a queen to follow into a war they expected and dreaded. Men won't fight for murky excuses and a leadership they don't believe in." I glance sideways at the Headmaster but don't offer any apologies. "A queen with a crown and the land's gift in her blood is an easier image to sell on the march to battle."

Iain inclines his head. "You are an ideal."

"I am an excuse," I reach for my wine glass, "for the nobility to do what to do what they do best. Spill blood, and feel righteous about it."

I set the wine glass down without drinking from it, a flush creeping up my neck.

"Rose..." Iain says softly, his words for my ears only. "I will be here beside you when the war begins."

I wrest my hand from his, the fight draining from me. I am tired and emotional and drunk. Though I meant the words, no good comes from me needling at old wounds. I am afraid—of war, of battle, and of how much I want to try my hand at it. Kingdoms has rendered me a bloodthirsty queen.

I try not to remember that the only way to gain the Warmaster rank is to win an actual war.

"I know," I admit. "I don't think I could do it without you." I eye the wine in front of me, deep red and alluring. I tug my hand from his. "I'm going outside. I need some air."

"Take a guard."

I slip away, the tone of his voice coming with me. Already, I regret the haughty words I'd spoken, lofted by the taste of wine and the weight of the crown on my head. Had I not taken lives by my own hand already? Whether by blade or flame, I'm just as much of a killer as the men and women I'd condemned at a dining table.

The cool air hits my face as I push outside, the damp scent of earth and gardens upon it. I breathe deeply, and my spinning head begins to slow. Soft dirt squelches around my boots as I pad deeper into the grounds and away from the glowing windows of the palace, laughter and decadence muffled within. A voice, which sounds very much like Netalia's, sounds in the back of my head— that I should not be walking the grounds alone. My steps cease and

I stand amongst a grove of darkened trees, near blind save for the moonlight filtering through the canopies. A thought hovers at the edge of my mind, has done since the prince approached my table.

I did not send any flowers.

And another phrase, a curious combinations of words I'd never inquired about, because the woman who'd spoken them was dead at the bottom of the stairs before I could.

Vine tangler.

I turn on the spot, spying the illuminated palace through the greenery. My heart pounds, emboldened by the remnants of the wine and my growing, dreadful realisation.

Every great and minor house is gathered within the stone walls. I'm a newly minted queen, with the eyes upon me judging the onset of my rule. The treaties and alliances that will begin tonight, between men and women who grow surer and drunker, revelling in their new government, will lay the foundation of the coming years.

It is the perfect scenario for disruption.

I take a few steps back, but a shadow detaches from the trees and blocks my path.

"No," Tyson says simply.

I halt, my chest heaving. My eyes search the pockets of darkness around us, and another familiar shape emerges against the palace lights.

"I'm sorry, Rose," my mother says.

I grip my stick. "What are you doing here?"

Tyson begins a sentence, but my mother holds out her hand. "You know."

Anger heats suddenly, made more fierce by my fear. "No, I don't know. At least, I hope I don't."

Tyson wears leather armour, close fitting and well made. A sword hangs in a sheath on his right hip, a large hammer on his left. In the deep shadows, I can't see his face, and I'm glad. I don't want to see his eyes when he wields a sword at me.

My mother is dressed similarly, but instead of a sword at her hip, pocketed pouches hang from her belt. I can see leaves poking over the edges, and she wears vines like gauntlets around her forearms.

I'd never asked what her speciality was, and the answer surrounds me. My mother is a vine tangler, and I have no idea how to fight one. More than that, I don't want to. But she sent the flowers, I'm sure of it. How else would they have known the plans for the evening?

"I would've sent invites to the coronation but I wasn't sure where to find you," I say, attempting to sound casual, though my voice trembles at the end. "If I'd known you were in Castor—"

"Don't," Tyson says roughly. "Don't do this with us, not *us*, Rose. We know you."

"Do you?" I shoot back, and anger steadies me. "Because I thought I knew *you*, knew the both of you! Yet you're standing against me like you want to draw that sword, Ty. What are you going to do with it? Cut off my other leg?"

He says nothing, but looks away and I turn on my mother. "And you... I bring you back to this world, to find me, to *support* me, and you instead turn and run back to the man who, a few months later, sent men to kill me in the streets."

"Rose, I didn't know—"

I stamp my cane, my heart thudding in my chest. "Are you *kidding* me? The man you pledged allegiance to, over your own child, makes a move to end the Lotherian monarchy and you're going to try to tell me 'I didn't know'? Either you don't care, or you're shit at observation, and neither of those bode well for the conclusion of this conversation."

Because it needs to conclude, I'm realising. If they're here, Kynan and his men are also likely sequestered in the trees, or the cellars. If I'm their target, I'm already dead; I barely fought off half a dozen of them in the streets with a full armoured guard and *Iain*, one of the most powerful war mages alive. My right hand aches for the ghost of the sword I should carry.

Fire begins to seep into my veins, and I remember I am not just words and a walking stick.

Tyson moves, and I hold a finger up. "Don't."

Neither of them say anything, and a breeze filters through the leaves above us. I watch my mother's eyes flick upwards, and I wonder what they're telling her.

Across the garden, the sounds of the party drift to us on the same breeze. Whatever plan we're standing at the inception of hasn't started yet.

"Why?" I ask simply, to the two people who should've loved me best. "Why did you choose him over me?"

At first I think neither of them will answer, but then Tyson lifts his head. "You broke my heart, Rose."

Confusion scours my face. "I... what?"

"Not like Petre broke yours. But you promised to get me home and then you burnt a town to the ground. You made a promise to a madwoman, and betrayed everyone who trusted you. Fairhaven lies in *ashes* because of what you did! Laela's family, gone!" His voices rises. "My shop, my home, gone! Everyone I knew, everyone I spoke to, every baker I bought bread from, every merchant who sold to us, *gone*. And you went home and left me to wallow in grief I had no idea how to manage. I lied to my family for you. I did irreparable damage to my parents, to our home life, to keep your secret. And when they knew I would never tell them the truth," his voice begins to break, "I saw the love leave them. They could never trust me again, Rose, because of my loyalty to you, and because of what we went through.

"They told me they were leaving Narralong. They moved, and they left me behind... I was no longer their son. And so I came back for the man who treated me as though I was."

Tears streak down my face, mirroring his, and I see the rage and grief mixing into bitterness as he stands against me. And the sick thing is, I understand him and I cannot fault him.

I would hate me too.

"I should've been there for you. It's wrong that I wasn't," I whisper.

He meets my eyes, but there is nothing in his gaze. "It's too late."

I nod. "I know."

"Rose," my mother begins, and my eyes linger on Tyson a moment longer, savouring the seconds before our friendship dissolves completely. "I loved Kynan from the moment I set eyes on him. He made me feel seen, and heard, beyond the blood in my veins and the gift that came with it. He didn't care what my last name was, or what ties to a great House I had. He *loved* me."

"No, he didn't. *I* loved you," I point out. "I'm your child. But you always looked at me like I was the reason we were alone."

Her breath hitches. "If I hadn't ridden north, to tell him of you... if I'd never made that journey..."

I can't miss the accusation in her voice, and blinding realisation hits me; my mother is wrong, terribly wrong about something, and her mind cannot be changed. It's a fracture that has threatened to crack between us since I was old enough to know my own mind and circumstances, and now it yawns, dividing us.

"You would've always chosen him," I say.

"I tried to deny it, Rose." Her voice trembles. "For nearly two decades I tried to forget him. But he's written into my blood. *He* is my life's story. I know he can be rough, but I can change him, given enough time."

Silence falls in the small clearing, and her words clear my mind.

For the first time in my life, I do not crave her approval, for I know she is unable to grant it.

"That's pathetic," I tell her quietly, and the surety those words grant me are worth more than the crown on my head. "And I'm going back inside now."

Tyson moves into my path, his hand out. "Don't, Rose."

The fire in my blood heats as I look from his outstretched hand, to his face.

"At what point have I given you the impression that I'd like to stay here with you both?"

He seizes my right wrist, and I look down at the contact. "You can't go back inside. They want to kill you."

"How noble of you to try and stop them," I hiss. "I suppose I should be grateful that the friend who denounces me, and the mother who doesn't want me, should try to save my life by having me hide in the bushes. Take your hands off me."

His grip tightens, as I knew it would. I pull my arm towards me, dragging him closer, and grip the pommel of his sword with my left hand. I draw it as I shove him away with my boot, the naked steel glinting in the dark as I step back. My cane falls to the dirt as I switch hands, but I know I've got a few standing minutes in my bad leg.

I just need to make them count.

The fire comes easily to my offhand as my mother raises her arms. Small vines whip towards me, but they crumble into ash as the fireball I summon soars over our heads, illuminating the clearing, then the grounds. It explodes overhead, turning it from night to day for a moment, and I hear answering shouts from the walls.

I tear my eyes from it as stinging branches sear my cheeks. I swing Tyson's sword up and slice them from my mother's control, but she's fast; already, more are bursting from the soil at my feet, tangling around my legs. I pull against their hold, but my leg is weakening rapidly.

Tyson closes in as I focus on trying to get free, his large body looming over mine. A moment of hesitation gives him the opening he needs, and then his sword is torn from my grip and thrown to the ground.

I don't know if I could've used it on them anyway.

He twists my arm behind my back, his overwhelming strength

easily gaining the advantage. My leg gives out and I buckle to the ground. More vines lash my ankles and wrists together.

I don't want to fight them. I don't want to hurt either of them, despite their words.

The fire within my blood stirs, but it's too easy to burn; Fairhaven dances in my eyes again, and I know I can't wield it against the two people I'm supposed to love most.

I dig my hands into the soil as though I can bury myself, the vines lashing my legs tighter together, Tyson's weight leaning on me.

I am utterly subdued, unless I want to reduce my mother and my best friend to ashes.

Tears grow as I hang my head, and the mirriam crown falls heavily into the dirt, embedding itself in the ground. And a stunning, surging realisation sets the runes on my arms to tingling, pearly white light beginning to flicker beneath my sleeves.

I'm the Lotherian Queen, and my queensgift is ready to serve me.

The clouds overhead rumble with harnessed energy, much as they had done over Fairhaven. When I open my eyes, my vision is laced with silver thread, illuminating the forms of Lydia and Tyson standing over me, but also the trees and plants around me; everything with a life force blazes brilliantly in my vision. The vines in my mother's belts, around her arms, sing to me and await their orders. The hammer at Tyson's side reaches for me. The lightning holds its breath, buried in the bellies of the low hanging clouds.

And inside the palace, the music stutters to a halt.

"Rose—" Tyson begins, and his voice is filled with sorrowful victory.

I throw my head back, connecting with his nose. There's a horrible crunch and he falls away, his voice choked by sudden blood, and I grab for the hammer. It meets me halfway, the metal calling to the Melacorean rune carved into my skin, fuelled by the blood that had once run in my mother's veins. I twist in his loosened grip, bringing my elbow up to connect with his head. I know at once that had I not broken his nose, he would easily have the advantage in this fight.

It is dirty, and it is unfair, and he sprawls in the dirt regardless.

I stand, holding the hammer, as my mother reaches for me. I lift my free hand and the vines on her person follow. Her face flickers with confusion, and then the tendrils curl around her, not as protective armour, but in the same constriction she'd held me in moments before. She struggles, her hand rising as mine had, but the little plants are overwhelmed by the queensgift that now commands them and they cannot hear her. When she loses her footing with a cry, they send roots that go deep, fastening her to the earth.

I know then that she never used the power Lotheria gifted her. If she had, there would have been many more sent to hold me.

Tyson struggles to his feet, blood streaming down his face, but as he takes a step towards me, he sinks. I concentrate, loosening the loamy soil beneath his boots carefully lest he be swallowed entirely. When he is buried to his chest, his eyes two dark pools of hatred, I relinquish the grains of dirt and turn to the castle.

"Don't follow me," I advise them. "I don't think you'll like what I have to do in there."

And I walk from the trees, my cane forgotten and hammer in hand, on two strong legs.

CHAPTER THIRTY

THEY'VE NOT YET POSTED guards around the palace they're overthrowing; I'm able to slip back in the same door. As I cross the small corridor, towards the throne room, I marvel in walking for the first time in over a year.

I pull up short as voices echo in the cavernous room beyond the half-closed door I'm approaching.

"—have no place here," Iain is saying. It's eerie, hearing one voice in a room of hundreds. There should be conversations buzzing, laughter, music. "I will give you one chance to leave."

There *is* laughter at that, but it is dark and unkind. My father's voice answers.

"We've come to pay our respects to the new queen."

My blood turns to ice, and I know I will hear his words in my nightmares if I survive.

I draw back from the door as Iain answers, my heart racing. I envision this situation playing out on a Kingdoms board—they will have archers or crossbowmen up high, likely on the gallery. They will not wear metal armour, lest I heat it and burn them again. Still, a group of armed non-magi against the nobility of

Castor, most of whom are graduated mages... They either have a death wish, or something I haven't thought of.

Unknown elements make me nervous.

In my mind's eye, I see the glass ceiling of the throne room. From my father's words, he sounded like he was positioned in the centre of the hall—directly below it.

There's no way he can know what the queensgift actually does. I'm an unknown element too.

"Her Majesty has retired for the night," Iain says, his voice carrying clearly, and I open my eyes, inching near the door with its sliver of golden light. "Perhaps I should send someone to fetch her?"

"Dismissed your puppet already?" Kynan calls. "Don't bother." There are low words I don't catch, and then I hear boots against flagstones, and a distant door slams. Presumably dispatched men to pull me from my bed.

Lillian.

She'll be waiting for me to return. Sweat breaks out on my forehead as I stagger, leaning one hand on the cold stone walls of the palace.

And my mind's eye *flies* through the building. For a moment, the images flash too quickly for me to parse, but then I recognise the library and it begins to slow. Slowly, my heart thudding as though I'm running, I manoeuvre towards my chambers. The image is blurred at the edges, spiking when a noise sounds from the throne room, as though my attention is splitting, but I refocus and soar through the stone.

Suddenly, I'm in my own bedchambers. Lillian has one candle lit and is laying out my nightgown. A soft sound mixes with the harsh words echoing beside me, and I realise she is humming.

I reach towards her from the stone, and she hesitates in laying out the gown.

"Hello?"

Run, I tell her. *Run and hide. They are coming.*

She stiffens, then looks towards the door. As my vision begins to draw back, my head pounding, she runs for the candle and blows it out.

I come back to where I'm standing in the antechamber, my chest heaving as though I've run the streets of Castor.

Warmth trickles from my nose and I brush at it. Blood smears the back of my hand as I withdraw the other from the crumbling remnants of the stone wall. I stare at the hole my hand has made, then shake the dust off.

It'll take me a while to learn the limits of this new power, but I don't have a while. I don't even have minutes.

"While we wait for the queen," Kynan continues, "I'd like to deliver a message from a good friend of mine."

I return to my post near the door, wondering if I've got the strength to follow through with my plan. My heart rate is slowing, but I can feel fatigue beginning to drag at my bones. The queensgift may be all powerful, but I, the vessel it is housed in, is not.

"The true Lord Araspire promises to make calls at the Houses Thoreau, Nithewaite, Greatcast, and especially Lyon, very soon. He regrets that he has not yet made his way to your vast lands and houses."

I can nearly feel Phoenix's anger, and likely would've if we'd been bonded. A surge of longing replaces the fear.

Don't do anything stupid.

But I finally have confirmation that my father is working with Aloysius Araspire as my grandmother hinted, the previous Lord of House Araspire and the orchestrator of the rebellion Kaya and her Halvers had joined

A perverse grain of relief swims through me; all my enemies are connected. I'd worried about splitting my focus, but a victory against one would be a victory against all.

Rising voices bring me back. The named Houses are returning the threats, and Iain's words are drowned amongst them. Unable to wait in the shadows, I pull the door open and walk inside.

Iain stands on the raised platform where we'd eaten only a short while ago. I approach him, and the voices begin to die down as the nobles recognise me. My heart begins to pound again, but I reach Iain's side before I turn and look down on my father.

The sheer number of men and women he has with him makes my heart sink. I'd wondered why they'd be foolish enough to take on a room of accomplished mages—as I look to the hate-filled glares of people I'd never met, I realise he intends to win by force.

Good. It means he has no other strategy.

"Your Majesty," my father says, and it's the most mocking thing I've ever heard with two ears. "How kind of you to join us tonight."

"My apologies, father. I went for a walk."

Kynan Alsain stands ringed by the soldiers he'd brought into the throne room, all of them armoured and armed. Sharp blades, mauls, and shields are held at the ready, and my chest tightens at the sight of a mace with spiked teeth, similar to the one that tore my leg from me at Deadman's Keep. Their armour is boiled leather, layered plates of it, tightly knotted together. I send a few casual tendrils of heat towards them, noting as they die without taking hold. I cannot roast them within their own armaments as I've done before.

My father is the best equipped of them all, and stands a head above even the tallest man beside him. He wears a sword on his back and, unlike the others, has nothing in his hands yet. The sight of him unarmed makes me nervous. I would prefer if he wielded the sword like a common threat.

Black leather makes him bulky and, as he walks forward a few steps, I sense the overwhelming power of him. Not through magic or any elemental whispering, but through sheer presence alone. For a moment, I understand why my mother was drawn to the centre of his gravity.

Gone is the stooped posture, the low growl of the blacksmith's voice. It is as though Craige never existed, and I wonder how I never realised this behemoth, my nightmare father, had been in such close proximity while I visited Tyson in the blacksmith.

His eyes flick to the door I'd entered through. "Where is your mother, and my boy?"

Sourness tightens my breath as jealousy sweeps through me. I say nothing, but toss Tyson's hammer at his feet. The clatter of metal on stone echoes through the hall, and I imagine him as my Kingdoms opponent; my features smooth and give him nothing as he looks up toward me.

His careful expression flickers slightly. "What did you do to them?"

"You should've had more men on the perimeter." A muscle twitches in his cheek, and I latch onto the tell. "Unless... you didn't have them. It must've been a chore, even for you, to convince these brave people to accompany you here tonight."

I make eye contact with a few of the newcomers. Most meet my gaze with steel, but one or two look away. I take my time as Kynan stands in silence, and when I turn back, I see him clench his jaw.

"Is this your first coup?" I ask.

"Enough!" He sweeps a hand, turning his back on me, and my eyes flick to my nobles. Orin and Amisha are standing nearest, and we look at each other for a moment.

Be ready.

Orin nods, and threads his fingers through Amisha's. She looks toward him as silent words pass between them.

"What are your plans here tonight, Kynan?" I continue, my voice ringing across the crowd. "Deliver a message from the former Lord Araspire? How kind. Consider it heard. You may leave, unless..." I place a finger to my cheek. "You're actually here to murder your own daughter."

There's a rumble at that, and even a few of the northern soldiers look uneasy. The intent was stated plainly when he entered the hall armed, but somehow the words are harsher than the implied threat.

Kynan turns towards me, and there's nothing of his blacksmith persona in the dark eyes that look through mine. For a moment, I'm lost for words as he holds me in that locked stare. A forgotten longing yearns through me, of sleepless nights, of unanswered questions, of fantasies and dreams imagined by a younger Rose who wore a question mark in place of a father's love.

I curl my fist and dig my fingernails into the oath rune on my palm.

We've walked too far down different paths to converge now.

Iain steps closer to me, and I steady at his familiarity.

"For what it's worth, I never wanted it to go this far," Kynan says, lifting his hands as though helpless. "I merely wanted to be heard."

"And we should've listened," Iain says, his voice cutting across my father's. "I received your letters. We should've negotiated, and I apologise to you and your countrymen."

Silence follows in the wake of his words. The noble men and women that Iain has held power over for his entire reign stare at him, and I, too, find myself lost.

Iain has apologised to me, in private, with quiet yet sincere words. Not once did I think I would see him in front of his people, faced with an armed coup, telling their leader that he should've done things differently.

A reddish hue climbs Iain's neck, but his gaze doesn't waver from my father. I can nearly feel what the words are costing him.

"Set down your swords, and we will negotiate now. In front of witnesses"—he sweeps a hand over the watching crowd—"and you will have my word that I will hold to whatever compromise we reach."

I look from Iain to my father. It is clear, in this moment, who has taken power back. Beyond Iain, Netalia stands with her fists clenched and her face is unreadable. Iain might honour whatever agreement he manages to reach, but his soulmate certainly won't.

A flicker of fire curls around my fingertips as my gaze rests on her.

Kynan, too, seems thrown. An apology from his enemy has manoeuvred him sufficiently—if he attacks now, he will cement support against his cause. He has no reason to reject Iain's offer of negotiation before any war begins.

Unless...

I look curiously at him as he seemingly struggles for words. I give him a few seconds, and then reach out a finger and touch the back of Iain's hand, the queenrunes whispering to him as they'd done to Lillian.

He cannot negotiate. He has not been given leave to by Araspire. He is a pawn, not a player.

Iain cannot reply, but he hooks his finger around mine for a second in acknowledgement, and then we part. I fix two thoughts in my mind.

Get Iain a sword.

The Thornsguard, outnumbered yet present, ring the walls. Above, in the gallery as I predicted, crossbowmen have them set in their sights. They can rest easily, firing at the slightest movement without having to draw an arrow. Their bolts, I know from experience, will punch through even plate armour.

I drop my gaze to the floor again, and note Amisha had followed my gaze. She'd majored in cartography but had taken to archery as I had to the sword. If I can get her a crossbow, she can use it.

Orin, beside her, is a fog speaker. I wonder if he's realised it yet, having been informed so by Arno upon discussion of my fire whispering.

In the crowd, I know Phoenix, Dena, and Theresa also wait. I doubt my Rune Master would attend the coup, having been the only one to speak for me during the meeting in the woods, and I can only hope this is the case. If we fight with runes, I will lose, even with the queensgift.

My second objective comes to mind as thunder rumbles again, chained to my will, and impatient.

"Last time I saw you," Kynan says to me suddenly, breaking me from my reverie. "You fled in tears."

The room fades away, and all thoughts of preparing my board go with it. Old rage and indignation flare at his words, but the Rose who would've snapped back without thought is gone. She has been sanded down, moulded, and shaped into someone else entirely.

"Of course I did," I say. "I'd met the man who was supposed to be my father, and found a monster in his stead."

He'd expected words of defiance; the sneer on his face was set to enrage me as I'd done him with my needling words. But I see the lines on his brow smooth in confusion, and I give him a moment of doubt before finally unleashing the power of the clouds above.

Glass shatters as the sky roars, the bolt lancing down to the stone. Fragments splinter and my father and his soldiers disappear as dust explodes upwards. Rain and wind howl into the room, and the lamps gutter, plunging the room into darkness and chaos.

But the queensgift sees everything. Some of the nobility flee, and I am grateful, but others remain, their own magic rising. I search through the outlines until I come across familiar steel, and draw it to me. The rune pulls hard on my skin and when the sword comes flying, it's with such speed that I nearly miss it.

But I catch it by the hilt and toss it to Iain. He catches it without a word, looking at me for a moment.

He can feel it, as I do; this night will change everything, as the Dawn Harbour Massacre did. This is my first venture into the nightmare, but he has lived it his entire life, and now it is happening again.

Sour flashes of light flicker within the battle below, and my chest tightens. I nod.

And then it's upon us—a blade swings towards me and I barely dodge it, the air hissing as it passes. It's wielded by a woman I don't recognise, her eyes wild. I have no idea who she is, but I know what she wants. Where my father may have wavered at the final moment, my death is firmly fixed in her mind.

When she swings at me again, I duck the blade and grab her wrist, straightening her arm unnaturally. Before she can push against me, I strike her elbow hard, the *power* rune lending unusual strength to the blow. She screams as her arm breaks, and I twist the sword from her grasp, still pushing against her elbow as I wind the sword and plunge it into her back.

She falls and I yank the sword free, the metal streaked with the blood of a woman who's name I will hopefully never learn.

Before I can move, fog begins to climb my person. I panic for a moment until I realise Orin is hiding me from view, ensconcing me in a cloud amongst the dust. But I have fire in my veins, and I burn the mist away. I will apologise later, but I won't run from my father again. The fog instead begins to spread across the room, obscuring those attempting to hide.

Streaks of light and magic flash around the room, illuminating the writhing mass of bodies and blades. The cries of the wounded and dying are deafening in the enclosed space. A man in the house colours of Nithewaite—brown and blue—staggers up the platform towards me, falling to his knees as though in supplication, his shirt soaked and his right arm missing. I start towards him but a crossbow bolt lances through his chest and he topples. I look towards the shooter, wondering if it were a near miss or an act of mercy, and pull the stone flooring from beneath his feet, the runes digging into my skin.

I hear his cry as he disappears into the rubble, crushed beneath the stone. His crossbow clatters aside, and strong hands swoop it from the ground. The bolt Amisha fires at me sails over my shoulder, impacting the chest of a man in leather armour who'd raised his arm to end me. I look to her and nod, curling my fingers as the remnants of my worked magic fade. She returns the nod, determination in her dark eyes, as she winds the crossbow.

I need to find the others, but I nearly trip over a body, catching myself at the last moment. Lord Olinius, the forger of my crown and my first friend in the capital, stares with unseeing eyes, his sleeves damp with the blood of other men. I crouch, using him for protection, as a band of men in leather armour pass near us, their steps heavy. With a clumsy hand, I feel for Olinius' pulse, but my fingers are slick with blood and his skin is clammy.

"I'm sorry," I whisper, and then take off running, my won sword in hand.

I'd underestimated the damage my father and his soldiers could do; with the heads of Houses—or representatives of—present, the chances of killing a lord, heir, or both are high. I'd gathered a room of targets together like piglets amassing for slaughter.

Even if we fend off the threat, we will lose. And if someone kills my father, despite my hatred of him, I think I will lose as well.

But I have a sword in my hand, and two legs beneath me for the first time in a year. Losses may be inevitable, but I can meet them fighting; I will never accept defeat without clawing for every inch of a possible victory first.

My vision darkens as I'm slammed bodily into the wall on my right, and my head clunks off the stone with a sickening crunch. I blink, dazed, and only catch the sight of a blade a moment before it begins to descend. Again, the Melacorean rune in my forearm activates, pushing the metal away. The wielder of the sword—a man with a snarl on his face—pushes against the hilt, trying to wend it down into where my neck meets my shoulder. I watch the trembling blade with wary eyes, unsure of how long my rune can hold out, or how much pressure will overwhelm it. For a moment, I see it snapping and slamming downwards, severing my left arm from my body much as the Nithewaite man had suffered.

The sword trembles like a violin bow and I decide I'm done humouring his attempt on my life.

He's failed to notice my own blade, and I know from the northmen we've fought before that their leather breastplates stop short above their ribs, so I wind my sword and step close, plunging it up and into his body. We are intimately close when he realises he's dying, and as his sword finally completes its arc, it draws his body deeper onto mine.

The fire of battle begins to light behind my eyes, and I am tempted to let it take over as three lives are extinguished by my hand. But I guide him to the floor and slide the sword from his belly, the metal slick with blood and black bits I don't want to know about. When his eyes fade, I take a crucial second to check his pulse, but it is still and he does not suffer.

The same can not be said for many around us.

The screams have become white noise to my ears, my brain padding them into a soft background noise as the thunder of adrenaline washes through my body, keeping me upright, keeping me fighting. My leg does not tremble yet, and I revel in the borrowed strength, though a kernel of concern is beginning to gnaw at my stomach.

I push through the bodies to the centre of the room, where the rain falls steadily, mixing the stone dust into tacky mud. Another flicker of lightning illuminates the two figures at the centre, and my heart stops.

Iain and Kynan, locked blade to blade. As I watch, they disengage and circle one another warily. Iain's war magic flickers down his sword like the lightning I'd summoned, but Kynan's weapon is dull and dark. He doesn't need war magic to lend him strength; the greatsword is nearly the same length as my entire body, and he wields it like I had Tyson's hammer. It seems to cost him nothing to hold it, and when he lunges at Iain, he may as well be barehanded.

Iain steps offline, guiding Kynan's blade with his own and attempts to bind, but my father shoves him away. Iain staggers, thrown off balance, and Kynan presses the advantage, closing in.

I don't realise I've moved until my sword chips the flagstones, having taken the brunt of my father's downward swing, knocking it off course.

My right arm nearly wrenches from its socket and my fingers go numb, but I hold onto the hilt as though it is a lifeline. I wait for the follow through, for a rough hand to push me out of the way, or the greatsword to wrench up. But the stillness settles for a second, and then another, and I slowly look over my shoulder at the hulking figure of my father.

And I see indecision. I see the eyes of the man who once tended my injured arm, who spoke to Tyson and I with gruff kindness, who swept us away from the flames of the Fairhaven fire. This is not the man I burnt in the forest, nor the tyrant who spoke words of hatred only moments ago. *This* is my first glimpse at the man my mother loves, and for the first time, I half-understand why she went back.

We look at one another as the rain falls upon us, and I know I cannot put my blade through his ribs. In a flicker of lightning, I see him reach the same conclusion, and we rest in a stalemate, our swords pinned together.

Then, I watch black fingers claw up his throat.

"No."

I drop my sword as Kynan does, his fingers going to his neck. The skin blackens and rots as I watch, and as he falls to his knees I follow him, my hands on his shoulders. My mind races, searching for any remedy, any magic I have that might save him.

When I look behind me, I see Netalia emerge from the dust, the rain streaking down her face. Her eyes are darkened with bitter magic as she chokes my father's life from him.

"Stop!" I scream at her, but she does not listen.

I turn back to him, tearing his armour from his throat as blackened chunks of leather. I don't realise I'm burning him until my fingerprints are scalded into his skin, but he is unable to tell me as his throat begins to open from a festering wound.

I told her I would burn her if she worked this magic again.

She has turned her poison hand to all members of my family now, but I am done being afraid of her.

And I turn, the fire at my fingertips eager to obey. The grey room is lit in golden flames and I see her eyes clear the moment before she is engulfed.

As she burns, I am already tending my father. I do not hear Iain's roar of pain until much later when the memories sear my dreams.

The hole in his throat gapes, the magic halted at the edges of his skin like burnt parchment. Words rasp from him, but they are unintelligible, so I pretend he is apologising.

I pretend he is telling me he always cared.

And as my father dies, he does so with my forgiveness, and my tears upon his cheeks.

CHAPTER THIRTY-ONE

NETALIA TAKES a long time to die. Dimly, I'm aware of people battling the flames, but I can feel what the fire does, and I know when the spirit leaves her body.

I know when the remaining nobility looks to me, holding the body of my traitor father. I slowly lower him to the flagstones with trembling arms, as the main doors burst open and the guards from the grounds flood the hall. Shouts echo as the remaining assailants are caught trying to escape, winding down the staircases from the gallery or fleeing through side doors.

And then silence falls across the room and the bodies, both living and dead.

I look up. Iain is gazing at me from beside the charred remains of his soulmate. He saw me burn her. He knows the side I chose.

Boots halt nearby—the Thornsguard look between us for orders.

"Her..." Iain says, his voice hoarse. "Arrest her. She did this."

I hold his eyes as his words rest upon me and the waiting guards standing amongst the bloody remains of my coronation party. The survivors look between us, waiting to see who they'll obey.

I go to rise, and someone helps me to my feet.

"Are you alright, Your Majesty?"

"Take my hand, ma'am."

Two Thornsguard hold me upright. I clear my throat, my heart pounding.

You are in control until you look like you aren't.

I relax, and square my shoulders. "Send word for every carrier in the city who can be spared. Organise the wounded in order of most serious to least. Find Dena, and any other student of healing on the grounds."

"What about them, ma'am?" A guard points to a woman in black leather armour, her face streaked with blood, clutching her arm.

"Them too." I meet her eyes. "They will have information we want."

Movement begins to rise in the room. Noble lords and ladies climb to their feet, some with weapons still in hand, others with charred sleeves from wielding magic. I look around as the Thornsguard begin to follow my instructions. At first I am looking for my friends, and I find them easily; Phoenix carries the feet of an injured nobleman, Orin his head. Amisha tears her skirts for makeshift bandages. And then my eyes drift back to the blackened remains of the Headmistress.

Iain is no longer beside her.

I flex my hands as a deep, yawning grief opens wide in my chest, but I temper it with impatience. Tonight is not over. I can feel it in my bones, as sure as the runes in my skin.

When dawn breaks across the city, Ser Neal hands me the mirriam crown. I take it with hands dirty with ash and blood, and place it on my head. I don't want to know what the rest of me looks like.

"They're in custody?" I ask him.

He nods. "Took us a while to dig out the young man, but both have been taken to the dungeons."

I seize his sleeve as he goes to disappear into the mass of people before us. "No one knows about them, Neal. See to it. Spread the rumour of their demise, but I'm entrusting you with their safety."

He bows his head sharply. "Yes, ma'am."

I move into the crowd, placing a hand on an arm here, an encouraging word there. My leg howls in its metal brace, freed of the influence of the queensgift, and I know my time standing is dwindling.

But a choice was made by the people here tonight, and I want to prove that I am the right one.

As the morning sun lances through the broken skylight above, the throne room begins to empty. But cracked stone streaked with blood remains in the wake of the night's events, and weariness lingers at my brow. My eyes are drawn, unwillingly, to the spot where Netalia died, and I approach it with slow steps.

My right hand tingles, the memories of the blazing fire at my fingertips. There is nothing left of her on the stone; her body was removed before I could see what my flames had wrought. But I've seen how men die burning before, and she would've been no different.

I feel nothing as I look at the stone beneath my boots. Netalia had been a cruel, unforgiving woman who had murdered my grandmother and my father, amongst others; I hadn't forgotten her story about her carrier. She had blooded my mother and threatened me.

I lift my eyes to the nearest side door. I might not regret her death, but I do regret what must come next.

⚜

"The entire city?" Griffin echoes, and I nod.

"He is a fresh half-soul," I tell him, wincing as Lillian begins to undo the brace buckles. Griffin keeps his eyes on my face as my maid works. "He won't be thinking clearly enough to formulate a proper plan."

"This is the Headmaster we're talking about, Rose." Griffin sits on the chest at the foot of my bed, and I forgive the impropriety. I can accept the bowing and scraping of strangers, but Griffin was one of the guards to return us from Riverdoor—he has seen me at my lowest. "Iain Nevalas is incredibly cunning. He will always have a plan."

"He had a plan for a lot of things," I agree, thinking on our games of Kingdoms. "But not this."

Carrier Bayde moves in as Lillian removes the brace. The two examine my leg as though it's a separate entity, and I look away.

"Close the gates. Post guards at any point of entry to the city."

Griffin nods. "They won't open the gates without my direct order. And the docks?"

I wince again as my skin is pinched. "Yes. Any ship leaving must be searched."

"Understood. I'll report back when we've spoken to the wall guards."

"Thank you."

He opens the door to leave, revealing Phoenix waiting outside. Griffin glances back at me, and I nod. The captain stands aside to let my former soulmate in.

"Are you alright?" he asks.

"No, she isn't," Bayde answers, straightening from my leg. "With all due respect, ma'am, I told you you can't use magic to fix this damage."

"I didn't use magic," I remind him. "It was the queensgift."

Lillian looks between me and the carrier standing over me. I give the dismissal she's silently asking for, and she whisks the brace away.

"Queensgift or not," Bayde begins quietly. "You cannot heal what is not there, Rose."

With a single word, I am no longer the queen of Lotheria; I am the student he healed in his office, having been whipped by the Headmasters. He was strict but fair with me then, and he is doing the same now.

"Heal it, no," I reply, looking out the window. It's a clear morning; I can see all the way to the main gate over the rooves of Castor. "Use it, yes."

He goes to speak, and I sit forward in my chair, resting my leg back on the ground. It shrieks in agony that refers up to my hip, but I ignore it.

"If I could not have walked or run or fought last night, Kynan Alsain would've done what he set out to do," I remind him. "He was there to behead the noble Houses and throw them into chaos. He half succeeded—we'll be dealing with succession crises for months. A Lotherian queen cannot be a cripple, Bayde."

The carrier looks at me, and adjusts his glasses. "No. But you are, Rose."

Phoenix bristles at my side, and I put my hand on his. "Then I need to find a way to be both."

"If you keep using the queensgift to allow you to walk"—the carrier moves closer—"you will live in agony."

My mind's eye clouds with memories from the previous night, sharpened and brittle without sleep. I see the woman, hear the blade of her sword sing past me, and feel her ribs part beneath steel as I bury it deep. I feel the warmth of my second assailant's blood gush over my right fist as he dies upon that same sword, and when I look down, I can see brown rivers of it still encrusted in my skin.

"I've lived in agony since Deadman's Keep," I murmur.

His stare is hard. "Then that is Her Majesty's choice."

"It is," Phoenix says. "May we have a moment?"

Carrier Bayde inclines his head, not an inch lower than he has to, and begins to pack up to leave. As the door closes behind him, I realise I'm alone with Phoenix for the first time since the garden.

"I'm glad you're alright," I tell him earnestly.

He kneels beside me and pulls me close, his arms around me. I try not to think of the ash and gore we're both covered in as I return the gesture, resting against his solid strength.

"I'm alright," he murmurs. "That was not the first fight I've been in."

"Nor I," I remind him. "But it was certainly one of the worst."

He pulls back, and sits down on the footstool I'd rested my leg on for inspection. "I'm sorry about your father."

I clench my jaw, then release it. "He was a traitor, and a murderer."

"And your father," he repeats gently. "Trust me, Rose, I know what it is like to be trapped loving someone you know has only blackness in their heart. It is a curse for children born into circumstances they could never repeal."

His father, Aloysius Araspire, had sent mine to die for him, with a message threatening war for my northernmost Houses. I will be forced to act against him, and my games of Kingdoms will move from the board to the battlefield.

"I did not love my father," I say, and feel sure of it, though guilt nips at me, his last moments playing in my mind again. "Will you fight against yours?"

Phoenix shrugs. His fine court clothes are in the same state as mine—torn and filthy with the remnants of a midnight battle. "I did so last night. I don't see why it will be different in the day."

"Because your father wasn't there last night." I sit forward and take his hand. "I need to know I can rely on you when he is."

Phoenix curls his fingers around mine, but before he can answer, my bedroom door is thrown open.

"Rose—Your Majesty," Griffin amends, seeing my soulmate sitting before me. "I've received word from the gate."

I go to stand, and Phoenix assists me, holding me upright as I tremble. My heart begins to flutter in my chest, and I brace to hear the news I knew was coming.

"They saw a man matching his description leave through the

gate." Griffin looks between us. "He got out before they knew to seal the city."

"Was he ahorse?" Phoenix asks sharply, and the captain nods.

"Yes. Which means he could be anywhere by the time we assemble."

"Not anywhere." In my mind, I can see the runes, glittering gold above my head. I remember Iain standing beside me at the Archives, the Lothericon open before me. His eagerness, his master plan, had never changed. Before, he had hope. But now...

I meet Griffin's eyes. "I know what he's planning to do."

CHAPTER THIRTY-TWO

THE SUN WANES on the horizon as the guards finally leave the palace grounds. I watch from my window high in the palace, lies fresh upon my lips.

"Iain wouldn't leave Castor, leave his soulmate's body... He's at the Archives. You'll find him there."

I'd put up enough fight to be believed, though Griffin had given me a look that lingered as he left. I'd dismissed Lillian, citing the need for sleep; that hadn't been a lie. I do need to sleep.

But it's a long ride to the Academy.

I begin to strip off the remnants of my dress, pausing for a moment with the filthy fabric laid across my fingers. Netalia had ordered this dress for me, and I'd killed her while wearing it. Something twinges deep in my belly, but I bury it. I have to deal with any guilt over her death, and the others I'd committed, later.

Right now my mentor was getting further and further from the city.

I wring a cloth in the bowl of warm water Lillian had insisted on bringing up for me, and quickly run it over my face and body. It doesn't come close to removing enough of the grit and grime, but as I pull on riding clothes, I do so with my mind slightly more centred.

My maid had taken the brace, but I fasten it back on, sending the pain to the back of my skull and burying it in a box with my guilt. The queensgift flickers through the rune scars lazily, and I know that, for now, it is done obeying me. An edge of concern cuts through the anxiety but that, too, goes into the box.

I will find another way to deal with Iain. My eyes fall on the sword the late Lord Olinius forged for me, and I buckle it to my belt.

Though if it comes to blades between us, I'll be better off putting it to my own throat and surrendering.

The palace hallways are quiet—most of the activity is in the throne room, removing bodies and scrubbing floors. I skirt it, using the servant's passages and casting my eyes downwards whenever staff approach. With my hair tied back and no cane in hand, they don't recognise me; they're used to seeing me in dresses, dwarfed by Iain's stature and presence. I haven't been queen long enough to be known by most people beyond the nobility.

The stables are busier, though I walk to Iotha's stall without being noticed. My limp becomes more pronounced the further I travel, and as I heave her tack down from the wall, my forehead is damp with sweat. I drape her saddle over the stall wall and rest against it, my leg shaking.

"Rose."

My fingers tighten on the leather before I turn to him. "I'm going after him."

Phoenix nods, moving closer. "I know."

I wait for the fight, the push to come with me, but it doesn't arrive. Phoenix folds his arms, his eyes on the ground.

"Is it dangerous?"

I think of Iain, the way he'd fought in the streets as we were attacked by my father's men. I think of the way he'd committed to beheading my best friend in front of our village.

"It's Iain," I say finally. "Of course it is."

My soulmate doesn't reply for a moment, then sighs and uncrosses his arms. Before I can say anything, he goes to one knee.

"What—"

"You won't get far on this," he says, and lays his hands on my leg. Warmth radiates through the fabric of my breeches as dull light glows brighter. His healing magic, though his lesser area of study, is potent; strength rushes into my leg like the ocean into a cove at high tide. I breathe deeply as some semblance of feeling comes back, and tears prick the corner of my eyes as my mind reminds me of what I lost, that day at Deadman's Keep.

"The day you catch up with Iain will be one hundred times worse than that," Phoenix murmurs.

My breath catches as he looks up at me, and silent understanding passes between us. Then I set my jaw, and nod.

"I have to do this by myself," I tell him. "I created him."

"You enabled him," he corrects, standing. "Iain was never the man you kept trying to make him out to be. He could never give you what you needed, Rose."

I look away, my vision blurring with tears. "I know. It was stupid to imagine."

"Not stupid." He reaches out and brushes away a wayward tear. "Wanting to be loved is never stupid."

More fall as I smile tightly. "It doesn't make what needs to happen next any easier."

"And yet I have no doubt you will do what needs to be done."

Phoenix saddles Iotha for me, and I try not to remember that my beautiful mare was a gift from Iain, nor think about the long days ahead of me. I'm returning to the Academy, to Fairhaven, where I swore never to return.

She's restless when he leads her from the stall, and we walk to the yard together.

"I need a boost."

"Of course." He hesitates. "I'll see you again."

"Hopefully alive." I manage a weak smile that he doesn't return.

"The guards will return soon," he says. "When they get to the Archives and realise he's not there. You have an hour at most. And then there's the city gate—"

"I can handle the gate." I gather Iotha's reins, ready to mount up. "Phoenix, I need to go. And I really hate goodbyes."

"I know." He kisses me on the forehead, then laces his hands together. "Foot."

I place my left boot in the cup of his hands, and hop as he lifts me. I land neatly in the saddle, and Iotha tosses her head, shifting beneath me.

"Thanks," I tell him. "Bye, Phoenix."

"Goodbye, Rose."

I don't look back as my mare walks forward, but the cold wind forces more tears from my eyes. I pull my scarf up over my mouth and nose as we approach the palace gate, but the assigned guards are talking intently near the guardhouse and we pass through without challenge. I breathe a sigh of relief as we begin down the winding road from the palace, but it is quickly bound up in my chest again as I realise the guards I sent to the Archives could round the corner at any moment.

I keep my head down as Iotha sets the pace, a brisk walk, though I can feel her straining at the bit, anxious to move. I know how she feels.

We cross the bridge into the city, and my eyes roll across the crowd that parts for us like they do any horse. No curious faces peer up into mine, no sudden cry sounds at my recognition. I am another rider in the twilight traffic of the capital city, and for a moment I relax in the anonymity.

Then a pair of guards watch me pass from the mouth of an alley, and I coil like a wound spring.

We begin to climb towards the gate, through the shanty town of refugees. Their structures are more permanent now, with posts embedded into the shallow soil of the city and thatched rooves instead of stretched canvas. The people here are more suspicious of a rider leaving the city near dark—their eyes follow me. I clutch Iotha's reins in one hand.

I can see the gate ahead; the large wooden structure looms within the stoney walls, the gatehouse arcing high above it. Small figures, silhouetted against the remains of the daylit sky, move within it.

The gate is locked and barred, and a line of armoured guards stand before it. My own orders. They won't stand down without permission from the captain of the city guard, even for their queen.

Iotha seems to know what I want her to do before I do. I feel her lean forward underneath me, and I follow the motion. She gathers speed, her hooves flying against the cobbles, striking sparks in our wake.

"Open the gate!" I yell.

The guards lift their heads, moving towards us with their hands on the pommels of their swords.

"Halt!"

I wait until they come away from the gate, then I raise my right hand and lean back, the fire igniting at my fingertips.

I think of black fingers crawling up my father's throat, of Netalia burning within my flames, and the broken man I've created.

I think of what I have to do next.

When the fireball roars overhead, it lights the area like the day for a moment. The guards cringe away from it, shielding their eyes, and I follow suit as it impacts the ancient wood of the gate with all the fear and regret I could muster.

The gate explodes outwards, splinters tearing through the air along with buckled metal braces. Iotha barrels into the smoke as the shouts of angry guards follow us, but when we burst from the other side, no arrows or bolts are fired. I look back over my shoulder, my horse rolling smoothly beneath me, and see a few brave souls trek through the destruction to raise their swords at us. But the pale mare is quick and they are weighed down by armour— soon, they give up. Besides, their job is to keep people out, not in.

I turn back to face the open road, the landscape sinking into the night. The greatroad of Lotheria lies before us, and I know what must happen at the end of it.

Gripping Iotha's reins, I make a promise to the people of Castor. As birds alight from the fields beside us, we ride north to Fairhaven.

CHAPTER THIRTY-THREE

WE RIDE into the night as the icy chill cloaks both of us. Iotha slows to a manageable walk, tossing her head as though indignant at the chase, and I lean forward to give her a scratch. But we're both nervous and it shows; she dances sideways a few times, the whites of her eyes rolling in her head, and I keep my own on a swivel, searching the dark trees that press close to the greatroad.

I've never travelled it alone; only with a riding party or caravan. I hug my arms around my belly, trying to conserve a centre of heat. Stars glitter overhead, courtesy of a clear sky, and I curse it as my breath billows from beneath my scarf. I decide against holding a tiny fire all the way to the Academy—I might be fireproof, but my gloves and my horse are not.

The cold sinks deep fingers to the marrow of my bones and my eyes begin to close, long languid blinks following each other. I'm truly exhausted, from the tips of my fingers to the core of my soul. I didn't sleep the night before my coronation, too anxious about what was to come—and rightly so, it turns out. But now I think of my bed at the palace and wish for but an hour within it.

Anything to make facing Iain easier.

I see his face again, the hands he'd thrown out as though he could fend off my fire before it reached her. I had told Netalia what would happen should she use that magic again, but the Headmistress had gambled with my word and sent poison to claw and tear at my father's throat.

I shake my head as images of the night replay in my mind. The men and woman I'd killed, the armless noble falling from the dais with a bolt in his chest, the shattering of glass and the roar of thunder.

Maybe Iain could've talked Kynan down. Maybe we could've negotiated right there and then. Waited for my wall guards, delayed by the extra soldiers outside, to do their job. Maybe one of the nobles had been formulating a plan—they were all trained and graduated mages.

I flex my fingers.

But I'd felt the strength of the queensgift and known I could use it for the first time since carving the runes into my skin with my mother's blood. Had it been mere curiosity about the power I now wielded, the drive to end the battle before it could begin, or had it been another, uglier reason; the push to prove myself, show off, in front of my people?

Don't walk this path, Rose, I hear Phoenix say. *You chose your course of action, and none other can apply. Hindsight is not a gift given in the present.*

I sigh, tucking my hands into my armpits, trying to find a semblance of warmth. I know he is right, but I fear the day when I don't second guess my choices.

Dawn begins to break as heavy exhaustion threatens to pull me from the saddle. Like a gift from the goddess herself, a wooden building appears in a small copse of trees off of the road, and I recognise the abandoned wayhouse. I sit up, Iotha perking her ears as her gait increases. But we're both disappointed as we draw nearer; as when Iain and I last travelled to the Academy, it is boarded and closed. I draw my horse to a halt outside the main door and chew my lip for a moment, then make up my mind.

I swing my leg over and drop as gracefully as I can, walking bow-legged for the first few steps. The brace digs painful metal fingers into my skin, and I ignore it; I hadn't lied when I told Bayde I lived in agony every day. It had as much power over me as I allowed it, so I allowed it none.

I tow Iotha around to the stables, hoping for some good hay that hasn't gone mouldy. It takes me a while to find some up in the hayloft, and climbing ladders was never my strong suit, even with two good legs. But I manage to toss it to the stable floor to the delight of my mare, and I have just enough strength to untack her and give her the worst brush she's ever had in her life.

The stable stinks of damp and mildew, the cold of a thousand nights lingering in the corners. I eye the main building, knowing I could get in if I really wanted, that there are beds on the second floor, maybe even some leftover bottles of ale in the dining room downstairs.

But then I fold my arms and seat myself against the wall of Iotha's stall, looking up at the horse.

"Don't tread on me," I tell her, and she barely pauses in her eating to acknowledge my words.

The sweet embrace of sleep wraps comforting arms around me, and the itchy bits of straw feel like the softest featherdown as blessed nothingness overwhelms me.

⁂

I wake from a dream of darkness to a world becoming enshrouded by it. I rest for a moment, pushing the heels of my palms into my eyes, as though I can massage the nightmares out of my head.

But in my experience, I'll be saddled with the memories of death and screaming for a very long time. It's as though my brain collects my worst moments and puts them on a carousel of dread —in a few years, I wonder if I'll sleep at all.

I go to rise, and fall back into the straw. Fear nips at my stomach as I examine my leg, still fastened into the brace and howling with pain after a day of walking, fighting, running, and riding. I grip my calf with both hands, imagining Phoenix's healing magic. But nothing happens, and so I quickly work the muscle as best I know, hoping it'll be enough to get me in the saddle.

I can't allow Iain to get too far ahead of me. I know what he's planning to do.

And an immortal tyrant, fuelled by anger and hate, is the last thing this war needs.

I climb to my feet using the wall, and stand on one leg as I throw Iotha's saddle over her. My balance wobbles a little as I bend down to buckle the girth, but I manage to hold it and wait until my treacherous horse, wanting to stay in the relative warmth of her stall, releases the breath she'd taken to make her belly rounder.

"Nice try," I tell her, doing it up tightly; I don't need to arrive at the Academy and have my saddle slide off sideways. "Echo used to do that too."

A pang of sorrow courses through me as I think of my old horse. But I shake it loose as I lead Iotha from her stall with little hops. Evening is falling over the old wayhouse, and the dark greatroad beckons once again. I shove back the fear beginning to beat a tattoo in my skull, and mount up using the wooden block at the edge of the grounds. A slight thrill sears off some of the edges of doubt as I realise I've managed to untack and tack my horse, dismount and mount, all by myself.

That bolt of confidence is what gives me the strength to guide her back to the road, reins in hand, as though I'm capable of facing what awaits for us at the end.

CHAPTER THIRTY-FOUR

A LIGHT RAIN starts as we draw closer to Fairhaven, and by the time we begin passing the burnt out remains, both I and my horse are soaked to the bone.

Lightning flickers deep in the black clouds above, illuminating the night sky briefly. Iotha's hooves ring out as leaves scatter around us, and I crane my head to look into the empty buildings that still stand, imagining unknown eyes peering at us from the darkness. A chill rises on my skin, and I force the fear down, resting my hand on the pommel of my sword. I am not only armed with a blade, but with the fire that burns within me and keeps the cold from burrowing too deep. And the queensgift...

I tug my sleeve back to look at the rune scars. Pearly light beats through them, in time with the rumbling thunder. The next lightning flash is tinged purple, as it had been at the Battle of Fairhaven. I know now that I caused it, though if I could've stopped it, I'm not sure.

Iotha leads me through the remnants of the once thriving village, and the Academy looms above us. We stop in the rain and watch the building's facade for a moment, but no light graces its windows, no candles burn in its depths.

And yet, there is not a single doubt in my mind that this is where Iain fled to.

I leave Iotha in the square where the Headmasters once built a wooden platform from which the villagers would be judged and punished. It's too easy to remember Tyson, hooded and bound, upon it. Too easy to remember the fire that had surged within me, and taken over. Arno had been the one to get through to me; his words had brought me back from the brink of complete and utter destruction.

But Arno isn't here now. And everyone who was supposed to love me had either let me leave or left me themselves.

I wait another moment in the falling rain, then climb the front steps awkwardly and push on one of the great wooden doors.

It opens a few inches, the lightning illuminating the soft carpet at the threshold in a brief flicker. I slip within and close the door behind me. Inside, the building is heavy and silent, as though waiting for the students, the merchants, the nobles to return. I recall the busy days, going from class to class, worrying about exams, looking forward to our next day out. Painful tears squeeze from my eyes as I remember walking these hallways with my friends, and suddenly a loss so great I can barely parse it grips me and threatens to never let go.

I clench my hands into fists, then draw my glove from my right hand.

Fire whispering works best with bare skin.

The brass sconces on the wall have been dead a long time, cold and lifeless in their brackets, but I lay my hand on one and easily find the dial on its side. I twist it, and there's a slight hissing noise; a touch of a flaming finger and the torch bursts to life, tinged green in its steady flame. The light throws the corridor into sharp relief, with long twisting shadows cast across the walls. I take a deep breath, driving back the ancient, primal fear of the dark.

Iain is here. I know it.

I walk the corridor, turning the gas dials on the torches as I go and lighting them. Warmth follows in my wake, and I take comfort from the glow behind me. All too soon, I find Arno's antechamber and step inside, craning my head to examine the sparkling shapes carved into the ceiling. I trace a design on my arm with my finger, and nod to myself as my eyes find the key rune again at the peak of the ceiling.

I'd always known the rune Iain had been searching for—I'd seen it the second he'd interrupted my conversation with Master Yoris Moon, standing in this very spot a few months ago. The shape had been etched into my dreams since, and I could recall it as easily as my own name. I had kept it from him in fear that he had not overcome his fixation on this power.

Now, it turns out I was right to do so.

I continue through the Academy, laying my hand on the bare stone as I peer up the staircase to Iain's quarters. A few chunks crumble away, and I pull my hand back sharply, a rune on my arm beating a pleasant tattoo. There are powers awakening in my blood I don't know how to control.

I have other problems; my leg trembles as I consider the climb before me, but I didn't come all this way to do a cursory glance at the building and leave.

When I get to the top, there is a light I didn't conjure casting shadows from under a door.

I rest for a moment, waiting. Part of me had been hoping I was wrong, praying to Belatha in all her absence that I'd misjudged Iain and he actually *had* gone to the Archives to read the Book of Blood. Part of me had been ready to return to Castor with a shrug and an excuse.

But the rest of me, the part of me that'd known Netalia had killed my grandmother, that Kynan couldn't treat with us, had known I'd find him.

The door to his office is open slightly, the crack spilling light across the floor. I press it open.

The room within is covered with discarded paper, as though a hurricane went through a library. A single candle burns upon his desk, the scant light illuminating the room weakly. At the centre, a hunched figure sits on the wrong side of the desk, his arm working frantically. I'm reminded forcibly of the last time I'd entered his office late at night, bleeding and broken. He'd comforted me and tended to me. This seems like a sick version of that tableau.

As I watch, another sheet of paper is thrown aside, a fresh one seized from a waiting stack.

Quietly, I reach down and collect one; the key rune is inked upon it, still wet. I glance up at the silhouette of the man. I know what he's doing; Arno had me doing similar every time he taught me a new, difficult rune—repetition is the only way to get the muscle memory required to inscribe the rune cleanly on your chosen object. I remember my first rune, how many pages I'd filled with the same, clumsy shape over and over. But it had worked, and I'd learned the importance of practice.

Another page is tossed away, and I let mine fall.

"Iain."

The scribbling pauses, but he doesn't turn. I step closer, resisting the urge to rest my hand on my pommel for comfort. My brace clinks with each step, shockingly loud in the silent room. The Headmaster remains cast in shadow, unmoving.

"What are you doing?" I ask quietly, still a few steps from him.

"Drawing."

His voice is low and coarse, barely recognisable. I let my right hand drift towards my belt as smoke begins to curl from my left. Every nerve in my body screams at me to leave the room, to run and hide.

But I remember the way he'd held me after Kynan's first attack, his smile when I'd first beaten him at Kingdoms. The deepening sorrow that lingers in my stomach brings tears to my eyes.

"Come back to Castor with me," I whisper. "Come back to the palace."

His head moves, drifting over the pages that litter his desk.

"No."

"Why not?"

His shoulders hunch and he seems to get smaller for a moment. "She's not there."

I clench my jaw, Netalia's burning screams in my ears. "I know. But I am, Iain, and I need your help. You said you'd help me."

"You..." He turns his face towards me, though it is still cast in shadow from the single candle. "You burned her."

"I did." I've avoided responsibility for my killings before. I know how it causes blame and doubt to fester. "I had to."

"You chose *him*," he spits, and suddenly dashes his hand against the desk. I flinch as papers go flying across the room. "Your father. The one who tried to kill you in the streets like a dog. Who marked you with a blade upon meeting you. You chose him over her."

"Iain, I—"

"*Why?*"

I take a step back, fresh tears on my cheeks. "Her magic, Iain, was wrong, I—"

He jerks towards me, the movement so sudden and unexpected that fire flares from my fingers. The sudden burst of flame is nearly blinding in the darkened room, but Iain does not flinch from it.

He is covered in blood. Jagged, torn skin weeps in the firelight; dozens of rough shapes that resemble every iteration of the key rune are cut into his face. It's horrific, and I lose every word I'd been about to speak. His eyes, once dark, are now pale blue, the icy grip of the chill beginning to overtake him. Kaya had fought hers, held it off, but Iain has embraced it.

"I've already lost everything, twice over," he begins, his words raw. Blood slides down the crease beside his nose and is lost within his beard. "She was all I had, Rose, the only constant, the only one who stood beside me through everything. I can't live without her, Rose, I don't *WANT* to."

I open my mouth but he stands, pushing his hands against his eyes as he draws a ragged breath. I step back as he towers over me, and when he lets his hands fall, his face is smeared crimson as the runes bleed openly. Fear nearly seizes me; I have no idea if they're active, if he can be fought and beaten.

Grief is giving him strength, and the runes may be giving him immortality. Even if I get him back to the capital, it would be like bringing back a powder keg and sitting it in the middle of a populated area.

My mind flies as he stumbles, searching for something in the room. I move around him, getting my back to the nearest wall as he rummages through his belongings. When he straightens, it's with sword in hand, and my heart nearly stops beating.

"Why do you have a sword, Iain?" I ask quietly.

He lifts it clumsily, like a drunk raising a toast. "House Araspire sent a man to kill us. I need to repay the favour."

For a moment, I am tempted. I am tempted to loose this grief-stricken, broken half-soul upon the lord who turned my father against me, who gave him men and weapons to enter the palace with, who forced my hand and caused the war before it could be settled with words.

But Iain looks at me with chill-locked eyes and I know that to do so would likely be to send him to his death.

And for some reason, I can't reconcile with that.

"Iain," I say. "Come back. We will go after the House Araspire, but together. We have a war to fight, together. I don't want to do it without you." My throat tightens. "Don't make me do this alone."

He goes still, closer to the door than me. His head lolls towards me, like a marionette on strings. His eyes are two pinpricks of ice in the darkness.

"I am alone," he says simply, "because you took her."

It hadn't mattered in the end; both Netalia and Kynan lay dead in the capital. Both of us are the remnants of their lives, the leftovers. But our broken hearts are seething and demanding retribution. Truthfully, standing in the building where Iain was the shadow that haunted my dreams, who dogged my footsteps and policed my friendships, makes it harder to remember the mentor he's been to me in Castor. It's easier to recall his looming presence in the hallways than it is to remember him fighting alongside me in the streets of the capital, sitting with me in the night as my leg ached, holding me when I needed support.

"I did chose him over her," I hear myself saying. "And you would chose her over me. We are who we are, Iain. Netalia made her choices and her threats, and so did I. I told her what would happen if she were to use that magic again, and she did. You taught me to keep my promises."

When tears streak down his face, mixing with the blood, I know the salt must sear his wounds. But the ruined Headmaster makes no sign that he's in pain, and new fears begin to cluster in my mind.

Even if the runes are not active, Halvers cannot feel pain. There is only one way I can put him down.

"You were supposed to be everything I wasn't," he whispers. When he draws his sword, he looks directly at me.

And his eyes are his own.

I barely have time to draw my own before he bears down on me. The clash of metal sings across the room as I clumsily guard against his first blow—the strength of it knocks me to the ground and I scramble backwards, trying to get my feet under me, as he straightens again.

He lifts the sword, and his eyes flicker with pale ice. "You were supposed to be the best of both of us."

I grip the hilt of mine, my hands still numb from blocking his first blow. I've never sparred with Iain. I never wanted to.

Anger and frustration heat my face, the exhaustion of the last few days peeling me back to the core, where I keep the quiet things I never say. "Haven't you learnt yet, Iain? I'm the worst of everyone who was ever supposed to love me."

His expression wavers for a second, then strangled red light sparks and flickers down his blade. His war magic is as broken as his soul though, and I take the opportunity to step forward, planting my feet to swing my blade at his left arm.

Shattered as he might be, he is still a master; he blocks and parries almost faster than I can follow. I throw myself to the side on my twisted right leg and stumble, falling against his desk. My hand refuses to let the hilt from my grip though, the oath rune digging against the leather wrapping, and every mistake, every misplaced atom of trust, every failing, suddenly crushes me with their weight.

How many times will I entrust myself to the wrong person?

Fire blooms in the twilight weary room, and I throw it forward. Iain barely dodges it, though his clothes blacken and smoke.

"Not like her!" he roars, and raises his sword. "You won't burn me like her!"

The sword arcs downwards and I duck forward under his right arm, my leg howling as I place my weight on it. Sweat clusters on my brow, and I know I'm running out of time to be upright.

I clutch my sword and swing it two-handed at his midsection, desperation fuelling the attack. But Iain was ready for it, and grips my wrist as I'm at full extension, and for a moment I feel the same panic that the woman at my coronation must've felt. My arm screams as it's straightened beyond its natural point, and I raise my left fist, punching forward with the fire conjured by my fear.

Iain narrowly avoids losing his head, jerking out of the way, but the fireball was large and strong, fed by the pain and terror. The fire, tinged with darkness, roils to the ceiling and blasts through it, raining mortar and stone down upon us.

Outside, the storm that had threatened to break has done so, and the elements surge into the room, much as it had done during the coup. Wind gutters the candle on the table and flecks of rain hit my face like ice-cold iron pellets. The similarities spur us both with fear.

Iain comes at me again in the darkness, and I use flashes of fire to illuminate his steps, dodging and weaving, raising my sword only when he leaves me no choice. The blades sing and spark as they clash, and my arms soon grow heavy. I was never a sword master like Iain or Phoenix; it's a miracle I've lasted this long. But as Iain hesitates after I step offline of yet another blow, giving me time to recover, I realise he isn't fighting me at all.

He's toying with me.

My chest heaves, exhaustion rampant in my limbs. Every ounce of me is covered in sweat, blood, or rain, and my leg has long since gone numb; only the brace holds me up now. A thousand stinging cuts, nicks and slices from being too slow to avoid the sword, cover my arms. The runes flicker as blood runs over them.

I make a decision and toss my sword to the side. Iain's eyes follow it before returning to me, the weapon thudding into the soaked carpet.

It's a tactic, a play, and he knows it; we've played too many games of Kingdoms for him *not* to be suspicious of any sudden actions. I flex my hands, hoping I haven't misread the signs from the runes—I'm fast learning that the queensgift is unreliable, at best. The Book of Blood named me unworthy, and apparently the rest of the land still agrees.

Except for when I take action to protect its people.

If Iain leaves this room, I think to nobody, *he will cause the deaths of thousands by beginning a war of vengeance with no end.*

The Headmaster lunges towards me, sword flashing in the dim light. I throw my hand up out of reflex, cringing away, expecting to feel the cold slice of the blade against my palm.

But instead, he's halted by an invisible force, and I realise I can feel the *mineral* rune tightened in my skin. The steel cannot advance upon me, much as I'd done in the throne room.

I was right. The runes are obeying.

I lash out with more fire, causing Iain to haul the sword back awkwardly; he was expecting to be able to either cut through or recoil with whatever parry I was able to come up with. But the dead stop caused by the rune throws him off balance, and I press my advantage, flames flashing in the darkness as steam and smoke rises.

Then Iain abandons his sword as well, and seizes me by the throat.

My fire dies immediately, plunging the room into rain-soaked darkness. I gasp, clawing at my neck as his hold tightens.

"You," he begins, his voice choked with tears, "were supposed to be the best of us. My *redemption*, Rose! I gave you a second chance. I brought you back, put a crown on your head... I would've followed you into war. I would've made you into a *queen*."

My vision is tinged black, his fingers digging into my jaw. He's lifted me so my feet barely touch the floor, and my neck is straining. I fumble at his grip with soft fingers, fighting to free myself. As my head swims through the last moments of consciousness, I summon every ounce of strength I have left for one last, desperate act.

My nail shreds the back of Iain's hand, moving swiftly in practised motion. I feel the second I complete the rune and close my eyes against the blast as he's thrown away from me.

I hit the ground and suck in a lungful of air, coughing as it burns my bruised throat. My ears ring with silence as I roll to my knees, struggling upright as I try to make out what became of my former mentor.

And I'm given no time to recover as he roars from the blurred darkness, picking me up bodily and slamming me into the wall.

The world blinks, and when it comes back, I'm sitting on the floor, legs splayed, my chin on my chest. Pain hammers every inch of my body and blood drips onto my shirt, from my nose or my lip, I'm not sure. My throat burns and I cough, sending droplets of red into the air. I can taste iron on my lips and wish desperately that I'd thought to carve one of the queensgift runes as a healing rune.

Iain wobbles into focus before me, examining his destroyed

hand. The rune blasted a hole in the centre, and his entire forearm is soaked in blood. The damage is catastrophic, and my stomach churns. I'd had no idea what the rune would do to organic matter.

"In the hands of a master," he says quietly, and my body seizes at the familiar words, "runes are the most powerful form of magic."

Arno's voice rings in my ears, and I squeeze my eyes closed, wishing for him to be here.

"I never realised how true those words were until you showed me the ones you carved yourself. Until I read your master's alphabet and realised they could defy, not just time, but the old laws themselves." Iain exhales. "And now I feel them myself, Rose. I feel nothing from my hand, or what remains of it. What power he created, here in this very building. My building, my Academy... Arno Veloquis was my student, and he created the most powerful magic since the queens."

Iain laughs, raising his hand to look at it again as though he can't believe his own immortality, and I struggle to rise, using the stone wall he'd thrown me against, the queensgift surging into my ruined leg and strengthening it.

"I can walk into battle and tear them to pieces," he continues. "No arrow nor blade can stop me, Rose. This is a gift. One I will use to make the world right."

His words fall silent and I feel his eyes on me. They narrow as I wipe my split lip, spitting blood aside.

"You bleed red," he says in a puzzled tone.

I'd noticed it too. Thought the queensblood had been white— gleaming, shimmering white—my own blood moved between the two colours seemingly at random. I look at the red and brown smears on my hand curiously and he approaches. I stiffen, raising my chin and preparing to summon more fire.

But Iain's eyes are his own now. When he reaches for my arm with his mangled hand, I let him, my breathing quick and shallow.

Did I get through to him?

"Your runes are sealed," he comments, and looks at the remnants of his hand. No rune remains there. Then he touches one on his face, and it bleeds anew at the intrusion. "These are not."

His runes aren't active; I can see that now. The lack of pain and sensation he's feeling is the chill, the curse of all half-souls, torn from their soulmates and gifted by the trauma of loss. I see disappointment crease his brow, and tears glimmer in his eyes.

"I can't even draw a single rune," he says.

I say nothing. I can draw the key rune. I could gift him that power.

And he knows it.

"Give me the rune, Rose. You have the queensblood. You could make it even more powerful than Arno's original creation. It could stop the chill from advancing, I know it." He squeezes my hand, a sensation so familiar I nearly bawl, and then lowers himself to one knee. "I would be your creature. I would pledge my loyalty, just... give me this gift, Rose."

I reach out and touch his face. One of the attempted key runes he'd tried to carve into his own skin calls to me, and I examine it in the scant light. I follow the path with my mind's eye, correcting it as Arno would one of my drafts, reading the amount of power it would take to power.

And I see the choice that lies before me.

Arno's time runes work because he happened to mark them into ancient walls, with thousands of man hours worked into the stone.

The more hours and effort involved in creating a material, the more energy the runes can pull from.

To carve this time rune into organic material would destroy the person it belonged to, unless that person carried the gods-gifted blood of a queen in her veins.

I stand before Iain, my leg strong and painfree beneath me. I will never walk again without this blood, this magic.

I run my hand down his cheek, and he closes his eyes, leaning into my palm. In this moment, he trusts me utterly and completely. The wall at my back is strong and smooth, and I make my decision.

I finish the rune within seconds, knowing innately that it is perfect—it cannot be anything other, for I have never drawn another rune so often.

It was my first, after all.

Iain's eyes open, and sees the hollow gouge carved into the wall, a rune he does not recognise, nor bear.

"What have you drawn?" His words are curious, not concerned. It is just a symbol in his walls, after all.

The rune flares behind me, illuminating my blood-soaked Headmaster in sheer white light. It dies away and I wait, dimly aware of the magic rippling throughout the building beneath my feet.

"At every turn," I begin, and he looks from my rune back to me. "I chose someone else. Petre used my feelings for him to bring me to the moors, and I lost my leg. Kaya saw me vulnerable and desperate, and used me for revenge. My mother used me to bring her to Lotheria, back to Kynan."

"I never used you," he whispers, and the floor begins to shake. "I could never."

Tears grow in my eyes. "You used me to replace the family you lost, and you used me to fix your mistakes.

"I am done choosing anyone else. I am being selfish." My leg sings with strength beneath me, and I straighten. "I am keeping the queensblood, for me, to replace what I lost. Because it makes me feel powerful. Because it makes me feel strong. The queensgift is *mine*."

His eyes bore into mine, his earlier anger surging back into them. "Rose—"

"That," I interrupt, my voice steady, "is my decision."

The building buckles, then heaves upwards, as the *burn* rune finds the pocket of natural gas, which feeds the pipelines of the entire Academy, below the dungeons. Super heated air roars in my ears as Iain disappears from view, and I close my eyes. Our conversation is done.

And I don't want to see Fairhaven burn a second time.

ACKNOWLEDGMENTS

Well, heck. This book has been a monumental journey, from its original beginning as a draft in 2018 to the book it ended up as in 2024. The length of said journey also means *a lot* of people were involved, so let's get this ball rolling.

For Wardog. Tom, you kicked me up the arse every week to make sure I was writing, and helped me get back into the habit. Your check ins and encouragement directly resulted in this book being published.

For Jonathan Maloney, my brother in publishing, for your companionship and sympathy, your insights and advice. Honoured to have your books sitting side by side with mine.

For the beta and ARC readers of His Throne of Embers - the beta readers had the tough but necessary job of being brutally honest when the first draft of this book wasn't up to snuff. They knew I could do better and they pushed me to be better. As a result, I'm very happy with how this chapter in Rose's journey closed. For my ARC readers, who waited patiently for nearly five years, and then signed up to receive early copies of the book. You reminded me that people still wanted this book after such a long gap in publishing, and I'll appreciate that forever.

For my partner, Kurtis, for letting me disappear on weekends to write, for bringing me coffee and snacks, and celebrating my achievements with me. For creating a safe space for my creative self to work and experiment, for dragging me out for breakfast to give me a break from the computer. Also for listening to my rants about publishing in general.

For my audio drama actors, who voiced the cast of Her Crown

of Fire and brought them to life better than I ever could. I heard your voices as I wrote this book and your incredible performances inspired many changes.

For the staff of SkyNation Publishing - Lydia Fuller, Reordan J Carey, Dayna Watson, Sean Gurr, Ashley Bravington... you all had a hand in pushing this book forwards. Lyd, your edits and feedback calmed me the heck down when I realised the book was actually done and coming out. Dayna for her beautiful cover as always. Sean and Ash for their logistics and financial advice. Reordan for always being a cheerleader and his beautiful rune work.

And lastly, anyone on stream or in Discord who pestered me about this book. You *would not* let this go, and I'm grateful to you. I hope you know how much I appreciate your love for my story and characters.

I promise Book Three won't take another five years.

Probably.

ABOUT THE AUTHOR

Renee April is the author of the young adult Molten Crown fantasy series.

In addition to being an avid reader and writer, she streams on Twitch and works in the video games industry. As a result, she spends far too much time in fantasy realms.

She spends most of her time making YouTube videos and lurking in her Discord server instead of writing.